T5-BQB-298

Navy Girl

Madeline J. Wilcox

To Jeff Arnold

Thank you

Madeline J. Wilcox

This book is a work of non-fiction. Names and places have been changed to protect the privacy of all individuals. The events and situations are true.

© 2003 by Madeline J. Wilcox. All rights reserved.

No part of this book may be reproduced, stored in a retrieval system, or transmitted by any means, electronic, mechanical, photocopying, recording, or otherwise, without written permission from the author.

ISBN: 1-4140-1331-0 (e-book)
ISBN: 1-4140-1332-9 (Paperback)

Library of Congress Control Number: 2003097258

This book is printed on acid free paper.

Printed in the United States of America
Bloomington, IN

1stBooks – rev. 11/18/03

I dedicate this book to Susan and Ron, who made it all possible.
To my husband for his patience while listening to the keys of a
Typewriter. To Carole whom inspired me to get the book published.

For every ending, there is a new beginning.
A chance to set new goals, to dream new dreams,
To rekindle the hope in our hearts.

For endings are a way of rediscovering
Ourselves of learning who we are
And what we need in life,
Of finding out where we want to go
And who we want to be.   Anonynonus

1

    The full moon showing down upon the boundary of the trees that surrounded the Reddy home spotlighted the girl pressing her face against the coolness of the window. "Am I going to regret today? She uttered as she looked out on the star spangled night. Having found sleep impossible the young girl had risen early. Her thoughts cluttered to what lie ahead of her for the day "Is mother right? Do I really know what I want?" Shaking her head, she continued to question her decision about joining the military. Taking a deep sigh, she moved away from the window and putting on a faded blue terry cloth robe and fuzzy worn out slippers, slipped quietly from her room and down the hall to the kitchen. Walking quietly over to the sliding glass doors that led to the deck off the back of the house, she took a chair sitting at the patio table.

    She again ponders over her troubled thoughts "When will I see this place again? Will Wellsburg ever change? The thoughts that had kept her awake through the night were still plaguing her. "I really do enjoy working for dad, but I want something more? Maybe being an engineman is not the right choice? But I do know a lot about fixing engines."

A sense of nostalgia and all that Wellsburg stood for began to torment her. It was a place set back in time, hardly anything ever changed as she begins to argue with her thoughts. Wellsburg was a place where the seasons and holidays were celebrated in grand style for the tourist to enjoy that found their way there.

Had it only been a year since she had walked into her Grandmother Reddy's office and told her of her plans? A smile crossed the often-moody face as she thought back to that day when she had made a rare visit during her grandmother's busy work schedule.

"Grams," she had started after taking a deep breath. "What would you say if I told you I was planning on leaving Wellsburg?"

With her glasses sitting close to the end of her nose and her eyes looking out over the rims, Maude Reddy, with her no nonsense stare looked at her granddaughter and stated. "Now why in the tar nation would you want to go and do a thing like that?" The daily reports she had been going over when Joan entered the room now forgotten, as she shoved the reports aside and gave her granddaughter her full attention.

Swallowing her nervousness, and trying to make light of the situation, Joan answered her grandmother with the stubbornness in which she could process with no problem when the need arose. "Because I don't see a future here in Wellsburg for me. You know me Grams; I am not like most of the girls whom I go to school with. I think there is more to life than getting married and having babies. I want to see the world. I want to travel and go places," she stated, having little breath left.

"How do you plan on financing these fancy ideas of yours?" Maude Reddy asked as she continued to stare down her granddaughter with the stubborn look fixed on her face.

"By joining the military," Joan quickly responded in a defiant stance.

"By what?" Maude snapped, almost falling from her chair as she slammed both her hands on her desk with a loud slapping sound and not believing what she had heard. "You wouldn't mind telling me who put this crazy notion into your head?" Asking as she tried to hold anger from her tone of voice while drawing her own conclusion as to whom Joan had been talking to.

It was best never to try and get around your grandmother with telling her anything but the truth, especially Grandmother Reddy. The Reddy grandchildren had learned that lying to her was not the thing to do along time ago, and now was not the time to start Joan sensed as she stood her ground.

"Uncle Matt said I would make a good engineman. That working with engines seems to be a natural for me? Taking a quick breath, Joan continued to plead her case. "Oh come on Grams, you know I am not happy here," Joan added hoping her grandmother would understand why she wanted to leave.

Sensing that it was not the time to argue with her, but to listen, Maude replied, "I am aware of the fact that you are not happy. I just don't think military is a place to solve your problems. Have you mentioned this crazy idea of yours to your father yet?"

Joan wanted to look away from her Grandmother's demanding stare, as she answered slowly. "No," and before her grandmother could say more, Joan added. "But I have checked into it, and I can go in after I graduate next year. I have a problem though…," taking a deep breathe, she continued with a forlorn expression. "I need someone to sign the papers for the 'Delayed Entrance Program'. I was hoping you would convince Dad to do it. Please?"

Still having a difficult time trying to comprehend this crazy idea of hers, Maude inquired with skepticism. "Let me think. You want me to convince your father to let you join the military, when I am not quite convinced that you are making the right decision?"

"Grams please!" Joan spoke with aspiration. "I have thought this through completely. I can get a G.I. Bill that offers to pay thirty thousand dollars of my college tuition and they allow you to either go to college while you serve, or you can go to college after you decide to get out?

Still not quite ready to agree Maude questioned. "What is wrong with you continuing to work for your father in his office?"

Realizing that her grandmother wasn't making it easy for her at all, Joan was determined to get her grandmother's approval as she stated. "Working for dad is something I have to do. Joining the military is something I want to do. Won't you please think about it?"

'You bet I will think about it', Maude replied, testing her granddaughter's determination with curiosity as to what this child whom was known to be very stubborn, might do. "And if I say no?"

"I'm hoping you won't," Joan's look almost pleading now.

With reservation, Maude answered, "We will see." as she smiled inwardly while she looked at Joan and thought. "I never thought I would see the day when one of my own grandchildren would stand up to me. But I should have known this gutsy young lady would?"

Having a sense that she was winning Joan ran around to where her grandmother was sitting and threw her arms around the very prim looking lady and gave her a hug. "I knew you would understand Grams."

"Now I am not making any promise's?" Maude sort of smiled at the pint size tomboy as she returned her generous hug.

Her grandmother had talked to her father. It had not been a pleasant discussion when he had called her into his office on that hot summer day a year ago. As usual Joan and Mrs. Johnson were in the office hours before her father arrived. Her dad always made a habit of having coffee with his mother, and making rounds of the job sights to make sure everything was running smoothly before he came into the office. Joan's duties were answering the phone, and doing the filing and taking notes in shorthand, while Mrs. Johnson managed the more important details of the day.

Joan was standing at the file cabinet when her father entered the office and gruffly spoke. "Joan, in my office. Now!" From the glare on his usual smiling face, Joan had a feeling this meeting was not going to be pleasant. Picking up her notepad to take notes she jumped when he commanded. "You won't be needing them young lady." and as she looked at Mrs. Johnson with a questionable stare to what might be wrong, Mrs. Johnson looked away from her.

Entering her father's office behind him, he continued to bark at her. "Close the door and have a seat." Trying to control his anger, Tom Reddy kept silent for several minutes as he stared at his daughter sitting now in the chair across from him as he stood behind his large oak desk, which was always cluttered.

"This is not going to be good." Joan thought as the scowl remained on her father's face and she had the feeling she wasn't going to like what he had to say as he cleared his throat and stated. "Where in the hell did you get this lame brain idea that I would agree, to you going into the military?"

"So that's it." Joan thought as a look of defiance crossed her face and she answered him. "From no one, sir."

"Don't give me that! And don't call me sir!" He glared at her. "Your brother was here not more than two weeks ago," Tom declared.

"So!" Joan dared to reply.

"So!" Her father continued to growl. "Of all the damn fool notions you two have come up with...I think this one beats the cake. I don't care how attractive Jeff may have explained it." Her father exploded. "The military is not the place for young

6

women. Especially where my daughter is concerned. Do I make myself clear?" His face turning red and his voice rising.

"Jeff didn't talk me into it," she spoke defending her brother. "As a matter of fact he reacted about the same as you." She was ready to argue with him. "I will be okay. You have always said that I have more guts than any female you have ever knew." she continued with little oxygen left. "And you have even agreed with Uncle Matt about me being good at fixing engines."

"I should have known," Tom spoke losing some of his fighting tone as he gave a regretted sigh and recalled several conversations with his brother about Joan's ability to fix almost anything that had to do with engines.

Seeing his changed expression, it gave her the courage to go on. "Dad I will be okay."

"I will be okay," she uttered not realizing that she had spoken aloud until she heard her father's voice.

"Up kind of early wouldn't you be?"

Turning she looked at her father and responded, "I couldn't sleep."

"I guess I couldn't either if I had facing me what you have ahead of you for the day. Thinking of changing your mind?" He continued since he too had doubts about her leaving. He had been wondering all night if signing those papers for her to join the military had been the right decision. What did she know about the real world? She knew nothing about young men or people. She knew nothing about how they could manipulate a person.

7

Looking still at her, he shook his head to the fact that she had always been raised in a protective environment. Even with Kathryn and her always at each other's throats, Joan didn't stray to far from the nest. Sitting a cup of coffee down next to her he said, "I thought you might be needing this."

"Thanks," she answered, continuing to look at him. "You asked if I wanted to change my mind? I doubt it. I am scared but I will get over it." She spoke with confidence and tried assuring him before she took a sip of the hot coffee that he had brought her.

"I am sure you will but if you find that you have made a mistake...you can always come back home."

"Thanks but no thanks. You do remember last night and mother. I don't believe she would be that eager to welcome me back." Joan stated as she recalled the going away party that her sister, Peggy and her best friend, Maureen Colby had surprised her with. Her mother, the social drinker, was in full prime as she declared, "Well don't think for a minute that anyone is fooled by your innocence. We all know why you are determined to leave here. You will no longer be under the watchful eye of your peers and God forbid your Grandmother Reddy. Well young lady if you find yourself in trouble...don't think for one minute you will be welcome back here with open arms!"

With defiance to her mother's declarations and wrath, Joan responded, "Don't worry mother I am not out to lay the whole damn fleet like you keep insisting that I plan on doing!"

As usual, her mother responded with striking her on the face and hissing, "Don't be disrespectful to me young lady," and turning she faced Maureen Colby and speaking with no uncertain terms, Kathryn had told her, "Take yourself and your friends out of her. Now!"

"With pleasure," Maureen had responded to Mrs. Reddy as she turned to Joan and pleaded, "Don't back out now."

Joan hadn't realized that she had put her hand up to her face until her father said, "It doesn't show that much," as he added, "I should have stepped in and stopped her but I had friends and family to tend to and I didn't think she would resort to her usual tactics."

"Me either," Joan sighed adding, "You asked why I was leaving. I think you know Dad," she said with some regret as she reached for her coffee cup again.

"Probably," Tom thought as he changed the subject with a forced smile. "I ran into Mayor Wilson. He thinks I should have more control over my tomboy daughter."

"Why because I blackened his son's eye? He was just lucky that was all I did," she spoke with malice.

Her comment brought back his thoughts of earlier. Her attitude alone would make any sailor back off. In addition, her chosen career to be an *engineman* still kept the tomboy in tact. But yet, he still couldn't help wonder. "How many fights would she be willing to face before the right young man comes along, then what?

2

Kathryn Reddy stood listening to the discussion between father and daughter. Staring at the two with a look of disgust on her face, she recalled the warning her mother had said, "You are going to have nothing but trouble with this child."

"Well how true that statement is." Kathryn thought, assuming why her daughter had made the decision to leave Wellsburg. It had nothing to do with her knowing about engines. And why did they keep on insisting that Joan was a 'tomboy'? Why for God's sake she was a girl!

"I should have never let Maude Reddy butt in on the raising of my daughter? Maybe then my daughter wouldn't be leaving today? . She has always seen to it that Joan has her own way," Kathryn continued to criticize. "Well she sure was surprised when her darling granddaughter announce she was going into the military."

"It was a disgrace. That's what it is. Why, no decent girl would join a military institution." Kathryn's mother had declared when she found out about Joan's wild decision to leave Wellsburg.

Why she couldn't even hold her head up when she was in town and faced all of their friends. The gossip was terrible. "Just terrible!" Kathryn's thoughts went on, "Well young lady I hope you understood my warning. For you never will be welcome back here!"

"I suppose you are still planning on going through with this crazy notion of yours." Kathryn spoke with contempt as she stepped further on to the deck and let her presence be known.

"Good morning Mother." Gritting her teeth for the first encounter of the day. Joan turned and looked at her mother and saw that her expression was clearly marked for an argument. "I really don't have much choice about changing my plans. Besides, even if I did I still would leave." Joan added with assurance and a defying look for her mother.

"Well young lady," Kathryn stated sharply, "you better remember one thing, if you get into trouble...don't think for one minute you will be welcome back here with open arms. Never! Do you understand me?"

"Yes, one thing I have learned...I know where I stand when it comes to your opinion of me," Joan chided as she rose and moved past her mother.

Kathryn started to reach for Joan's arm but Tom stepped between the two as Joan moved towards the house. "Give it a rest Kathryn! I think you have said enough on the matter," Tom looked at his wife with repugnance as he took her arm and held her back.

"Leave it to you to take sides with your precious daughter." Kathryn accused as she shook off her husbands hold on her. "Just remember this wasn't my idea!" she spat at him while taking the seat Joan had occupied.

"Nor mine," Tom sighed as he looked away from the house and out across the field of trees beyond his home. His thoughts of the little girl that used to run and play forever amongst the trees, The tomboy that would climb to the top and call out "Look at me Dad," and he would find himself holding his breath until she was back safely on the ground. "That little girl is gone," he continued to think as tears moistened his eyes.

As Joan entered her room she saw her sister dumping her tote bag out onto her bed. Her mood rancid from having a run in with their mother, she snapped at Peggy. "What are you doing?"

Startled by her sister, Peggy jumped at the sound of her voice and insisted, "I was just putting your things in a neat order."

"Well don't. They are just fine the way they are," Joan spoke with aggression, starting to put her things back into her tote bag after taking it away from Peggy.

"I'm sorry," Peggy rejected her sister's sharp tongue.

Moving away from her she turned and started to leave the room that was plain compared to her canopy bed, ruffles, silk flowers, and soft colors. Joan's room was decorated in plain colors and plaids. Nothing in the room connected with a girl.

12

There was something in her sister's voice that made Joan stop her from leaving. "I am the one that should be saying I'm sorry. I really didn't mean to snap at you. It's just that mother and I are off to our usual start for the day." Joan made the attempt to apologize.

"Maybe after you are gone for a while, Mother will realize how much she misses you." Peggy commented stepping back into the room and making herself comfortable on the end of Joan's bed.

"Dream on, Peggy. Mother has no intentions of missing me or caring about what I am doing." Her look severe as she turned on her sister who resembled their mother in looks with green eyes and red hair. How many times in the past had she heard, 'Oh that Peggy sure is a pretty thing.' or 'Peggy made the 'Honor Roll' again. And 'Peggy is so talented!' The list seems to go on and on to what accomplishments her sister could do. Fighting the thoughts that always seemed to separate her sister and her, she turned away from Peggy to stare out across her room.

Peggy, having seen Joan's face of envy, made the effort of changing her mood by asking, "Are you excited about leaving today?"

"Scared would be more like it," Joan confessed while finally smiling.

"Surly you don't plan on backing out now. Do you?" Peggy stated with concern.

"Not hardly," Joan assured her as this morning with her mother still fresh in her mind. "Anything would be better than staying here."

Seeing her sister's face fill with confusion, Peggy then told her, "Do you realize how many girls would like to have the courage you have? I don't mean joining the military, but leaving Wellsburg. Believe it or not sis, but you are the envy of a lot of girls."

"Oh sure Peg! They were all lining up last night just to come to my going away party. Over half of the girls in my class didn't even know I existed. So don't tell me they wished they had the courage to leave this God forsaken place!" Joan stubbornly replied.

Ignoring her sister's usual negative approach, Peggy added, "They figured that you would back out when the time came for you to leave. Especially when it came to Grams and your leaving."

"Grams? What does Grams have to do with my leaving?" Joan questioned.

"Well you know how Grams is. If she doesn't like something, she expresses her opinion and the subject is dropped." Peggy declared, taking the stance that their grandmother would.

"Sometimes, but this is different. Grams has always been there for me, and has supported me all the way."

Smiling, Joan told her sister about the promise that she had made their grandmother. "I told her I would leave the sailor's alone until I am thirty."

"You have to be kidding. Why in the world would you make a promise like that?" Peggy asked, shaking her head in disbelief.

"I'm not sure. Probably because I have always been teased by the guys in school. Did you know they called me 'Miss Iceberg'?"

"I knew, most of the time I ignored it." Peggy admitted." "But I think if you drop that tomboy appeal, some guy will sweep you off of your feet," laughing Peggy added "You know it could happen?"

Yeah, if could happen. Maybe not in my lifetime, but it could happen?" Joan replied as both girls broke out into laughter when Peggy stated.

"Oh wouldn't I love to be around to see your face when it does. But first, you will have to do drop that tomboy attitude of yours."

"Why couldn't we have been closer?" Joan wondered, as the two of them relaxed and actually was holding a decent conversation. "Peggy, how come we are so different?" Joan asked, the younger sister by one year. Peggy, always seemed older, more sophisticated.

"I don't know," Peggy responded, as she thought about what the kids would say behind Joan's back at school, some of the things not so nice. How at times she wanted to defend her, but she would only ignore some of what they were saying and agree at other times with them. "You will write me?" Peggy asked to change the subject.

"Yes," Joan responded as she looked at her watch and stated. "It's almost time for Petty Officer Levin to show up." Then turning Joan stuffed what few remaining clothes were still laying on her bed, into the tote bag.

Entering the kitchen Joan looked for her mother who seemed to be nowhere in sight, but her father was coming through the dinning room into the kitchen. "I was just coming to get you. I am afraid it's that time. Mr. Levin is outside talking to your mother in the driveway." Tom spoke as he reached for his back pocket to pull out his billfold. Seeing her father's intentions, Joan placed her hand on his arm and told him. "Dad, I have everything, including money."

"You sure/" Tom spoke with difficulty as tears stung his eyes, and turning to Peggy told her. "Better make it a quick goodbye."

As the two girls hugged each other, and made promises to write, Joan's mother came into the house, without saying a word to Joan she walked on passed Peggy and her and into her sewing room, closing the door behind her.

"Tell Petty Officer Levin I will be out in a few minutes," Joan told her father, as she turned to leave the kitchen and walked across the hall to her mother's room. Knocking on her door, Joan heard her mother sharply express. "What!"

"I am leaving," Joan answered. "Mom, I am sorry about this morning, but I will be okay," Joan added in an apologetic tone through the door, and heard her mother answered. "Whatever," Kathryn answered, never making the attempt to come to the door to tell Joan goodbye.

Fighting the tears that stung her face, Joan shrugged her shoulders and turned and left the house.

3

Taking her seat on the bus a sense of loneliness settled over her as she made a final wave to her Uncle Matt and her grandmother who had came to the bus station to see her off. Fighting the notion of being lonely, she scolded herself 'Now is not the time to start getting homesick.' Then laughing to herself, she recalled telling her brother. "Jeff you can bet your last dollar that I will never be homesick?" That was after he had insisted that she would be. Also, he had reminded her to do something about her attitude. "It's getting to be the pits," he had declared when she had last talked to him.

"My attitude?" She had informed him, "Is not any different than yours."

"Maybe, but I know how to control mine. You don't," her brother had replied as she recalled Peggy also stating this morning that she needed to change her tomboy attitude. Deep in thought, she didn't pay much attention to who was beginning to sit beside her until he spoke. "Think you are going to miss the old place?" Dave Wright questioned the girl who had graduated a year behind him in school and had heard rumors that she was joining the military. Seeing her this morning in Petty Officer Levin car, he had smiled at her, only to get an impartial stare from her.

Madeline J. Wilcox

Groaning inwardly, she acknowledged Dave Wrights presence. Turning and looking at him she complained. "Isn't there a vacant seat somewhere else for you to sit in?"

Grinning at the girl who always had the disposition of a rattlesnake, Dave Wright answered, "Now is that anyway to talk to an old friend?" Looking her over slowly and thinking there had been some major changes in her appearance. He had a hard time believing this was the same person who had decked his friend Bruce Wilson. 'Iceberg' fit her well, a name the guys had tagged on her in school. "Bruce Wilson said to tell you hello," he antagonized knowing she had a quick temper and an attitude to match.

Turning she looked at Dave Wright and eyed him suspiciously. "Am I supposed to be flattered by that?" she coolly remarked.

Ignoring her reprisal, Dave asked. "Who taught you judo?"

"Jeff. He just didn't know I would use it," she spoke with impertinence.

Feeling that he wasn't scoring any points by testing her sense of humor, he changed the subject, "I understand that you want to be an engineman?"

"Wrong. There is nothing about my wanting to be an engineman. I am going to be one," she corrected him.

"Really now? Hasn't anyone ever told you that it's a man's job?"

"Probably, but I never let what other people say bother me," she declared, taking the offense rather than being forced into a defensive position. Then not letting him get the best of her, she remarked. "I thought you would be making wedding plans by now?"

"What? What gave you the idea I was thinking about getting married?" His look perplexed.

"Why Betsy of course," she flippantly replied, "she told everyone at school that you had proposed."

"She wished," he denied her comment.

Knowing that she was pushing the right buttons, she added. "Didn't you get a Scholarship?"

Looking at her like maybe she had just lost what brains she had, he answered. "With my grades? I don't think so."

"What happen to the job at the Soda Shoppe?" Joan asked next.

"Actually nothing until dad gave me the option of going to college, joining the military, or the street. I enjoy having a roof over my head and food on the table, so I joined the military. What is your excuse? I thought you had a good job working for your old man?" he asked, finally getting a chance to ask the questions.

"I probably did, but I wanted something with a little more excitement than having to spend the rest of my life in Wellsburg and I sort of like the idea of adventure."

Which he doubted that she would ever find, as he remarked. "Adventure? I must have missed something in the brochures. Besides, you wouldn't have been bored if you had dropped your cold shoulder," Dave commented with an ear-to-ear grin.

Contempt seething in her voice, she sternly stated. "Why is it that all guys think if they get laid, they are set for life. Well I have you to know there is more to being married and having kids? Which seems to be the ultimate goal for most of the girls in Wellsburg?"

"And what is wrong with that?" Dave responded.

"I don't know, why don't you ask Betsy? I am sure she would be more than glad to fill you in on her career goals?" Joan asserted with disgust.

Ignoring the subject of Betsy, Dave found an opening to taunt her with, "do you know what the guys called you in school?"

Not wanting to admit she had heard rumors, she answered. "No, but I bet you are dying to tell me?"

Not knowing when it was best to shut up where Joan was concerned, Dave continued. "Miss Iceberg. Want to know something else?" Dave stated. "The only adventure you are going to find with your attitude is a ticket back home!"

"You wish," she turned glaring at him.

Since they were arriving in the middle of the afternoon, they were taken to a hotel that was close to the MEPS Center. "You will be staying the night here," Petty Officer Stevens told them as she had met their bus. "You are not to leave the this building for any reason. There is a restaurant in the building where you will be eating supper. Feel free to order whatever you like, the military is picking up the tab." Then before getting to far from the young people, PO Stevens turned back and told them. "There is security on each of your floors."

Spending the night in a strange place, a strange bed, a scared seventeen-year old girl laid in her bed crying. The girl in the bed next to her was also going into the military as well. (But not joining the same branch of military service.) She looked over at Joan and asked. "Hey girl, you alright?"

"Yes," Joan answered sitting up on the side of her bed and looking over at the girl who had told her, her name was Mary Ann Webster. "I tried calling home to let my parents know I had arrived okay. My mother wouldn't except my phone call."

"You have never been away from home before?" Webster asked, in disbelief.

"Never. I live in Wellsburg and we didn't go very many places." Joan admitted.

"Wellsburg? I think I have heard of it. Isn't it a tourist attraction somewhere in the Southern part of our state? I believe it's close to Brown County?"

"One and only," Joan answered back.

"You do know what is ahead of you? Cause girl if you don't, then you are in for a lot of problems." Webster declared, looking at Joan who was probably around seventeen or eighteen, and looked very young and naïve for her age.

"Really?" Joan stated wondering what possibly could happen to her.

"Yes. So you will want to close your eyes and get some sleep because tomorrow is going to be extremely busy." Her roommate informed her.

The next morning at 5:30 am as promised by the petty officer, the young men and women were awoken. After eating a light breakfast of cereal, donuts, fruit, milk, or coffee, the group of young men and women were told to hop on the bus waiting outside the hotel to take them to the MEPS Center.

Of course Dave Wright was among the group, and as he walked past Joan, he stopped and spoke to her. "It's looks like you didn't sleep to well last night?" as she looked sort of worse for the wear.

"I didn't, if you must know," she snapped at him.

"What missing mommy and daddy all ready?" Wright continued with his antagonizing humor.

"No," she continued to be opposite with him.

"Sure could fool me," Wright insisted, as the guy behind him spoke. "Come on man, leave the girl alone. There are others waiting to get on the bus." Brian Matthews stated, as he looked at the girl with the bluest eye he had ever seen. As he followed the guy who had been talking to her, he asked. "Do you know her?"

"Yeah, we come from the same town,' Wright answered. "Her name is Joan Reddy and the coldest person you will have ever run into."Wright also informed him.

" Really! Well she just hasn't met the right guy yet," Matthews smiled.

"Don't get your hopes up," Wright added, "she has a black belt in judo, and there is a guy in Wellsburg who will testify to it."

"Why, what happen to him?" Matthews wanted to know.

"Let's just say he is limping around and having a hard time looking out of one eye." Wright replied with a sarcastic tone.

"She doesn't look like she could fight her way out of a wet paper bag, let alone beat up some guy?" Mathews stated back as he recalled the girl with the blue eyes, pouting lips, and perk nose. All in all she did look a little young for someone going into the military? "How old is this person?" Matthews asked, not recalling her name.

"Seventeen, or maybe she is eighteen by now. Who cares," Wright insisted, as he turned to watch the scenery going by.

About a block or so later, they were pulling up to the MEPS Center. Once in side the building they were taken to what was called a holding area and told to wait, that a personnel man would come and get them.

Feeling restless, Joan walked around the room reading different pamphlets for different branches of the military. Above the table for the Navy, a banner stated. "Navy---It's not just a job…It's an adventure) "It better be," Joan mumbled, as a guy came up behind her and asked. "Going into the military?"

"No just visiting," she curtly replied, not bothering to look at the person speaking to her.

"Thought so, for you look to young for anything else," Brian Matthews answered checking the girl out more closely as she finally looked at him with a cold hard stare. WOW! She was even cuter than he had imagined, he thought, as he took a closer look at the girl with the stunning blue eyes. "So do you have a name?" Matthews asked her, and wasn't quite ready for her response as she told him.

At first Joan was ready to ignore him, but that hadn't worked with Wright, so maybe she should try a different approach. "Yes," she indigently replied. "Puddin' tain'. .Ask me again and I'll tell you the same?"

"Did you have a second bowl of bitch flakes this morning?" Matthews grinned, thinking that he wasn't going to be so bored after all.

"Yes," Joan continued to be indifferent towards him.

"Oh darn and I was hoping to find out your name," Brian Matthew's insisted as he heard his name being called and the girl went back to reading the pamphlet she had picked up off of the table. "If you find anything of interest in that pamphlet Puddin-tain'," he told her before walking away, "let me know about it when I get back." he quickly added.

"You bet," Joan mumbled under her breath.

Reporting to the personnel office and filling out all of their paper work and beginning to sign their lives away to the United States Military, it became a situation of waiting for what they had been told would be a large scale of psychoanalysis tests and be given a complete physical.

Within the hour Joan was about to change her mind as far as the adventure went. She was beginning to wish she was anywhere, but where she was. Nothing could have been more humiliating when the statement was made. "Well we have a virgin. That condition won't last long!" after she had completed her pelvic exam. Being told to dress and return to the holding area, it was all she could do to face the girls standing behind the privacy curtains and having to listen to

24

some of their snickers and comments spoken in low whispers. What she really wanted to do was continue past the holding area, out the doors and go home.

Entering the holding area she was surprised to find so many people there. Everyone who was joining the military was seated in the room, all waiting for orders to take them to other designated areas in the building where they would have to pass security clearance, and talk to a career counselor. Trying to decide where would be a good place to sit and be alone came close to being impossible as she made her way past the rows of chairs already filled. Taking a seat on the outside of the last row, she opened the pamphlet she had picked up off the table near the door. Starting to read Dave Wright asking interrupted Joan. "Anybody sitting here?"

"Yes," she curtly answered, without looking up at the person since his voice was familiar.

Well it doesn't look like there're here now," Dave insisted, taking the empty seat and once again spoke to her. "I take it you are still pouting?" since her mood was pretty much the same as it had been earlier on the bus.

"I doubt it,' she declared, glancing at him as he continued to speak. "I take it you are still in the running?" he made the comment once he had her attention again.

"Yes, and I had hoped that you were back on your way home," Her sarcasm well defined in her voice as she answered him.

"Sorry to disappoint you, babe, but I am staying," Dave grinned at her.

"Too bad," she expressed, bending over and picking up her tote bag. Standing she moved away from him to wait for her name to be called. What seem like hours later, she finally heard her name and moved to the front of the room where a personnel man was sitting and told her? "You are to report to the career area," then he gave her directions on how to get there.

The rest of the morning a career counselor informed her about 'schools' after boot camp. Which according to him came under the heading of 'A schools', which taught you basically about everything you needed to know about the Navy and where you would fit in as far as your career went. 'C Schools' were more advanced, and you had to pass 'A schools' to get there. There were other schools, but he doubted if she would even have to worry about them he insisted, as he pushed a contract that needed her signature. (It was signing the contract that the guy found became a problem.) When he suggested, "We will put down as your first choice; Yeoman, second choice, engineman, and if these two fields are closed, as they sometimes are…what would be your third choice?"

"Boiler Technician," she replied, smiling as she gave him her answer.

Writing in her third choice, the counselor couldn't resist saying. "For all physical appearance, you seem to be a girl!" Then pushing the contract towards her, he told her with a precarious look. "Sign on the dotted line."

Having been warned by Jeff to read everything carefully, she corrected the counselor. "Excuse me. I would prefer that it read; engineman, boiler technician, and then yeoman."

"Even if I did change it to you're liking. I doubt very much if you would receive your choice. Not when they look at your physical stature," the counselor said with annoyance.

Her attitude well intact she looked back at him and stated with assurance, "then I guess you won't be getting my signature."

Great! Just what he needed this morning, a temperamental female? Reaching for a new job application he gruffly remarked, "Okay we will do it your way," commencing to type in the two finger fashion of hunt and peck. Signing the new document for job qualifications, Joan couldn't resist saying as she got up to leave. "Have a nice day!"

Looking at her the guy only grunted a greeting, as he thought about what his superior officer had said this morning, "we need to increase our female quota's."

With the rest of her day being filled with presumptuous questions and signing papers, she smiled when the security officer remarked, "you are so clean you squeak. Didn't your parents allow you to do anything?"

"Yes sir. Breathe," she couldn't resist answering.

Although the security officer had troubled keeping a straight face, he did comment under his breath, "for some reason I believe that." Looking again at her, he sensed something naïve and fresh about her.

Telling her to stay seated, he walked over to a computer busy giving prints outs. Knowing what it would read, upon returning to his seat, he told her. "I need you to read and sign this document on the dotted line. Then it's 'welcome aboard."

It was sometime later before she stood with what seemed fewer people in the holding area. Looking around she did see Dave Wright and the guy that had been persistent in talking to her. "I wonder what Dave Wright told him?" she thought as they glanced over in her direction and the guy tipped his hand in a salute to her. She was about ready to respond but was halted by the officer in the room speaking. "Attention!" Then he told them. "Raise your right hand and repeat the oath hanging on the wall behind me."

"I…do solemnly swear (or affirm) that I will support and defend the Constitution of the United States against all enemies, foreign and domestic; that I will bear true faith and allegiance to the same; and that I will obey the orders of the Uniform Code of Military Justice. So help me God."

4

Joan Reddy's orders had stated she would report to the USO Booth upon arriving in Atlanta Georgia, Finding the USO Booth, looking around she realized she wasn't alone. Never having really interacted with other people, she was unsure as to how to approach any of the other girls and introduce herself. Having always been a tomboy and being teased about it, and feeling different, she had developed a very-low self-esteem, and had developed an attitude to defend herself. Plus, she stood about 5ft 2.5 inches, with blond unruly curly hair, and had always felt she was a plain Jane.

Standing a little ways from the group of girls, she was surprised when one of the girls left the group and walked over to her. "Hi, my name is Lori Logan, and I am from Texas." the girl who stood about 5'7", dark brown hair, warm brown eyes, and a perpetual smile, spoke.

"Hi," Joan responded, telling her, "my name is Joan Reddy, and I am from Wellsburg Indiana."

"Where?" Lori Logan asked.

"Hicksville, USA," Joan added, with a nervous laugh.

"Oh," Lori laughed, "Your not far from where I live then," as both girls started laughing and talking about their hometowns.

"Do you really dress like pilgrims?" Lori stated, finding it hard to believe there was a place so quaint.

"Yes. My grandmother insisted that the towns' people play the part of the past. All of the stores had the vintage look inside and out." Joan informed her.

"Wow, how neat." Lori responded, and asks. "Is that why you joined the military, to get away from a quaint historical place?"

"That and other things, which I care not to talk about," Joan replied, as their attention was directed to a person in uniform. "When I call out your names, " he began to speak loudly. "I need you to walk over to those doors," pointing as he spoke, "and get on the bus waiting outside which will take you to Orlando Recruit Training Center. Also, as you walk pass me I need to hear your last name and social security number. That way, I know I will have the right person and you won't be getting on the wrong bus." Then the guy proceeded down the list in alphabetical order of calling out names.

"Well this is comfort," Lori stated taking a seat and motion for Joan to sit next to her. "Do you wonder what it's going to be like?" Lori went on to ask questions.

"Yes," Joan replied, and added. "Are you scared?"

"No, are you?" Lori responded.

"Some," Joan answered, "As she added. "Have you ever been away from home before?"

"No, but that is what makes it so exciting." Lori laughed, "I am going to look at it like a job, something that I would have to do and learn anyway. Besides, just look around us at all the neat guys we can meet?"

"Oh sure," Joan sighed, as she made herself comfortable and taking the small pillow she had found in the seat and curled up to go to sleep for the next couple of hours.

A sign that stated: "WELCOME ABOARD. You are a member of the UNITED STATES NAVY. The tradition of the service demands your finest efforts! Give it willingly." greeted the young men and women as they stepped off the bus in front of the INDOC Center at the Orlando Recruit Training Center.

"I think they mean it," Lori Logan stated, as she walked pass the sign and read it.

"Probably," Joan replied, as she followed Logan in to the building ahead of them.

As they entered the bay area, they were told they would be spending the next couple of days there while they waited for the rest of the young people to arrive from other MEPS Stations across the United States.

They were awoken early in the morning, and to their surprise, they were told. "You will be getting your first lessons in marching. Form a line of four across and follow me," the petty officer in charge told the girls, and as they did so, she called out. "Starting with your right foot, mark time in place," as she proceeded to show them how. Just when the girls thought they had it right, she called out. "Forward, march." For their first time marching, it was stepping on heels and trying to keep in step with the person

31

marching next to you. They found marching not so bad while they noticed the guys were not doing so great either.

"Ready Halt!" the Petty Officer in charge gave the command to stop. "Just what do you females think you are looking at? Because I know you don't have your eyes on those 'TREES'. For the next eight weeks I suggest that you consider all male recruits as just that, 'TREES'. Any and all fraternization is absolutely, no shape or form, tolerated. When you march you will maintain eyes forward at all times. Being caught doing otherwise will cause you to start back to day one."

"That's it, I want to go home." Logan replied, as others expressed their opinions to that little bit of news also.

"Well that is going to be pure torture," a long legged girl by the name of Ann Warner expressed, as she turned and looked longingly at the male recruits who stood a good distance from them as they waited to enter the mess hall.

"What? Going back to day one, or not being able to look?" Temaillia Jones insisted, as she looked over at the guys also.

"Both," Warner replied, as she turned her head back to face forward

While in the holding area they had been given a green card, a bed roll, and a packet which contain, stamps, stationary, and a postcard to be sent home letting people know they had arrived okay? Something else they were told after being given brown wrapping paper, string and tape to wrap any articles not military issued to be sent back home "That included makeup along with "Don't forget those curling irons, hair rollers, and any personal clothing in which you have brought with you," the petty officer in charge informed them as she walked down the marked red line on the floor and made sure they followed her orders.

It was a lot of grumbling and complaining as girls packed headsets, personal items, clothing and whatever else they were told to send back home. "How am I going to look good for all the new guys I am going to meet?" One girl groaned, as the petty officer walked past her.

"Trust me. You won't have time to primp or worry about 'trees'." the petty officer declared, checking the girl out to make sure she packed all the items that were not military issued. By the time the petty officer was finished with the girl, the only thing that was taken out of her suitcase was her underclothes, toothbrush and the items she needed for hygiene care.

"And just what am I suppose to wear?" The girl questioned as she was instructed to remove the clothing she was wearing.

"Oh I don't know. I thought I would have you finish the day in your underwear," the petty officer in charge, insisted, getting a blank stare from the girl. "I believe you were issued PT gear, I suggest you put it on, and do it quickly for your new company commanders will be here shortly."

At the end of their first week, day five, the first Friday of their training cycle, all one hundred and twenty-five girls were now ready to meet their company commanders. (Better known as C.C.'s.)

TD1 Betty Benson and AQ1 Margaret Greene were both in their mid-thirties and veterans when it came to training new recruits. Both stood aggressive and stern as they were introduced to the new recruits. "Ladies," Company Commander Benson started. "I would like to welcome you to training unit K-100 Division nine. Company Commander Greene and I are here to make your transition to Navy life as easy as possible.

We will for the next eight weeks be your friend, your mother, and your worst nightmare. We are here to instill in you things that you will remember through out your career with the Navy. We want you to be proud to serve as members of the Armed Forces. The things you will learn here will carry you through to be outstanding citizens. You will learn discipline and instilled habits that will automatically teach you precision and the ability to respond to orders quickly." Her voice carried as she looked over the new group under her lead command. Her eyes stopping now and then as she made first impressions of each girl. A habit in which she had acquired over the fifteen years as a company commander, and usually her first impression of someone was correct.

"Well this should be interesting?" C.C. Benson mused with her eyes falling upon the young girl standing before her. Reading the name, 'Seaman Recruit Reddy', her eyes went back to the face that showed a definite sign of animosity. She didn't need trouble facing her right off the top. But yet, she felt with this person there would be problems. Continuing to walk back and forth, the symbolic riding crop tapping either her hand or against her thigh, she again looked at the unit as a whole. "I expect each and everyone of you to be homesick. But you had better get a grip on it! I am not here to be your babysitter. Do I make myself clear?" Her words ringing out to each girl who stood a little straighter as the riding crop made the clicking noise and the c.c.'s eyes fell upon them. No words were spoken or needed to be with the eye contact made as C.C. Benson continued to speak. "Ladies, you have twenty minutes to vacate these premises and move into your new quarters." With that final statement made, C.C. Benson and C.C. Greene got into each girls face that looked lost and confused, and yelled. "Now move! Move! Move!"

The girl who had been made 'Recruit Training Petty Officer', then stepped forward and called out in a whining nasal tone, "You have twenty minutes to vacate this barracks."

"Oh please, someone teach her how to talk?" Ann Warner insisted, as she placed her hands over her ears. "We have eight weeks to listen to this?" she added, as she picked up her tote bag to fall in line with the other girls. Before they were marched to their new barracks, they were issued their allotted clothing, and other paraphernalia they were told by the Navy, 'would make you sailors'.

Their first cultural shock came, when they were told they would be getting haircuts. "Yes haircuts!" C.C. Greene stated, to the surprise expression on the girls faces.

"I paid fifty dollars for this perm," Ann Warner declared, as it came her turn to sit in the barber chair.

"You paid too much," Lori Logan commented sitting in the chair next to her.

"Well you just don't know style?" Warner insisted, looking over at the girl as the barber began to cut at her hair, and the replied. "Maybe not, but I do know what a comb is used for," Logan snickered, as she turned on the girl whom always appeared to be better than the others.

"And you think I don't," Warner continued with insistence as she looked at the person talking to her. Lori Logan, she asserted was well liked by the other girls in the unit, and she seemed to take everything in stride. She probably was considered average in her part of society? Blue collar would be what her family would call her, as Logan answered her. "You said it not me." Logan stated as C.C. Benson stepped in between the two girls. "Would you two like to finish this conversation elsewhere?" the C.C's voice stern.

"No ma'am," both girls quickly answered.

"I didn't think so?" the C.C.s remarked, as the barbers finished doing their hair. Not only were the two girls making comments, someone else was complaining. "It looks like a bowl was set on my head?"

Having heard enough of complaints, the C.C. told them not missing any words. "You will be happy with these short haircuts when you are standing outside and the temperatures are in the hundreds."

"What did she say?" Some of the girls waiting outside the barber shop asked, when one of the girls had stepped outside with a dumbfounded look on her face. "Look at it this way," Logan answered following the girl who seemed in a daze. "We have just entered into hell!"

Struggling with gear they had received in the past days, some were finding the task of moving not so easy. They stumbled, staggered and finally in some cases of desperation, dragged the paraphernalia they had received down three flights of stairs.

With the procedure of marching tall people in front. Short people in the rear, Ryan and Reddy found keeping up with the unit a difficult task. Not only were they last in line and being yelled at continuously to 'move it'. Reddy and Ryan tried not looking at the 'trees' they passed. "We do not talk to tree's," was a very important warning if they wanted to stay with their units and not in the holding area. Undoubtedly the trees had not been informed of the ruling before hand, as the 'trees' companies had made a sudden stop and dropped to do pushups. Bearing the trouble it would bring down on them, the girls found them swallowing giggles as they made efforts to march on and keep their mouths shut.

Reaching their new building several complaints started about having to carry sea bags, hatboxes, and whatever else they had been given up several flights of stairs. "They could have at least put in elevators," Reddy complained, finally making her way up the steps and into her new barracks. Looking around the huge room in which they would be spending out the remainder of boot camp, she questioned the move. "Why did they bother moving us? This building is identical to the one we just left?" Grey seemed to be the favorite color of the Navy. With a trim of beige to off set the gray. About the only thing bright in the whole room were the emergency doors. They were painted a blood florescent red. "At least we will be able to find our way out of here," Seaman Recruit Reddy commented, as she continued to search for her rack. Each bed was double racked, with a bin and locker at the end of each for storing your belongings.

Seaman Recruit Reddy and Seaman Recruit Ryan felt a break was in order before handling the task of putting anything away. Since neither chairs nor tables had been seen upon entering the barracks, the girls used their sea bags in which to rest upon. Talking, they didn't hear the order given to come to attention as C.C. Benson and C.C. Greene were announced on deck. Continuing to talk as their numbers were called, they answered from where they were sitting.

Seaman Recruit Perkins sound off "thirty-five", following Seaman Recruit Ryan answered. "Thirty-six," with Seaman Recruit Reddy following with a "thirty-seven". In the seconds that it took the girls to stand, C.C. Benson was towering over them. "Oh please, don't stand up on my account, that would be like showing respect for my rank!" her voice stern, her expression austere, "As a matter of fact you may drop and give me 30."

"We were resting," Seaman Recruit Reddy was quick to explain as to why they were not standing on the red line.

"You were what?" C.C. Benson calmly replied, while both girls felt the quake of her tone clear to the toes of their new chukkas. "We were resting," Seaman Recruit Reddy managed to repeat, although her voice wasn't as loud as she added. "We didn't hear the command to come to attention!"

Letting Seaman Recruit Reddy answer pass by C.C. Benson asked. "You do know the procedure when Company Commander Greene and I enter the deck? Or am I to assume that neither one of you can see the other girls standing at attention?"

One recruit managed a weak "no ma'am," while the other complained about having to carry her sea bag up two flights of stairs and her new chukkas were killing her feet. With her face only inches from Seaman Recruit Reddy's, as she continued her push-ups, C.C. Benson spoke in a monotonous tone. "Am I to believe that we should have hired a moving van to bring your things over here?"

Figuring it was already too late to make amends, Seaman Recruit Reddy didn't hesitate to answer the C.C. "It would have helped."

With her face stern and her actions full of authority, C.C. Benson straightened. Taking note of the fact that neither girl had stowed her gear, she didn't think as she gave the reprimand. "Pick up your sea bags. Since you two love them so well, you will really enjoy what you are about to do next?"

With some difficulty both girls complied with the order. Hugging their sea bags close to their bodies for support, their expressions strained, they waited for the next order." I don't believe I said anything about making love to them! I said hold them!" C. C. Benson commanded, as she took both girls arms and brought them straight out in front of their bodies. Their sea bag now held in a tight grip of their hands. "You will retain this position until I tell you otherwise," she spoke tight lipped. Then stepping away from the girls she went into her usual speech for new recruits.

"What! You thought the pushups were not enough," Ryan whispered to Reddy

"Sorry," Reddy managed, as she concentrated on keeping her hands gripped to her sea bag, and listen to C.C. Benson at the same time.

"I will expect top performance out of each and everyone of you, being second best does not cut it with me. If you cannot comply with this . . .we will have problems. Believe me ladies, I am good at solving problems," her steps deliberate, her look and her composure meaning to be comprehensible. The riding crop clicking against her pant leg as she continued to say." When you are given an order, I expect you to follow it without reason or why. Don't expect praise for something you learn and are expected to know. As a unit, you will learn the term teamwork. You will come to rely on this word. For only as a team will you make this unit work. Do I make myself clear?"

With her stride moving up and down the line each girl felt the fear of God being put before her. Their bodies were drawn to erect position and their eyes stared straight ahead. No one dared to flinch or look directly at Company Commander Benson and her commanding voice, but they did have their own thoughts. "Eight weeks of this…?"

Letting her words sink in, C.C. Benson glanced towards the two girls being reprimanded. One looked very much in pain and was crying. The other held a look of defiance and was standing stead fast, if not with some difficulty. You may defy me now young lady, C.C. Benson found herself thinking of Seaman Recruit Reddy. But in the end…you will find that I am the victor. Then taking her eyes away from the two girls she continued to tell the unit. "Junk food is not permissible while in training. For those of you who smoke? Bummer. There is no smoking any where on base. Talking, using the phone and some other privileges has to be earned. You will be encouraged to write home and keep in touch with your families. You will only be able to send mail when the mailbox is not secured. You will receive mail call each day after 1800." In finishing her lecture, she looked down as the two girls still holding their sea bags. Walking towards them, and standing in front of them, she spoke. "Do you two think you could come to attention when the order is called?"

"Yes ma'am!" one replied, with difficulty, while the other cried even harder.

"You may then set down your sea bags," C.C. Benson informed them, then turning she started to walk away.

"Well it's about time," Seaman Recruit Reddy grumbled, dropping the sixty-pound sea bag with a thug to the floor. C.C. Benson turned so quickly that Recruit Reddy didn't have time to blink or think about what she had just said. C.C. Benson face came so close to Seaman Recruit Reddy's that their noses almost touched. "What did you say?" Her voice a choked whispers, but deadly stern.

Now was not the time to show panic, Reddy thought quickly as she answered in a voice stronger than she thought possible. "I said, it was about time."

"Oh really?" C.C. Benson asked it as a question, and Reddy didn't think she wanted a response as she too steadily looked back at C, C. Benson with the look of defiant still posed on her face.

Returning to her stance of authority, it became a standoff between the company commander and the new recruit. Looking directly as Seaman Recruit Reddy, C.C. Benson informed the other recruits. "Seaman Recruit Reddy will be giving you your first order of the day. I want this deck policed until every nook and cranny shines. Do I make myself clear?" To Seaman Recruit Reddy she added. "You will stand fast while the others do the work for you."

"Excuse me ma'am. I believe I should be working along side the others." Seaman Recruit Reddy couldn't resist not having the last word in.

"Oh no I couldn't let you do that. You need to continue to rest." C.C. Benson glared at her. Then again having her face directly in front of hers, her voice lowered. "Don't push it. For I am sure you wouldn't enjoy the consequences." C.C. warned, before turning and making a motion for C.C. Greene to take over charge of the deck.

Somewhere in the middle of the day, the company was then taken to receive their dental records, vaccination shots, and dog tags made. After that, while standing outside the personnel office, they were taught how to stand in formation.

Once back in their barracks, they were handed notebooks and shown a blackboard that would have the duties of the day wrote on it and they were to copy this every morning. They were also told that they had to memorize the chain of command from the President of the United States all the way down to the company commandeers and be able to recite it at a moments notice. If you could not recite it, you would have to do push ups.

As a matter of fact, you had to do push-ups anytime you made a mistake. One thing you learned was that attention to detail was extremely crucial in the Navy. From making your bunks a certain way to folding your clothes a certain way to even making sure your 'gig line' was straight. The 'gig line' is where your shirt buttons are lined up to the zipper on your pants and the edge of your belt buckle was lined up to the button on your pants. If this wasn't even close to a straight line, you were doing a lot of push-ups.

During weeks one through four the company learned survival at sea, the history of the Navy, the rights and responsibilities of the Navy, and physical training at 0500.

Physical training alternated with calisthenics on one day and running on the other. Reddy preferred the calisthenics. For some reason every time she ran, she puked. Some of the other girls said that it was because she didn't breathe right. What ever that meant? She ran and then she breathed rapidly, then she would throw up. The company commanders said it was because she was just getting excess air out of her lungs due to never running before. What did they mean? She ran up and down the hills of Brown Country.

Her first glimpse of people coming off of the grinder, as the track was called where they ran, looked like they had just ran the Boston Marathon. The problem of not being able to run would become the focus of all of Reddy's problems in boot camp.

5

The routine was basically physical training of a morning, and when the sun was at it's hottest point, you set in an air conditioned classroom learning the procedures of the military. Well this isn't so bad after all most of the girls thought. But for those who were finding being away from home the pits, the transition to military life was unbearable.

Sitting down and starting to eat, most of them were to tired to talk or complain after spending two hours on the drill field learning how to march and carrying rifles. Which for some was a difficult task as the terms: right flank, left flank, double time, march, were orders they were not a custom too. Seaman Recruit Hill was bawling as usual and Warner was finding it hard to digest her food to Hill's constant sniffling. "Why is it every time we sit down to eat, you end up bawling?" Warner yelled at Hill. "Do you have any idea of what you are doing to my appetite? Why hel!, I don't need to go on a diet, I have you to make sure I don't eat."

"I can't help it if I want to go home!" Hill whined.

"Well hell, don't we all." Warner declared, "but you don't see us bawling at every meal."

"Oh leave her alone," Logan came to Hill's defense, and spoke out to the girl who seemed aloof to the other girl's feelings. "She is just homesick and having a hard time being away from home.

"After three weeks? Damn, she needs to get a grip on life," Warner snapped, as some of the others agreed with Warner.

"Maybe if you were a little nicer to her, she would?" Logan suggested, looking over at Hill, and couldn't help inwardly to agree. It did seem that Hill was always crying over one thing or another and if she didn't get a grip on military life, she would be sent back to the holding area, soon.

"That would be an improvement for Warner," Reddy butted in who had been targeted a few times by Warner as being a daddy's girl, and needed to grow up.

"Excuse me. This is an A and B conversation. So why don't you C your way out of it," Warner sitting next to Reddy warned her.

"I would if I could see around you," Reddy snapped back, as the rest of the girls worried about a fight breaking out. Logan sitting across from Reddy warned. "It's not worth going to IT over." Thinking about it, Reddy backed down from Warner, but not before assuring her. "This isn't over?"

The weekends found the girls cleaning barracks, shining shoes, and studying their 'Blue jacket Manual'. If you had a good week, the company commanders would march you to the commissary so you could stock up on shampoo, soap, and other personal articles, or call home. Which today was what Company K-100 had the privilege of being able to do.

As Reddy was making the call collect, she kept thinking 'let them be home'? It would be great hearing her fathers voice again, Seaman Recruit Reddy thought as she waited for someone to answer the phone. Finally someone picked it up and she heard her mother say to the operator. "Yes?" speaking with discord to be interrupted from whatever she had been doing. After the operator explains the call, Reddy was surprised to her mother's reaction. "Tell her to call when she can pay for it!" then there was silence as her mother hung up the phone.

Fighting back tears she turned to Logan who had been waiting in line behind her. "I guess there is no one at home." she mumbled, stepping away from the phone booth.

Returning back to the building, they received mail call. Taking a seat on the deck next to her rack, she begins to shuffle through the stack of mail she had been handed. A couple of the letters were from home. There were two in which she didn't recognized the handwriting. Who do I know at Great Lakes? She wondered as again she checked the return addresses. Her call home almost forgotten as her curiosity rose and she begin to open the first letter from Great Lakes and begin to read:

> "Hi. Bet you are wondering who would be writing you from NRTC? Think back...Indiana! The guy who was persistent in trying to talk to you. Now do you remember? (Not really, she thought continuing to read) Well if you don't I really can't blame you. But

anyway, I was wondering if you have found Navy life to be a great adventure? I sure haven't. I could think of a million places I would rather be than having my butt chewed on every day. How about you? Or maybe it's different when you are a girl in boot camp?

In case you are bored here is something to think about. There are ninety guys to one girl up here. Don't ask why I felt compelled to tell you this little bit of news. Since I saw you first. Oh by the way, my name is Brian Matthews. I got your address from Dave Wright, who says he knows you quite well. I hoped you don't mind. If you care to answer this, please do so. It gets pretty lonely around here when mail call is called, and you don't received letters.

Then Brain Matthews went on to tell her that he was from South Bend, Indiana, and other personal things about him. Like what kind of music he listens to. What kind of hobbies he likes. Even down to why he had joined the military. At the end of the letter, he again begged her to write back.

Brian? Who do I know by that name? Trying to place a face with the name. Picking up the next letter with the same markings, she wondered if Brian what's his name had wrote two letters. Looking at the name on the return corner of the envelope, she grumbled. "What in the world does he want?" when she saw who it was from. Suspicious, she opened the letter from Dave Wright and begins to read.

"Hi. I didn't know you met someone at MEPS? Well anyway this guy by the name of Matthews ask me for your address. I gave it to him; I figured you probably needed a little excitement in your life by now.

Look if you are having a good time don't answer this. This place has to be the pits. I mean you almost didn't get this letter. The damn mailbox is always secured. I called the folks. They thought Great Lakes, was another state in a remote area. I had a hard time assuring them it wasn't. Mother did her usual crying and wanted to know if they were treating me okay. I told her I was fine. Dad was thrilled to know I was surviving and wouldn't be back home for a while.

Speaking of home, how about a date when we get leave? We should be getting it about the same time. At least give it some thought, after all we now have a lot in common. That is if I haven't gotten kicked out of here. There is a good chance I may be. We have the meanest, roughest, company commander that God ever put breath into. When he yells the other companies snap to attention. My rifle and I are well acquainted. I feel naked without it. Even had to sleep with it a few times. It was not by choice, I can assure you of that.

I am very good at getting up. Let me tell you I am now the first person out of his rack and standing on the line. It took one treatment of sleeping in for me to realize when reveille is called, you have better be up. I sleep on the top rack. Do you know how quickly my eyes came open when my company commander dumped me; I mean mattress, blanket, sheets and all. I thought my nose was broke.

I told the guys about you, so I better get a letter back. Take that as a warning, Dave. P.S. I wrote Peggy for your address."

Reading the last line she mumbled, "thanks Peg, just what I wanted, the biggest jerk from Wellsburg writing me? Not only is he writing me, but also he handed out my address. She continued to complain as she tried remembering who Brian Matthews was.

Even though she rejected the thought of Dave Wright letter, she found herself walking over to her locker and taking out pen and paper. A letter to the guys, then to the folks, she smiled to the idea. Her first letter was off to Dave Wright:

"Dear Dave, I must admit I was surprised to hear from you. Heaven only knows what you probably have said about me? I am not even sure why I am bothering to answer your letter. I guess I am bored.

About company commanders, I am still trying to figure ours out. Let's say I do a lot pushups and standing at attention. I too have found that sleeping in doesn't make a C.C. day. But this beats being in Wellsburg any day. I have friends, something that I didn't really have in Wellsburg, maybe except for Maureen.

About the folks, I tried calling home but mother wouldn't accept my call. But I am getting letters so I know that everything is okay. Peggy is keeping me informed about all the things that everyone is doing. It's funny she didn't mention any thing about you wanting my address, ha.

Peggy says mother has lightened up on her and she is doing a lot more dating and going places. But, I am sure you already know this. I will leave it up to you if you care to continue to write. Joan."

Now for what's his name, a smile broke across her face even though she was still having trouble putting a face with the name?

"Hello Brian, you are right about one thing. I don't remember you. Please don't let this keep you from writing for I enjoyed getting your letter.

Let's say that this adventure is different. No I don't enjoy being yelled at all the time either. As far as being somewhere else, would it be any better? I really wonder if it would be any different? We would still have to take orders from someone. I choose to be here and for the next four years, it is up to me to make the best of it. That is if I make it through boot camp. I came here very naïve about a lot of things, and I suppose I am spoiled in some ways, as well as having been protected by my family. Some of the things I hear the girls talking about, I can hardly believe.

Even if Wellsburg was a place out of time and their parents controlled every teenager, things weren't as bad as some of the girls in my company had it. Even with mother and I always having different opinions, I knew what a home life was like. Several of the girls in our unit didn't even seem to have that?

I don't know about you, but I never was raised around African Americans. Here I am learning to live with them and to find out that they are just as equal as you and I. They want the same as us, a future in an every-changing world

And hoping to make something of their lives and to be independent without welfare and to be respected, as they should be, I feel that we should all come together as one, when it comes to our lives and our country.

About the odds being ninety guys to one girl? They can stay that way. I have only one goal in life for the time being that is to make it through the next four years with no commitments to anyone but myself. I promised my grandmother that I would wait until I was thirty, before I had a relationship with someone. Probably being a tomboy and the career I have chosen, no guy will want me any way?

As she continued to write Brian, she also told him about her likes and dislikes. She realized that she was saying things to a total stranger and as she signed off the letter, she thought only for a second as to what he might think.

During the third week, they realized that learning about chemical warfare, survival, evasion and escape, came under the term teamwork. That learning some things about being in the military could almost be fun.

Chemical warfare consisted of going through a chamber of tear gas. They had been told before starting to put their facemask on to make sure it fit properly. You will go through the chamber twice once without the mask, once with the mask. Do not touch your face or any exposed area of your body at any time. I repeat. Do not touch your face," the instructor warned, adding. "You will hold the belt loop of the person in front of you. Do not let go of this person for any reason. In your other hand, you will hold your mask. See we do make it easy for you to keep your hands away from exposed area. Is everyone ready for the first trip through?" What looked like a space invasion one hundred and sixty young men and women in chemical warfare suits nodded their heads, yes. "Move out," the instructor called next.

This isn't too hard, the girl in Company K-100 thought as they made the first trip through. The second trip was a different story. Their eyes watered, their mouths became dry and choking was easier than breathing." Are we almost there?" Several girls tried saying? Seaman Recruit Reddy was literally shoving the girl in front of her as those behind kept up a steady push for the nearest exit.

Going through the hatch door, they were told. "Turn your face towards the wind." What wind? Several girls thought as they turned in every direction. They were in Florida, there was hardly any wind, heat yes, but no wind unless a storm was brewing. Which unfortunately wasn't the case today.

Their second step in survival found them in the pool area. The object: Learning how to stay afloat by using their clothing as a saving device. "Should you find yourself in the water, the most important thing to do . . .is to remain calm. If you see any floating debris nearby try and latch on to it. Otherwise, remove and inflate your trousers," the instructor informed them as he pointed to several people standing around the edge of the pool.

"Don't worry ladies and gents, if you find yourself in a panic we will save you!" Then he begins to explain the procedure to the young ladies waiting to hit the water. "Once in the water, rapidly but calmly begin to remove your clothing," the instructor told them, as the people who were in the water, showed them the procedure in which to save themselves.

"I am going to drown," Hill whined watching the guys in the pool.

"Hell, I want to drown," Warner stated speaking in a whisper, to Logan who was standing next to her. "Boy do I know that feeling," Logan answered back. "I really don't want to drown, just come close to it?" she laughed. Looking at some of the guys in the pool.

"Oh well here it goes.", Reddy thought as it came her turn to jump into the pool fully dressed, shoes and all. It took some struggling and drinking half the pool before she managed to get her pants off, tied in knots and gathered around her neck. Climbing out of the pool, she saw C.C. Benson standing close by. 'Oh please don't tell me I have to do it again?" Reddy thought as she started pass C.C. Benson. "You can do some things right," C.C. Benson stated, as Reddy came by here.

'I try," Reddy was thinking, as she answered. "Yes ma'am."

The last lesson of the day for survival came under evasion? Evasion, avoiding the enemy at all possible cost. Obviously the most important consideration in evasion is knowledge of where the enemy is," as the instructor told them, "Survival is a state of mind. If you panic, you will be caught. Try at all times to keep your wits about you. This is a major lesson in survival. It is your determination to live and your ability to make nature work for you that are the deciding factors. The best way to reduce the shock of being isolated behind enemy lines is to remember to keep calm, and value living."

They had been given a ten-minute break as Logan walked up to Reddy and asked. "Having fun yet?"

"Loads of it," Reddy giggled, as she asked Logan. "How did we get in a desert?" as she recalled the instructors talking about being lost in a desert? "I thought we were on ships?"

Logan agreeing with her commented laughing. "Well they do let us off the ships once in a while!"

"I'm glad you cleared that up for me. I thought maybe we had been shipwrecked?" Reddy answered, as a guy moving closer to Reddy interrupted the two girls. "Haven't you heard? Camels are the ships of the desert?" Seaman Recruit Rourke remarked, moving yet closer to the girl whom he had been taking notice of on several different occasions. Her look fierce, her voice low, but stern she told him. "Do you mind?" stepping away from him. It wasn't the first time she had encountered him, she realized as she recalled one other incident when entering the classrooms, and he was standing close to where the girls had to march by. His way of looking at her, had made her feel very nervous, and in a way that she hadn't cared for.

Once more Reddy felt the hair standing up on the back of her neck, as this character looked her over like maybe she had forgot to dress. She was relieved when time was called and they had to report back to the classrooms. "Do you know him?" Logan inquired as they walked back into the building.

"Heavens no," Reddy quickly replied in a whisper so not to draw attention to Logan and her for talking.

It was a different instructor and they were told, "This is part of your basic seamanship which covers the learning of ropes." For the next several hours they became familiar with knots, bends, hitches and whipping that had anything to do with ropes and ships.

That evening sitting on the deck the girls practiced ropes. Several comments were made about how they had wished they had paid more attention to their mother's and learning knot tying. "I don't know what this has to do with engines?" Reddy complained having problems with a round turn and two half hitch.

"I can remember my mother sitting for hours and making all sorts of art and crafts with ropes. She made end tables that were extended from the ceiling, plant hangers, and wall decorations. Dad was beginning to think we had moved to the jungle." Hill spoke up.

"My mother was into arts and crafts for bazaars," Warner told them. The girls that once were fighting with each other were now friends. Sitting off in one section of the deck, talking quietly. Helping each other remember the general orders for watch standing. Talking about home and how they were beginning to accept being away from home.

Brown, who was the only African American girl sitting among the small group told them. "I got a letter from my mother. She is finding it hard to believe I am not parked in front of a television."

"My mother is finding it hard to think I don't have a radio going full blast," Logan added.

"My mom it really finding it hard to believe that we are not going to a mall, and hanging out," Warner laughed.

"Boy wouldn't that be fun," Logan joined in., as the others agreed, as Logan looked at Reddy, who had become awful quiet. "What does your mother say about you not listening to music or watching television?"

With bitterness, Reddy stated. "My mother could care less about what I am doing."

"Boy, I wish I could say that," Hill remarked, "My mother worries about me all the time," and added "I am not surprised that she hasn't called the base commander?"

"She probably has but you just don't know it," Stevens. A girl whom seemed always to be listening in on everyone's conversation mentioned, as she spoke up and looked down upon the girls talking. "Well I guess we just found out what your problem is Hill? You're a mommy's girl!"

"Yes, I am. So what is your point?" Hill declared, and shocked everybody by finally standing up for herself. "Hill!" Warner stated. "You are finally standing up for yourself, and you are not crying?" Warner stated, which brought laughter from the others girls still sitting in the circle.

"Yes, aren't you proud of me," Hill smiled.

"Now if only we could get Reddy's attitude under control," Logan suggested in a teasing manner.

"That will be our next project," Warner insisted, as she stood and looking at her watch told the others, "Taps will be playing soon."

It was the next morning after breakfast that the girls in the front of the line came to a direct halt and caused commotions through out the entire company as those following the lead bumped into, stumbled and stared in disbelief at the barracks which they had left in a neat order. The barracks had been turned into total chaos. Every bit of bedding, clothing, you name it was thrown on the deck.

Some where in books, unknown to recruits in order to react to orders, you must not question the authority of your C.C.s. That any orders or punishment they handed out, you accepted. That the company commanders were there to teach you to react to any given situation. They started by breaking you down, then building your character stronger. It was the brow beating and verbal abuse, that was to make you stronger and make you react quickly. "You have twenty-five minutes to have this place back in order." Company Commander Benson commanded the company as they stood in shock to the chaos. "I suggest that you get moving. We have general inspection in thirty minutes." she added, before leaving the deck.

"I wonder who pissed her off," Logan grumbled, reaching for a mattress and throwing it back upon her rack.

"It wasn't me this time," Reddy declared, searching through her stuff, and folding her clothes as quickly as she could.

"I think this is what they call a drug raid," Someone else suggested.

"Oh! Who would be so stupid to use drugs," Warner remarked, as she stood making her rack.

"Who knows," Hill complained, as she proceeded to put her things back in a neat order.

It was by some miracle that the girls managed the feat of having the deck cleaned by the time the company commanders came through with the 'Commander of the base,' and she gave her approval to almost everything. In their haste to do field day, and stand attention in a neat and orderly fashion, they forgot to check their clothes to make sure their 'gig line' were in order. Out of the eighty-five girls about half of them were unsatisfactory.

You could tell by the grim look on Company Commander Benson's face that she wasn't to please about them, and they all knew that they would probably be standing at attention for a while. Sure enough, the order was called and for four hours they stood on the red line. Some of the girls passed out from locking their knees up.

It was the weekend and looking at the blackboard which told them what they would be doing each day, the girls groaned when they realized it was the Saturday where they would compete for the 'Over all Sports Award', against the other companies. They had to compete in an obstacle course, tug-of-war, volleyball, swimming, and various track and field events.

Darren McCall had been keeping his eye on a very cute girl, with striking dark blue eyes and very unruly curly hair, in his sister company. Her height couldn't have been more than the minimum height allowed. Not saying anything to her but just watching, more often than not she was chosen to run in the relay races. "There was something about her that spoke of innocence." Darren McCall thought to himself as he walked over to where she was getting ready to run again.

For some unbelievable reason they had her posted to run in the relay races again. Thank God, Brown was running after her, and the fact that she had long legs, maybe she could take up the slack, Reddy was thinking as Brown spoke. "Don't think about winning, just run. I'll do the rest," It wasn't a great distance that Reddy came upon her with, but taking the baton, Brown managed to put distance between the other girls and she had kept them from losing the heap.

With her sides hurting and her breathing difficult, C.C. Benson told her. "Walk around." Walk around? She's got to be kidding, she couldn't even breathe let alone walk!

She wasn't sure how far she had walked when she heard. "Nice day for running?"

Slowly lifting her head she looked up to see who was dumb enough, or willing to repeat the past few weeks. It was he! The 'tree' with the friendly eyes and warm smile Reddy took note as she felt the color rushing to her face. "So we meet again?" McCall grinned, to the shy repose of the girl who he had been searching for in the galley, on the fields and in the classrooms.

"It would seem so," Reddy stammered, beginning to feel very nervous as she looked around to see where the company commander's were.

Seeing her nervous reaction to him standing so close, McCall smiled as he said. "I think we are safe?"

"I sure hope so, for I wouldn't care to repeat any of the past few weeks," she groaned as she stood up to her full height.

"Been that bad?" He mischievously grinned.

"Let's say I have had better days," she declared with sobriety, and realized that she was actually talking to a guy without being tongue tied and all nervous.

"Is that why the RCPO was so nice to you a few minutes ago?" He asked, with a light chuckle.

Thinking about how Cunningham had yelled and called her names before she lined up to run, was anything but nice she declared. "You sure could have fooled me," she answered him.

"Should have told her to take a hike," McCall insisted, continuing to talk to her while they had a fifteen-minute break before moving on to the next events.

"I don't think that would have been a good idea," Reddy assured him looking around again.

Thinking that maybe she was having a rough time with the RCPO, McCall reminded her. "You don't have to take her mouth, she is one of us?"

"That may be so," Reddy answered, "But I am walking a thin line right now," she admitted to him, as both of them heard the whistle for breaks to be over with.

"Guess I had better be going," McCall stated, as he turned and walked away, with only a few inches from her he turned back around and told her. "By the way my name is Darren McCall."

With the weekend behind them, physical training, school, and keeping out of the C.C. hair were Seaman Recruit Reddy's main objective as far as getting through boot camp.

It seemed she was still having problems with the company commanders. That she always had a comeback to their ideas or suggestions. Once more her attitude would take precedence over everything she was told to do. Why she was making so much trouble for herself, she couldn't understand. Especially when she was enjoying what she was learning. It seemed that everything was going against her. Not only was she creating problems for herself, but also for others in her company. Her morale was dropping and she didn't help matters as she let her attitude take perseverance to prove the company commanders right about her.

Feeling extra sleep was entitled to her since she had stood watch until 0500; Seaman Recruit Reddy had ignored the call to reveille and covered her head. Ryan seeing that Reddy was still in her rack tired getting her up. Shaking her, Ryan insisted. "Time to rise and shine."

"Forget it Ryan. You rise forget shine. I am not moving from here," Reddy mumbled from under her covers and vowed to herself to get more sleep.

"Doing her morning inspections, C.C. Greene upon reaching the spot where Seaman Recruit Reddy should have been standing. Inwardly groaning as she saw the person in question still in her rack, she took steps to stand beside Reddy's rack. It took only one lift with her hands to dump bedding and girl to the floor. "What in the hell?" Reddy sputtered as she quickly opened her eyes and made the attempt to sit up right. Untangling herself from her mattress and bedding, and looking up, she came one on one with Company Commander Greene standing over her. Letting out a louder groan and knowing she was in trouble she mumbled." Look out holding area here I come?" Knowing that her day was ruined.

Stepping on the red line Reddy stood waiting for the order of her reprimand. She didn't have to wait long as she and Seaman Recruit Ryan were told. "Give me twenty," by Company Commander Greene. Dropping to the deck, Reddy and Ryan began to count off, 'one company commander. Two, company commander," the count continuing until they reached twenty-company commander. When the girls fell back into rank Company Commander Greene made the point of saying. "I hope you two don't plan on holding us up and longer?" One gave the reply of, "no ma'am." The other was still bent on having the last word replied. "I stood watch until 0500. I figured sleep was entitled to me."

"What did you say?" C.C. Greene was in her face.

Her expression not changing, Reddy repeated what she had said. In a chasten tone, C.C. Greene spoke. "I keep for getting that you expect special treatment,' and with the next order Reddy was told to stand at attention until told otherwise. Of course this meant that the whole company had to do the same.

As they girls were preparing to leave the barracks for classes Ryan spoke with vengeance as she told Reddy. "Stay away from me. I am tired of taking punishment for your stupid mistakes."

"O…oh! And you think you're so perfect?" Reddy rejected Ryan's remark.

"Yes," Ryan snapped as she added. "I wish you would grow up so the rest of us wouldn't have to suffer for your stupidity."

"Well excuse me for living," Reddy retorted, fighting back tears as she got plenty of looks and comments in agreement with Ryan.

Finding friends was few as they insisted she was a spoiled brat and a daddy's girl. The letters that she wrote home more than expressed her feelings.

"Dear dad. Help! Get me out of here. I have no friends and I am beginning to believe this was a big mistake. Mother was right about one thing. I don't belong here. Joan"

If things weren't already at their worst for Reddy several days later when she was standing duty, she was suppose to get Sanders up early because she was in special drills squad. Reddy tried waking Sanders up on time and Sanders refused to get up so Reddy kept waking her up until she threaten to punch her if she didn't leave her alone. Leaving her alone,

Reddy didn't realize that she would be the one in trouble for Sanders being one hour late for drills.

The next morning, during muster Reddy received word from the RCPO that C.C. Benson wanted to see her.

Company Commander Benson waiting for Seaman Recruit Reddy thought about the phrase that company commanders were told over and over. "Before you can lead, you must have followers. Before you can be a good leader, you must have willing followers. Both Company Commander Greene and her were finding this phrase difficult as they tried to teach Company K-100 to be good followers. Telling them over and over. "You need to learn discipline. Standards of conduct in which you are expected to follow…that the chain of command exists to ensure you did. They found that this phrase needed to be repeated to some more than just a few times.

Having the feeling that she was about to make Company Commander Benson day from the fumigating glare she was receiving, she wasn't to shock when Company Commander Benson commented. "I knew you would be trouble. I just didn't realize that I would be seeing you more than the others. I understand that you made Seaman Recruit Sanders late for drills?"

"No ma'am," Reddy corrected her, thinking she was given permission to reply.

With a look of disgust, C. C. Benson questioned. "Are you saying that you are not the reason that Seaman Recruit Sanders was late for drill?"

"Yes ma'am. I woke her up several times and she told me to leave her alone. So I did."

Already knowing the reason, C.C. Benson continued to stare at Seaman Recruit Reddy as she thought to herself, 'okay young lady I can play your game. Let's see how well you do with IT?' "I am recommending that you be sent to IT. I believe this will help you to change your attitude." Her sternness holding in her voice as she added. "That will be all Seaman Recruit Reddy." As Reddy left her office, C.C. Benson shook her head at the thought. Usually I am here to inspire young people to do their best. With this one, I am finding it more of an order. But yet, I have been wrong about her, I feel that she will make a very good sailor! As she recalled on several different occasions she had seen Reddy helping others who were dragging behind.

IT consisted of people doing drills in winter clothing, leggings, wool caps, and a backpack on their backs. They went through marching drills, pushups, and whatever else the drill instructor could throw at them. This method of discipline did nothing to improve her attitude as she more than once thought of undesirable names for the C.C. Drawing the conclusion that things were not going to improve for her, she once again thought. "Dad, get me out of here?"

After completing IT, returning back to her unit she was surprised when Seaman Recruit Logan called out to her during free time. "Hey Reddy, why don't you join us?" Reddy was ready to walk on past the group that always seemed to be together. Why not? She then thought as she turned and walked back to the group. "How is it going?" Logan asks, as Reddy took a seat next to her on the deck.

"You really don't want to know," Reddy grated with malice in her tone. "One thing for sure, I owe Sanders one?"

Not sure of the reason why Reddy had been sent to IT. Warner spoke up. "Try getting up and you won't be having problems with stepping on the C.C. toes," lightly laughing as she remembered Reddy being dumped from her rack several days ago.

"Right!" Reddy glared, giving Warner the impression that maybe she was pressing her luck. Not taking too much heed to Reddy's attitude, Warner continued to tell her. "Really Reddy, if you would change your attitude things around here would go much better for all of us, including you?"

"My attitude? Well let me tell you there are plenty of others with the same problem," Reddy declared, still throwing threatening looks at Warner.

Logan having heard enough of Reddy's whining added her own opinion. "Maybe so," she interrupted. "But they know how to keep their mouths shut, you don't."

"Oh really?" Reddy chided, as she proclaimed. "I don't expect to kiss ass . . .Now or never."

"I don't think anyone expects you to kiss ass, but you could comply with the rules. Do you know how impossible you are making it for all of us?" Warner declared again.

"Well excuse me!" Reddy stormed, jumping up and with quick steps walked to her rack. She was offended by the idea of there thinking she was the only one causing trouble. That night she let the tears flow freely. She had five weeks left of training and she was beginning to think she wouldn't make it.

6

They had been told that during their fifth week, they would be doing what was called workweek. Work week, was where you worked in different areas learning what it was like to work in the real Navy. Company K-100 and their brother company C-101 had drawn the lucky number by starting in the galley.

Working in the galley, you seated companies and cleaned tables. After showing the companies where to sit down, (while they stood at attention) they would say. "Welcome to the galley. You have 20 minutes and 20 minutes only to eat your fine Navy chow! Take your seats!"

After everyone had been served, and the galley was empty, you got to clean the tables, the deck, and the bulkheads. It was during this time that Hill, was sent on a bullshit errand to locate 'bulkhead remover' (Wall remover) she thought it was a spot remover to clean the walls with. It took her 2 hours before she caught on that the guys were playing a joke on her.

Work week, was also the unofficial time to pick up dates for the graduation field trip to Circus Land, or better known as 'control weekend,' Also it was one time that the company commanders weren't around you.

They even had humor thrown in as the guys complained more than the girls. " I don't see how anybody could catch a damn thing in the military. Why were all so clean we squeak," Thomas grumbled as he cleaned tables.

"I am surprised that we are not polishing the silver," Warner added to the complaints as she too washed down tables. "I never had to do this at home," she stated, holding up her once neatly manicured nails. "I don't believe my hands will ever look the same?"

"Will you two shut-up," Rourke warned, and before he could finish the last word, the 'petty officer in charge', walked over to where the three were working. "Is there a problem?" He questioned with rigor.

"No sir," all three answered as they quickly went back to scrubbing the tables. As the 'petty officer in charge' walked away, Rourke glared at Warner and Thomas and mumbled something about how he wasn't going back to day one. Not for anyone.

"Planning on going UA?" Thomas laughed, not caring whether the PO heard him or not.

"Maybe," Rourke couldn't resist saying in a low tone.

"Good luck. You are going to need it," Thomas added.

"Will you shut-up?" Rourke snapped, as he scrubbed harder on the deck.

"Careful, you don't want to raise the varnish," Thomas continued to make comments as he looked at Rourke and knowing he was pushing buttons where he was concerned. It was quickly learned in the barracks that Rourke was a hot head, and that he was close to being sent back to day one.

When break was called the girls collapsed in the nearest spot they could find. "I have a friend who does this for a living as a waitress. I think I will write her and tell her she would love the military?" Logan declared, removing her chukkas and rubbing her feet.

"I think I prefer marching to this," Reddy spoke up and got quite a few looks form the other girls. For marching was one thing Reddy did plenty of complaining about as she had to march in the last row.

"Boy if only my mother could see me now. She would be in shock, I don't know how many times she yelled at me to keep my room clean." Hill stated as the girls looked at each other and realized they were changing. With this in mind the girls began to share the reasons as to why they had came into the military. "I wanted something more out of life than staying on the welfare row," Brown expressed. "I have a little girl back home that is living with my parents. I feel that I can take better care of her after I get out of boot camp."

Hill next explained why she was there, "As I said, I spent most of my time in front of a television. I guess mom got tired of seeing me just hanging around the house and supporting me. She insisted that I get a job, or a life, only she didn't expect me to join the military."

"You call this a life," Logan laughed, as she added. "I don't think my mother was to happy about me joining the military. I lost a brother in Lebanon, and a father in Vietnam. I guess I felt the need to follow in their footsteps. Not that I am planning on dying or anything."

"I guess I have the least reason to be here," Warner spoke next. "I was at this party playing a game called, 'truth or dare'. I pulled a dare, which consisted of me joining the military. No one actually thought I would go through with it?" Which in saying she received a lot of curious stares and Logan made the comment. "I guess when you are rich and bored, why not?"

Instead of saying something to start an argument with Logan, Warner stated. "I am not sorry I took the dare. I have met some very nice people whom I consider my good friends."

Reddy being the youngest among them felt out of place as it came her turn to speak. "I came into the military to get an adventure, and probably to get away from my mother." the words came so easy that admitting the truth startled her.

"And to grow up," Logan added, giving her the thumbs up, to let her know that she finally was doing okay.

"That too," Reddy smiled as time was called and they had to get back to work.

By noon they had the place looking shiny and bright, only to have to do it all over again after lunch. The only thing that made workweek bearable was to know that on Saturday they would receive their first liberty, and that Darrin McCall and her were making plans to spend the day together.

They had been able to talk during breaks and had shared a lot about each other. She knew that Darrin was from Iowa, that he had a brother in the military. They he went to collage. That his brother had suggested he join the military. Telling her this, on their next break he had said. "You have ten minutes to tell me all I need to know about you?"

"It might take a little longer than that to explain me," she had stated looking at the guy who had a warm friendly smile, and an easygoing manner.

"Better start talking then," Darrin answered, settling back to listen to the girl with the intriguing blue eyes and a unique husky soft voice.

Keeping her hands clasped, her eyes avoided looking directly at him, she begins. "You know I come from Wellsburg Indiana. That I have a mother, father, brother and a sister."

Pausing, trying to think of something else to say as he asked. "Got hobbies to go along with the family?"

Slowly smiling, as she answered him, "I like swimming. Walking through the woods," she began and continued to tell him. "Enjoy a warm spring rain. Don't mind snow, I like ice skating and roller skating."

"Let's see if my memory serves me right? You did okay in school, so I guess we can skip that," then looking at her in a tantalizing way, with hesitation he asked. "No boyfriends?"

Feeling a little uneasy to his question, she became defensive in her answer. "No there are no boyfriends?"

Even though he sensed her mood had changed, he couldn't help sense there was more to the answer than she was admitting. 'Hell McCall, what difference does it make? This isn't going to be a long and lasting relationship'. He corrected himself, pushing his thoughts from his mind for the time being. "Anything else I need to know?" he then asked with a smile.

"Not that I am aware of?" she said glancing back at him, the warm eyes smiling, teasing, meeting hers as silence began to prevail. She hadn't realized she had let out a deep sigh, until time was called, and they both rose from where they had been sitting to return back to work.

Hell week, consisted of taking your final test, of having your barracks inspected on a minute notice, which you usually failed. Also final PT tests were done, and knowing that if you didn't pass you could be sent back to day one. Everything was going smooth until the morning of the PT testing; the calisthenics' were the easy part, as far as Seaman Recruit Reddy was concerned. It was the running the five-miles that scared her.

The company had agreed to put Reddy in the front row to stay. Out of fear of letting her company down, (Since they all had worked with her to try and improve on her running) Reddy managed to stay in front for the first 3 miles. During the 4th mile, she begins to drop back to the last row but stayed within the company during the last lap. Reddy had just dropped to just behind the company, when C.C. Benson fell in beside her and threaten. "So help me God Reddy, if you fail this you will end up in my company which starts in two weeks. Don't you even think about failing this run?" With that in her mind, Reddy started throwing up. She stayed with her company but she continued to throw up the entire lap and still managed to pass, thanks to the girls in her company encouraging her on.

Coming off the track, and passing by C.C. Benson, she heard her say. "Good job. Now go back and clean up your mess." So much for praise, Reddy thought heading for the head. Entering the head she was greeted by Logan and Warner. "You did it! The two girls stated, giving her the high-five sign.

"I---I did?" Surprise filling her voice, she never felt more exultant, or taller as she realized she had done it. It hadn't been by much distance, but she hadn't quit. She had not let her company down.

Back in the barracks and doing 'field day' for inspection, for once Company K-100 was not complaining, put actually talking, and laughing as the task of doing windows, cleaning the heads, and scrubbing the decks enjoyable.

Sitting later as mail call had been called, Reddy eagerly shuffled through her mail and smiling she laid the letters from home aside to read the letters from Great Lakes Training Center.

"Hi, Sorry I have been slow in answering your last letter, but things have been hectic around here lately. It seems they have been throwing everything at us this past week. I think they are calling it hell week?

I take it things have been going better for you? You don't seem to be complaining as much. Like you, I feel that I can depend on myself in any given situation. I too, never thought I could do that. I guess its part of growing up.

I think I understand why you joined the military. Did you really have to dress like pilgrims? I think I would have a hard time adjusting to the real world and I would have rebelled too.

I wrote my parents and ask them if they had ever heard of Wellsburg? Dad wrote back that mother and him had been there several times. Dad also said that they had taken my sister and I there when we were younger. Yeah, I have a sister; I just don't talk about her very much. She died when I was sixteen in a car wreck.

Hey! Dave Wright said you plan on becoming an engineman. Great! I may be seeing you again after all. That is my MOS also, and if I make it. I will be taking my training right here at Great Lakes. Good luck, I hope you make it here. Brian."

Her next letter was from Dave Wright, although she was eager to read what he had to say, she would never admit it to him:

"Hi. Have been getting your letter regularly. Well as regular as they can be. I was wondering if you were till thinking about going out with me? It seems you are avoiding the issue. Just because I come from the same hometown, don't let that stop you from saying yes. I have changed, trust me! Now do you feel better about saying yes?

You may not have to worry about me anyway. I have been thinking about joining the SEALS. I know all I have done is complain about how I hate boot camp, but no one said I had brains. But I like excitement and I think they do a lot of it?

Glad to hear you have finally gotten your act together. Who kicked your butt? Or should I say who dealt with your attitude? I wrote Bruce Wilson that I was writing you. He wanted to know why? I told him you had changed.

For some reason, I don't believe Bruce believed me. Take care, and keep the letters coming. They seem to make my day a little brighter. I will write Peggy, to find out where you are and to let you know where I finally end up. Dave."

After answering the two guys, Joan picked up her mail from her family. Her sister Peggy wrote about the usual things going on at home, and how she now was working in the Community Hospital as a candy striper. Her grandmother's letter was, telling her about the family and how everyone was doing and wondering how she was? Her father's letter was long and breezy about missing her, and how his construction company was putting in a bid for the new shopping center. "Just think Kitten, I finally may make it to the big times?" It had always been her father's dream to have a construction company that was known, rather than have it attached to the small lumber company which was family owned. Finishing her father's letter, she had enough time left to brush her teeth and turn in for the night.

With hell week almost behind them the girls of Company K-100 was beginning to come together as a unit. Their military bearings were sharper. As a unit they were showing great progress when it came to working as a team. Even Reddy by some miracle was staying on the good side of the company commanders.

It was Friday the last day of their seventh week. They were taking their placement test for A-Schools. This is going to be a breeze, Reddy thought tackling the different sections with determination to succeed. Her thoughts were confirmed when the career counselor told her. "With your scores there are several fields open to you." With her mind being made up since day one to be an engineman, she stuck to the idea of doing just that. The career counselor shook his head at her idea of being an engineman, telling her. "You will know you're A-School by the end of the next week. Don't get your hopes up too high. They sometimes close out schools to females."

"I am aware of that," Reddy spoke back and received a rather stern look from the career counselor as he again shook his head at the very determine young female sitting before him. Making the comment, "from all appearance you do look like a female," he then told her that she could be excused.

Every thing that they had been through the past week, had been worth it, or so they had thought as they listen to the company commanders going over the rules for 'controlled weekend'.

7

Controlled weekend…the girls soon found out; meant their company commanders would be going with them as they visited the local attractions around Orlando Florida.

Reddy wasn't too happy when Logan told her. "I have a blind date for you. It's one of Matt Thomas's friends. You will like Kevin Rourke, plus he is kind of cute," Logan insisted when Reddy tried backing out. After listening to the rules given by the C.C. Reddy figured there wouldn't be any problems with Rourke.

"As you are aware of tomorrow is controlled weekend ladies? We have rules, which we expect you to follow. You will show the public that you are able to handle yourselves in a dignified manner at all times.

Representing the United States Navy, you will not make a public spectacle of yourselves." Then with warning, she added. "We will be watching you! Summer whites are permissible. Do not get a sunburn, and above all else. . . Do not miss your buses."

"Gee-Whiz, why bother to let us go?" Logan whispered to Warner as they listen to the rules, and was standing, 'at-ease'.

"I was thinking the same thing," Warner answered back hoping not to draw attention to Logan and her as Company Commander Benson continued to speak. You may wear light color lipstick. No heavy makeup is permissible, so I don't want to see a bunch of clowns walking out of here. If I do, you won't be going. Do I make myself clear?"

Reddy was wondering if they gave the same speech to the guys. Sure hope so, she thought after realizing whom Logan had set her up with. It was the same person who always made her feel uncomfortable. Again she had done her best to get out of the date after Logan had pointed him out in the galley. Logan wouldn't hear any of her excuses. "Come on Reddy, what harm is going to happen with all the C.C. going with us?" Logan had declared, as Reddy looked like a scared rabbit about ready to run. Then laughing she asked her in a low voice. "Have you every dated before?"

"Does the prom count?" Reddy shied away as she started walking towards her rack.

"Stop," Logan called out to her, "you turn yourself around and you come back here?"

"Why so you can laugh at me?" Reddy retorted.

"No, so we can talk." Logan answered, as Reddy slowly turned and walked back to where Logan and the small group was beginning to gather, and the conversation turn to the usual of home, family, guys and sex.

"You have never dated?" Brown asked Reddy with doubt.

"She went to the prom," Logan answered for Reddy.

"Well actually I didn't make it to the prom," Reddy stated. "The guy I went with had second thoughts, and tired parking. I carry a black belt in judo," she added with avenge. "He was lucky that all he ended up with, was a black eye."

"You belted him in the eye?" Hill asked in disbelief.

"Probably his eye and a few other places," Logan laughed, as Warner stated. "I bet you are a virgin?"

"She is," Logan, stated, as she told them about what Reddy had said, about being examined at the MEPS.

"Thanks Logan," Reddy stared at her in plain disgust.

"Oh hell, I knew there was a reason why you were always grouchy," Warner chuckled. "It's no crime to be a virgin, just unique."

"Yeah, real unique," Brown joined in agreement, and still with doubt added, "Are you really a virgin?"

"Come on Brown, can you believe other wise with her attitude?" Warner laughed, as Reddy continued to glare at Logan and Warner.

Brown for some reason still doubted Reddy innocents as she asked. "How did you manage to stay a virgin? I mean after all anyone who looks like you surly dated?"

Her face turning a scarlet red from being the main topic of conversation, her voice hardly audio, Reddy managed to say. "With a mother like mine, it was easy."

"Hell girl, my mother was strict. I just climbed out the window," Brown insisted.

"Not with my mother you wouldn't had," Reddy stated, as the girls looked around at each other as Reddy continued to say, "my mother could hear a leaf rustle," her expression remaining in a straight pose, her look still consistent towards Logan.

"They did have guys were you lived?" Hill wanted to know.

"Yes, just none that I cared to get involved with," Reddy replied, as she added. "I wanted out of Wellsburg. Being pregnant and barefoot is not my way of having fun. I am not ready to make a commitment to anyone just now."

"I am curious, does the good-looking babe that has been hanging around you know about your plans and not making commitments?" Logan questioned with raised eyebrows, since she had a feeling that this guy had some major feelings about Reddy.

"Why would I share my feelings with him, we are just friends," Reddy replied.

"You do know about birth-control pills?" Brown quipped.

To their surprise, tilting her head downward, Reddy answered. "My mother wouldn't let me take sex education classes. I had to sit outside the office during that class."

"Was your mother nuts?" Warner stared at her in disbelief. Then remarked. "No wonder the hunk is keeping his distance. You stand out like a sore thumb with your innocence."

"What is that suppose to mean?" Reddy stammered. Before Reddy dumped her attitude on Warner, Logan remarked rather serious. "I think we should clue her in on a few things.

For the next hour with laughter and some serious talk, the girls who spent a lot of time together whenever possible clued Reddy in on the facts of life from their point of view, with their last warning being. "Get the pill and have safe sex."

The next morning found the barracks of Company K-100 in total chaos, as girls repaired to go out. "My God," Warner exclaimed, in stress. "You would think I was the PX, and we were getting ready for the prom. Don't ask me for anything else," she yelled out loud, turning back to her bins she searched for a pair of panty hose, which she was sure she had.

"Do you realize how long it has been since we have had the privilege to look like girls?" Brown stated looking at Hill who was complaining about her uniform being to big for her now. "Does anyone have any pins?" she asked, hoping some how someone would come up with a suggestion on how to make her uniform look presentable for standing inspection.

"Too long," Several answered Browns comment.

"Tell me," Warner agreed, as she asks loudly. "Does anyone have an extra pair of panty hose?" Her voice strained.

"Here," Logan answered, throwing a pair at her. "They have a runner in them, but if you wear your 'tropical' it won't show."

"Gee thanks, I wasn't planning on wearing slacks, but I guess I don't have much choice. "Are they clean?"

"Yes. I wouldn't have offered them to you otherwise," Logan stared at her in disbelief.

"Seeing her expression, Warner stated flatly, "Well I was just checking?" Again she thanked her just as Reddy passed the two girls and turning Warner asked her. "Don't you want to borrow something, everyone else has?"

"Only a gun. You got one?" Reddy replied, looking directly at Logan with a dire expression.

"Sorry I can't help you," Warner smiled as she added. "Who knows Reddy you just might have a good time?"

"It would be the first," Reddy remarked somberly, as she continued on down to her rack to make sure everything was ready for inspection.

———————————

Arriving at the USO compound they were told which bus to board for the excursions in which they had signed up for. "Don't forget you're with Rourke," Logan reminded Reddy as they fell out of line.

"You just had to remind me?" Reddy grumbled looking for the bus heading for 'Sea World'. Three buses down the line she spotted Rourke, or did he spot her? Whichever way it was she had the feeling from his expression that once more she had forgotten to dress.

Not bad, Rourke was thinking as Reddy walked to where he was standing. Letting his eyes travel slowly over her, he asked. "Ready to make my day for me?"

"Don't get your hopes up too high," she expressed as she stepped past him to get on the bus and didn't care how he felt about her answer.

"Did we have a bad morning?" Rourke inquired with humor to her undoubtedly bad mood.

"It could have been better?" Reddy retorted taking a seat next to the window and saw McCall waiting in line to get on the same bus as hers. Why did I let Logan talk me into this? She questioned, the reason for being there as McCall boarded the bus and moved towards the back. Her thoughts were lost to him, as she wondered why he hadn't followed through with their plans to be together? Being lost in her own thoughts, she hadn't heard Rourke speak until he tapped her on the arm. "You do remember you are with me?" His look contentious for a moment as he reminded Reddy she was with him and who seemed to be looking for someone else.

"I haven't forgot," she declared sliding down in her seat and sulking like a child would. She was sure Rourke was still talking so she had to ask. "Did you say something?"

"Only to myself obviously," Rourke stated his voice curt as he looked towards the back of the bus where a group of guys from his company was sitting. Okay, which one of you jokers does she have the hot's for?" were his thoughts as he stared at the six guys. Then it dawned on him who it probably was? McCall, he assumed, for he had seen him sitting with her on different occasions during workweek. Looks like he lost out, or was it her? He wondered as he again turned his attention back to Reddy and figured McCall had probably changed his mind, but why?

"So you want to tell me where you are from?" Rourke then asked her.

"Wellsburg Indiana," she answered hoping her voice sounder more pleasant. "What about you? Where are you from?" she turned the question back to him.

"Virginia. I plan on going back as soon as I can. Well in four years anyway?"

"What did you choose as your MOS?" Reddy then asked next.

"Gunner's mate." Rourke answered flatly.

"What made you join the military?" Her next question since it was obvious he wasn't happy about being here.

"I let Thomas talk me into it," Rourke grumbled, as he turned the questions to her. "Why did you join?"

"Adventure!" She smiled.

"Adventure? Found any yet?" Rourke looked at her dumbfounded.

Her eyes wide, her face glowing she smiled as she answered him. "Yes.' Like what?" Rourke wanted to know for he sure hadn't found any adventure in his company.

"Like meeting new people. Getting a chance to travel and see the world," Reddy answered him.

"You haven't left boot camp yet," Rourke reminded her.

"But I will. Then it's off to Great Lakes Naval Training Center."

"Doing what?" Rourke continued with the boring questions.

"Becoming an engineman," She spoke with pride.

Rourke sat up and looked at her with surprise. "Why in the world would you want to do a man's job?"

"Excuse me, but I don't believe it's for males anymore?" She answered, ready to give him some of her attitude. "Women have just as much rights as men do when it comes to picking a field. Plus, I know something about engines."

"What turning the key?" Rourke remarked, adding. "Don't you think you would be better off sitting behind a desk and letting us guys appreciate the view?

Rourke had just pushed the right buttons to get her going as she answered. "If it's a view you want . . .May I suggest you take up sightseeing?"

"I thought we were?" Rourke followed with a cynical laugh as he added, "did I happen to step on your toes?"

"Probably, if you think women are for docile jobs only?" she exploded.

"Whoa! There's no need to lose your cool," Rourke continued to laugh, as he made her sulk more.

Once they were at Sea World, Rourke did admit that being with Reddy was rather different. She seemed amazed at everything they did or saw. "Didn't you get out much?" Rourke questioned as they ate lunch.

"I guess I am acting like the tourist," She admitted becoming embarrassed by his remark.

"A little I would say," Rourke prompted. "So what was living in Wellsburg like?"

"You really wouldn't care to know," she stubbornly replied, thinking that she didn't need to hear anymore-snide remarks from him.

"Oh come on! I am curious as to why they would let a country bumpkin get away?" Finding it hard to believe that out of three hundred girls in boot camp, he had to pick the hick! "Tell me something Reddy. Just how naïve are you?"

"Excuse me?" She answered, hoping that her complexion would remain a normal color, since she was almost positive as to what he meant.

With a satirical expression, he stated. "I am sure you heard me. But just in case you didn't, let me make it clear for you?" Rourke's laughter was full of contempt "You still a virgin?"

"Go to hell," gritting her teeth, she shoved her seat back to stand and to get as far away from this jerk as possible. "I'm not finished," Rourke stated, reaching and taking a firm grip on her arm and stopped her from getting up from her chair. "I am making a bet with you," He added with a smug look. "That you will be married or in a serious relationship before the year is out?"

"Don't wait around to collect," she stared at him in disgust as she tried freeing her arm, only to have his grip tighten as he continued. "Maybe I should. I saw you looking at some guy getting on the bus. Baby, you wanted him in the worst kind of way?" By saying nothing to him Rourke continued. "I take it by your silence, I am right?" the satirical grin again appearing on his face.

She didn't respond to his words only struggled harder to be free of his grip. "You can relax. I won't be the one collecting the bet, but I am sure the poor slob who does will pay highly for it," Rourke assured her, as he released his grip finally and standing.

Reddy also stood, her fury becoming blacker by the second, she raised her hand to slap the smug look from his face. "Now! Now! We wouldn't want to make a spectacle of ourselves," Rourke reminded her as he blocked the move of her arm, his stare cold.

"Go to hell," she repeated glaring at him and turning away from him, she started to move away from him.

"I probably will babe," he responded back to her.

What was left of the day, Reddy had caught up with Hill and Brown as they explored the rest of 'Sea World' and had the time of their lives doing so.

Getting on the bus later, she heard someone ask behind her. "Have a good day?"

"Why would you care?" She turned to face him. With her attitude in place, turning she almost knocked him back off the bus with her elbow.

Recovering his balance and watching her storm down the isle to find a seat, McCall smiled at his next thoughts. "Must not of had?"

8

Eighth week, day four, parents night. To some it meant seeing parents. To others, it meant getting past their final physical training test. To add pressure to that idea Company K-100 company commanders were hoping for the 'Commanding Officer's Award for Excellence'.

Doing field day for their final inspection, the tension was high as they waited word on whether or not they had made 'Honor Company'. The tension didn't ease as one by one the girls received word that their parents were waiting for them. Dressing for the final inspection, each girl made sure they looked her best by checking and being checked by another person.

When word came to stand at attention, Company Commander Benson and Company Commander Greene were proud as they escorted the Commandant of the Orlando Training Center down the row of girls standing straight and tall on the red line. The area was policed and spotless. Clearing her throat, Commandant Brooks stood before Company K-100 proud to announce that they had been chosen as 'Honor Company'. Looking at them each face maintained the stance of attention. Calling 'at ease' ladies," Commandant Brooks made another announcement. "I would like to be the first to say, congratulations to, "Seaman Recruit Lori Elaine Logan for making honor recruit." Then with a rare smile, she told them, "Tonight when you march into the USO Compound, march proudly. You deserve the recognition. "You have earned it fairly," then she saluted the unit as they snapped to attention and returned her salute.

March proudly, Company K-100 did. When they made the corner of the building heading for the USO they were synchronized in step; their shoulders squared, their arms swinging in unison. Eyes were straight and heads were erect. They were proud and it showed.

Parents were not the only ones who watched Company K-100 enter the compound. Several other company commanders also watched with envy. "Looks like Benson and Greene have done it again?" they commented to one another. "It makes you kind of wonder how they always managed to come out on top?" Some expressed their feelings aloud to what the others were thinking.

Parents and family members were straining to see their sons or daughters as they had been told to stay put and let the sailors find them. It was cries of, "over here, Tom, Peter, and Mark," as sons were spotted, or you heard, "Susan, Jane, Lois," as girls were spotted. There were plenty of oohs and aahs as parents stared at their son's and daughter's in uniform. The words of praise, the sound of pride and the sound of surprise were heard as parents realized that the sailor standing before them was their child.

Standing under a large tree a distance from where the companies were coming in to the compound stood Tom Reddy and his family. Tom Reddy was busy dealing with his youngest daughter who was pleading with him to let her go and find her sister. "Please dad! I want to see Joan before she sees me," Peggy begged her father.

"Now Peggy. You know we were told to stay put," Kathryn sternly scolded her daughter. Wondering where Joan was, as the heat was unbearable and she just wanted to get back to the motel where it was cool.

"I really don't see what harm it would do," Maude, remarked, "as long as the rest of us stay put," turning to her son and speaking.

"I guess then it would be okay," Tom agreed with his brother and gave Peggy permission to go and find Joan.

'You would put your two cents in? Kathryn bitterly thought, looking at Maude Reddy and thinking how comfortable she looked in her peach colored lightweight gauze material, with a matching wide brim hat. "Nothing bothers her," Kathryn grated with envy as she fanned herself with the program they had been given when they entered the USO. Her two-piece pantsuit made of linen felt like it was sticking to her in every place possible. Removing her jacket, her white cotton shirt seemed to cling to her more. "Where in the world were the girls?" she complained looking up at Tom from the picnic table she was sitting at.

"Honey, I am sure they will be here soon," Tom stated walking over to where Kathryn was sitting, and made the suggestion. "Why don't you go back in to the USO Building and wait for them. I think you would be more comfortable?"

"What and miss Jeff and Linda when they arrive. Why I wouldn't think of it," Kathryn baited.

"Whatever," Tom mumbled, as he turned and walked back to where his mother was standing and mentioned, "Do you think Joan will have changed much?"

"Oh I think so," Maude chuckled, thinking of the young girl who had left Wellsburg months ago, and now seemed so grown up in her letters.

It took some doing before Peggy spotted Joan searching the crowds. "Joan! Joan! Over here!" Peggy screamed, waving her arms and jumping up and down. Turning to the sound of her name it took Joan only seconds to see her sister bobbing up and down in the crowd of people.

Working her way though the crowds, she finally made it to Peggy. "You're taller?" Peggy declared looking at her sister and thinking how neat she looked in her uniform.

"I probably am," Joan responded as the two sisters hugged. When they started walking again, Joan asks. "Where are mom and dad?"

"Sitting at a picnic table, over by a big nears the USO Building. I'll warn you now that mother is in her usual frame of mind, thanks to it being so hot.

"Was I expecting it to be any different?" Joan stated, more to herself than to Peggy.

"It's about time!" Tom declared, catching his daughter in his out stretched arms.

Through tears of joy, Joan choked out, "I have missed you so much," then looking over her father's shoulder she added. "I have missed all of you."

"We have missed you also," Maude Reddy laughed as Tom released her and she moved towards her grandmother. "Thank you for being there for me," Joan whispered, giving her a hug.

"You're welcome, but I don't believe I had anything to do with this," Maude exclaimed as she held her granddaughter out away from her and looked her over closely. "I believe you were on your own with this adventure," Then still glazing at her, Maude spoke in awe. "Oh how I wish your grandfather could see you. He would be so proud!"

"Think so?" Joan smiled, as once more she hugged her grandmother.

"Oh yes," Maude lightly chuckled, and added. "He always believed that everyone should follow his or her dreams. And I think young lady you have a good start on yours."

"Well I am trying," Joan answered, "for there have been days when I sure had doubts about making it to this point."

"Well you did, and I think you will be going the rest of the way with no problem?" her father spoke, as he whispered. "Don't you think you should say hello to your mother?"

"Got it," Joan expressed, as she moved away from her grandmother and father and walked over to where Peggy and her mother were sitting at a picnic table. Moving closer to them, she over heard Peggy saying to her mother. "Doesn't she look great, mom?"

"Oh I guess she looks okay," Kathryn replied, her voice strained as Joan walked towards her. "Hello mother," Taking a step closer to her mother and wondering if her mother was going to respond with a hug, or remain sitting on the bench seat.

Kathryn remembering Tom's warning, "You are not going to spoil this weekend?" didn't make the effort to reach out to her oldest daughter but remained seated. "You look nice," she did manage as she continued to wave herself with a folding fan, and making complaint of it being so hot. "Oh how I wish I had stayed back at the motel. This heat is unbearable."

Trying to ignore the fact that her mother didn't seem all that pleased about being there, Joan remarked. "I know it can get terribly hot down here. We have to do a lot of our PT's in the gym because the temperatures were into the nineties by nine o'clock in the morning."

"Well you are a lot younger than me and can tolerate it better," Kathryn declared, wishing there was some sort of breeze to keep her cool. She couldn't help but think how she must look with her drooping hair and sweat insisting on running down her face. "I will get even with you Tom Reddy, for insisting I come here!"

Sensing her mother's obvious restraint, Joan shrugged her shoulders slightly and moved back to where her father and grandmother were. "You okay Kitten?" Tom asked, seeing the forlorn expression on her face.

"Yeah, I am okay," Joan forced a smile, as she turned back to her grandmother and commented. "Thanks for all the letters. I believe I was the envy of everyone when mail call was called. It sure helped when I couldn't do anything right," Joan confessed to them.

"Didn't I tell you to quit fighting the system and things would work out?" Jeff Reddy spoke stepping up behind his sister. "Jeff! Jeff!" Joan's scream could be heard for miles as she turned to face her brother. "Oh God! You are here?" She squealed in delight and threw her arms around him.

"You didn't think I would miss this?" Jeff laughed, reaching down and swinging his sister around. As he sat her back on her feet, he took a good look at her and recalled the last time he had seen her. She had been chubby with long unruly hair. You've changed," he remarked continuing to excess her appearance.

"So Peggy tells me," she laughed, as she turned and acknowledged the person standing beside him. "I hope you are Linda? For it not my brother is in big trouble," she remarked with a smile, as she looked at the very pregnant person standing beside her brother.

"I am," Linda answered, and added. "I enjoyed your letters. So how are things with McCall, Rourke, Matthew's and Wright? Did I miss anyone?"

Madeline J. Wilcox

"No I think you named them all. McCall is not speaking to me. Rourke I could care less if he spoke or not. Matthews will be at Great Lakes when I get there, and Dave Wright has joined the SEALS from what I understand," she answered Linda as her mother stepped up to the group and interrupted their talk. "I thought you weren't allowed to talk to the young men?" Her mother's look cautious and stern.

"We could talk to them during work week," Joan sort of stammered in reply.

"Mother, Dave Wright is from Wellsburg," Peggy informed her mother hoping to ease some of the tension that was beginning to be felt, and Jeff quickly spoke up asking. "I am ready for something to drink, how about the rest of you? Plus, I don't think Linda should be out in this heat for very long."

"That sounds great!" Peggy eagerly replied, along with her dad and grandmother as they turn and begin to walk towards the USO, following Jeff, Linda, Kathryn, Peggy and Joan.

As the two girls walked towards the USO, Peggy was full of questions. "How could you stand it, knowing that you couldn't socialize with all of these good-looking babes?"

"I was easy, I didn't care to repeat boot camp," Joan answered, as she reminded her sister. "This is me we are talking about. Remember I don't mingle to well with the opposite sex?"

"Then how did you meet McCall and Rourke?" Peggy questioned, a little confused by her sister's answer and knowing from one of her letters that guys were called 'trees' and they couldn't talk to trees.

98

"McCall, I met at the sports competitions meets. Rourke was a blind date for controlled weekend. Matthew's was a person who knew Wright from INDOC. And also met me there, only I didn't remember him nor at the time I didn't know his name. Wright! Well you know who Wright is? Thanks for giving him my address." Joan laughed.

"You're welcome. Betsy said to tell you that he is still her boyfriend," Peggy replied, laughing.

"Tell Betsy that she has nothing to worry about. I am interested only in making it through the next four years."

"Still full of questions, Peggy then asked. "Who fixed you up with Rourke?"

"Logan and I promised her that someday I would get even," Joan stated, as the two girls stepped up to a long line waiting to get drinks from the soda pop machines. That was after, Jeff had told them. "You two get the drinks, and the rest of us will find a table to sit at."

Continuing to talk Peggy caught Joan up on what was going on back home. Who was dating whom, who was getting married and who was planning on going to college in the fall. "Can you believe I will be a senior?" Peggy was saying when her eyes widen and her mouth stopped moving as she found herself staring at the guy with the sandy colored hair and light blue eyes. "Hi you all. How's it going?" Kevin Rourke spoke as Joan turned around to see whom Peggy was staring at. "What do you want/" Her voice was unmistakable annoyed as she spoke to Rourke.

"I was thinking maybe I could apologize for the other day," Rourke grinned, taking another look at the stunning red head with Reddy. Man! She was a looker! Having seen the two enter the USO together, he assumed that Reddy knew her. "Why don't you introduce me to your friend?" Rourke insisted, turning and ignoring Reddy's obvious attitude.

Looking at him with repugnance, she told him. "Why don't you go crawl back under the rock you came from?"

"Now is that anyway to treat someone who wants to make amends," Rourke satirically smiled at her.

"I doubt it that is your intentions," she declared becoming infuriated with him. "Now if you will excuse us. People are waiting for us to move in line." Dismissing him, she snapped at Peggy. "Come on we've have held up this line long enough," as she took steps to move in line. Minutes later with soda pop in their hands, the girls were trying to figure out how they were going to carry coffee also. "We could come back for it?" Peggy suggested.

"Look I would like to spend some time with dad, and the rest of the family? Not running errands," Joan snapped at her.

Walking over to where the coffee and tea were sat up on a table, Peggy continued with excessive chatter. "That guy was cute. Who was he, McCall?"

"Hardly not, McCall is nice," Joan, snapped in reply.

"Well I know who Dave Wright is, and Matthews is at Great Lakes, so that leaves Rourke?" Peggy stated, answering her own question.

100

"Yes!" Joan conceded still snapping as she all but threw a bottle of pop at Peggy to carry so she could get the coffee cups.

"Hey!" Peggy yelled at her, "I don't care to wear pop all over me!"

Then pay attention to what is going on," Joan told her as she heard a familiar voice say. "It looks like you could use some help?"

"Really!" Joan coolly accepted his offer to help.

"I see you still have your attitude?" McCall grinned, looking at her with a quizzical stare.

"Yes. Now if you will excuse me, I have people waiting for these drinks?" she answered, trying to pick up three hot cups of coffee. "You are helping?" she stated, looking at McCall.

His eyes unwavering, he answered. "Oh I thought you didn't need my help?"

"You're right I don't," She remarked, as she told Peggy. "Come on we can come back and get the coffee."

As McCall reached for the cups of coffee to help, he was stopped by a hand reaching in front of him. "I believe my sister poured those?" and turning McCall looked at the person talking to him. His voice caught in his throat to the stunning girl with the long red hair, green eyes and a face full of freckles. She was stunning to say the least, and had a soft Southern accent to go along with the good looks. "I am helping her," McCall finally said finding his voice, then turning he told Mark Greene. "Give us a hand!"

"No problem," Mark Greene responded, as he too had been staring at the girl with the auburn red hair and stunning looks. As Peggy handed the other guy a couple of bottles of pop she found herself looking at a guy with red hair the same color as hers, freckles and a smile that was contagious.

"Hello, Mark Greene at your service," the guy spoke with a clear smooth voice.

"Peggy...Peggy Reddy," Peggy found herself replying, as she guys green eyes held hers in conquest. Peggy was glad now that she had decided to wear the light green sundress, with spaghetti straps.

"You two are coming?" McCall said turning his attention back to Reddy and told her. "Show us the way."

"Are you Reddy sister?" Mark Greene then asked the stunning red head.

"Yes," Peggy answered, with a question for Mark Greene. "Where are you from?"

"Seattle Washington," Mark answered, and soon the two were in a deep conversation of finding out about each other.

"Well it's about time?" Jeff Reddy was the first to speak when his sisters returned and brought along two sailors with them. "We sort of got side tracked," Joan stated, handing her brother his coffee.

"So I noticed," Jeff grinned looking at the two guys helping Peggy hand out the other drinks. "Your friends?" Jeff chuckled, questioning Joan.

"Was?" Joan answered, avoiding to looking at her brother. Put Jeff had already saw the perplex look on his sister's face and had the feeling she was feeling envious of her sister to all the attention she was getting. "Want to introduce us?" Jeff asked her next.

"Not really," Joan responded as McCall walked around to where she was standing. "This is Darrin McCall," then she moved on to hand her mother a cup of coffee. "Want to tell me again that you weren't allowed to talk to young men?" Kathryn stated, accepting the coffee from Joan and giving her a look of displeasure.

"Does it look like I am carrying on a conversation?" Joan spoke with taut nerves, and to avoid her mother's usual biting tongue, she moved on to her grandmother and handed her, her coffee. "Here Gram's, I hope it isn't too cold?" Joan said, sitting the coffee down in front of her grandmother.

Chuckling, Maude told her in a soft-spoken tone. "I am sure I won't even notice. Your friend McCall is a very nice looking young man," Maude continued to give her approval.

"Is he?" Joan stated, looking to where Peggy, her father, McCall and Greene were standing and talking with Jeff and Linda "Isn't your company K-100?" Maude questioned, drawing her attention from whatever she was thinking.

"Yes," Joan responded as her brother motioned for her to join them.

"Come on Gram's," Joan stated, and as her grandmother stood Joan slipped her arm through the crook of her grandmother's and leading her over to where everyone else was standing as her mother had turned to talk to some lady sitting at the table next to them.

"We just heard that your company made 'Honor Company'." McCall stated when Joan had joined them with her grandmother..

"Trust me I had little to do with it," Joan spoke with sullenness.

"Why don't I believe that/" Jeff chuckled, looking at the young man who Joan had wrote about in her letters to Linda. Was it possible that this person had finally awoken his sister up to the fact that she was a girl? Continuing to listen to the conversation that was being held between Linda and Joan. "I have been meaning to ask you about 'street marks'?" Linda spoke to Joan.

"It's slips of paper that you hand the C.C. when you are told to do extra field day or IT training. Street marks, get you cleaning up the areas around your barracks. Also, street marks could give other company commander's permission to reprimand you. IT training was something else all together. "Joan told them.

"So how many did you get?" McCall asked, coming in to the conversation, his eyes teasing as he looked at Joan.

"Enough," Joan stubbornly replied.

"I can believe that," McCall smiled, looking at the girl with the stunning blue eyes, and the pouting face at the moment.

Seeing the cantankerous look on her granddaughter's face, Maude asked. "What were your first weeks like?"

"Other than being yelled at---different," Joan answered, as she told them about some of the training. We did calisthenics one day, and the next we ran the grinder. I know about ropes?" she added, as McCall interrupted her. "I had better be getting back to my family or my brother will send out the shore patrol to find me."

Before he got to far, Tom asked him. "Did my daughter tell you she plans on being an engineman?"

Looking at Joan with raised eyebrows in somewhat curious interest. McCall answered, "No, I think she forgot to mention that fact?" Then giving her a slight salute, he took off to join his family.

After McCall left Joan told them some of the antics of being in the barracks. "Jones would sing to the unit at night. I think she did it to keep from crying. The first weeks that's all you could hear, girls crying. I know for I was one of them," Joan admitted, as her brother jumped in to the conversation and teased. "Didn't I tell you, you would be homesick?"

"Want to get out?" Her father wanted to know?

"No," as she told them. "I got Great Lakes for my A-school"

"That's great, you will be close to home." Peggy stated with glee.

"Yeah, close to home, but not close enough," Joan smiled, as she turned to her brother. "Did your transfer come through?"

"Not yet, and we hope it's not until after the baby's are born. Oh I forgot to tell you that Linda is carrying twins." He spoke like a proud father.

"Well I guess then it runs in the family. Your Uncle Matt two youngest boys are twins." Maude expressed, as she turned to Linda and added. "Boy you are going to have your hands full. Do you have any idea as to what they might me?"

Not yet, and I think I will wait and be surprised.

"Should have waited on a few others things," Kathryn muttered, just loud enough for the rest of the family to hear her. It was Jeff who responded quickly to her. "Yeah, S----, happens." His voice low, but sternly correct. Tom would have stepped in to tell him to apologize to Kathryn, but Joan interrupted them saying. "Taps."

As the young men and women came to attention in the USO compound, all you could hear was a bugler playing taps through the intercom system, and the soft stirring of a breeze blowing through the trees.

Before joining her company, Joan reminded her mother, grandmother and Linda to wear hats. "It's really going to be hot."

9

The next morning the sun came up hot as usual. The weather was promising to be another scorcher for Florida. Each company commander was giving last minutes instructions to their units. In the bleachers families of the graduating units took their seats.

In one of Company Commander Benson's rare moods, she took her company aside from the others. "I have yelled. I have lost my patience on several occasions, but I couldn't be any more prouder of all of you as I am right now. You have come a long way since the first week of training. I am informing you now that the hard work has paid off. Not only are we the 'Honor Company' but also we have won the 'Outstanding Commandants Award'.

As the band started playing the Naval marching song, the representations of the fifty flags were carried out on to the parade field, followed by the honor guard, the Naval choir, and then the eight graduating companies.

Pride was felt knowing your son or daughter was standing on that field. Knowing they were about to take on a challenge of a lifetime, your heart soared as you watched your son or daughter's company snap to attention when each unit sounded off. In the back of your mind you hoped no wars would break out during their stay in the service. That the Middle East problems wouldn't break out into a major upset.

"Do you see Joan yet?" Peggy continued to pester her brother who was looking through field glasses.

"Cool it Peg," Jeff warned her for the umpteenth time. Scanning the group of companies coming into his line of view. It took some time before he finally spotted his sister. Smiling to the uncomfortable way she looked holding her rifle, he mentioned to his father who was looking through his camera lens. "See her yet dad?"

"Yes, and I even took her picture, which I doubt she will appreciate," Tom chuckled looking again at his daughter and the awkward way she was holding her rifle. She looked more like Daniel Boone, than a sailor at the moment. Turning to his wife, Tom asked. "Did you find her Kathryn?"

"No," Kathryn snapped, adding. "How much longer do we have to sit in this heat? I really should have stayed back at the motel."

"Didn't I tell you to bring your hat?" Tom stated, turning and looking at her.

"Well there is a good one. I was so rushed this morning that I am surprised I found time to finish dressing?" she despicably declared, fanning herself with the program she had been given.

Tom giving her a scathing look turned to Peggy. "Here you can use these," handing her a set of field glasses that he had brought for Kathryn to use and who had plainly stated. "What do I want them for?" Then he told Peggy where she could find Joan standing. "Look towards the end, She is the second person in."

Spotting her sister, Peggy laughed as she handed the field glasses to her grandmother. "You can't miss her gram's. She looks like she would like to toss the rifle she is holding."

"Now where did you say she was standing?" Maude questioned, as she scan the sailors, and wasn't sure which unit was Joan's.

"She is in the very first unit," Jeff stated, pointing across the parade field, and told his grandmother. "Here Gram's take mine, they are stronger."

Taking the glasses that Jeff had handed her, Maude found Joan in no time, and her thoughts were. 'There I stand, only years younger?' Awed at the fact that Joan resembled her so much. Oh my dear, you are going to give them hell! She inwardly chuckled, giving the binoculars back to Jeff, she commented. "I hope the Navy is ready for her?"

"If not, they will soon be," Jeff commented, as he turned back around and handed Linda the binocular and was pointing Joan out when his view became blocked. "Excuse me," making eye contact with the girl, his voice somehow dropped. "Whoa!" His mind registered, dropping his eyes over the view. At first he didn't recognize Maureen Colby until she spoke to his grandmother. "Hello Gram's," Maureen said, as Maude Reddy made room beside her for Maureen to set down.

"You made it?" Maude smiled to the young woman now sitting beside her. "Joan will be so happy to see you?" Maude commented, patting her hand.

"How is she? Her letters have been far and between my schedules." Maureen inquired of her friend whom she had missed for a while, but with everything going on in the hectic life she was leading, she really didn't have time now to miss anyone.

"She is doing rather well. As a matter of fact you will see quite a change in her," Maude informed Maureen.

"Really! Then I guess I won't complain to much about not hearing from her." Maureen answered, as she caught a cold stare from Kathryn Reddy who had turned to look at her. Nodding her head to say hello and whatever, Maureen thought to herself. "Sorry lady, but we still are friends!"

'Well this day is completely ruined. I was hoping that the distance between those two would have ended their relationship', Kathryn thought, posing a stance of disapproval at Maureen.

Looking away from Joan's mother, Maureen's attention turned to Jeff Reddy. "Hello Jeff," she spoke smiling to his obvious stare.

"Hello Mo," Jeff answered, recovering from her stunning looks. This surly wasn't the same Maureen Colby who had been tall and lanky? Who was Joan's best friend in high school?"

"I heard you got married", Maureen returned his friendly smile only to be "ssss," by the rest of the Reddy's as the graduating program begins. Once the invocation and National Anthem was over, Jeff turned again to Maureen and introduced Linda. "This is my wife, Linda, and as you can see we are going to add to the population of the United States."

"Hello," Maureen responded holding out her hand to Linda and adding. "I am glad to meet the person who finally cornered Jeff."

Feeling anything but attractive as the moment, Linda sort of snapped. "Hello,' but she did except the girls welcome, as she forced and took note of the girl who probably had the latest hairstyle and fashionable clothes on, all of it blending to enhance her dark brown eyes and creamy complexion.

Maureen's concern was genuine as she said, "Should you be sitting in this heat?" as she noticed that Jeff's wife was very pregnant. Making the motion to stand, she was stopped by Maude asking. "You leaving so soon?"

"No, I will be back shortly." Maureen stated as she excused herself.

It was a few minutes later that Maureen reappeared and told Jeff and Linda to follow her. Following Maureen they found themselves sitting in a tent out of the sun. "Isn't this better?" Maureen asked, before leaving to join Joan's parents again.

'Glad I'm not in uniform, for I would have to be saluting all these officer's' Jeff thought, as Maureen had somehow managed to get them seats in the reviewing stands.

The whole program lasted several hours and kept the spotters busy by young people passing out in the companies. The heat becoming unbearable as the temperatures rose. "Ouch! That is going to hurt," Jeff commented watching as a young man fell straight forward, the flag in which he was holding now an imprint in his face. turning to Linda, Jeff asked. "How are you doing?" Concern showing on his face "We're all doing okay at the moment," she answered him, then smiling she added. "Remind me to thank Maureen."

"Will do," Jeff answered as the call for the companies came for them to 'pass in review', 'About time," Reddy thought, as they were given the command to move out, and thinking about Hill who would be spending the rest of the day in the barracks for passing out. They had been warned that if they locked their knees, they would pass out, and that they would be staying in the barracks for the remainder of the day. (Put then Hill always was passing out when they had to stand on the red line for a long time. Plus, when she finally came to, she had to do pushups for the time she was out cold).

Once the ceremonies were over they were told they could spend the rest of the morning with their families and to return back to the barracks at '1300'.

Tom Reddy watching his daughter's unit march past, turned to say something to Kathryn, then stopped, as he noticed her wiping her eyes and reaching over he took her hand. "She will be fine Kathryn," he whispered with assurance.

Letting her guard down for a second, Kathryn answered. "Do you really think so? She looks so young compared to the others that are in her unit?"

"Young but tough," Tom chuckled, as they watched the rest of the companies go by.

Joining her family, Joan let out a scream when she saw Maureen standing with them. "You came! You actually came!" Joan stated as she stared at Maureen in disbelief.

"For a reply, Maureen told her. "Peggy said I couldn't touch you?"

112

Navy Girl

"Stupid rule, but no you can't touch me," Joan sadly acknowledged. "So how have you been? How long are you in Florida? What are you doing tomorrow?" Joan threw questions at her.

Laughing, Maureen tried answering Joan's question all at once. "Have been doing okay. I will be in Florida for a couple of weeks. I don't have any plans for tomorrow, why?" Catching her breath as she answered Joan's questions.

"Good. Spend tomorrow with Peggy and I at Disney World?" Joan asked, as she turned to the rest of her family. "So did you like the program?"

"We could have done with a little breeze," her grandmother answered, as Joan looked at her mother and shook her head. "Mom, why didn't you wear a hat?"

"Because your sister and your father were in a great hurry to get here," Kathryn snapped, as she received warning looks from her husband and son.

"I'm sorry," Joan, mumbled, as she said louder, "anyone hungry? Because we made Honor Company, we get to eat with the officer's over at the Armory and all of your are welcome."

Following Joan, the Reddy's soon found themselves in a long line waiting to get into the National Guard Building where tables were set up for the dignitaries, the company commanders, and the honor companies, and the out standing sailors with their family members.

113

"Isn't that McCall?" Peggy questioned Joan as she looked across from their table to the head table. Sure enough there sat McCall talking to an officer, which Peggy recognized at the guest speaker this morning.

"Yes," Joan answered, following Peggy's direction of point, as Maureen asked. "Who is McCall?"

"A friend of Joan's," Peggy continued, "and boy is he good looking!" Peggy also informed Maureen, as her mother reprimanded her in a low voice. "Peggy we are in the company of officer's. We don't act like heathens from the back woods?"

"Sorry mother," Peggy stated, as she quickly looked down at her plate.

Before dinner there was a small awards program, and then every one was served with their choice of Chicken or a shrimp dinner. After lunch the girls had thirty minutes more to spend with their families. As the Reddy's stood outside the National Guard Armory talking under the shade of a big oak tree with Joan's company commanders, Jeff noticed the young man who had helped Joan with the drinks last night walking towards them. "Heads up ladies," Jeff laughed since he knew what the response was going to be.

Maureen Colby, turning held here breath to the good-looking guy about to tap Joan on the shoulder. Even the guys that modeled with her didn't look this good, and to beat all! Joan knew him.

"Sorry for intruding," McCall spoke in his deep smooth voice, "I just wanted to say congratulations. Your company really pulled it off," laughing, as he added. "Do you think your family would mind if I borrow you for a moment. There is someone I would like for you to meet." Darrin explained to her shy repose, and questionable stare.

Having heard the young man's question, Tom Reddy spoke for Joan's. "Go ahead kitten, I think it's time we got these ladies out of the heat."

"Thank you dad," Joan answered, as she turned to Maureen and again asked. "See you later?"

"You can count on it," Maureen whispered, as she rolled her eyes towards McCall and remarked. "I do want to hear all about him!"

Following McCall seconds later they walked up to a group of people standing underneath a large maple. One gentleman in the group was an officer, and snapping to attention when he turned to face McCall, Joan remembered Peggy saying that this person was the guest speaker.

Since Reddy had returned his brother's salute, Darrin sort of groaned, when he had to do the same. Then he told Joseph McCall. "Sir, I would like for you to meet the person whom I have been talking your ear off about."

"You must be Seaman Recruit Reddy," The captain grinned and telling her she could relax. His eyes like his younger brothers were filled with mischief.

"I am sir," Joan acknowledged.

"I see from the red stripe that you are going into the fireman field. What field have you chosen for your career?" The captain went on to ask

"Engineman. I soon will be going to Great Lakes for A-School," she answered his question.

"Great Lakes has excellent schools. They can teach you all you need to now about engines. Proving you don't let other things get in the way," Captain McCall spoke with pessimism as he thought about how the young woman looked, and he figured that she would be far from being unpopular with the young male sailors.

Hearing the skepticism in his voice, Joan quickly assured him. "I doubt if I will let other things get in my way. Making the most of A-School is my top priority."

Inwardly Captain McCall chuckled, his brother was right. She does have something of an attitude. One thing for certain her look was determined to prove him wrong in his thinking. "If you happen to pull duty in San Diego aboard a ship, we just may meet again," he suggested, telling her. "I am commander aboard the USS Holster, a repair ship."

Not if I can help it, Joan thought as the Captain gave her a look of amusement. "You did say you wanted to be an engineman?"

"Yes," to the unmistakable delight on the captains' face, prompted Reddy to say. "I take it you find my choice of careers amusing?"

"What?" He spoke sternly, somewhat thrown off guard by her replies and quick responds. "Are you sure you can handle the pressure that you will be under? The work that you will be required to do?" Once again his look filled with skepticism.

"I can assure you that neither my sex nor my size will hold be back," she contradicted to whatever he was thinking of her.

"That will remain to be seen?" Keeping a stern sound to his voice, although he was again chuckling inwardly to this girl's gutsy attitude. She wasn't even out of boot camp and already was willing to take on an officer. Wouldn't I love to have her in my fire room? Yes, that would be quite a treat for me to see Senior Chief Dawson's reaction. Surmising that she would have Dawson working buttonholes within a week, if not sooner. Why his so called efficiently ran fire room would be total chaos.

"We have to be going," Darrin spoke to the rest of his family and he motion to Joan it was time to leave. Turning to his brother he spoke in a low voice. "Didn't I tell you she was different?"

"I believe so," Captain McCall whispered back, before turning back to the young lady and saying. "Hope to see you again Seaman Recruit Reddy?" then he gave her a salute, which she returned rather smartly.

Walking away from his family, Darrin shook his head at Reddy and stated. "In case you didn't notice my brother out ranks us?"

"I noticed. So what?" She stubbornly replied.

"So what? He could cause you some major problems," McCall warned her.

"Big deal," she added, not knowing when to quit. "If you think I am impressed by his rank. Think again." she stopped walking and turning, placed her hands on her hips and dared him to say more. McCall didn't back down as he said in a commanding tone. "I think you and I need to talk!"

Not knowing when to shut-up she stated back. "This is not the company picnic?" to her comment he replied sharply with a demand. "Tomorrow, Disney World. Be there!"

10

This is really stupid the girls of Company K-100 complained as they waited for the results of their final advancement test to be posted. Knowing if they hadn't passed they would remain in boot camp. "One thing for sure we know what it is to graduate," Hill stated as the RCPO posted the test results. It was shouts of joy through out the barracks as the girls read her name on the list. "Well ladies, I guess its goodbye to all of you," Company Commander Benson and Company Commander Greene expressed later as they excused them to join their families for the evening. "Remember you have to be back here at 2400," C.C. Benson reminded them. "And no one had better be intoxicated."

"She is such a spoiled sport," Warner remarked as Logan and her headed towards the door. Then Logan stopped and looked around, "where is Reddy?"

"How would I know, the last time I saw Reddy she was with the hunk." Warner stated, as she also looked for Reddy,' then poking Logan she told her. "There she talking to C.C. Benson."

"Oh no, I hope McCall's brother didn't make a complaint?" Logan sighed as she told Warner. Let's wait outside for her.

"Okay, but you got to promise to tell me what happen with McCall's brother, who ever that may be." Warner expressed.

"You do remember the guest speaker? Logan stated.

"Yes I remember him. He was rather cute for an older guy." Warner commented.

"Well he is also McCall's brother. This afternoon McCall introduced him to Reddy. Well you know Reddy and her mouth. She felt it was necessary to defended her choice of career to a Captain."

"You must be kidding?" Warner laughed, "Reddy told a captain off, and she isn't even out of boot camp?"

"Something like that," Logan replied, not finding humor in it at all.

"I think she still has a few street marks left," Warner continued to laughed.

Glancing at her watch and Reddy still hadn't showed, Logan commented. "Good I think she may need them."

As Reddy was leaving the barracks, Company Commander Benson has called her aside. "Yes ma'am," Reddy said coming to attention. Afraid that maybe Captain McCall had make a complaint after all.

"Seaman Recruit Reddy," C.C. Benson started. "Normally I don't give out praise. But I have seen you making an effort to over come your shortcomings. I feel that you are intelligent and I would like to see you use it to your advantage," then pausing she added. "I met your parents earlier. I think I know where most of your problems lay. If you truly want this career, you will let the problems at home not become an issue."

Then she told her she could carry on.

"What was that all about?" Logan and Warner ask as soon as Reddy stepped outside. "I am not sure," Reddy answered, looking back at the building and still a little puzzled by C.C. Benson comments.

"Well I take it McCall's brother had nothing to do with Company Commander Benson talking to you?" Warner stated with curiosity.

"Nothing at all," Reddy answered, as she told them what Company Commander Benson had to say.

"Wow Reddy! You really did make points with our company commander?" Warner chuckled.

"Well I agree with our C.C.," Logan let her know. "Reddy you have come along way since the first day of boot camp. As far as you being intelligent, I think you probably will go further than some of the other girls in our company."

"Gee I wish I had that much confidence in me," Reddy deeply sighed, as she again thought about earlier, and McCall and the Captain!

Joan sat at the pool edge her feet dangling in the crystal clear water. Her thoughts elsewhere's she heard her grandmother speak to her. "You look deep in thought. Would I be intruding if I sat down beside you?"

"You're always welcome," Joan answered, looking up at the gentle lady who was her mentor, her best friend.

"So do you want to explain the long face/" Maude smiled, although she was concerned that it might have to do with her parents.

Giving her a doubting look Joan explained. "Darrin McCall would like for me to spend the day with him tomorrow. I really don't care to pick up where we let off this morning," she said, explaining what had happen between his brothers the Captain and her. "It seems that I am always opening my mouth to the wrong person. Why do I insist on defending my choice for a career?"

"Are you sure it's the career? After all, we have always encouraged you to be a tomboy. Have you thought maybe it's the young lady fighting for a chance to prove herself?" Maude looked at her carefully, and realized that Joan was no longer the tomboy that had left home. Somewhere in the training to be a sailor, a young woman stepped forward.

"Do you think so?" Her look deploying as a smile broke out across her face.

"Yes." Maude continued to smile as she added. "Especially when such a nice young man is letting himself be known."

"But Darrin isn't going to be around," Joan stated, a little confused.

"I know dear, but it doesn't have to be him. He just made you aware of the fact that you are a young lady," Reaching out and resting her hand on her granddaughter's "Don't be afraid dear, they all don't bite."

"But you told me to wait until I was thirty?" Joan looked at her in puzzlement.

"Well maybe not thirty, but until you are ready to make a commitment, May I be frank with you?"

Joan looked at her grandmother, and with a smile and some thought as to what she probably was going to say, answered. "Go ahead."

"There are several commitment you can make, one to your career, one to yourself, and one to some young man. When you make a commitment to a young man, I hope it is for love and not loneliness."

"Gram's are we talking about sex?" Joan asks, trying not to smile.

"Yes my dear, I guess we are." Maude answered, with a sheepish smile.

"It's okay gram's. Some of the girls in my unit have already discussed sex with me. They were very blunt about it, and they told me above all things get the pill and have safe sex."

Maude was silent for a while and Joan having some idea as to what her grandmother might add, said to her. "I love you gram's. You have always been willing to listen to me. You don't criticize, but try to understand."

"That's why I am your grandmother and not your mother," Maude replied, thinking that Kathryn was missing a lot, and that it should be her sitting beside her daughter, and not her.

Joan still confused somewhat about her wanting to defend her career again brought up the subject. "Gram's I don't think I am fighting because I finally realize I am a girl. I think it's because I am a female in general, and I am afraid they won't give me a chance to prove I can be an engineman?"

Halfway agreeing with her, Maude smiled, as she said. "God help the Navy!"

It was later riding back to the base with her father that he told her. "I thought I would give you time with the others. I think it worked, you seem in a better mood?"

"It probably was the long shower I took. It was long overdue," she smiled and turned in the seat to look at her dad. Then she told him about what had happened between Darrin's brother and her.

"You could make amends by saying, I'm sorry," Tom suggested.

"Why should I apologize for something that I believe in?" She questioned her father's motive.

"Heaven help the Navy!" Tom grinned, seeing the determination set on his daughter's face.

"Dad, I am serious. Why should I take a back seat to the men just because I am a female?"

I doubt it you will be taking a back seat, not with that attitude of yours? Tom thought, but didn't express aloud. But he did say, "Kitten I think you should remember that girls have only been in competition with the men for a short time. They are still adjusting to the fact that women can do other things besides sitting behind a desk. Just be patient, don't go making to may waves," he added, lightly.

"You have heard of equal rights?" Joan snapped. "That women are among the minority. I do believe that means we must be given a chance?"

"I've heard, I just hope the Navy has," grinning to his daughter's peevish remark.

"Oh I am sure they have," she continued to be obstinate. "Only now they are about to learn the meaning," she declared as they pulled into the USO parking lot.

"Do me a favor, Kitten. When you start making your pitch for equal rights. Don't tell them I am your father," shaking his head and looking over at her. Knowing she could be very strong headed when she wanted to be.

"What's the matter dad, afraid I might embarrass you?" Hurt to think he might think just that. Then wanting to keep a good mood between them, she added. "Couldn't you just see me picketing the Pentagon?"

"For some reason I can," Tom sighed, showing no humor at all to her comment. "You will give me fair warning so I can leave the country?" He did finally manage a smile.

"Sure. But you better leave mother behind. For you know she is going to keep saying, 'I told you so'."

"I will try and remember that," Tom finally laughed giving her a final hug before she got out of the car and saw Peggy walking towards the car with her new friend, Mark Greene.

Tom watching his daughter had the feeling the daughter he once knew, no longer existed. That this daughter was making plans to go far in what wants was an all male Navy.

Maude was waiting for her son in the restaurant. Seeing him, enter she motion him towards where she was sitting. Taking the booth across from his mother, Tom laughed when his mother ask. "So what do you think of your daughter?"

"I am proud of what she has become," and with a chuckle he added. "You wouldn't believe what she has planned for the Navy?"

"I am not to sure about that. You seem to forget I help mold that child," Maude reminded him.

"Good, then you will be willing to take the credit for her when I am asked. "Who is responsible?"

"With pleasure," Maude assured him speaking with pride in her voice.

11

Entering the bus for Disney World, Joan searched for a familiar face. Resigning to the fact that McCall wasn't on the bus, she shrugged her shoulders and took a seat. Why should I expect to see him after yesterday? Damn, why didn't I go with Jeff and Linda? But she hadn't been able to change her plans with a last minute notice.

Her eyes closed to the pressing headache that was beginning she missed seeing the young man running to catch the bus. Just making it as the driver started closing the doors. "Calling it pretty close their son," the driver claimed as McCall jumped for the open door.

"Yes, I know." McCall grinned, looking the crowd over and seeing the person he was searching for. Walking to where she was sitting in a whisper he asked the girl sitting beside her. "Do you mind if I sat next to her?" Beings that there were other empty seats, the girl didn't object to moving as she rose and McCall told her, "thank you."

Taking the seat, he spoke. "I believe we were going to talk?"

Joan didn't have to open her eyes to see who was speaking, she knew who it was. "About what?" she chafed, without turning to look at him.

"About me," Darrin stated looking at her and adding. "When I talk to someone I prefer they look at me," and taking his hand he placed it on her chin lightly and turned her head towards him. As she slowly opened her eyes, he found himself in a predicament in which he wasn't ready to deal with. Her eyes were misty; her bottom lip quivered, and there was a very innocent look about her. "I believe it's my turn to clue you in on Darrin McCall," he added, having a difficult time with the words.

"It really doesn't matter…does it?" She solemnly spoke, her eyes making a contact with the warm brown eyes and the face that had a gentle smile on it.

"Trying his best to avoid her eyes, the soft tone in her unique voice, clearing his throat he began again. "Now about me, I have five brothers. Joe is the oldest. No sister's, a mother and a father of course," which in saying, she interrupted him. "With that many brothers I sure hope so," a smile starting to form on the pouting lips.

McCall looking still at her, wondered if it was possible for a person to fall in love with someone in just a few weeks? The question plagued him, the reality of it being possible, hitting him as he tired finishing what he was saying. "I like to swim, dance, play football. Love walking in a warm summer rain. I don't care too much for snow, had to shovel it too often."

"What about school?" she asked, relaxing.

"What about it? I was salutatorian in my senior class. Made the dean's list a few times in college."

College!! Her ears perked up and she tried remembering what Greene had said about McCall and him. What was it? But she couldn't remember so she questioned him. "What in the world are you doing in the Navy if you have a college education?"

"Let's say there are enough college kids out there looking for jobs. I took a short cut. I get paid, get to travel, and learn at the same time. My brother---You remember him, the captain?" A mischievous smile played at the corner of his lips as he recalled his brother to her. "Had a lot to do with my being here. Not that he pulled strings to get me in; I had to do that on my own. He just did some heavy talking to convince me it was a good choice."

Her look demure, her memory of his asking about a boy friend, her eyes focused on him, she asked. "Any girlfriends back home?"

"All depends on what you classify as a girlfriend?" His own look tempting.

"Probably in the same respect that you asked me," she reminded him, her words spoken with difficulty to the abysmal stare he gave her. His eye holding hers, after some minutes passed he answered, " there is no girl back home."

Feeling unsure of herself at the moment, Reddy was lost for words and was saved any further conversation as someone called out. "We're here!"

Getting off the bus Joan met up with her brother Jeff, Linda, Peggy, and the guy whom Peggy had met at 'parents night', Mark Greene. It was a trip across the lagoon before they got to the main island of Disney World, and in that time, Jeff and Linda found themselves being surrounded by the United States Navy recruits of Orlando Florida.

"I wouldn't believe this is how I would be spending my weekend," Jeff stated looking around him.

"What being the chaperone to a bunch of Navy recruits?" Linda laughed.

"No the sailors are on their own, babysitting my seventeen year old sister," Jeff commented, as he looked for Peggy and her friend Mark."

"Relax Jeff, I am sure they are okay. After all, we are on a open boat" Linda again laughed.

"I hope you are right," Jeff sighed, as he looked to where Peggy, Mark, Joan and several others were standing. Joan's expression at the movement didn't look like she wasn't having a good time. I wonder where McCall is? Jeff thought, as he finally saw him and another sailor several feet from the group.

"So you really want to be an engineman," McGuire was saying to Reddy. "Why would you want to do a man's job?"

"I suppose you have different ideas as to what I should be doing?" Reddy glared at him.

"Probably. I believe women belong in a house, barefoot, pregnant and making us poor humble males happy?"

"I suppose your mother taught you that theory?" She indignantly replied.

"I think so, she does it every day," McGuire expressed with persistence.

"Good for her," Reddy cursed, wondering how she had got into this debating predicament with McGuire. The answer was easy; she couldn't keep her mouth shut. Nor was she going to let him have the last word for something that she believed in. "I will have you to know that I am very experienced when it comes to…" Cutting her words short, McGuire cunningly grinned. "I hope you are going to say engines because we all know it's not the other?"

"Other what?" she questioned, as her face turned several shades of red when she realized that she had just asked what the other was.

"I think McGuire is over loading his mouth again," Bain spoke to McCall who was standing next to him and being one of his friends, knew that McCall sort of like the little minx that was taking the heat from McGuire.

McCall was about to step in when he heard Reddy declare, "Look I would hate to make a spectacle of myself, but trust me, I won't hesitate to do so."

"Whether McGuire realizes it, he is about to go swimming," Bain pointed out to McCall, who started moving in the direction of Reddy." Not if I can stop her, he won't," McCall answered back, just before stepping in front of Reddy.

"Trust me, he's not worth the trouble you would be in," McCall warned, as Reddy looked at him and he saw the hurt in her eyes. "Come on why don't we join your brother and his wife." McCall suggested, taking her hand and leading her away from McGuire.

What a crazy day was beginning as the sailors explored Disney World. The ride on Space Mountain was everything the brochure promised, and more. The sailors were delighted with suspense as the cars made their way through total darkness to the bottom. Well some love the ride; some weren't so thrilled to be high up in a building that you couldn't see where you were going?

"Don't you love it?" Reddy squealed, as they headed out into the darkness.

"Yeah a blast a minute," McCall muttered, sharing the same car with Reddy. Taking his hands from the side of the car, he placed them around her. At first, she was about to reject to his hold, but relaxed when she felt him shaking and realized he was terrified. His scream piercing her ears as he yelled, "Where in the hell are we headed?"

"To the bottom," she laughed as they twisted and jostled around on the track; taking sudden plunges downward, around curves, straight a-ways, the car rumbled on in the dark. McCall tired telling Joan that he wasn't finding the ride a bit amusing, as yet they made another descending plunge toward the bottom, the drop being straight down. His phobia of darkness and the ride making him rather tense McCall ask, "Is this damn ride almost over with?"

Seeing the light ahead of them and patting his hand like she would a child, she told him. "Almost,"

"If you say anything about me being scared, I will choke you," McCall made a light threat to her laughter as he helped her out of the car.

"Would I say anything?" she commented, adding. "Ah, come on, you have to admit it was fun?" her laughter continuing.

"Maybe for you," McCall complained as Greene hollered out. "Anyone for going again?" As her sister Peggy and Mark were already heading up the ramp to go again.

"Why don't you take your brother?" McCall suggested to Joan who was about to suggest another ride down Space Mountain.

"Chicken," was her reply as they walked towards Linda and Jeff.

"Not always," McCall conceded as they reached Reddy's family and Reddy snapped at her brother. "You want to go on this ride with me?"

"I don't believe I should," Jeff anticipated looking at his wife who looked miserable since she couldn't enjoy the park like she would like to.

"McCall and her can go on the monorail," Joan suggested as it went by above where they were standing. "I am sure it's a smooth ride?" and to her disbelief McCall agreed with her, as he said. "Why not," then to Linda he asked.

"Would you like to ride the monorail with me?"

"Sure," Linda had responded, as Jeff looked at her, and with a wink, told her. "Behave yourself, see you when you get back."

"I'll try," she smiled up at him, as he told McCall. "Meet us back here."

"Will do," McCall smiled as he fell into step beside Linda.

Standing in the long line for Space Mountain, Jeff asked his sister. "You got a problem?"

"Nothing that I can't handle," Joan insisted snapping at him again.

"Yeah it sure sounds like it," Jeff answered with concern, "Did McCall make a pass at you?"

"Don't I wish," she tossed her head in aloofness.

"Should I feel relieved to know that?" Jeff sort of smiled at her.

Her attitude not changing, she assured her brother. "Don't worry I am not about to screw up. Nor do I plan on making a commitment to anyone."

"Hell I know that, for if you relaxed a little you would become a human being." His expression changing as he looked steadily at her.

"And what is that suppose to mean?" she glared at her brother as they took the next car and were getting in it.

"You are a snob," Jeff answered, before the car took off on its twist and turns towards the bottom.

It was after several rides that Teddy begins to notice McCall was avoiding her. Regardless of the distance McCall was putting between then, she made the effort to enjoy herself. After awhile she didn't even mind as she started enjoying herself with the group of other sailors that had joined them.

Leaving the park, Joan again wished that she were riding back to the base with Linda and Jeff. "Hey kid, you in there?" Jeff spoke breaking into her thoughts.

"Yes," she answered then giving her brother and Linda a hug, she told them. "Have a safe trip home. Tell everyone I love them and I will call when I get to Chicago."

"I am sorry that Maureen didn't show," Linda said, giving Joan a final hug.

"So am I, but I guess she was busy." Joan sighed, realizing the fact that she really hadn't missed her.

"Well kid, guess we had better let you go," Jeff stated, giving her one last hug and telling her before he motioned for Peggy who was saying goodbye to Mark Greene. "The worse is behind you, now it is time to show them how good you are."

For a moment there was doubt in her eyes, and before he left her, once more the big brother, told her. "You're my sister I know you can do it."

Getting on the bus, Joan saw McCall sitting to back of the bus with his friends. At first she thought about joining them, then on second thought she took a seat near the front.

McCall having seen Joan get on the bus. McCall thought about joining her, but instead he decided that it was best they leave things the way they were. Hope you have a great adventure, he thought as he joined the guys in a conversation about what was in store for them during the next four years.

12

This is it; she had her orders, her pay, and her final instructions from Company Commander Benson. Picking up all the paraphernalia that made her a sailor, she headed for the bus waiting to take her and the others to the airport.

As the small group of sailors boarded the plane for Chicago, Joan Reddy took her seat thinking that another phase of adventure which had been promised was about to begin. "I sure hope A-school proves to be what I expect" Her thoughts apprehensive, excitement seemed to build at the prospects of getting her hands dirty.

She longed to turn an engine until it purred. Mentally her mechanically inclined mind went over the aspects of what made an engine run. Being deep in thought, she didn't notice the person starting to sit down, until he spoke. "Seat G-23. Yes, this is my assigned seat," James McGuire mumbled, throwing his carry on bag into the overhead rack.

Glancing down to see that he would be sitting next to his face brightens. "Well good-morning sunshine!" His mood was cheerful as he spoke.

Turning sideways, Reddy took note of the person about ready to plop himself beside her. "Was," she murmured. Turning her back to McGuire, her attitude flared as she thought about how she had made a fool of herself with this character. Of all the seats on this plane, his has to be next to mine," she thought of the guy with the deep red hair and hazel eyes, tall and lanky. All in all he wasn't that bad looking if you liked Howdy-Doody?"

Hearing him talking again, she surmised what she didn't like about him, his opinion, and how women should stay at home and have kids. "Didn't I say we would be seeing each other?" McGuire reminded her.

"You probably did, I just wasn't listening," she replied, becoming more discouraged. Turning away from him, she again turned her attention to the window and what was going on outside the plane. "I wonder if McCall is leaving today? I wonder if we will ever see each other again?" she thought, as she was pushed against the interior of the plane. "Do you mind?" she complained sharply.

"No," McGuire chuckled leaning even further across her to look out the window. "I was just wondering what you found so interesting out there?" He stated, turning his head this way and that. All he could see were guys driving luggage carts up to the planes. "Where you hoping to see McGuire?" Sorry, he left early this morning for Quantico Virginia. Not sure what he will be doing though." McGuire informed her still leaning against her, his face only inches from hers as he looked at her. "Will you get off of me?" she protested, shoving him back into his own seat.

137

Sulking she pondered, why should I care where he is? We definitely will not see each other again?" thinking again as McGuire spoke. "Are you always this grumpy of a morning?"

Her glare intensified, her voice grating, she answered. "Only when I have to face a chauvinist male after standing watch for four hours with no sleep. So will you please shut-up?"

His eyes holding a hit of laughter, his voice cordial and being persistent, McGuire stood and called out loud and clear. "Hey we need a flight attendant. Bring coffee with you make it black and quick. We have a person going into early morning withdraws."

Logan sitting in the seat in front of Reddy had also been trying to get some sleep. Rising from her seat and turning around she stared at the guy giving Reddy a hard time. "Do you plan on wearing it?" Logan quizzed him.

"Now why would I wear it?" McGuire smiled at the dark haired girl turning around to talk to him. "I ordered it for my friend here," McGuire continued as he heard a familiar voice tell him. "Why don't you do us all a favor and sit down and shut-up?" Thomas growled from where he was sitting next to Logan.

"Hey Matt, I didn't know you were going to Great Lakes?" McGuire stated looking over the back of the seat in front of him, and down at Matt Thomas.

"I think they send most of the Gunner Mates there," Thomas replied, as he added. ""I think you need to take your seat, the 'fasten seat belts' light just came on.

"Is that right?" McGuire asked, turning his attention back to Reddy and poking her arm several times, after he fasten his seat belt.

Having accepted the fact that he wasn't annoying her any longer she had made the attempt to close her eyes. Now he was poking at her. "What!" she snapped at him.

"You really don't do mornings?" he smiled, at the grumpy expression on Reddy's face as she stated. "You really wouldn't want to find out," she warned with obstinacy, then insisted. "Isn't there another seat you could sit in?"

"Nope. This is my assigned seat, so I guess it means you will have to tolerate my good humor?"

"Don't press your luck," she sarcastically replied, as he continued to harass her. "Well let me see? You have an attitude problem and you don't do mornings. I guess I will have to think about dating you?"

Feeling that to continue this conversation was a waste of effort so ignoring him as the plane begins to taxi down the runway, she placed headphones on and turned on the radio, which she had dug out of her backpack, glad now that Peggy had remembered to bring it with her. Tilting her seat back she closed her eyes and let the song *'Along comes a woman'* by the group 'Chicago' sink into her mind.

As she listened to the radio, Reddy wondered if her folks had made it home okay? Even if her mother had been offish, she had been glad to see her. Linda said she was seeking help from a doctor. I sure hope it helps? Dad looked good and so did Peggy. Then she smiled, recalling Peggy saying. "No one is going to believe this is you when I show them your pictures. You look so neat in your uniform. What did you say the red stripe stood for?"

"Fireman. I am now E-3 Fireman Reddy," Joan had told her.

"Is that a raise?" Her grandmother had inquired.

"I think so. If I do well in school I will become a petty officer. Didn't I tell you dad that I was going to make rank fast?" laugher followed when Jeff commented. "Don't make it to fast. I don't want to salute you to soon?"

"Boy wouldn't I love that," she teased, looking over at her father who was looking at the two and glowing with pride.

McGuire sat back in his seat giving into defeat for the time being and leaving Reddy alone. Having placed headphones on he assumed she was no longer turned into the surroundings. Staring at her he thought no wonder McCall was intrigued with her? There was something about her aloofness, her stubborn attitude that made you aware of her. Could it be the deep blue eyes? Maybe it was her charisma?" His thoughts rambled as he studied her. How could anyone who looked like her want to do a man's job?" He thought staring at her.

Sensing that she was being stared at Reddy opened her eyes to McGuire looking at her. "Oh please! Don't let him start talking again?" she inwardly groaned. "I would like to enjoy this flight by relaxing and not defending myself."

"It's her attitude?" McGuire finally settled on. "It's the feeling underneath that tomboy exterior a woman prevails. Especially when she lowers those long lashes. Girl, whether you like it or not, I am going to know you better?" Then he started talking again. "Are you still pouting?"

"I doubt that I am pouting," she declared, folding her arms in a resistant manner across her chest, much to her distress McGuire continued to be a nuisance. "You know if you went out with me, you just might change your opinion of me?"

"I doubt that, Zebra's are known not to change their stripes!" Reddy insisted avoiding to look at him.

"How do you know? Have you ever seen a Zebra?" McGuire chuckled.

"No! But I have seen pictures and they all look the same! Now will you please leave me alone," she found herself almost begging.

Logan having tired sleeping rose and turned, glaring at McGuire she spoke sharply. "Why don't you give her a break? She undoubtedly doesn't want to carry on a conversation with you. Plus we around you would like to get some sleep."

"But she is so cute!" McGuire insisted as a flight attendant stopped by their seat. "Is there a problem?" The lady asked.

"Yes," Reddy opened her eyes and sat up. "I am being harassed by this person."

"Sir would you mind moving to a different seat?" the flight attendant requested, with Logan agreeing with Reddy that McGuire was causing problems.

"Sure, no problem," McGuire answered, getting up out of his seat to follow the flight attendant, but not before telling Reddy. "We are not finished."

As Reddy once more tried to close her eyes, she felt someone sit down beside her. He's back? She thought, and slightly opening her eyes she turned slowly and looked at the person now sitting next to her.

Moving towards the last seats in the plane, the flight attendant had stopped at a young man's seat and asked him if he would be willing to trade seats with the guy standing behind her.

Sure why not, Drew Adams thought, since the over-sized person sitting next to him, was snoring louder than the engines, and getting any sleep was close to being impossible. "Your new seat is eight seat forward," The flight attendant informed him as he had pulled his carry-on bag from the overhead rack and started moving forward. Sitting down after placing his bag in the overhead rack, he took a glance at the girl sitting next to him that was curled up in the seat with her head resting next to the interior of the plane. 'Well she is military?' he thought to her appearance in uniform, "Navy to boot. Probably fresh out of boot camp," Adams also thought, as he closed his eyes and tried to stretch his six one frame out the best he could with what little space they allowed you to sit in.

She awoke slowly as her arm felt like pins and needles were going up and down it. Trying to turn, she felt weight on her arm. Opening her eyes, she looked at the top of a person's head lying on her arm. Moving she shoved the guy back towards his seat and in doing so she awoke him. Mumbling "Sorry," Drew Adams abruptly sat up; rubbing his eyes he tried to work the kinks out of his body, and turning he stared into the deepest blue eyes he believed he had ever seen.

She couldn't believe it, she was looking at someone who in the past couple of hours had been sleeping against her and all he could say was 'Sorry?' Keeping her attitude in tact, she answered. "Hope you slept well?"

Catching her mood, Drew Adams answered. "A bed would have been better?"

"No doubt," Reddy uttered, turning to face the seat in front of her as she smoothed her skirt out, and wondering how much longer it would be before they arrived in Chicago?

"Take it you are fresh out of boot camp?" Adams inquired, as he continued to look at the girl sitting beside him. The girl who looked more likes a kid, than a young woman in the military.

"Yelp," she simply replied, turning to look out the plane window and noticing it was late evening. Turning only when she heard the flight attendant moving down the isle with a cart. "Would you like something to drink, Miss." the flight attendant ask Reddy as she stopped the cart even with their seats. "Yes a coke, please." Reddy replied, as then the attendant ask the guy sitting next to her if he would care for something also. "Rum and coke," the guy answered, and the flight attendant then asked for some ID.

Reaching for his billfold, he pulled out a military ID card, which Reddy happen to notice as the flight attendant handed it back to him. Handing the two young people their drinks, the flight attendant asked the young man. "Is this seat better?"

"Much better, thank you.' Drew Adams stated, "I even managed to catch some sleep."

"Yes I noticed," the flight attendant commented, before she moved on to the next seats.

"What branch of military are you in?" Reddy asked the guy as she held her coke, and continued to look at him.

"Navy," Drew Adams grinned as he added. "Do I pass inspection?" Since once more the girl seemed to be looking him over.

"You will do," Reddy answered, feeling her face turning a deep shade of red as the guy continued. "Are you heading for your base, or on your way to a school?"

"A-school at Great Lakes," Joan informed him. "What about you?"

"I am going home to visit my family. I have been out to sea for quite some time and it will feel good to put my feet down on soil for a while," Adams smiled, enjoying the girl with the unique voice that was soft, but sort of throaty.

"So you can tell me what it's like to be on a ship?" Reddy then asked next.

"Wouldn't have the slightest idea. I have been on a sub for the past six months." Adams again smiled at the girl and wondered what she would be doing for the Navy." Probably a personnel person?" Drew surmised taking in the appearance of her size. "Oh," Reddy expressed, as once more he was looking at her back as she turned her attention back to the window. Taking a sip of his drink Adams sat the glass in the holder and again closed his eyes.

Hours later, as they were making a final approach to O'Hare International Airport, Reddy heard the guy remark. "Sure hope Jenny remembers to pick me up?"

The group of sailors heading for Great Lakes Training Center waited in the terminal for their transportation to the Naval Training Center discussing what they figured A-school would be like. Some hoped it wouldn't be as strict as boot camp. Thomas being one noticed Reddy standing off from the others. Turning he spoke to McGuire. His voice loud enough for Reddy to hear him, he declared. "I have a friend who thinks the same as you do about Reddy. Reddy turned a cold shoulder to him also. One thing about her," Thomas declared," She is one cold bitch." Thomas concluded looking over at Reddy as McGuire added. "Yeah, I think I will have to agree with you," his attention also drawn to where Reddy was standing.

Overhearing her name, Reddy turned looking at Thomas and McGuire talking. It didn't take much to assume they were talking about her, as they both seemed to be staring at her. Moving towards them she was ready to set Thomas straight on a few things. Walking up to Thomas she began poking him, and declaring. "I am not a bitch. Furthermore, I did not encourage your friend into anything," appalled to think he would say such a thing about her.

"Did I mention names, or is your conscience bothering you?" Thomas insisted sarcastically, stopping the movement of her hand against his mid-section.

"Yes!" she snapped back, adding. "I believe my name is Reddy and you were speaking loud enough for the whole area to hear you. Do I make my point clear?" she stated looking directly at the two guys.

"Rourke is okay. You just didn't give him a chance to prove it," Thomas spoke, defending his friend.

"Well! If you think he's so great, why didn't you date him?" Reddy spoke with animosity.

"Not to be undone by Reddy's snide remark, Thomas threw back at her. "He's not my type."

"Gee I wonder why not? You both seem to think alike," she resisted, finally freeing herself from his grip on her wrist. Still angry, she added. "In case you are wondering he's not my type either," needing to have the last word with him.

"Is that why he made the bet with you about your virtue?" Thomas snickered as Reddy moved away from him.

Her anger rising, taking steps she lost no time in facing him again. "Don't you ever assume that my virtue is nothing but honorable," her voice low, threatening. "Plus if you insist on keeping tabs on me...Logan will no longer have to worry about you...!"

"Am I suppose to take that as a threat?" Thomas declared as he added. "What are you Reddy a snipe dike?"

Not knowing quite what the words meant, but the tone was insinuating raising her hand she hit him across the face. From the crack of the sound you could have heard a pin drop it was so quite. When Thomas recovered from her hitting him, with threatening eyes and a low threatening tone he told her. "I will let this go for now but don't you ever touch me again!"

"Do I look scared?" Reddy answered, not backing from him as she turned and holding her head high strutted away from him. She maintained her cool until she reached the high windows overlooking the landing strips. Staring out she let the tears flow freely as she wondered why she let Thomas get to her. Her hand finally rose to brush the tears away. "Damn!" she thought about the next four years ahead of her. "I don't want to spend the time defending my choice of career, nor do I want to continue the time defending the way I have been raised?"

13

Arriving late evening they were given orientation by the 'Officer of the Deck' on what was expected of them. The dos and don'ts in which they were allowed. "No men on the second or third deck. No civilian clothes are to be worn for the first thirty days. Muster is at 0600 for the next eight weeks. I don't have to tell you to be there, other than that you are on your own. When crossing the quarterdeck have your id's present. In addition you will have purses and any parcels checked. Your BDQ (Barracks Duty Officer) is 1st Class Petty Officer Barton. You will meet her in the morning. I am passing around a clip board," the guy said looking over the group of women standing before him. "I need you to sign your names, rank, and social security number for bedrolls." When the clipboard was handed back to the OOD, he told them which company and platoon they were in. Reddy's was Company 183, Platoon 3, room 347.

Third deck meant she had two flights to carry her luggage up, Reddy thought to herself, as she also heard the OOD tell Logan she was on the third deck also. Still out of sorts with Logan for not coming to her defense this afternoon at the airport, she wasn't too thrilled when Logan tried carrying on a conversation as they struggled with their luggage up the stairs. "All I want is a hot bath, good food, and no more orders for the rest of the day," Logan remarked coming up beside Reddy.

"Good for you, then maybe you'll shut up," Reddy complained continuing to climb the steps and dragging her luggage behind her. "Gee, with all the money this wonderful United States Navy spends on us you'd think they could throw in an elevator" She grumbled.

"Na that would make it too easy for us. Besides, with all this climbing we could become the future Seal's." Logan confirmed with a smile.

"Don't patronize me, Logan. I'm not in the mood," Reddy grated, stopping she gave herself a rest before she climbed any further.

Logan. use to Reddy's attitude, seemed a little taken back by her attack on her. Her mood quickly changing she snapped. "Well who stole your lollypop?"

"You probably did," Reddy retorted as Logan and she continued on up the next flight of stairs.

"What? What did I do?" Logan questioned her.

"If you don't know then I am not going to tell you," Reddy insisted as they finally reached the third deck. Their rooms were halfway down the hall and unlocking the door to her room, Reddy's mood didn't change as they entered what would be their home for the next six months. "Well field day should be a breeze," Reddy thought looking around the eight by ten room. There were four desks, sitting in the middle of the room; four lockers along one wall and bunked racks took up the space, what there was of it. A small window up in one corner offered light and some breeze.

"I think we are going to be crowed," Logan laughed, as she asked Reddy which of the two empty racks would she like. Top or bottom?" Noticing that each rack had an empty bed.

"It doesn't matter," Reddy stated continuing to move into the room and walking over to an empty locker with no lock, she finally sat her things down and dropped into the nearest seat. She didn't know why, but the tears seem to sting her face and she was wishing her grandmother were around so she could feel a comforting arm around her. So this is what it feels like to be on your own?"

"It doesn't matter to me either," Logan objected placing her hatbox on the closest rack that was empty and near the door. "You sure you don't want this rack?" Logan asked, since it was a bottom rack.

"No!" Reddy's answer sharp as she looked again around the small room that she would be sharing with three other girls.

Having had enough of Reddy's attitude, Logan snapped at her. "Would you mind telling me, why you are mad at me?"

"You do remember the airport?" Thomas?" Reddy glared at her.

"That was her problem?" Logan thought to herself, laughing she commented. "If you mean that trifle between Thomas and you? I thought youre doing pretty good holding your own." Then before Reddy could answer, Logan added. "Besides, who cares what you do before you are thirty?"

"My mother," Reddy stated without giving much thought to her answer.

"Oh hell Reddy, by then she will be more concerned about whether or not you are going to be an old maid," Logan continued to laugh.

"She probably won't be the only one wondering," Reddy shook her head in despair, thinking about how she was always ready to take on a fight with the guys.

Seeing the forlorn expression on Reddy's face, Logan tried assuring her. "Trust me there is someone out there for you," and in a lower voice, she said to herself. "And God help him when you do meet him?"

Only hearing the first part of Logan's reply, Reddy answered, "Sure," sighing deeply with doubt. Picking up her purse she then asked Logan. "Want to go find something to eat?"

"Sure," Logan answered back, as she then remembered that she was to meet Thomas at McDonald's.

Starting to leave the room, the door opened and a girl about 5'10" came into the room. Reynolds look was stern as she spoke to the two new girls in the room. "Oh look! The new boots have arrived? Just remember who has seniority boot camp and you'll be fine."

"Oh I am sure I will remember that?" Reddy retorted, as another girl entered the room. She had long blond hair, which was piled up, on top of her head, and a perpetual smile. "You have to ignore Reynolds," the girl chuckled," She thought she was going to get laid last night and it didn't happen. My name is Nancy White and you two are?" as the girl who had came in the room first turned from where she was standing near her locker and gave White a look of revenge as her eyes narrowed to slits, and stated. "You wished!"

White catching Reynolds last words snickered as she responded. "You don't have what it takes?" Which confused both Reddy and Logan, but gave them the feeling that these two didn't care for each other, as again White asked. "You two are?"

"Joan Reddy and Lori Logan," the two girls responded feeling the tension rising in the room. "We are hungry. When the bus brought us in to the training center I thought I saw a McDonalds?" Logan asked.

"McDonalds! Oh it's easy to find, just look for the golden arch. After you cross the quarterdeck and leave the building, turn right, go to the end of the block, make a left, go across the street. It's at the end of the block. You can't miss it." White directed them.

White was right about one thing you couldn't miss it. Cars were lined bumper to bumper at the drive though area, and the building seem to be over pouring with sailors.

"I don't think we are going to get in there," Reddy stated as she noticed that Logan's head looked like it was on a swivel. Her expression excited as she declared. "Can you believe this? We have got to be the luckiest two girls in the world. Why Reddy even you will be able to find some guy here?" Logan stated, continuing to stare in every direction at all the guys. Some were babes; some were average and some…well! "I have died and gone to heaven," Logan declared, as she answered several 'hello greetings'.

"Die you may but I doubt if you will reach heaven," Reddy finally smiled, then it quickly changed as she saw Thomas coming towards them. His mood obviously had not improved since this afternoon as he ranted at Logan. "Where in the hell have you been?" then looking at Reddy he added. "How come you brought the 'tag-along' with you?" and in a no uncertain tone, he also declared. "I am not buying food for you?" his look tedious as he turned to Reddy.

"Don't believe I asked," Reddy retorted throwing her head high, and answering with animosity towards him. Moving away from Logan and Thomas, she picked the shortest line inside the building to stand in. After several opportunities and rude comments to make several sailors happy, Joan finally reached the counter to place her order.

Moving past people who didn't want to move she did some balancing with her food tray in an over crowded building. Minutes later she didn't see the person about to stand. Being shoved again her efforts to stay up right became futile as again she was pushed and fell against a person coming upright from a booth.

"Judas," Tanner swore as the wet, cold chocolate milk shake sprayed across him and to his disbelief, he was shoved or knocked back into the booth and a girl in a Navy uniform was lying across him. "Your food, I assume?" he stormed, in a fumigating stare at her.

"It was," Reddy relented with her own impartial stare as she tried standing. Embarrassed, and not quite sure how she ended up in the guys lap, she accused him. "If you hadn't been sitting with your feet in the isle, I wouldn't have fallen over you. Plus, you owe me five dollars for my food!"

"Really?" Tanner arrogantly implied, as he shoved at the girl to put her back on her feet and off of him. Taking a tyrant pose once back on her feet, she informed in no uncertain terms. "I am in no mood to play games. You will pay for my food. If it hadn't been for your clumsiness in that seat, I would be eating it?"

Tanner speaking continued with insolence towards her. "Glad to hear it. Now if you will move," dismissing her like one would a child, he walked past her once he was out of the booth.

Not giving him a chance to put distance between them, Reddy took a hold of his sleeve. "Just a minute," demanding his attention. "I believe you owe me some money!"

What! Tanner couldn't believe this person was still pestering him. Looking at the girl who had a tight grip on his sleeve, Tanner declared, "Other than a bill for a new uniform which would be mine, I owe you nothing?" Taking her wrist he then pried her hand away as his buddy Dan Crawford looked on with amusement on his face. "Obviously this girl wasn't going to give up? Crawford chuckled to himself.

Not to be undone by this jerk, her temper begin to seethe. Having drawled attention to them Reddy didn't seem to care if they were making a spectacle of themselves. She was determining to get the money owed to her. Following him to the door and directly stepping in front of him, she began to attack his midsection with her finger. "You will pay for my food and the cleaning of my uniform," she stated, stomping her foot and placing her hands on her waist as if to make a point, and she firmly stated. "Give me your name and building?'

Getting tired of this tyrant person, Tanner informed her. "Look kid, get the hell away from me," side stepping her as he did so.

"We're not finished?" Reddy called after him, stomping her foot in anger as she spoke.

Looking at the map she had been given of the training center, Reddy knew she needed to get her uniform cleaned before the stains of chocolate set in. What she didn't know after making a change of clothing and finding the cleaners that it was going to cost her ten dollars for one uniform. "That jerk, will pay me back!" she uttered aloud as she unlocked the door to her room and entered.

"Well look the new bootie didn't get lost," the girl with the short boyish styled hair and stern looks commented, as Reddy walked over to her locker.

Turning to look at her, Reddy remarked. "No, they taught us how to read maps in boot camp," laying her purse down on the desk near her. The girl with the stern looks continues to speak in a commanding tone. "Excuse me," Reynolds said, reaching across the desk from where she was sitting. "That desk is mine," speaking rather sharply, she added. "Yours is on the other side," Before Reddy could respond, Reynolds threw her purse across to the other desk. "See that you keep it there," Reynolds said, pointing at the desk where now Reddy's purse laid.

"Thank you for letting me know which desk was mine," Reddy glared at her. She had a sinking feeling this person and her were not going to get along. Never! I think I need to get some fresh air, as she picked up her purse and walking towards the door left the room.

Getting permission to cross the Quarter Deck, Reddy felt her good mood slowly dissipating. First, I have a run in with McGuire, then Thomas. If that isn't enough I ran into a jerk who ruined my uniform. Then to top everything off I have to deal with a new roommate. Gee what can happen next? She questioned, as she left her building with map in tow to explore the base. It really wasn't a bad place to be, Reddy thought, as she walked through the streets of what would be her home for several months. The streets were lined with trees and some shrubberies planted here and there. For amusement there was a theater, a bowling alley and several clubs for your pleasure. Continuing to walk she passed a post office, a PX, the brig, and main headquarters, and the convention center where she had received orientation to the base earlier. The bowling alley was one place she had never been before, and opening the door, she stood for a minute just inside the building as she watched in amazement as people threw balls down a large lane and hit pins at the end.

Getting shoes and a ball she found the alley in which she had been assigned to. Changing shoes, she took a few minutes to watch the person in the alley over from her bowl. At least the guy at the counter had shown her how to hold the ball when she had asked. Also, he had told her how to keep score, but he didn't tell her how to step off or throw the ball.

Drew Adams home on leave had decided he needed some time alone. Having chosen the bowling alley for a little R&R, he was getting ready to bowl when a ball came whizzing past his head. "Whoa!" he declared, as a girl in a Navy uniform ran past him to retrieve the flying ball. "Sorry," the girl called out when she walked back past him with the ball in her hands. Drew Adams still a little dazed, decided to watch her bowl for a few minute. She hit more gutters than she did anything else and walking over to her, he offered to give her a few pointers. What he didn't expect thought was an attitude. "Excuse me, would you like a few pointers as to where the pins are?" he asked in a teasing manner.

"No and I don't care to carry on a conversation either," Reddy implied to the guy with the neat rugged looks as again she repaired to throw the ball. Once more the ball took off in the wrong direction as it slid off her fingers.

"You sure you don't need lessons?" Drew Adams declared, as the ball this time landed directly in front of his feet. Bending and picking up the girls ball and coming face to face with her as he handed it back to her, he realized it was the girl whom had sat next to him on the plane. Once again he was amused by her snappy tone as she told him. "No!"

"I think you do, or do you plan on busting up this alley?" He laughed to the girl who was cute in a tomboyish way. Her hair, unruly curly was a natural blond, incredible blue eyes, and pouting lips. In conclusion he figured her to be about eighteen, as she asked. "May I have my ball back?"

"I don't know. I am beginning to wonder if it would be safe," Drew smiled at her.

"Trust me, it will be," she declared avoiding now to take the ball from him. Instead Joan sat down and began to remove the bowling shoes.

"What! You are giving up?" Drew teased thinking that the evening was turning out to be interesting after all, as she turned on him and stated.

"Look! I have had a bad day and I don't need for it to continue to be so. A conversation I don't need. A date I don't need. And I would prefer to be left alone," Reddy insisted standing and picking up the shoes, her purse, she left the guy holding the bowling ball.

"Sure I couldn't buy you a coke for the entertainment?" Drew laughed as the girl strutted past but still in hearing distance.

"No," she grated looking quickly at him, but continued to move on.

"Oh well don't say I didn't try," Drew continued to laugh, even if he was thinking that she was a little young for him, but interesting?

Beings that she still hadn't ate she was wondering if she dared give McDonalds a try again. Looking at her watch she figured she had time as it was going on 2100. "The place shouldn't be to crowded," she thought turning the corner to cross the street that led to McDonalds.

Getting her food she checked the narrow isles before taking steps to find a seat. What few people there was in the building most of them had their noses stuck in books. So this is where you come to study? She thought, as she begin to eat.

158

Logan was pacing back and forth in the room. "Where in the hell is she," she spoke with concern regarding Reddy not being in the room. "Are you sure, you don't know where she went?" Logan asked Reynolds.

"No," Reynolds answered and made the comment. "Why should you care where she is? You're not her mother."

"No, but I am her friend," Logan stated, "and there is something you must know about Reddy. She is not use to being on her own?"

"So that doesn't make you her bodyguard?" Reynolds insisted, looking at Logan and giving her a stupid smile as she asked. "What is your sexual preference?"

"Not you," Logan turned on her and with warning added. "You even think about touching me or anyone else in this room. You will no longer be in the military? Understand."

Taking her threat seriously, Reynolds backed away from her just as the door opened and Reddy walked in.

"Where in the hell have you been?" Logan screamed, grabbing Reddy and shaking her.

"Out," Reddy stared at her as Logan continued to shake her, which Reddy rejected, "Will you stop," she shouted at Logan.

"Don't you ever scare me again<" Logan declared letting Reddy go.

"Thank you for being concerned but you are not my mother," Reddy smiled still surprised that Logan was worried about her.

"I know your mother would have belted you," Logan relaxing now that Reddy was in the room and okay. Laughing she asked next. "So, did you meet anyone special?"

"I'm here aren't I," Reddy laughed.

"Yes, now be a good girl and go to bed," Logan stated, as she climbed into her own rack. She was five years older than Reddy, and for some reason unknown to her she did feel like her mother.

14

Standing muster at 0600 and listening to your BDQ (Barracks Duty Officer) telling you, you would be standing muster each morning outside your barracks, winter included. That you had better be there unless you were on leave, in sickbay, or the brig; That they would be standing watches on Wednesday and every other weekend and that they were expected to do field day on Fridays, and that they would have inspections without notice.

"Well isn't this going to be fun?" Seaman Apprentice Shaw complained, as other girls expressed their sentiments also after they were excused for breakfast.

Brian Matthews having just entered the mess hall turned to hold the door for the girl behind him. At first he just glanced at her, then turning and taking a second look; he felt there was something familiar about her. "I know her," he thought as he asked. "How was Florida?"

Reddy was about to tell the person what he could do with his question. Her mouth dropped, her eyes opened wider as she recognized Brian Matthews from the photograph he had sent her. "Brian!" she screamed glad to see a face she knew.

With heads turning in their direction, Matthews figured everyone in the galley knew who he was. Smiling at her surprised expression, he again asked. "How was Florida?"

Laughing with embarrassment Reddy answered. "Oh you know how it is at a summer resort. You get to do all sorts of fun things.'

"Yeah I bet," returning her smile, he added. "Wouldn't you have loved sleeping in late just one morning?"

"Yes," Reddy answered wondering, I hardly know him but yet, I feel like I have known him for years she continued to think as Logan tapped her on the shoulder. "I take it you are not eating with me?"

"No," she answered as Logan raised her eyebrows in question and Reddy made the introductions. "Lori Logan, this is Brian Matthews."

"The guy whom wrote you while we were in boot camp?" Logan asked looking a little bit curious and wondered if this was the person whom Reddy may have been out with last night?

"The one," Reddy acknowledged as Brian interrupted the two girls. "I think we should find a table instead of holding up this line much longer, You are more than welcome to join us," Matthews told the girl standing next to Reddy.

"Thank you, but I think I should leave you two alone and let you get reacquainted," Logan remarked, picking up her tray and leaving the chow line, looked around for Thomas.

Walking along side of Matthews Reddy took note of his appearance; he had blond hair, what there was of it. Light blue eyes, and what once was a stocky built was now a firmer masculine look. Still big, she thought continued to assess him. She also noticed that he had a friendly smile. As they found a table and sat their trays down, Reddy took up the conversation again. "In your last letter you suggested something about controlled weekend and filling me in on it?"

"I did, didn't I?" Matthews answered as he got a felicitous expression on his face. Then his voice softened, "what I can remember of it, it was different."

"I am to assume it included the person that you wrote about coming to your rescue?"

"Very much so. Her name is Jenny Adams and her father is an instructor here at the base," Brian spoke with feelings.

Boy she really must have come to his rescue, Reddy thought of the special look on his face. "So do I get to meet her?" She inquired next.

"Sure. How about tomorrow evening?"

Well she hadn't quite expected to meet her that soon! Wondering why she felt this tinge of jealously and feeling quite uneasy she said." I am not so sure about tomorrow. I don't want to make any plans until I found out what our schools are going to be like. Maybe this weekend would be better?"

"Probably you're right. It would also give me a chance to tell Jenny you are coming over. She has an apartment close by here and she works during the day." With that sort of settled between them they spent time catching up on how rough learning things the military way had been.

"I thought I wasn't going to make it through boot camp," Reddy declared telling him about some of the more climatic experiences she had been put through.

"But you did make it," Matthews smiled.

"Just barely," Reddy admitted to him.

Still smiling at her, Matthews told her. "Our buddy, Dave Wright, said to tell you hello and that he would be waiting out in California for you."

"Wright's in California? That must mean he got Seal training? She spoke with awe.

"That he did," Matthews stated as he added and not knowing even why he thought about bringing up the subject? Was he one of the guys that made the comment about you being an 'iceberg' in school?" Which Matthews found it hard to believe for she seemed friendly with him?

Her stare turned cold her voice reserved as she answered Matthews. "I suppose it was common knowledge in your barracks about me?"

"I wouldn't know. Wright told me about you when we were at the INDOC Center in Indianapolis." Matthews admitted, now wishing he hadn't said anything to her and had ignored his own curiosity.

"Glad to hear it," she stated suddenly rising and stubbornly walked away leaving him still sitting at the table. "Joan! Joan! Wait!" Calling after her Matthews couldn't understand why she was angry with him.

With her head down and her thoughts preoccupied, she didn't see the person blocking her path until it was too late. "Damn," Tanner cursed, as the contents of his tray spilled onto his white uniform. Looking at the person responsible, he found himself curing even more. Especially when she said. "You owe me ten dollars."

"In your dreams maybe?" Tanner declared, trying to move around the girl.

"In yours," she stormed standing up to him. "But you will give me ten dollars for my cleaning bill?"

"Look kid I am not paying you for anything. Now move before I move you." Tanner blasted wondering even why he was bothering to continue this conversation.

"Not until I get my money," she again took a tyrant pose in front of him.

"You have to be joking," he spoke to her with annoyance.

"I never joke when it comes to money," she crisply insisted as their eyes locked in an unspoken battle.

"Neither do I kid," Tanner looked at her cunningly and wondered if she really thought he was going to give her ten dollars. Maybe I should if it would get her out of my face and off my back. Instead of handing her money, he declared. "If anyone owes money. It's you?"

"Should I ask my parents?" She smugly snickered since he insisted she was a kid.

"I don't give a damn who you ask?" Tanner rejected, as he turned to Dan Crawford, who again was finding the situation with this girl amusing. "I take it we are leaving," Crawford chuckled.

"Yes," Tanner exploded, stopping to clean up the spilled food and to pick up his books. Standing again Tanner looked around for the girl. "She's already left," Crawford informed him.

"Like I care," Tanner grumbled looking at his watch and realized he wouldn't have time to eat, change his clothes and make it to school on time.

"You are changing?" Dan Crawford couldn't resist asking his friend.

"Yes," Tanner snapped, and almost leveled Dan's head with his shoulders.

The adventure is beginning, Reddy thought listening to the PQS Mr. Morton giving them a lecture on what was expected of the students sitting in the auditorium. "This is your basic military requirements. Only we will be going further in depth in addition to what you have already learned in boot camp. For the next two weeks we will cover the duties and conduct expected of shipboard entries and fire watches, whether it is while you are in school, on ships, or shore duty. Also, we will be covering first aid emergency, and at the end of the sessions, you will receive a certificate saying that you have passed this course."

In the days that followed Reddy did work details during the morning and classes in the afternoon. On the last day of classes, Instructor Morton informed them of what was expected of them once they started school. "You will be expected to maintain a score of eighty-five to stay in school. As always you will be expected to go through the chain of command for any questions or problems you may have. There are two night classes for you to attend if you need extra help. One is voluntary and the other is mandatory," he informed them as he gave the two room assignment numbers in which to report to. "If you are told to attend either of these classes, you had better show up," he warned as he paused for effect.

Then beginning again, he told them. "On Fridays you will be given a test. This test will determine whether or not you stay in school, and to see if you receive liberty. Which, I am sure none of you want to miss," again he paused as comments were made in low voices from the students. Clearing his throat he brought the large group back to order. "As I call your names, you may step forward and received your certificates."

That weekend Reddy and Logan were standing their first of many watches. Their first watch consisted of checking exits, making sure they were clear. Check doors to make sure they were locked and writing down room numbers for those that weren't' when they made out their watch reports. They did this ever four hours through out the day. "Isn't this fun?" Logan commented when they returned to their room s after the final watch in the morning.

"Loads," Reddy answered yawning and wanting to craw into her rack for some sleep. "Set the alarm," she then told Logan "I am going to sleep."

"You're not going to chow?" Logan asked her.

"Food I don't need at the moment, I want sleep. You know where you close your eyes and your body relaxes?" she continued to grumble. It seemed she had just fallen asleep when she felt someone shaking her. "Time to get up," Logan was telling her, when she turned over and looked at the person who was interrupting her sleep. "Time to rise and shine," Logan spoke again.

"You rise, forget shine," Reddy declared, not wanting to move from the comfortable position she was laying in.

"Come on Reddy, I don't want to be late for watch," Logan insisted, as she threaten to dump her out of bed. "I'm moving," Reddy groaned, as she sat up and jumped down off her rack.

Signing the logbook the two girls had pulled watch on the quarterdeck. Beginning the check of ID's, purses, clothes and liberty chits. Also they had to check any parcels that were brought across the quarterdeck they found little time to talk, as they were kept busy with an endless stream of people. Beings that it was also the weekend, the girls had to deal with a few intoxicated people, who meant they called the 'mater at arms', the same if you happen to find drugs on a person. By the end of the watch they had sent four people to the brig on various charges and several were written up for no valid chit request.

After standing watch, Reddy decided to make a call home, once more she was listening to her mother telling the operator. "Tell her to call when she can pay for it." Hanging up the phone, Reddy fought the tears in her eyes as she turned and left the lounge and walked back to her room.

White, who was becoming good friends with Reddy and Logan, looked up as Reddy entered the room. "How is everyone back home?" White asked.

"Wouldn't know, no one was home," Reddy lied, as she walked over to her locker and taking out books that had been assigned to her for engineman classes which started Monday, Taking a seat at her desk and opening the first book Reddy soon became lost in the subject of engines and didn't realized it was lunchtime until Logan asked her." You are eating this time?" Logan questioned Reddy who for the past four hours had seem glued to her books.

"Yes," Reddy replied getting up and walking over to her locker, where she placed her books and grabbed her purse.

Since Logan was broke the two girls decided to take their lunch in the galley. "Do you always stick your nose in books?" Logan questioned Reddy.

"Probably, it's the only way I learn things," Reddy insisted, as Logan cut her short and stated. "Now there is a guy that wears the uniform like an advertisement. He is such a babe!" she continued to stare across the room near the galley entrance at some guy.

"Who is a babe?" Reddy wanted to know since most of the guys looked almost the same with the short haircuts and identical uniforms.

"Him!" Logan responded with this look of aspiration on her face, as she pointed to the person whom she was staring at.

Following her arm, Reddy eyes sprung open with exaggeration "Him! Why! Why he is the biggest conceited jerk I have ever run into."

"You know him?" Logan asked with doubt.

"Not personally. He just keeps me at the cleaners," Reddy stated sharply.

Still laughing Logan added. "But you have to admit he is still one good looking babe?

"In your dreams maybe?" Reddy said doubting Logan opinion of men.

Continuing to laugh, Logan told her. "I swear Reddy you have got to be the greenest person I know. If I remember correctly McCall was nice looking?"

"McCall was human, this person isn't," Reddy retorted. "And further more I did think McCall was cute?" To change the subject Reddy wondered aloud. "I wonder where McCall went or where he is stationed at?"

"I believe Matt told me that he was sent to Quantico Virginia."

"Yeah, I think you are right. I think McGuire same something to that affect. By the way where is McGuire? I haven't seen him around lately. You don't suppose he got kicked out already?" A slight smile crossing her face to think he might be gone.

"Sorry, he's still here. He is just hanging out at a different place called 'Snipe's Castle'. I have been there a few times. You should go there once in a while and mingle. If would do you good to have a smile put on your face," Logan antagonized her friend who hardly ever left the room.

With loathing in her tone, Reddy rose from where she was sitting and throwing her head in aloofness she firmly stated to Logan. "I don't need anyone to put a smile on my face as you put it."

"Oh damn Reddy you are such a snob!" Logan declared rising and following Reddy over to the area where they put their dirty dishes.

As Reddy turned to tell Logan what she could do with her thought she didn't see the guy that she was about to collide with. Wham! She was smacked with a tray and was sent sprawling to the floor, her tray contents following her.

"S…O…B," Tanner swore as he was hit with food. Looking down to the person sitting on the floor, he stared in disbelief. "I should have know?" he uttered in a menacing tone. "Damn girl! What is your problem?"

"I was wondering the same about you?" Reddy spoke with a hostile stare. It became a standoff between the two as personalities clashed and tempers flared. Standing back on her two feet, she demanded, "You are helping me clean this up?" as she bent to clean of the dishes and the spilled contents that were in them.

With out intentions of doing so, Tanner also stopped to help her. "I am not the klutz here, you are?" Tanner strongly spoke.

"What? It wasn't me who made this mess," she assured him as she quickly rose to a standing position and started to leave him to clean the floor alone. She would have succeed in leaving if a person from the galley hadn't came out with a broom and dustpan. Handing them to her the guy with the apron tied around his waist insisted. "You make the mess, you clean it up!"

Reddy couldn't believe it as she stared at the person and thought of the burly portrayals that you often seen in the movies of the guy working in the ship galleys. She also would have laughed if the klutz hadn't been snickering at her. Grabbing the broom and dustpan she was tempted to hit the jerk, but then she didn't need a Captain's Mast on her third week at school. With fury she cleaned the food up and all but threw the broom, dustpan and its contents at the over weight civilian person who had emerged from the galley.

Sitting in the room later and trying to study basic military requirements Logan seem bent on tormenting Reddy. "Are you sure you're not bumping in to that guy on purpose?" Logan stated, sitting down across from Reddy.

Her words seething, she gritted her teeth to keep from giving Logan a piece of her mind. "Oh hell yes, I have nothing better to do with my time but run to the cleaners," Reddy retorted as she looked up from her books to see if the other two roommates were in the room as Logan asked. "Did you see how he looks at you? Trust me Reddy he is interested?"

"In what. Killing me?" Reddy rejected staring in disbelief at Logan and shaking her head. "He doesn't even know I exist as a person. He thinks only of me as a kid."

"Sure," Logan laughed, as she repaired to leave the room and cross the hall to take a shower.

Come Monday they were finally getting their first day of school and the training they had been waiting for. Entering the classroom she was nervous about what was going to happen. Looking around she groaned inwardly when she saw the seating arrangement. In the line of five rows across there were tables with two chairs sitting at each. Realizing that she was the only girl in the class, she was ready to declare defeat. Her next thought was could she be as smart as the guys when it came to knowing about engines? There were even a few senior people it rank sitting in the classroom. Seeing them, she wondered how they would treat her and the others? Seeing the books on the desk and feeling intimidated by them she was beginning to have doubts about how she would do?

Their first instructor was Mr. Hamilton who was a civilian. Looking around the class his stance relaxed, but his look stern as he started the lecture. "This is your firemen course, you will have eight weeks of assignments in here. This course will cover your duties on a ship and on shore. You will learn where you fit into the organization as a fireman. You will be expected to maintain a score of eighty-five or better to stay in school. As always you will be expected to go through the chain of command for any questions or problems you may have.

There are two night classes for you to attend if you need extra help. One is voluntary and the other mandatory," Instructor Hamilton informed them as he gave the two room assignment numbers in which to repot to. "If you are to attend either of these classes, you had better show!" he spoke pausing for effect as again he looked around the classroom.

"On Friday," he began again. "You will be given a test. This test will determine whether or not you receive liberty. Which I am sure none of you want to miss," again he paused as comments were made in low voices from the students. Clearing his throat he brought the class back to attention, "You will be given pop quizzes without notice to see how quickly you learn and how you are doing, any questions?"

Everyone seemed to sit mute as he then continued to speak. "Your first assignment will be getting to know what is expected of you as you fit into the organization as a fireman. Since you will be serving in the fire rooms aboard ships, your main objective will be the engine room area. This department is headed by the engineering officer and usually is a master chief petty officer.

There are two division in which you will be working in. "M" Division where they operate and maintain ship propulsion machinery and associated equipment such as; pumps, distilling plants, compressors, valves, oil purifiers, heat exchangers, governors, and etc. "A" Division, maintain and repair machinery such as: steering engines, anchor windlasses, cranes, elevators, laundry equipment, galley equipment, and air conditioning and refrigeration equipment.

The nature of your duties depends largely on the type of ship or station to which you are assigned. Repair ships and tenders furnish other ships with spare parts, repairs and other services that are beyond the facilities of the ship's crew.

Looking at the only girl sitting in his class, Mr. Hamilton went on to tell them. "The duties of an engineman assigned to a repair ship or tender may consist mainly of repairs and other services to ships assigned to the tender or repair ships. All repairs beyond the capability of other departments are handled by engineering. The ship doesn't move until you have done your job properly. Please direct your attention to the front of the room. The slides, which you will be seeing, will inform you how you go through the chain of command and some of your duties as a fireman. Lights please."

You could hear a pin drop for the next forty minutes that the slides took on describing the ships organization and the publications which were the basis for the organization. The next set of slides described the functions of the various departments of a ship and an aircraft squadron and the duties of the various people assigned to these commands. Their learning objective: Know the chain of command, its essential elements and its application to members of the organization.

Lights back on Mr. Hamilton walked to the front of the room and started telling them. "In case you can't make muster there is a number to call, 555-4748. Don't use this number unless it's for a good reason," he emphasized with his eyes roaming the class. "And that doesn't include your forgetting to put in a wake up call from the motel room!" Which in saying brought some muffled laughter from the class. Ignoring the comments made, Mr. Hamilton went on. "Your school hours are 0715 to 1600 with lunch being at 1130 to 1230. You will receive ten-minute breaks every two hours. You may be excused. Break rooms are across the hall," he ended the lecture with.

Walking in to the room, which was marked 'break room', they found there were no table or chairs in which to sat at, it was standing room only. Turning to Matthews Reddy remarked. "They sure don't expect us to be comfortable,"

"Looks that way," Matthews agreed, and then asked. "Did you get most of what Hamilton was saying?"

"Most of it, why?" Reddy smiled as she reached into her back pocket where she had stuck her notebook, pulling out the notebook she started to open it as Matthews asked. "Wouldn't mind refreshing me up on some of it? That is the slides of course," Matthews then mentioned as he had recalled her taking notes.

"Where you sleeping?" she teased, since he did have that sleepy look about him.

"Na, I was just setting there with my eyes closed," he answered, yawning and stretching out his huge frame.

"Here take my notes. You can give them back to me tomorrow," she mentioned without thinking she handed him the notebook.

Leafing through Reddy's notebook, Matthews shook his head as he handed it back to her. "I can't read these chicken scratches?"

"Oh sorry," she laughed then added. "What? You didn't take shorthand in school?" tucking her notebook back into her back pocket.

"I don't think it was a required subject for my choice of career," Matthews answered with a puzzled look. Wondering why she had chosen engineman for a career if she knew shorthand? "I tell you what," he grinned, "you sat with me at lunch then we can go over our notes together," as time was called and they had to report back to class.

"That I can do," she accepted his offer.

Reporting back to class instead of Instructor Hamilton, they found a new instructor. "Good morning people. My name is Mr. Collins, my job is to make sure you understand the network of the ships in which you will be working on." Mr. Collins started off with and he looked around the room and saw the girl sitting among the men. "Okay," he begins walking towards the table she was sitting at. "Who is the first person you report to?" As hands went up, he called on the girl. "I hope you were paying attention?" he spoke to Fireman Reddy, as he repeated the question.

"The section leader, who happens to be enlisted," Reddy replied, as Mr. Collins questioned the others in the classroom. "Does everyone agree with her?" With the class agreeing he turned back to her and remarked. "Miss Reddy, I hope you keep on paying attention," Then he continued to throw questions at them for the next two hours.

Their next lecture was explaining the apprentice program. "If for some reason you leave school and don't finish there is an apprentice program which if you qualify, you may apply for. You must strike for this position," he informed them as hands were raised, and someone asked. "What do you mean?"

"I was getting to that," Mr. Collins spoke with impatience as he went on. "By striking you put in a chit giving your descriptions, your qualifications for the job. It's like putting in a resume for a job. If no one with higher rank is striking for the same position, you must may get it," Mr. Collins added.

"If we prove ourselves what are the chances of getting back into a school? That is, if we are dropped?" Matthews asked.

"A lot would depend on your E-vales and your chiefs," Mr. Collins answered him.

"E-vales?" The class seems to speak at once.

"Yes. You are graded by your performance, your conduct, your attitude and military bearings." Mr. Collins informed them as he listened to more moans and groans. "Yes this is a grading in which you will received advancement in rank, along with a test," he added, as more groans seemed to pervade through the class with a few comments thrown in. "Well I can plan on being a recruit for a while," came from one corner of the room while another person added. "I will be lucky even to stay a recruit," and yet another comment was made. "Guess I had better learn how to kiss ass quick!" Which brought a warning look from the class master-at-arms.

When the class had resume silence, Mr. Collins made the effort to assure them. "You have made it this far so don't throw in the towel as of yet?" Smiling as he settled his eyes on the female in his class. "You may have a problem…?" He spoke directly to her.

Reddy wasn't sure if he was kidding or being serious as she returned his doubtful stare. But one thing for sure, she would prove him wrong in his thinking, he could count on that? She thought as he turned his look away from her and continued the lecture.

As they were introduced to each new instructor they also were introduced to routines that would teach them where they would fit in to the organization as a fireman.

"Holy cow! They must think we are all genius?" Sanders argued as they sat in the mess hall eating lunch.

"No, but I think they expect us to become one," Lang suggested looking at the girl who was in the class. "Hey doll, why don't you forget about being an engineman and help me study? I am sure we can find something a bit more exciting than what the military has to offer you?" Lang's look suggestive as he stared at Joan with this stupid 'come heather' expression.

"No thanks," Reddy rejected his offer in a no nonsense manner. Her eyes rolling as she did so.

"Ah, come on. Don't waste your time by being an engineman. It's job for us men," Lang continued not realizing he was about to get an attitude adjustment from Reddy. "I doubt if I am wasting my time," she turned on him. "At least not when it comes to studying. Dating you might be a different story," she further

179

charged. "Don't ever underestimate me with your egotistic, stupid chauvinist views. I plan on being the best, therefore I suggest you had better study something other than me."

"Well aren't we Miss High and Might?" Lang declared with a smirk on his face which was followed by the others laughing. Reddy began to feel totally out of sorts with herself as she shoved her chair back. Looking at the guys with total disgust she picked up her books and food tray to find a different table to sit at.

Matthews throwing glares at the others also rose and followed Reddy. "You okay?" Matthews asked as they took their seat at a different table.

"Yes," she snapped then giving a deep sigh of regret, she told him. "I'm sorry. I didn't mean to snap at you."

With a slow easy manner, he teased hoping to bring her back to a better mood. "I guess this means we are not sharing notes?"

Looking at him with a dismal expression she opened her books and for the remainder of the lunch hour they reviewed their notes from the morning classes.

As the next three weeks passed Reddy became the bookworm her sister had warned her not to be. The only association she made with the opposite sex was in the mess hall and classes. Even that was beginning to create problems. "So how do you feel about being the only girl in the class now?" Sanders wanted to know as he closed his books and looked over at Reddy.

Reddy looked at him seriously and replied. "Since we are all after the same career, I can see no problems as far as my being the only girl in this class.

"Doesn't it bother you to know that we might out do you?"

"Not in the least," she smiled "After all I am the one who's notes you are always eager to see."

Lang wasn't about to give her credit for know anything, nor was he going to be put down by her again, as he told her, "we do that only because we are trying to figure out what makes you tick? We know you don't date? At least not with us," Lang insinuated raising his eyebrows at her.

"And your point is?" Reddy glared at him, almost sure to what he was getting at?

"Well at least we know Wright was right about one thing," Lang snickered, "You should have been in a nunnery instead of the military!"

Glaring at him and speaking to all the others sitting in the group, she didn't waste words at she told them. "I am not here for your amusement and furthermore, I don't give a damn what you think about me. Just step back when I make my move to become the best!" Having spoken her piece she shoved her chair back. Standing she strutted away from the table. Although tears were stinging her eyes and she had to bit her lip to hold them back, she was determine not to let them know they had touched the right buttons with her.

"What's her problem?" Sanders asked, as he watches Reddy walk towards the entrance to the galley.

"Maybe it's the way you jokers are treating her," Matthews spoke up following Reddy with his eyes and shaking his head as he thought to himself. "She had better get a grip on her attitude or all of this is going to be impossible to achieve."

15

Five weeks into school and the weather for September still clung to the hot muggy days of summer. Having donned her gym clothes for the day Reddy decided to do some running after learning they would be doing PT on Tuesday. Following a path after running out of sidewalk she found herself on the beach of Lake Michigan. Sitting down in the sand she felt the sinking feeling of being homesick stronger than ever.

Here things were different than being in boot camp. Here you were on your own unless you made friends easy, something in which she didn't do very well. Logan was busy with her own social life and school. The other two girls were already settled into a routine that didn't include her. Not that she cared what Reynolds did with her life, but White did seem to be friendly at times. Fighting the tears of loneliness her hands tucked under her knees, her chin resting on her arms, her thoughts turned to family and home. It was then that she remembered the letter tucked in her back pocket. Reaching around behind her she pulled the letter out. Opening it she begin to read the letter from her sister Peggy.

"Hi sis. Having a great time I see? From what letters you have wrote I Would say you are sticking your nose in your books? Doesn't Matthews know of anyone you could go out with? But knowing you, you wouldn't go out on a blind date anyway? Speaking of dates do you remember Mark Greene? I have been receiving letters from him. He even sent me a picture; I have it sitting next to yours. Mark is in Tennessee going to school. I am not sure what he is learning though.

Hey guess what, I passed the SAT test. Dad is already talking about college and wanting to know which school I would like to attend? I have been thinking about Indiana University. It's close and I can come home on weekends.

Mom and Dad are going to a marriage counselor. I think its great that they are willing to give it a try. Mother doesn't seem to be as edgy lately. Gram's says to write or at least give her a call. I wish you could be here, but I know you can't. Please answer when you can. Love Peggy.

Well this sure makes me feel better, Reddy thought closing the letter and tucking it back into her back pocket and returned back to her position of her chin resting on her knees. Letting her eyes drift out across the water, she watched as the sunbeams sparkled and danced out across the water. The water tempting to take a dip in, "Why not?" she questioned aloud, removing her shoes and standing she headed for the edge of the water.

Drew Adams had stepped away from his parent's home on the lake, when he saw the girl and felt there was something familiar about her. "Might as well check this out," he thought moving closer to the girl. "You do know that you are off limits?" speaking and startling the girl as she turned around to face him.

"You!" They both spoke simultaneously. Then recovering her attitude she asked," "who says?"

"Probably the sign back there at the beginning of the path," Drew Adams replied, letting his eyes slowly move over the girl in the PT gear and thinking how different she looked from the time he had seem her at the bowling alley a couple of weeks ago where she had made the attempt to bowl and had missed him by inches. "Been bowling lately?" grinning he asked her.

"No," she answered impertinently.

"What happen did they bar you from the bowling alley?" He couldn't resist asking.

"Not hardly," her attitude was striking as she turned away from the person whom she considered as being very persistent about carrying on a conversation with her.

"Well since they are still letting you into the bowling alley. Maybe you wouldn't mind getting a few pointers on how to bowl?"

"I don't need lessons," she coolly replied, continuing to walk and trying to ignore the fact that he was walking along side of her.

Finding the girl intriguing, with the unusual husky voice and temperamental attitude, Drew Adams continued to talk to her. "How would you like to spend the day with me?"

"I wouldn't, besides I have other plans," she added scathingly, beginning to move away from him.

"Does this mean no?" Adams persisted, since he had only a few days left of his leave and was avoiding his sister who had told him earlier that she had invited a girl for him to meet.

"I think so," Reddy answered to the person whom she thought of being cute in a rugged looking sort of way. He had black curly hair, cut military style, but not real short. Blue eyes that sparkled with a mischievous gleam in them, and a smile that made you feel good as he looked at you. Shaking her head from those kinds of thoughts, she wondered just how old he was? She already knew he was in the military, Navy of course.

"You look cute when you smile," her thoughts were interrupted by the guy speaking again before he turned and started walking towards a row of houses, which she had missed seeing earlier. Turning she began to follow the path in which she had been on earlier. Looking down as she walked she saw a sign lying in the tall grass. Reading it, she couldn't resist smiling, 'Off limits to enlisted personnel, Officer's only!' So you are an officer? She thought, as she continued to walk back towards her building.

Matthews was about to give up when he saw Reddy coming down the sidewalk towards her building. "Where have you been?" Matthews begin to chew her out.

"We have PT Monday and I was out running," Joan lied as she started to apologize for having forgot she was to meet Jenny today.

186

"You were to meet me over an hour ago," Matthews stated once they were walking across the street and Matthews was steering her towards a car parked across from her building. Objecting to his pulling on her arm as he maneuvered her across the street, she declared, "Do you mind?"

"Look I have called Jenny twice already and tried to explain why I was late, so don't give me a hard time," Matthew's stormed at her once they wee in the car and he had started the engine. Ten minutes later they were pulling up in front of an apartment complex.

Jenny Adams stood looking out her apartment window, "where is Brian?" she complained again. "He has probably made different plans," she continued to speak as feelings of jealousy plagued he. "Why would I think otherwise when all Brian has done is talk about Joan? Friends? Sure Brian, who are you kidding?" Then there was her brother who undoubtedly was going to be late as usual. Starting to turn from the window, she finally saw her car pull into the parking place. Brian was the first one to get out, and then she watched as the passenger door opened. The person getting out was petite in size and had short blond curly hair. Brian and her seemed to be arguing about something. Whatever it was, the girl didn't seem to be too happy. "Probably didn't want to meet me?" Jenny mumbled as she turned to walk into the kitchen.

Joan continued her bickering with Matthews for not letting her change her clothes. She was still harping on the issue when he let them in to his girlfriend's apartment. "Look I will explain everything," Matthews assured Joan with annoyance as she walked past him into the apartment.

"You better," Joan commanded.

"Drop it, Joan." Matthews spoke with warning, having heard enough of her complaining.

"Never." she assured him with her usual stare of stubbornness.

Ignoring her, Mathews called out, "Jenny! We're here!"

"In the kitchen," Matthews heard her answer, as he turned to Joan and told her, "make yourself comfortable." Matthews told Joan before he headed for the kitchen. "Are you coming out to meet Joan?" Matthews asked when he reached the kitchen. Jenny was dressed neatly as usual in kaki walking short, and a sleeveless blouse the color of light yellow, her long red hair tied back from her face in a matching ribbon.

"Sure," Jenny answered wiping her hands on a towel, which she laid up on the counter as Matthews stepped, further into the kitchen and begun to apologize for being late. "Sorry babe about being late. I had to wait on Joan." He made the effort to apologize.

Joan stood in the same spot where Matthews had left her as she looked around the living room, and felt uneasy about being there. I wonder if this speaks of the person? She thought, taking in the view. The soft colors were in hues of light green, light mauves, and sprays of blues. These colors were chosen for the over-stuffed pillows, which covered the white rattan furniture. Large pictures hanging on a wall of huge flowers were done in contrasting colors to accent the bright cheery mood, which the room sat off. Observing the room she didn't notice that Brian and Jenny had walk into the room until Jenny spoke. "Hi, you must be

Joan? I have been anxious to meet you since Brian has spoke of you often." Now looking at Joan, Jenny understood why Brian appeared to be protective of her. She looked like a kid of thirteen, and also looked like she was about ready to spring from the room. *Maybe I should have seen a picture of her before I told Drew I had a blind date for him?*

"I hope it's all been good?" Joan smiled at her and then added. "I'm sorry about us being late. This morning at muster they informed us that we would be doing PT on Tuesday. Running is something I don't do very well, and in the five weeks I have been here I have not done any running."

"Think nothing of it, Brian already told me why you were late and that he wouldn't let you change clothes." Jenny added.

"Yes and I don't think I will forgive him for that," Joan stated, looking at Brian with a glaring stare as the doorbell rang and Jenny walked towards the door. "That is probably my brother," she informed Brian and Joan before she opened the door to let him in.

Again Jenny caught Joan dire expression before she turned to open the door, scared would be an understatement for her expression.

"Joan moved over towards Brian and whispered. "You didn't tell me someone else was going to be here?"

"I'm sorry, I just found out a few minutes ago myself," Brian looked at her with an apologizing stare as Jenny spoke to the person on the other side of the door as she opened it. "Well it's about time?"

"Now is that anyway to speak to your brother," Drew Adams asked as he whispered. "So where is this person I am suppose to meet?"

"Here," Jenny smiled as she stepped back and let her brother enter into the apartment. Well this was a pleasant surprise; Drew Adams thought spotting the girl from this morning. "So did you see the sign?" His eyes teasing, his smile broadens as he held out his hand and introduced himself. "Drew Adams."

"Yes," she snapped and added. "I usually don't pay much attention to signs laying in the grass." Joan stated, avoiding to accept his hand as she also told him her name. "Joan Reddy." as her voice seems to crack since she was nervous to think she had been set up with a blind date, Remembering what she had read on the sign, she too was nervous to think he was an officer?

"You should it might save your life someday?" Drew continued speaking to the girl, as his sister asked. "You two know each other?"

"Not really," Joan beat Drew to the answer.

"Well not personally anyway," Drew continued to look at Joan and smile as he placed his hand at the small of her back and directed her towards what Joan assumed was the dinning room.. "I think I have held up dinner long enough," Drew stated turning his head to look at his sister as Brian and her followed the two towards the dinning room.

They had been sitting at the table for sometime when Drew Adams make the remark to Joan about not eating. His eyes once more holding a look of satisfaction, Drew asked "Not very hungry?" drawing her attention away from whatever she was thinking.

"You really should try the food, it's very good," he said as he watched her pushed her dinner of Chicken Cacciatore served over noodles, with steamed broccoli and cauliflower as the vegetable around on her plate.

"Really?" Her attitude was defensive as she stared at Drew Adams.

Drew Adams having to deal with attitudes in his line of work for the military ignored Joan's. Turning towards his sister telling her. "I think you have out done yourself again. I may never get married again if you keep cooking for me."

"Thanks for the warning. I quit as of today," Jenny laughed at him and for what it was worth, both Brian and Joan sensed the closeness of the brother and sister as the brother answered. "What! Who will cook for me now?" then winking at his sister, he turned back to Joan. "Do you cook?"

With out thinking of how it would sound, and really not easy for her to come back with something smart, Joan answered. "I am not accepting marriage,"

"Did I ask?" Drew replied trying hard to keep a straight face as Reddy's face turned a crimson color to the insinuation of her remark.

"That's not what I meant?" she forced the words out.

"Sure sounded that way to me," his teasing became annoying to her, if not unnerving.

"You have to excuse my brother. He can be a big tease when he wants to be," Jenny spoke up covering for her brother.

"Now you tell me," Joan forced a smile as Jenny added. "Anyone for dessert?" Dessert was Baked Alaska with Strawberry ice cream baked in the center, and fresh strawberries as the decoration.

Walking toward the refrigerator to retrieve the dessert, Drew stopped her. "Hold it sis, I think we should hold off dessert for a while. Someone still has to clean up her plate."

"I am not a kid?" Joan flustered stammered at him.

"Really! Well it is common knowledge in my family that if your plate isn't clean, do dessert." Drew continued to antagonize her as his sister butted in. "You have to excuse my brother. Sometimes his job gets the better of him?"

"And what would that be?" Joan inquired; as Jenny went on to inform her. "My brother works with NIS."

"NIS?" Joan questioned.

"Naval Intelligent Service," Drew answered before his sister could.

"I hope you're not an officer?" Joan sighed her food totally forgotten.

"I'm working on it," Drew grinned, knowing he was really causing frustrations where she was concerned as he added. "I think we have found someone willing to do KP."

"We will be in the living room," Jenny chuckled as Brian and she stood to leave the two alone.

How did she get into this predicament? She was wondering as she stared at the sink. "You will find the dish soap under the sink," Drew interrupted her thoughts. "I take it I have nothing to say about doing dishes?" she turned ready to argue with him.

Drew Adams fighting laughter at her dire expression, answered, "I don't think so. You wash, and I will dry since I know where things go."

Finding herself in soapy water up to her elbows, she started washing the dishes as Drew began throwing questions at her. "Where do you know Brian from?"

"Don't worry, your sister is not in any danger of losing him," Joan quickly answered.

"I wasn't concerned about my sister's love life. I was just wondering why he was so protective of you," Drew commented with raised eyebrows.

"I am sure you're wrong there. Brian doesn't protect me from anything," she swore answering, "We met in Indianapolis at the INDOC Center."

"Indianapolis? Is that where you are from?" He asked, relieved that her attitude had changed somewhat.

"No," she snapped, her mood changing again.

"Should I be ducking?" Drew found himself laughing.

She smiled, actually laughed. "Turning she faced him. "I guess it all depends on how you value your life?"

"I value it," Drew Adams said. Having a hard time with his answer. She had thrown him off guard with her deep husky laugh. For a girl it was an unusual sound and coming from her it was rather unique.

"That's good to know," she couldn't resist adding, as she began to relax.

Wanting to know her better, Drew persisted with questions. "Why don't you tell me where you come from and why they would let someone still tied to her mother's apron strings loose?"

Not knowing that he had hit the right button, she was provoked by his insistence that she was still a kid. Her glare sharp, she spoke with assurance. "I am anything but a kid and still tired to my mother's apron strings, as you put it."

"OOP's. Sorry I guess I misjudged you. But you do look a little young to be serving in the military. What are you? Eighteen and fresh out of boot camp?"

"No nineteen," she quickly snapped back as he handed a plate to her and stated. "Want to try washing it?"

Already loathing the idea of having her hands in dishwater, continuously under fire, her nerves jagged she grabbed the plate. Scrubbing it she all but threw it back. "There! Does that satisfy the officer?"

"I am not an officer since I work for a living, but a chief. And yes I am satisfied that I won't be eating leftovers," Drew charged a deep laugh clearing his throat as he watched her tackle each dish like it was a matter of life and death. "So are you going to tell me about the girl that wants to be an engineman?" Drew asked, wanting still to know all he could about her.

"Why should I? You probably will only laugh at me," she insisted.

"You are aware of the fact that being a female you shouldn't get your hopes up too high, not for the job in which you have chosen for yourself anyway."

"So I have been told," she declared," but that will not stop me."

"No? Then I think you should understand something. There are certain ships in which you can be deployed on. Woman are not allowed into battle zones."

"In time I am sure that will change. Or do the men fear that women will out do them?" she argued.

"I doubt it. I think it's a matter of being able to perform jobs to the best of their abilities."

"Are you saying that women could get in the way?"

"Yes," Drew antagonized with a shake of his head. "But not in the way you might think?"

"And just what may I be thinking?" She edged him on with a curious stare.

"I feel that men will overlook their own safety in order to protect a woman," Drew stated.

"Not if they are well trained," Joan assured him with a positive look.

"We do train the best," Drew grinned at her, his eyes once more lit with mischief. As much as he hated to admit it, there was something about her tomboy impression, her relentless attitude that kept him intrigued.

"So then what is the problem?" she questioned his motive.

"Probably none," he felt himself answering her as his sister walked into the room. "You two about done?" Jenny asked.

"Finished," Drew answered as he placed the towel back on the towel rack.

"Good. Brian and I were wondering if you two would like to leave for the beach before it gets much later?" Jenny asked next.

"I don't think so," Joan quickly answered not wanting to spend any more time with this person and all of his questions.

"Might help unloosen those apron stings," Drew suggested, winking at his sister and as he walked past Joan, he commented. "Relax I am not going to pounce on you."

"Do I look worried?" Joan couldn't resist saying.

"Maybe," he grinned as he suggested to his sister. "Why don't we go to the Crow's Nest instead?"

"Hey I like that idea even better," Brian agreed, walking into the kitchen to see what the hold up was.

"What is the Crow's nest?" Joan questioned, looking at Brian.

"A place to dance and drink," Jenny answered.

"I don't drink," Joan let them know.

"That's good. I think you are still a little under the age in Illinois," Drew grinned as he once more placed his hand at her back and led if not slightly, pushed her out of the kitchen.

"Are you okay?" Jenny had the chance to ask her brother before they left the apartment. Laughing, Drew responded. "Stop me if I look like I am getting in over my head."

"Wouldn't dream of it. I love to see you sweat," Jenny chuckled, and then added with concern. "Look out big brother. I think she is dangerous?"

"Danger she isn't. Innocent is more like it?" Drew corrected his sister.

"Probably, but Brian says she eats guys for just saying hello," Jenny laughed, although Drew had a feeling his sister was sending out warning signals.

"I think I can handle it," Drew shook his head in wonder as they left the apartment and caught up with Brian and Joan. Joan started towards the car, which she had taken to Jenny's apartment, when Drew stopped her. "I believe you are riding with me," pointing to an older car.

To hide her uneasiness she commented. "Is this thing safe?" as they stepped up to it and Drew held the door open for her. "It gets me where I am going," Drew answered to her comment about his 55 Chevy. "I have you to know this is an antique and I love her very much. Her engine purrs like a newborn kitten regardless of the miles on her. As you can see the upholstery has been kept in mint condition." Drew stated, as if the car was brand new and had just rolled off the assembly line. As he turned the key and started the engine, Joan had to agree that the car sounded exceptionally smooth for its age.

As they drove to the Crow's Nest Joan asked. "How long have you been in the Navy?"

"Too long," Drew answered without looking at her.

"You were married?" surprised that she was beginning to feel relaxed with him.

"Something like that," Drew replied with bitterness.

"Take it things didn't work out. How long were you married?" She then inquired, wondering how he like all the questions.

"Long enough. Now can we change the subject?" His tone was harsh?

"What's the matter? Don't you like the shoe being on the other foot?" she smiled to the fact that he didn't care for the questions.

"It all depends on the subject," Drew spoke with discord.

"Gee! Did I hit a sore spot?" she chuckled.

Drew looked at her and she couldn't avoid smiling at the glaring look on his face and she added. "I believe I did," she found herself laughing.

"You think you're cute?" speaking as angrily as he felt since his divorce had finally been finalized just weeks ago. After a long battle with custody hearings, his two-year-old daughter now was living with his parents. As they pulled into the parking lot of the club, Drew not wanting to stay on the bad side of the girl sitting across from him, he asked. "Ready to have a good time?"

"Ready," she stated slowly, a little nervous about being in a dating situation with Drew. She wasn't sure of what she was feeling, but one thing for sure she didn't feel threaten by him, as he held the car door open for her.

They had been sitting at the table through several songs. Words were absent as Drew got the feeling Joan was avoiding him. She had been that way since they had stepped inside the club. "Would you like to dance?" he finally asked knowing it probably would get her to react in some way as he had thought about her having a Jackal and Hyde, personality.

Her look amusing, she rose from where she was sitting. After several songs, she realized that Drew Adams was a good dancer. Taking a short break to get something to drink, they had walked back to their table. Taking a drink of her pop, Joan thought it tasted different, sort of sweet? She was about to say something to Drew, but he was urging her to hurry that his favorite song was playing. Finishing her drink, she let him lead her back on to the dance floor. At least she was dancing, something which she enjoyed doing, and it had been awhile since doing so.

Never having flirted with a guy before and usually on the defensive end, she showed Drew Adams a different side of her. Her look kind of coy, kind of shy, her thought were running wild about the kind of evening she had been spending with this rugged handsome person. Now for paybacks, she let her moves become sultry, seductive, as she moved to the beat of the music, and the song, *'strutt'* by Shenna Easton.

As the music changed so did she. With his arms around her, their bodies somewhat close, she laid her head on his shoulder, the move making them even closer, very close, her lithe movements being synchronized with his as they went from fast songs to slow songs.

His nerves becoming rattled, Drew spoke softly but sternly. "You wouldn't want me to take you up on your offer?

In a soft whisper she answered. "Why I haven't the slightest idea as to what you mean?"

"I am not one of the farm boys," Drew cautioned her.

Her laughter soft,   her look demur, she answered. "Really?"

"That's it! We are leaving," he grated with regret and frustration. Regardless of her age and her rank, she was playing havoc with his nerves.

"Coward!" she continued to laugh, throwing back her head and lowering her lashes, her voice tempting him.

"Not hardly," he snapped taking her hand and leading her back to where they had been sitting with Brian and Jenny. "We are leaving," Drew snapped at his sister as he picked up Joan's purse and handed it to her as she laughing, insisted. "But I was enjoying being away from the apron stings.

"Not at my expense," Drew grated under his breath almost yanking her along." It was then that he realized she was slightly drunk and turning to his sister he asked. . "Did you give her something to drink?"

"Do I look stupid," Jenny answered, as Brian shook his head 'no' also.

"Well someone did?" Drew expressed, as he looked around the area and wondered who knew Reddy and who had fixed her drink. Then turning back to Brian, he asked. "Know anyone sitting close to us who might have fixed her Coke?"

"Not really," Brian answered, although he saw McGuire sitting up at the bar. He didn't even think McGuire knew Reddy for when the guys from school complained about her, he never put his two cents in.

Not far from where they were sitting, James McGuire sitting up at the bar was watching the scene unfold at the table where Reddy had been sitting. He had seen her come in with a guy and some couple, the guy he knew from being in the same barracks with him. He had sat waiting for the moment when he could walk over to the table and pour two shot glasses of whiskey into the glass he had seen Reddy use.

. "Come on Drew the music is still playing," Joan insisted as she tried getting him to go back on the dance floor.

"Yeah, I know." Drew grumbled as he put a strong grip on her hand and walked towards the exit doors.

As he was putting her into the car, she slipped her arms around his neck and before he could resist she kissed him. Unwrapping her arms from his neck he was glad that he was leaving for Washington in the morning. To himself he admitted that this tomboy of a girl was having some major effects on him. He didn't need another female at the moment to screw up his life again now that he had it straighten out. Dropping her off at her building he did tell her. "Take care, Joan."

"Plan on it," she snapped and he had the feeling that Hyde was back as she slammed his door and rattled his windows.

16

For the next several weeks Reddy was finding out what it was to learn things the military way as they continued to cover assignments from their 'Bluejackets' and 'Basic Military manuals'.

Instructor Collins had traded places with Instructor Hamilton after break. "Good morning ladies and gentleman," His usual greeting before starting his morning lectures on ship organization. "Today we will be covering Navy policies and programs. Which I am sure some of you will note. You have already covered the basic in your 'Bluejackets' manual. Only now we will cover it more in depth."

Generally you could tell by the moans and groans from the group who had studied and who had not and by Friday, Instructor Collins knew who was going to be in his class and who wasn't one of them was Fireman Lang as he watched him rise over his desk and whisper something to the girl sitting in front of him.

Lang knew he was failing and leaning over his desk, he whispered to Reddy. "How about giving me your notes at break?" She was about to turn around and tell him no, when Instructor Collins stepped up between the two. "Miss Reddy and Mr. Lang, do you have something that you wish to share with the rest of us?"

"No sir," Lang was quick to answer.

"How about you Miss Reddy? Would you care to share with us whatever Mr. Lang whispered to you?"

"It was nothing of importance," Reddy responded, sitting up straighter in her chair.

"Let me be the judge of that?" Instructor Collins sternly commanded, as he stood posed over Reddy and looking down at her as he waited for an answer.

Lang had put her in a very awkward situation and she didn't like it as she looked back at Instructor Collins. "He ask to see my notes at break." She finally answered.

"Oh he did? And what notes would that be since I see none on your paper?" Instructor Collins stated with intimidation.

Not to be undone by him, Reddy answered the instructor in a firmer tone. "The ones I will be taking on Navy policies?"

"Oh really!" Then he turned and firmly spoke to the Mr. Lang. "Mr. Lang, if you are having problems, there are night classes in which you can attend. Miss Reddy, I think you would prefer to watch the front of the room rather than listen to what is being whispered into your ear!"

What is it with this character?" Reddy wondered as Instructor Collins walked away from her and called. "Lights please."

Instructor Collins being retired from the Navy had come back to teach. He still couldn't accept the fact that they were letting women in to fields, which were definitely male dominated. His assumption of women was that they didn't belong in the military. Nor did he approve of girls being in his classes and every time one failed he was joyous. They could never expect special favors from him. He didn't care how much they thought they knew?

It hadn't been enough to be humiliated by Collins in front of the whole class. At lunch she had to sit and take the same jeers from her so-called classmates.

"Hey Reddy, you could have gotten us wrote up," Lang insisted looking down and across the table at her in the mess hall.

"Excuse me? I wasn't the one who started it," she rejected.

"Yeah, well you could have kept your mouth shut," Lang then accused.

"Yes, I could have and you could have kept yours shut and left me alone." Reddy retorted. "Besides, I think I saved your ass," she added as the guys who had been looking at her notes laughed.

"Hey Lang, man I think she just told you off," Saunders commented to his roommate and waited for the retaliation. Lang stayed seated keeping his mouth shut for once, but even remaining silent he vowed to get even with Reddy for making him look like a fool in front of his friends.

Having picked up her tray Reddy stormed away from the table. She fought back tears as she headed for the dish tank area. Lost in self-pity she paid no attention to who was also headed towards the tank area. It was a collision of trays, food contents and a spewing of words that sent her to the floor as they collided at the tank area when they both tired putting trays on the conveyer belt.

Glaring up at the person she had collided with her temper was well in place as she stormed at him. "I wished for once you would watch where your going?" she provoked in anger.

"Excuse me, I am not the klutz here?" Tanner insisted with a satirical grin.

"Oh! And I am to assume I am?" she spoke between gritted teeth as she made the effort to stand and retrieve her books.

"Well I am not the one on the floor!" Tanner insinuated turning to Crawford and telling him. Let's go,' as he dismissed the girl like one would a child as he moved pass her.

"And I thought I was going to eat? What was I thinking?" Crawford complained following Tanner towards the door of the mess hall. Continuing to complain, he remarked. "You might need to shed a few pounds but I am rather happy with my weight. Thank you so very much?"

"Why don't you just shut-up," Tanner retorted as he looked back at Reddy, for a moment their eyes met in conquest. Whatever was taking place neither one was ready to deal with it.

At 1800 the girls in building 332 were getting ready to go out for the evening, those that had made plans for the evening, that is. After having a trying day in school Reddy didn't care to listen to Reynolds usual report about another one of her conquest for the evening. Her details leaving nothing to the imagination as she talked about her date. Some of the details were absolutely discussing. "I think you should be more discreet about who you date?" Reddy commented as Reynolds took a pause in talking.

Looking at Reddy, Reynolds rolled her eyes and expressed with a snicker. "What's the matter baby, can't your virgin ears take it?"

"I am not a baby?" Reddy protested. "And I doubt it my hearing has anything to do with your details of your date. I just think you would be more concerned about your reputation." Reddy insisted as she picked up her books and grabbing her jacket on the back of the chair, she made the motions to leave the room as Reynolds stopped her. "Were not through yet?" Reynolds spoke sternly.

"As far as I am concerned we are?" Reddy rejected as she made the move to move around Reynolds who was blocking the door. "Well aren't we Miss high and mighty? What makes you think you are so much better than me?"

"I think you just told us," Reddy answered, looking up at Reynolds and not budging from her obnoxious stare.

"Here we go again," Logan, murmured looking at White who was getting ready to go out for the evening.

"Tell me. I bet we are the only ones who have a slut and a virgin in the same room," White whispered back to Logan.

"Probably," Logan answered waiting for the fist to start swinging. To their relief Reddy made it around Reynolds and left the room with Reynolds yelling after her. "One of these days you are going to regret knowing me?"

Walking to the library had not changed her disposition as she pondered over how much she had been taunted by being so naïve. Feeling sorry for herself, she didn't pay much attention to the person sitting on the other side of the table that she had chosen to sit at. Preparing to study she arranged her books in a neat and orderly fashion. Shoving a few books lying on her side of the table out of the way as she pulled items from her backpack.

Tanner had hoped for a quite evening so he had chosen the library to study. Glancing up his eyes open wide to the person who was demanding the whole table. "Excuse me, but I believe I was here first?" Tanner spoke with malicious to the girl who had been giving him a few restless nights.

Taking pencils and a notebook out of her backpack, Reddy didn't bother to look at the person speaking as she answered. "Maybe so, but I am taking my half of the table!"

His patience was already thin after having a run into with Chief Molson this evening, the last thing he needed was to be intimidated by some chick, this one especially? "How would you like to study from the floor?" he made the threat picking up her books.

Her glare was fixed, her attitude aroused, she stared unbelievable at the person sitting across from her. "You! You! You wouldn't dare," she stammered provoked by anger.

"Taking a glance at her name first, Tanner proceeded to make good his threat. "I am very good at dare's" he assured her making a sweeping move towards the floor and knocking her books off the table.

Stomping her right foot, her blue eyes blazing to his astonishment she threw his books to the floor also. "Pick them up!" Tanner demanded, his voice rising.

"No problem," she spoke with indignation. Bending and picking up her books, she left his laying where they had landed. Standing again, she came face to face with the person in charge of the library. "I suggest you two children take your little game elsewhere," the guy's annoyance showed as he added. "Or the next time I might feel obligated to write the two of you up!" As he held out his arm and pointed towards the doors.

Tanner couldn't believe he was being thrown out of the library. To make matters worse they were being escorted to the door. His temper was far from being under control as he turned on the little minx once they were outside. "You are a spoiled brat!"

"Me! Me! Well I don't believe your actions speak any different." she accused, as she looked at him, the fathom of the dark eyes holding hers.

"Wrong their kid. I wasn't the one demanding the whole damn table. I was minding my own business as I recall,' Tanner exclaimed.

"Oh! Right! Who threw books to the floor first? It sure wasn't me," she exploded with rage.

"Never let it said you were not warned, Tanner declared with a sardonic smile, adding. "Didn't anyone warn you that the military is not a place for kids?"

"Kid? I wish you would quit referring to me as a kid! I have you to know I am nineteen," she ranted as she absentmindedly begins poking him in the chest with her index finger.

"Maybe then you shouldn't act like one," Tanner belligerently stated, grabbing the hand making an attack on his midsection, the move brought her very close to him.

Reddy continued to argue with him. "I suppose you think your actions are any different than mine? Well don't waste your time calling the kettle black?"

"Baby, I am not calling anything black," Tanner declared gripping her arm tighter. There was something about having her close that his senses were stormed with the scent of a soft fragrance. He almost forgot about being angry. Changing his tone to a more normal level he suggested. "Why don't we settle this over a soda?"

"In your dreams maybe," she spoke with animosity. Her thoughts becoming confused, she felt the need to put distance between them before she did something stupid. Clutching her books in one hand, her other hand was in his grip. It left only her feet free, without giving it a second thought she kicked him hard in the shin.

It took only seconds for the pain to reach Tanner's dazed mind. Feeling pain in the area of his shin, he cursed. "Damn you," and released his hold on her. With warning he told her. "You are gong to regret ever knowing me!"

"I doubt it," she declared, calling over her shoulder as she rapidly moved down the steps that led to the library. Instead of following her, he shrugged his shoulders and turning limped toward his car. Grumbling a few words about getting even, he unlocked his car and looked around to see if he could see her, he found her nowhere in sight.

For once Reddy was glad to find the room empty. Laying her books on her desk, she caught a glimpse of herself in the mirror. Her hair was a mess; her face flushed yet she never felt more feminine and couldn't understand the giddy feeling that seemed to envelop her. Laughing at the jubilant feeling, she walked over to her locker and took out her radio and headphones. Placing the headphones on, she began to dance around the room and sing to the song *'Strut'* that was playing.

Being engrossed in the music playing Reddy didn't hear anyone enter the room. White opened the door quietly so as not to disturb Reddy who generally was asleep by now. To her surprise she found Reddy up and dancing around the room and trying to sing. "I knew you were spending too much time in this room," White laughed tapping Reddy on the shoulder. Reddy jumped, screamed, and doing a quick turn around faced White. To Reddy's startled actions, White couldn't resist asking. "Did you get laid?"

Embarrassed at being caught, Reddy turned away from White and murmured. "Don't I wish?" Her reply not so low that White could have missed it. Still laughing, White asked. "Anyone I know?"

"I doubt it," Reddy insisted, slowly removing the headphones and cassette player and placing them back into her locker and reached for her pajamas.

"Are you sure? I seem to know a lot of people," White stated, thinking that maybe she could find out how Reddy felt about Tanner. Once Jay Reed, her boy friend and Tanner's roommate found out that White was Reddy's roommate the questions flew. "What was she like? Was she seeing anyone? Did she have a boy friend back home? How old was she? Well now it was her turn to ask some questions in a round about way. "Could it be the guy that's keeping you on the floor in the mess hall?" White persisted looking at Reddy who was pulling a pajama top on over her head. Reddy didn't answer her so White went on saying. "Let me guess, you haven't noticed what a babe this guy is? White stated rolling her eyes at Reddy.

"Who?" Reddy questioned, as she had paid little attention as to what White had been saying. Staring at Reddy in disbelief, White shook her head as she exclaimed. "You haven't heard a word I've said?"

"Some, Reddy yawned, getting an impatience look from White, who then asked. 'Aren't you getting tired of setting in this room?"

"Yes, but I don't know that many people here," Reddy seem to whine, "and Logan and you are always gone."

"Excuse me--But Logan and I are not here to baby-sit you," White insinuated. As she suggested, "why don't you try going over to the Snipe's Castle? There are a bunch of girls your age that go there?

"Maybe I will," Reddy sighed, before turning her back to White and pretending sleep.

In the building next door three guys were finding sleep impossible as the fourth person whom they shared the room with kept pacing back and forth in what little space was left of the floor. "Tanner will you go to bed?" Reed complained, wanting to sleep.

"Or get the hell out of this room," Morgan added as Crawford suggested. "Why don't you go and see Warner, I am sure she can relieve some of your stress?"

"I can do that," Tanner grumbled picking up his coat, he left the room. Walking down the hall from his room, Tanner half expected Chief Molson to step out into the hall. Passing the lounge, Tanner changed his mind about leaving the building, instead, he decided to give his brother, Mike a call.

Letting the phone rang several times, Tanner was about ready to hang up, when he heard his brother's voice. "Tanner residence, how may I help you?"

"Hello Mike," Tanner responded to his brother's voice.

"What's up?" Mike questioned, once he heard his brother's voice. "Nothing, I just thought I would check in and see how things are at home," Tanner replied.

"Okay," Mike answered with doubt as to why his brother was calling. Steve had been in school for six months, and this was what? The second time he had called home. "You still in school?" Mike couldn't avoid asking.

"Yes," Tanner smiled to his brother's question.

"Good! So little brother what is the real reason you are calling?" Mike questioned. "You need money?"

"Not hardly, I just got paid," Tanner answered as he tired to figure out why he had called home in the first place and as usual he was getting the third degree from his brother. Then he laughed, "Mike what would you say if I told you I have found the girl for me?"

"I would say you were crazy. I thought you were after a career with the Navy?" Mike reminded him.

"I am, but I can't let this person get away from me," Tanner stated, almost imagining his brother's expression, and knew once he was off the phone, he would be calling their father, as Mike stated further. "I thought you had only a few months left to go there, then it's off to Florida?"

"I do," Tanner agreed with him.

"So where does this girl fit into the picture?" Mike continued to question his brother logic.

"She doesn't. At least not yet and probably never will," Tanner answered, confusing his brother as he went on talking. "She has this incredible attitude. I don't think she trusts anyone. I believe she is around nineteen?" he added before his brother could ask how old she was.

"Little young wouldn't you say?" Mike asked, to his brother's age of twenty-three.

"What's four years?" Tanner commented, since there was ten years difference in his parent's age.

"Probably nothing," Mike grumbled, as he added. "Just remember why you are there?"

"Haven't forgot," Tanner, replied, as he told Mike. "I've got to go,." tired of getting the lecture from his brother who was ten years older than him.

17

It was the usual of taking notes, of learning about what they would be doing aboard ships or on shore duty. Their learning objective for the day: To identify sources of pollutants, their effects and aspects of the Navy's policy and procedures for pollution abatement. From these it was identifying various ships and what their characteristics and functions were.

At break, Matthew's and Reddy were talking about how quickly the weeks seem to have passed by. "Can you believe it, we have only one week left in here?"

"Thank God," Reddy responded, as she turned and looked out the window. It was the middle of October, and for the past few days it had done nothing but rain. The weather was beginning to match her mood and she wasn't sure why she was so moody lately.

"Don't tell me you are worried about going on to A School?" Matthews turned and looked at his friend with a smile on his face, for she should be anything but worried, she was standing at the top of the class.

"Who me? Never. It's only that I heard the instructors are tougher on the girls though." Reddy mentioned with a deep sigh.

"I think you can handle it. You have a way of letting them know that you are here for the duration?" Matthews chuckled.

"I take it that is a compliment?"

"I meant it as one," Matthews assured her as he added. "Drew called Jenny's over the weekend. He said to tell you hello."

"Oh really. Did he mention anything about the fact that he spiked by drinks?" Joan questioned him.

"He didn't spike your Coke," Matthews stated defending Drew Adams.

"Yeah, right!" Joan uttered not believing him. Getting back to the other subject as to it being their last week in basics she told him. "It really hasn't been as bad as I thought it would be."

"You can say that after all the hassle you have been getting from the guys? Plus I don't think Instructor Collins has been that easy on you?"

Reddy's expression turned serious as she said. "I guess maybe if I was a guy, I too would feel the pressure of having a girl in my class. Especially when she knows what she is doing. But Brian, I am here for the same reason that they are, to be an engineman. As far as Instructor Collins goes, he is from the old school. No girls allowed.

It was the beginning of their last week in basic, Instructor Collins started the day's lecture with: Standard organizations are regulations of the United States Navy. "If a sailor had to learn a new set of regulations and an entirely different organization every time he moved from one division, department or one ship to another, he would waste valuable time. This information in which you are about to receive is classified material and is on loan to you. You must know and familiarize yourself with the general regulations. You must read all of the regulations and sign a statement to the effect that you have done so and that you understand them.

Your daily and weekly routines aboard ship will be governed by these instructions, also the organization of your division and your department."

"Holy cow!" Lang complained, "There are seventy items to remember?"

"Yes. And you will know all of them by the time you report aboard a ship," Instructor Collins assured him.

"We do get to keep this material?" Another person inquired to the copy of standard organization and regulations that had been handed to them.

"No, these copies are not to leave this room." Instructor Collins assured them as he added. "You will receive your own loaned copies when you reach your ships. For now we will be studying them this week, and also I need to inform you that what you learn in here this week you will not discuss with anyone. Does everyone understand?" As heads where shaking yes, some were complaining. "I got to learn this in five days?" Saunders complained as lights were called.

Having been avoiding the usual group of guys from her class, Reddy was quite surprised when Matthews asked. "Sitting by us?" at lunch.

"Need to see my notes?" She smiled back at him.

"Na, I am getting pretty good at understanding what is going on. I just thought maybe you would like to sit with us since this is the last week we all will be together." Matthews answered with a smile.

Taking a seat next to Matthew it didn't take Lang long to start in on her. "Aren't you lost?" he questioned Reddy who usually sat alone. Ignoring Lang, and not knowing he was no longer in school, she didn't have any idea that he was ready for paybacks. "Wright was wrong about you Reddy," Lang started. "He just didn't know a diesel dike when he saw one. You should have gone into the nunnery, instead of the military?"

You could hear gasps from the group as they looked at Lang, then at Reddy. Knowing that Reddy wouldn't let a statement like that go by without some reaction from her. The group didn't have to wait long as Reddy slid her chair back and standing she walked over to Lang. Raising her hand as Lang turned around to look at her, she connected with his face. It was a crack of thunder that followed as she open handed slapped him. You could hear a pin drop in the vicinity of the two as dead silence followed.

"Whoa!" Crawford uttered, seeing the commotion a couple of tables over from where he was sitting. Turning to Tanner he made the comment. "You know the chick that keeps us from eating in here? I don't think you should press the issue of her paying for your dry-cleaning. She just wallops a guy. I mean she really let him have it." Crawford chuckled, as Tanner turned around in his chair and looked back to where Reddy had been sitting. He caught the next scene though as he heard the guy state loud and clear for all to hear. "Bitch!"

"Yes and don't you forget it," Reddy swore at Lang with looks to kill

"I don't think he is winning," Tanner stated, turning back around to eat.

"Still want to find out who she is?" Crawford pressed on.

"I know who she is," Tanner responded, "Fireman Joan Reddy."

"What? And you haven't made a date with her?" Crawford stared at his friend in amazement.

Turning back around Tanner told him. "I think she is a little young for me."

Laughing Crawford remarked. "She must be of age or she wouldn't be here."

"Probably," Tanner answered picking up his books, the incident forgotten.

Reddy had moved to a different table. Blinded by tears she was furious to think she had let Lang make a fool of her again. Pushing her food around on her plate she decided she wasn't hungry after all. Rising she made the move toward the tank area. Again she was on a path to destruction. "What the hell!" Tanner swore, fighting to maintain his balance as he started to rise from his chair and found a girl in his lap. "I should have known?" He spoke to the person who seemed on a destiny to ruin every uniform he owned. Shoving her back to her feet, he continued to stare at her.

Her stance was straight, her attitude well in place even if her knees were shaking. In a rebellious tone, she stormed at him. "Go to hell!"

"Go to hell you say? Well baby, I think you are doing a good job of trying to put me there!" Tanner stated, his brooding glaze holding the girl's attention.

"Not my intentions I can assure you," she spoke with aloofness stalking around him she continued to head for the tank area.

"I think she would be quite a challenge," Crawford commented, watching Reddy also.

"Think so?" Tanner questioned casually, his eyes also watching Reddy but only for different reason. Something happen a few minutes ago and he wasn't sure if he wanted to pursue the feelings.

"Yes," Crawford answered rather serious. "That is one person I don't think you would want to get involved with. There is something about her that is different from your usual run of the mill?" Crawford added with some slight warning to his voice.

"You seem to forget that Reddy and I have already had one, no two confrontations," Tanner reminded him.

"Yeah and I also remember you saying you lost both times?" Crawford chuckled.

"Not funny my friend," Tanner added with no humor as the two left the galley.

Reddy was doing her best to study and ignore the comments being made about dates and who was sleeping with whom. It seem that her roommates favorite topic were guys and sex. Finally having heard enough she slammed her books closed. Storming over to her locker she pulled out her dirty clothes. "Going to do your laundry?" Logan asked.

"Yes!" Reddy snapped as Logan asked. "Wouldn't mind doing mine also?"

"Sure why not I have nothing better to do?" Reddy complained as Logan got up from where she was sitting and walking over to her locker, threw a bunch of clothes into a ditty bag and handed hem to Reddy. "I like bleach in my white's" Logan stated, trying to keep a straight face to Reddy's sour expression. "Wouldn't want to do mine also?" White added, before Reddy could get out the door. "Sure, why not?" Reddy insisted, as White handed her a ditty bag full of clothes. "They all better be marked," Reddy grumbled, as she added. "I need money for your clothes."

"What! You are not paying for them?" Logan laughed, as she reached for her purse and searched through it for money to give to Reddy. Searching diligently though her purse, she looked up at Reddy. "I seem to have missed place my money?"

"Sure," Reddy laughed, as she added. "Don't worry, I've got it." as she walked over to her locker and pulled out a jar where she kept extra money, which she tucked into her back pocket of her dungarees.

"Mine too," White asked, as she started to hand Reddy ten dollars.

"Maybe next time," Reddy answered, as she picked up her books, and all the ditty bags.

She lucked out for a Thursday night to do her laundry the place was almost empty. After throwing her clothes in a washer, she found a seat to read what Collins declared was a need to know. "No wonder I never did well in physics. This stuff is confusing," mumbling she reread the article on Newton's Law's. Still puzzled to what she was reading, she laid the book aside and rubbing her wasn't aware of the person who had been watching her for some time.

"You look like you could use some help?" Tanner spoke walking up to where Reddy was sitting.

Raising her head, she found herself looking at the jerk. "I probably do but I don't expect it to come from you," she insisted in a restrained tone.

Ignoring her ill temper, Tanner continued saying. "I heard you talking to yourself. So what do you need to know about Newton's law's?"

"Whatever it is, I am sure I can figure it out on my own?" she told him still speaking with animosity and not sure about the tightness she was feeling in her stomach, or the way he was looking at her. The deep fathom eyes seem to know everything she was thinking.

"Fine!" Tanner coerce, turning and started to walk away from her, her attitude finally beginning to get on his nerves. "Wait!" she stopped him from getting to far away. "I'm sorry. I do need help with physics," she told him thinking help from him would do know harm.

At first Tanner was going to continue walking, but something in her voice made him change his mind and moving back, he told her. "It's been a while but I think I can remember enough to get you by," grinning, he reached for her book and reading the note attached to the page, he looked back at her. "So you need to know everything?" he repeated what he had been reading in bold letters on the note attached to her paper.

"Everything," she repeated as he stood next to where she was standing folding clothes. "I am almost done with this load," she added folding the last article of Logan's and putting it into her ditty bag.

"Why don't we go sit down?" he suggested as he moved towards the chairs along the window and took a seat. With her following him she took the chair next to him as he began. "First law, an object will stay at rest, if at rest. An object in motion continues to move at a constant speed along a straight line. Unless in either case the body is acted upon by an outside force," he said making a diagram for her as he talked.

"Second law, it an object is acted upon by an outside force, causing that object to accelerate in the direction of the line of force. The acceleration is directly proportional to the force and inversely proportional to the mass of the object," Tanner continued to write as Reddy forced herself to listen. Even if her thoughts wee else where and to what White had remarked about him being very good-looking. Not only was he good-looking, Reddy now thought but also he had a voice that had a baritone ring to it.

"Third and important law," his voice rising brought her back to the present and caught him looking at her. "You do need to pay attention," he spoke rather sternly. Then he went on to tell her. "For every action there is an equal and opposite force. Their does that explain it?" Tanner asked giving Reddy a little boy lopsided grin.

"Not really," she replied still puzzled by what he had told her. "Isn't there some other way you could explain it?" She found herself asking.

"Let's see if I can explain it this way. You have a ball lying on a table. It's at rest until something moves it. It will go straight until acted up on by some unbalanced force. In other words if it hits something, or is hit by something it will move.

Unless I am mistaken what you need to know is how to figure out velocity. Speed is the term used to designate the magnitude of velocity. You can get this by doing a speed-time diagram." Which he showed her how to draw? "You need to remember that speed equals distance, divided by time. There have I completely confused you?" He asked, the boyish grin returning, as he looked at Reddy for the first time and was caught off guard by her stunning blue eyes, the sensuous lips, perk nose that sat in the lean face. She was cute being an understatement.

"Probably," she found herself smiling at him, and breaking into whatever he was thinking. Then trying to absorb what he had told her, she went back over his notes. "So what you are saying in terms that I need to know, is the force that is applied is called, input and the velocity are called output?"

"Did I say that?" a deep throaty laughed followed his question.

Wary to how she was feeling and being mesmerized by his eyes, which demanded your attention she fought the strange emotions that were surfing. "I don't need to be laughed at just because I don't quite understand something," she retorted, standing from where she was sitting and walking over to the washers and took out White's clothes to dry.

Following her Tanner insisted. "Baby, I wasn't making fun of you," as he was drawn into the unique husky voice, for coming from her it was quite sexy. "How would you like to spend the weekend with me?" He found himself asking. "I could show you the sights of Chicago and China Town?"

"I am not into dating someone I don't know," she insisted, using her attitude to warn him off

Tanner was caught off guard by her coolness, since only seconds ago she was giving him this very coy look. "I think we are well acquainted," he replied as again the boyish grin crossed his face. "You do remember the galley?"

"Yes," she answered nervously as her face turned a crimson color.

"So what do you say? Do we have a date?" Being a little persistence.

"I---I don't know your name and you want me to go with you?" she stammered apprehensive to the rising nervous feelings as she looked at him.

"Steve Tanner," he answered as she in return answered, "Joan Reddy."

Steve Tanner? Why does that name sound familiar? Where had she heard it before? Then it dawned on her, Reynolds? No way was she dating anyone that went out with Reynolds. Then she looked again at him, from all appearances he sure resembled her description of him. He had alluring and had aristocrat looks. A perfect built body, which in thinking again brought color to her cheeks. Although she was blushing, she flatly stated. "I wouldn't date you on a bet?"

Usually he couldn't care less about what a girl thought, nor would he be this persistent. But lately his nerves had been on the ragged edge due to her. "Who's making a bet?" His glaze intensified on her face, their eyes once more locked in an unspoken battle. It was there to tantalize them, the inordinate magnetism that seems to draw on their senses.

She stood before him chastised, her stare unblinking although her emotions were running a race with her heart. No way was she going to let him know that he was getting to her. She could always come back and get her clothes, she suddenly thought. Breaking the stare she gathered her books. Quickly turning from him she all but ran out of the Laundromat.

Watching Reddy, Tanner thought, "Baby! You may be giving me the cold shoulder, but I saw your eyes. You want me as bad as I want you."

The next morning rising at 0530 the girls in room 349 were in their usual state of panic as they prepared to stand muster. "Reddy! Where are my clothes?" both Logan and White yelled at Reddy who was searching her locker for something to wear. Backing away from her locker, she had a stunned look on her face. "Ooh my gosh---I'm so sorry! They are still at the Laundromat," Reddy tried to apologize. Completely forgetting that she had done Logan's and White's clothes with hers.

"What?" Both girls yelled at her. Not believing that they had heard her right. "They are where?" Logan demands an answer.

"At the Laundromat," Reddy answered in a timid voice.

"And what am I suppose to wear this morning?" Logan argued, slamming her locker door shut and pointing at her, and demanding "Go get them…NOW! And you better hope they are still there. Otherwise you are paying me for several sets of dungarees and underwear?"

"Yeah Reddy," White included. "I really don't want to stand muster with nothing on." As the girls continued to demand their clothes, a knock came to the girl's door. Reynolds being close to the door opens it. The 'messenger of the watch' stood holding three ditty bags. "These were left for Reddy," the girl spoke dropping the bags inside the room.

"Your ass is saved," Reynolds snickered, as she reached down and retrieved a note pinned to one of the bags. Reading, "we are not finished, Tanner," kicking the ditty bags towards Reddy, she waved the note. "You want to explain this?"

Reddy leaning down to pick up her ditty bag as White and Logan did the same, she answered. "You read it, you explain it?'

"You were out with Tanner?" Reynolds spoke with contempt, as Logan and White ears perked up and they both looked at Reddy as they waited for an answer.

"Not hardly," Reddy flatly stated. "I was minding my own business at the Laundromat when he came over to me."

"Then why would he say you two are not finished?" Reynolds continued to doubt Reddy.

Feeling she owe Reynolds any explanation but to avoid a conflict with her, she answered. "He ask for a date and I refused."

"Yeah right!" Reynolds baited but she turned and left the room.

Once Reynolds was gone Logan and White started in on Reddy. "You what?" Both girls stated, finding it hard for anyone to turn down Tanner for a date. "What happen did he make a pass?" Logan couldn't resist asking knowing how naïve Reddy was.

"If he had you wouldn't have gotten your clothes back," Reddy stated with no emotions to her voice.

"Then why did you turn him down for a date," White asked a little confused.

"Because he knows Reynolds," Reddy answered, as Reynolds came back into the room and the girls clamped up and finished getting ready for muster.

Reddy had decided not to sit in an empty room for the next two days. Leaving her room she stopped first at the lounge to make a call home. "Hope mother doesn't answer," she thought making the call collect. To her surprise Peggy answered the phone. "Yes, yes!" Peggy screamed when the operator wanted to know if she would accept the call. "Oh my gosh! It's really you?" Peggy continued with excitement upon hearing her sister's voice.

"Yes," Joan laughed as she added. "Who were you expecting the Pope?"

"Well I could say Mark, but I talked to him last night. Got your letter, you sound bored. Aren't you allowed out of your room?"

"Yes," Joan responded.

"So are you trying to tell me there are no guys there?" Peggy asked with doubt.

"There are guys here, just none that I want to date?" Joan responded knowing that she was about to get a lecture from her sister.

"What abut the guy you keep running into? Have you noticed what he looks like?" Peggy asked with curiosity.

"I haven't taken the time to notice. I am always busy running back to my room to change my clothes. I don't need to get caught unsat." Reddy informed her.

"Liar," Peggy stated, as she heard something in Joan's voice that hadn't been there before.

Sensing that her sister knew she was leaving out something, Joan told her. "Okay, he is tall. Now are you happy?" She insisted laughing.

"That's all?" Peggy sighed with rejection as she felt her sister wasn't telling her all.

Knowing how pretty Peggy was and how plain she felt she was, Joan wasn't about to let her know how good-looking Tanner was. What she did tell her was. "Look! I really didn't notice his appearance after I found out who he was. He is a jerk and will remain a jerk." Reddy stated as she said in her next breath. "I've got to go."

"Okay," Peggy answered as she added. "Take care and don't be so boring."

"Sure Peg," she grumbled hanging up the phone. Walking back to her room she also remembered Logan saying something about her being boring. That all she could talk about was what she was learning in school. "You need to get out of this room," Logan had told her more than once.

"Once she was back in her room she walked over to her locker. Just the other night she had brought some clothes that were unconventional for her. Might as well wear something beside work dungarees. Looking through her wardrobe, she had a limit choice to choose from. She had brought a couple pairs of jeans, a few agile sweaters, two pairs of dress pants, one navy blue, and the other black. Guess this will do, she thought to herself as she pulled out a sweatshirt that had Navy written across the front, and a pair of jeans. Taking a look into the mirror with a brush in her hand, she groaned as she tackled her hair. Pulling a brush through her curly locks, Reddy uttered,

"Defiantly got to do something with this hair?. Changing her train of thought as she searched through her locker again she found the makeup that Logan and her had bought at the mall. "Maybe makeup will help?" With care she applied the makeup. Stepping back from the mirror, she looked again at herself and decided to forget the makeup she didn't need to look like a clown, as she started to go and wash off the makeup.

Nancy White had quietly entered the room and had stood near the door watching Reddy for several minutes. "Want some help?" White asked and almost caused Reddy to let out a scream as she quickly turned around. Recovering, Reddy asked. "How long have you been standing there?"

"Long enough," White laughed, "so whom do you want to impress?" White added, as she began to tackle the mop of unruly curly hair after telling her to "have a seat!"

In answer to White's question about impressing someone, she answered. "No one but my sister and Logan think I am rather boring."

"That I will agree with," White declared figuring there wasn't much she could do with Reddy's hair. You need to get this cut and styled," White suggested. Taking an overall look at Reddy. "Let's redo your makeup," she then suggested. Reddy had a natural innocent look about her, so White choose soft colors that more or less enhanced her features with her eyes being her focal point.

Looking in the mirror Reddy gasped at the results. "Is that really I?"

"I think so," White uttered as she also told her. "You are really cute when you have makeup on. Not that you aren't okay with out it, but makeup seems to bring out your fine features more." All Reddy wanted to know was, "do I look older?"

"Some but I don't think you would want to look too much older," laughing, White couldn't resist saying. "You got that special look that sort of holds guys off at a distance."

"Well I guess then I should be relieved that no one wants to date me," Reddy answered sort of puzzled, since she was suppose to meet guys not scare them off.

"Would you like to know where Tanner hangs out?" White asked next.

Reddy looked at her curious. "Where?" she shyly asked.

"At the Crow's Nest," Nancy informed her, as she added. "I am headed that way would you like to go?"

"Why not," Reddy responded, as she picked up her purse and followed White to the door.

Walking in to the Crow's Nest, Reddy realized that she didn't remember the place. It's funny that I never noticed the surroundings? She thought to the place that was decorated like a pirate ship. Ship netting was laid out across the ceiling. Filling it were shells and starfish of all sizes. On the poles were ships steering wheels. The bar area took on the appearance of a galley on a pirate ship. The guy standing at the door checking ID's was dressed in pirate grab, eye patch, and black hat with a large white feather plume. His clothing consisted of a billowy sleeve shirt with ruffles down the front, and tight fitting suede pants and a sword tucked across his waist by a large cloth belt. He stopped Reddy from entering the room by holding his sword out and asking for her ID. When she showed him the card, he then told her. "Hold out your hand, and to her surprise, he stamped her hand.

"What was that for?" she asked White following her to a table where a group of people were sitting. "It lets the waitress know you are underage to drink." Nancy informed her, as they walked up to the table. Nancy began to make the introductions, "Dan Crawford, Lowe Martin and his girlfriend, Phyllis Hunter, Jay Reed," smiling Nancy introduced Joan to the group. "Joan Reddy." Before she sat down across from Crawford she looked around for Tanner, not seeing him as she pulled out her chair, she looked at Crawford with a curious stare and wondered where Tanner was?

"Tanner will be here," Crawford stated as Nancy took a seat across from him. "He had a meeting with Chief Molson." Crawford added as he looked at Reddy. Cute! Was what he was thinking as he asked her. "Would you like to dance?"

Well it's now or never to change Reddy thought as she accepted Dan Crawford offer to dance. Letting him take the lead, she wondered if he ever relaxed, for his movements were almost stiff. Dance this guy couldn't do to a fast song. Slow songs she realized weren't too great either. As they were about to dance to another fast song, Dan was relived when Tanner tapped him on the shoulder. "Mind if I cut in?"

"Be my guest?" Dan answered, stepping aside so that Tanner and Reddy were now partners.

Madeline J. Wilcox

"You do know how to dance?" Tanner asked, once he became Reddy's partner.

"I do know how to keep rhythm," she flatly replied, as *'Along comes a woman'* by *'CHICAGO'* started playing. To Tanner's surprise, Reddy could dance. Move was an understatement as their movements became synchronized.

Reddy loved dancing and it was something, which she had been doing little of lately. Moving to the beat of the music, she let herself go. Her moves became sultry, seductive as they danced to one song after another. Pulling her in for a slow song Tanner couldn't resist saying. "You do want to keep on dancing or do you have something else in mind?" as she was beginning to play havoc with his nervous system.

"I am dancing," she stated looking up at him. Something about the look on his face made her think that she might be getting into uncharted waters, realizing this, she said. "I think maybe we should take a break?"

Joining the others at the table again, Joan excused herself as she picked up her purse. Tanner thought she was headed for the restroom. To his astonishment and disbelief, Joan walked toward the entrance door. "You going after her?" Crawford asked, a little surprised at the girls actions also.

"Why?" Tanner shook his head slowly not quite understanding why Reddy had left.

"Because I think she likes you?" Nancy informed him.

"You sure about that?" Tanner asked with doubt.

"Yes." Nancy smiled, as she added. "You seem to forget that I share a room with her.

"Good, why don't you tell her I said to take a hike," Tanner insisted as he picked up the beer in front of him and took a drink.

"I think she did," Martin uttered, as he turned to his date and suggested they go somewhere else.

With luck there was a cab dropping off a group of guys as she walked out of the Crow's Nest. Quickly taking their place Reddy told the driver, "Naval Training Center, please." Not realizing that the short trip to the base would cost her ten dollars. "I could have walked for that price," she grumbled paying the driver.

After crossing the 'quarterdeck' she went to the lounge and placed a call to her brother's home with hopes that Linda would answer the phone. To her disappointment it was her brother who accepted the call. "You will pay for this," Jeff told her when she came on the line.

"Don't I always," she replied as she asked. "Is Linda around?"

"Nope, her mother and she went shopping. What's up?"

"Nothing much. I just wanted to talk," Joan lied.

"At my expense," Jeff teased her.

"You will get your money," Joan snapped at him.

"Wow! Are we in a mood?" he chuckled, "So who stepped on your toes?"

"No one," she replied her attitude not changing.

"I think you need to sound more convincing. Talked to mother lately?" he continued to taunt her.

Hardly I just had some free time so I thought I would give Linda a call, that's all." she sighed to the fact she wouldn't be able to ask her for some advice.

"Sure and I am the Poe. This is your brother, remember?" Jeff reminded her as he heard her take a deep sigh. "You in trouble?" he couldn't avoid asking as he recalled reading a letter the other day that his sister had written his wife. Linda was very upset when she had caught him reading it. "Jeff, that letter was not meant for you to read," Linda had stated clearly taking the letter from him. To the silence he finally heard his sister answer. "No."

"Good. I would hate to see you throw a career down the drain for someone who wears a 'Cracker Jack' uniform."

"Get real Jeff. Stupid I'm not," she was ready to argue with him.

"Hope so," his tone serious as he added. "I am pretty good about not having a bias opinion if you would care to talk to me?"

Remembering how he had always been there for her, she was ready to confide in him. "I met this guy---and well I think things could get complicated."

"And your are holding back, because you are afraid you might turn into what mother has accused you of being?" Jeff questioned her.

"Something like that." Joan agreed with him.

"Remember boot camp? I told you then that you were on your own. Guess what? You are. Quit waiting for mother, dad and even Grams to tell you how wrong you are."

"But Jeff," she was ready to argue again.

"But Jeff nothing. I think I know what you are trying to say. I won't think less of you if you truly love the guy. I also know that relationships in the military are not easy. Even Linda and I have problems sometimes," Jeff told her hoping he was making some kind of sense.

"But Linda and you are married," she stated, as if that would make a difference.

"That we may be but some dates won't match up to nine months," Jeff remarked reminding her that Linda and him had to get married.

"I don't think I can cross that line?" she answered her brother as she fought tears and couldn't understand why she was even crying.

Jeff hearing his sister tone of voice drop, he said. "Maybe I am not saying the right things to you. Why don't you call Linda later?"

"Maybe I will," she said as a 'messenger of the watch' entered the lounge and asked. "Are you Joan Reddy?"

"Yes," she replied to the girl.

"You have a visitor on deck," the girl let her know.

"Jeff I have to let you go. I have a visitor on the quarterdeck."

"Don't kill him," Jeff laughed as he let her go.

Hanging up the phone, she didn't figure it would be Tanner. "Probably Matthews," she muttered to herself. Crossing the quarterdeck after the OOD told her the guy was waiting outside. The minute she walked through the door, Tanner grabbed her arm. "What kind of game are you playing?" he assailed her with. His dark eyes brooding as they leveled with hers when she looked up at him.

"Let me go," she demanded trying to pull herself from his grip.

"Not until I get an answer," he stormed not understanding why he was so angry with her.

How could she explain to this person whom for the past three months had been invading her dreams. How could she explain the turmoil he was causing? She herself didn't understand her strange feelings. "Please let me go," she begged as tears started to fill her eyes.

With reluctance Tanner dropped her arms. Once again he told her, "We are not finished." Turning he let her go back into her building as he stepped off the steps and walked towards his building, which was next door.

19

Rising Saturday morning as usual Reddy was alone in the room on the weekends they were not standing duty. Sitting her feet on the floor she sat for a moment looking around the small room. Usually she was up and doing 'field day', but today she had a change of heart, she would take a shopping trip in to Lakehurst Mall, or maybe make a trip into Chicago. Either way it would be a change from what she normally did.

After taking a shower and was back into her room, getting dressed she had to throw a robe on as a knock came to her door. Unlocking her door and opening it she again faced the 'messenger-of-the-watch' who was holding a large flower box in her arms. "I was told to give you these?" the girl stated, handing Reddy the box. After closing the door, she walked over to her desk and sat the box down and stared at it. It took her several seconds before she picked up the card tucked under the red ribbon, which was tied around the box to hold it together. Opening the card slowly she began to read. "This better work. Meet me downstairs in ten minutes. Steve." Opening the box she was dazzled by two-dozen of red roses. Great! What do I put them in? Then realizing that she didn't have much time to dress, she put the cover back on the box and walked over to her locker. Shuffling through her clothes she was about ready to cry. "I have nothing to wear," she grumbled throwing one outfit after another onto the floor, finally deciding on a light blue sweater and dark blue dress slacks and shoes that had two inch heels to them.

Normally she would have stopped and put everything back into it's place, but this was not the time to worry about being neat, she told herself as she scooped up the clothes that had formed a pile on the floor, and threw them into her locker.

Once outside, she looked around for Steve, feeling a little desponded she figured that maybe he had gotten tired of waiting and had left.

As she turned to go back in to her building, she heard her name being called. "Joan! Joan, wait up." Turning she saw him coming off the steps that led into his building. Watching Tanner walk towards her, she smiled inwardly, he didn't just walk, he strutted. "Sorry I am late, Chief Molson was set on giving me his usual lecture," he smiled, the smile that enhanced his good looks. "I'm hungry. Have you had breakfast yet?" Tanner then asked.

Hungry! She didn't think she could eat a bite. Not with her heart beating so rapidly that her knees felt like they would crumble at any moment as he told her. "I have a car parked across the street."

His car was a Chevy Blazer, a sport model that in a way fit the owner. Once they were settled and on the road he asked her. "Where would you like to eat?"

Lakehurst Mall had been the only place she had been since arriving at Great Lakes. She had eaten at a restaurant with Logan; only she forgot the name of the place. "Any place you have in mind will be okay with me," Joan replied.

"Okay, I can handle that," Tanner replied, looking over at her as they waited for the traffic of cars headed off the base. No makeup today he noticed as she turned to look at him, and he asked. "Where did you live before joining the Navy?"

With a soft laugh, she answered. "I don't know if I can really explain Wellsburg, Indiana. Wellsburg is not your typical small town. People seem always a little out of step with time. Have you ever seen pictures of "Currier and Ives?"

"Several," Tanner smiled, thinking for some reason he could picture her living in that type of sitting, as she went on to tell him. "Then you have some idea of where I live,"

"What does your father do for a living," he continued with the questions wanting to keep her talking as he became intrigued with her soft husky voice.

My dad has a small construction company. I worked for him when I wasn't in school. I did secretarial work," she explained as he gave her a surprised looked and asked. "What made you choose a career like engineman, if you have a secretarial experiences?"

"A choice with the Navy I had. Working for my father was something I had to do. We weren't allowed to sit at home and watch television, or listen to the radio. My mother was a true believer that a busy child was one that stayed out of trouble, plus it beat sitting around and wishing I was doing other things," she shyly acknowledged.

"Didn't you date?" The question sounded ridiculous after making it, especially when anyone looked like she did. She looked more like a girl, than a girl should look. She had this innocent quality about her. Surly, she didn't expect him to believe she didn't date. Then he smiled at his next thought, but then she did have this attitude problem,

Seeing his expression, she flared. "What?"

Glancing over at her seeing her usual temperament, he asked with a light chuckle. "You did date?"

"Does the prom count?" she answered giving him a straightforward look.

"That's it. The prom?" Doubt was in his voice.

"Yes," her voice dropped as she turned and looked straight ahead and mumbled "and I doubt it you could count that as a date?"

Overhearing her, Tanner's curiosity rose, "Why didn't the guy show up?"

"Yes," she snapped finding her attitude.

"Want to tell me about it or is it something in which you care not to discuss?"

"What do you want to know? That I walked home," her voice having a cutting edge to it.

"Where was your date?" Tanner asked, trying to hold back laughter to her furious expression. He could almost picture her walking down some country road, her attitude well in tack, and her mood rancor. He couldn't resist asking as he recalled the scene in the galley not to long ago when she decked some guy. "Is this person still alive? He asked, again chuckling to himself.

"Not by my choice," she flatly remarked.

His laughter filled the car as he parked it. "I think you are going to be quite the challenge," he stated getting out and walking around to her side of the car.

"Oh really!" she proclaimed her attitude ruffled by his laughter.

"Really," he grinned, as they walked towards 'Denny's' restaurant. Waiting to be seated, he told her to order whatever she wanted. Being led to their seats and being handed a menu, she told him. "I am not very hungry." Tanner was hungry and he wasn't going to let her attitude defer him from eating.

Realizing that she was snapping at every word he spoke, she apologized. "I'm sorry, I guess I am a little nervous," she slowly admitted to him.

"Why! Were not in the galley," he grinned, as he relaxed and added. "Why don't you explain Joan Reddy to me?"

"I don't know if I can?" She replied, feeling at ease with him.

"Sure you can, you have ten minutes to do it in." Tanner told her doing his best to avoid looking into the tempting blue eyes, which had this sleepy eyed look about them.

"Ten minutes?" she stated, as she recalled another person saying that to her once before. "Ten minutes, I hope you don't time me," she slowly smiled at him as she began to tell him. "I have a brother in the Marines. A sister, who is a senior in high-school this year." She talked of her grandmother, her father, and her Uncle Matt, who had helped develop her interest in engines. "I was known as a tomboy around town," she finished with.

No kidding, he looked at her smiling inwardly, not wanting to rouse her attitude again, he then asked. "Are your parents divorced?"

"No," she quickly answered. "It's just that my mother and I are far from being close. She may have given birth to me, but a mother that doesn't make her as far as I am concerned," she spoke with bitterness.

Okay we don't talk about mom, Tanner made a mental note as Reddy said. "I have been doing all the talking. What about you?"

Tanner waited a few minutes before answering Joan as he gave the waitress their food order of two Western omelets, hash browns, and sausage gravy, toast and coffee. Once the waitress was gone Joan started to reject the fact that he ordered for her, but she didn't want the day to start off on the wrong foot, so she let it go as he said. "So I have ten minutes to sum me up? Well I guess it depends on whom you are talking too. Chief Molson would like to see me out of the Navy. Chief Adams, keeps telling me, 'Tanner, white is white. Black is black, why not try reading it that way? But there is also the gray matter in between," Tanner answered with this decisive look about him.

"Nancy White says your are very intelligent?" Joan informed him.

"Jay's girlfriend," Tanner commented, as he remembered who Nancy White was. Then laughing, he told her. "I understand you are the person who keeps the room in a turmoil?" Then before she could respond, he added. "I know one other person who you share the room with. Her name is Kathryn Reynolds," he spoke with disgust now.

"Yes, I know," she mischievously smiled at him.

"What!" He glared at her amused expression.

"Oh nothing," she responded continuing to smile.

"You might as well tell me," he insisted, taking up a defensive attitude.

"I doubt if you would really care about what Reynolds has to say about you? Although," her eyes lighting with mischief as she looked at him and continued, "some of what she does say seem to apply quite nicely to you."

"Do I want to know what that is?" Tanner ask, as he watched the color rise to her face. When she recovered she turned the questions again to him. "What makes you tick?"

Giving her a little boy grin, he answered. "I thought you knew what makes me tick?"

"Other than what I know," she slowly smiled, realizing that she felt very comfortable with him, but then they were sitting at a table across from each other, which brought laughter from her lips.

Thinking that she was laughing about something that she didn't want to share with him, he became quite serious when he told her. "Trust me. I have never been out with Reynolds. So whatever she has to say, didn't come from being with me!"

"Ouch, did I hit a sore spot?" Joan continued to smile.

"I am sure you are old enough to know what I mean," he provoked.

"I probably am," she assured him with a straight face. No wanting to stay on the defensive side with him, she said. "Remember you have ten minutes to tell me everything I need to know about you."

Tanner slowly let the boyish grin appear. "Ten minutes? Every thing? It may take a little longer than that to sum me up."

"Then I guess you should start talking," she laughed.

"You should do that more often," he remarked, looking at her and realizing that he was really enjoying the morning.

"What?" she couldn't resist asking him?

"Laugh. You have a very intriguing laugh." He told her, as he continued to tell her in his precise English. " I originally come from Maine. My parents move to Oklahoma after I finished high-school," he spoke as pain seem to flash across his eyes, and wasn't missed by Joan looking at him. "I have an older brother also, his name is Mike and he is an attorney along with my father. Mike handles the law firm in Oklahoma while my father handles the business in Maine. My mother, is an architect, and has her own business in Oklahoma." While he paused to take a drink of coffee Joan asked. "Are your parents separated?"

"Not that I am aware of. Why do you ask?" He almost choked on the coffee he was drinking.

"Your father lives in Maine, your mother lives in Oklahoma." She answered, as again the irresistible grin crossed his face. "Guess I need to clear my statements a little better, but I have only ten minutes to sum me up and I am trying to make it as short as possible. Now where was I?" Pausing as if he had forgotten. "Trying to keep your parents together," she answered, as again he was intrigued with her soft husky laugh.

Being caught off guard again by her, he found his heart taking up a different beat. Shaking his head as if to clear his thoughts, if was a few minutes before he could continued. "Oh yes, now I remember," he said collecting his thoughts. "Dad has a law firm in Oklahoma also. He travels back and forth between Oklahoma and Maine. There is that better?"

"At least I won't be jumping to the wrong conclusions," her tone serious, as she added. "White says you were in college?"

"Yelp, been there, done that?" Tanner responded, as Joan saw once more a quick flash of pain cross his face.

"Didn't you finish?"

"Yes," he answered with a sober expression.

"Then why are you just an enlisted person?" Sensing that he came from an altogether different background than most of the people who join the military, of course unless they were officers.

"Would you believe I became drunk one night and enlisted?"

"Not really," she casually remarked, not taking his answer to serious as she noticed the sober expression on his face and wanting him to return to his good mood of earlier, she quickly added. "Must have been some hangover?"

For a few moments Tanner remained silent, then he answered. "Coming out of it was quite a shock. Crawford keeps telling me, I owe you one."

"Do you," she gently remarked since the pain was still in his eyes.

"Yeah, I probably do. Crawford and I come from along way back. We went to the same prep school and college. His father handles our business in Maine.

"Oh Crawford dad is a lawyer also?" Joan questioned.

"No," Tanner spoke rather sharply. "He is the CEO for our boating company." Again Joan saw the pain in his eyes and wondered what had happen to bring so much grief to the dark probing eyes. With him becoming silent, brooding, she felt it best to change the subject. "We could talk about something else if you wish?"

Ignoring her, he continued in a sober tone. He told her how disappointed his father had been when he had not joined the family practice. For along time he was the family outcast. It wasn't until he had finished boot camp that he fell back into the good graces of his family. "The reason being I made outstanding recruit." He told her.

"How did you manage that?" She teased, since she felt that his attitude in general, was as bad as hers.

"With my charming ways of course," Tanner grinned.

With eyebrows raised, and a teasing smile, she couldn't resist saying. "Yeah, I bet."

"Don't push it," he spoke with irritation, then thinking twice about it, he added. "I can be civil when it's to my advantage."

"Now that I can believe," she spoke with subtleness, knowing she was getting to him.

"You do have a way of saying things," Tanner mentioned, being a little put out with her reply.

Giving it her best Southern accent, she answered. "My daddy always says it's better to say what you think, rather than hold back the truth."

"Really? What would daddy say if I made his daughter walk back to the base?"

"Probably would say, she's done that before," she quickly asserted.

He couldn't understand it. One minutes they were on friendly terms and next---they were snapping at each other. Maybe Crawford was right. Maybe he shouldn't precede this relationship with her. But there was something that seemed to draw him to her. "Would you like to see Chicago?" he then asked as they finished up their breakfast.

Trying to remain halfway sociable she fought to control her attitude. "What?"

"Never mind what," he smiled as he pushed back his chair. "Trust me, you will enjoy it?" Steve Tanner figured he hadn't walked so much and enjoyed it more as the day seemed to go by rather fast as they explored Chicago. Their first stop was the 'John G. Shed Aquarium, it had more than two hundred tanks that displayed more than one thousand wonders of the deep. From there they went to the planetarium. For two hours they watched stars as he picked out the different constellations in the sky. Taking a break after leaving the planetarium, Tanner couldn't resist asking. "You did leave Wellsburg once in a while?"

Looking at him seriously, she answered with exaggeration. "No, we were too busy entertaining the tourist."

"Must have been a lot of rebellious teenagers?" Tanner laughed.

"Must have been," she rejected his sense of humor. "And if you must know, I am not going back," she spoke with determination. "I am going to be the best female engineman the Navy ever saw!"

Knowing how quick her moods could change, Tanner answered with a straight face. "Somehow, I believe you will be."

"You can count on it," she added to any doubts that he might be thinking.

It was going through the submarine, 'Silversides', that Joan Reddy saw the real Steve Tanner. To be the best mirrored in his eyes, as he studied every detail of the submarine from World War II. This is I; this is what I am being trained for. Nothing she felt would stand in his way of his career.

Later walking along the shoreline of Lake Michigan, Steve began to talk about how he came to love the sea. "When I was younger, my grandfather would take me out on his boat." He spoke with longing as he explained. "I always spent what time I could with my grandfather. He was my mentor." There was sadness in his eyes, his voice almost breaking at times. "You don't have to say more,' she expressed as he paused for a few minutes.

Realizing that he was sharing with her something that he had blocked out for quite sometime, he continued to speak. "It's okay, really." Turning he looked at her, his voice filled with sentiment and pride as he said. "My grandfather built boats that you could put your soul into. You got callous from the shaping; you built arm muscles that you didn't even realize you had. He taught me life, Joan. He taught me without respect you had nothing, that your word is your greatest asset. I learned from him things you could never learn in school." Then he became melancholy, as if what he was about to say was very difficult. "I was seventeen, the end of high school behind me and looking forward to college in the fall. My grandfather invited me along on one of his trips to the Caribbean Islands. Let me tell you," he paused. "This was not a pleasure trip. I paid with blisters, sore muscles and a body that fell into deep sleep from being blessed with tiredness. I scrubbed decks, learned ropes, cooked meals. I became one of the crew carrying my own weight so to speak." Then with a shyness that she didn't think he could convey, he added, "I learned about women that summer. Grandfather said it was my initiation to life."

Madeline J. Wilcox

"Was it?" she interrupted trying to keep a straight face.

"Let's say what I didn't know---I was taught," the color changing in his face. The boyish grin returning as he continued to speak. The amusing look only lasting a few minutes as his tone of voice changed and resentment filled his voice once more. "He didn't say goodbye---Damn him. Didn't he know how much I loved him?" The probing eyes, searching as he turned on her. He spoke with deep conviction as cold chills ran down her spine when he added," no one will ever get that close to me again…!"

Although he didn't say, Joan felt the sense of loss and knew that Steve's grandfather had died. "I am sure he meant to say goodbye," she spoke gently trying to disperse the feeling of rejection from him.

"What do you know about it? You weren't' there," he hurled at her. Within minutes she found herself quickly stepping as she tried keeping up with him. "Do you mind?" she assured, panting as they raced along to his car. Catching up with him at his car, her mood now matched his. She spoke with antagonism as she said, "well this is much better. Thank you for waiting for me!"

"It's the least I could do," he snapped getting in on his side of the car. She had to knock on the window to let him know that her side of the car was still locked.

Driving for several miles in silence, it wasn't until he turned off the main road that she finally spoke," "where are we gong?"

"To the lake." Tanner answered.

"Becoming dubious to his intentions, her defensive attitude rose. "I am not parking?"

252

"Don't get your hopes up," he sarcastically replied.

"I wasn't. I just thought maybe you were," her own haughtiness filled the air.

Tanner laughed a laugh that came from deep within. Turning, looking at her he saw that putting lips fixed in a stubborn pose. His senses were aroused as he caught the defiant look on her face. Even from what little light the dashboard gave out, he could see her peevish attitude was going to warrant problems, especially if he wanted to continue this relationship further, he thought again.

The further they drove in silence, the more the tension built. By the time he turned off the engine, her nerves were on the edge. "I---I take it...You have changed your mind about ---parking?" She stammered, her senses charged by unexplainable emotions that begin to rise out of nowhere. She didn't like feeling trapped, not having an alternate route to take, not in the middle of the night anyway, as he moved towards her.

"Afraid of me?" His voice husky, reaching out he touched her face gently with his hands. Moving his fingers, he gently traced the outline of her lips. The dark eyes held hers in contact as he moved yet closer to her. Lowering his head, he began to touch her lips gently with his own. So much for self-control, one taste and all logical reasoning went astray as his heart took up a different beat. With a gentle exploration by his lips, he found fighting the urge to take the kiss deeper as again a physical awareness strongly threatened his senses.

She knew it would be like this. Her first kiss, was tender, and yet demanding. Dizzy and a little drunk from the effect, she swayed against him, her arms going up around his neck. She didn't know what she had done wrong, but the next thing she knew he was pushing her away from him. Moving back to his seat under the steering wheel he started the car. She had a feeling of what it was like to ride with terror as they drove back to the base. He only slowed as they neared the main gate.

Pulling up in front of her building, she again tired to find out what she had done wrong, but he didn't say much, only told her to "go." Standing outside her building she watched as he took off down the street.

Since it was Sunday and having nothing else planned for the day, Reddy dressed in her uniform and made plans to go to the chapel. As she started out of her room the 'messenger of the watch' greeted her. "You have a phone call in the lounge,' the girl informed her as she turned and started walking away from her.

She didn't know anyone who would call her, her parent's maybe? But no, they didn't have any numbers to the lounge. Curious, she asked answering the phone. "Hello?"

"It's about time. What did they have to do, get you up?" Tanner snapped.

Surprised as to who it was, she answered back. "I thought you didn't want to see me again?"

"So much for thoughts. So what are we doing today?" Tanner continued to snap.

"Well I don't know about you, but I am going to the chapel," she informed him.

"Chapel!"

"Yes. Would you like to go?" she answered, almost imagining the look on his face and what his answer would be.

As his mood changed, laughing he told her. "I guess for you I could take my uniform out of moth balls," Although mentally he told himself, 'as long as it doesn't become a habit?' Church, God and him had parted ways after the death of his grandfather. Yet, he wanted to be with her. If it meant going to Chapel, he could do it this once. "Meet you out front in about ten minutes, he then told her.

Nothing could have prepared her for the sight of Steve Tanner in his dress blues. His appearance breath taking, he was alluring, totally awesome with his aristocratic looks. As her friend Logan had put it, he wore clothes like an advertisement. "I take it, I pass inspection?" Tanner smiled to Reddy's embarrassment of the scrutiny of her eyes as they passed over him. The smile lingered as his gut tighten to the feelings he was beginning to associate with her. The warning that Crawford made the night before flashed across his mind as the expression on her face changed. With indifference, she told him. "You will do!"

"That's it. I will do? And I worked so hard to impress you," he laughed with a hint of mischief playing behind the dark eyes.

Impress her? That was something he would never find difficult to do for anyone. There was something about Steve Tanner's mannerism that reeked of authority. Realizing that she was staring the color rushed to warm her face. "I think we should be going," she stammered.

Like Orlando, Reddy found the Chapel at Great Lakes, overwhelming in its presence to make you feel welcome, if not reverent. Usually she had no problems following the sermon, but then she didn't have Steve Tanner standing beside her causing problems with her concentration. Why is he wasting time with me? Her doubts begin to rise. If I looked like Peggy, I could understand his interest. But I don't!

Tanner momentarily forgot about the services as he sensed he was being stared at. Turning his attention to the girl standing next to him, he was met with intense blue eyes. A puzzled expression on her face made him wonder what she was thinking about. Once more Crawford warning struck him as he thought about her innocence. I don't need this! Puzzled by his last thoughts, Tanner wondered which he didn't need. Reddy or being in a Chapel.

It took some force on her part to turn away from him looking at her. The eyes with the deep fathomable look held her in conquest. Again the color rose in her face as she made an effort to listen to what the Chaplain was saying. Leaving the chapel later, Tanner remarked. "Yelp! It's still standing?"

"You say that like you didn't expect it to be," she made a small laugh.

"I was having my doubts. I think my mother would be rather proud of me," he added with conviction.

"Why is that?" She had to ask.

"I was in chapel today," he sighed as he remembered the last time he had been anywhere neat a church or anything closely resembling one. "Are you okay?" Reddy became concerned about his grave look that was clouded with pain.

"Yes," his answer sharp as he quickly began to lead her away from the chapel. Sitting in his car, he turned and said. "How would you like to see the rest of Chicago?"

Again the girl being naïve impressed Steve Tanner. He took her to the "Industrial Museum of Science', they did a tour guide of 'China Town', where he literally had to pull her along.

As dusk gave way to the night Tanner who had been raised in the culture of finer things in life, was not quite ready for the girl with him as she stared up at the Sears Tower. "You haven't seen nothing yet," he insisted as he took her hand and lead her into the building.

The view at night from the 103rd floor gave them dazzling lights, which played a spectrum of colors across the sky. "Oh Steve," her voice full of wonder as she walked around the sky deck and looked out over the city below her. It was hard for him to believe a person like her actually existed. Her face was in awe to all she saw; her eyes wide open to everything. "Peggy would love it up here," Joan had remarked several times.

Remembering that Peggy was the artist of the family, Steve wondered if she could capture the look of radiance on her sisters' face. She seem peerless to anything he had ever known or knew. "It's about time for them to close." he remarked as he took her hand and led her back towards the elevators.

With his arm protective around her and the lull of a soft rock station on the radio, Joan closed her eyes and had no intentions of falling asleep but to savor the adventure of the evening.

Tanner smiled to the sleeping girl lying cuddled next to him. For some reason he felt a life time would pass and still he would never truly know the girl with the brilliant blue eyes. Nor could he understand his next thoughts. It would become a battle of wits to maintain the career he was after and to keep her at his side. With a regretted sigh, he woke Joan and put the strange thoughts from his mind. "We are almost to the base. You need to slip into a seat belt," he informed her.

Rubbing her eyes to wake up she apologized for falling asleep. "I don't normally do this or a date," she spoke in a soft whisper to hide her embarrassment.

"So you told me. I bet it beats walking?" The alluring grin appeared on the handsome face as he turned and looked at her and asked. "Can I see you tomorrow night?"

"Yes," she answered him as he left her to go to his building.

Crawford turned as he heard the key turning in the lock, to his surprise Tanner walked into the room. "You lost?" Crawford couldn't resist asking, since this was the last place Tanner would spend a weekend if they were not standing duty.

"Not hardly," Tanner replied, as he removed his clothes and prepared for bed.

"Come on old friend, this is Crawford you are talking to. We are on stand-down and it's still early. What is the matter, Wagner and you fighting?"

Again Tanner mentioned. "Not hardly," throwing his clothes into his locker and reached for his cassette radio and headphones. Placing them on he hit the play button for the tape player. He was soon listening to 'Chicago', a group that he enjoyed. "*A long comes a Woman'*, was playing and he couldn't agree with the words more. How could anyone with her attitude, her innocence get to him? Usually he was more cautious. But…there was something about her that drawled him to her?

Removing the headphones, he asked Crawford. "What did you think of Reddy?"

"A commitment," Crawford replied quite serious. "Why?"

"I have been with her for the past couple of days." Tanner answered with a troubled expression on his face.

"What?" Crawford stated in surprise. "I thought you were going to stay away from her?"

"Tried but after that evening when I ran into her at the library something changed." Tanner admitted shaking his head in disbelief as to the way she made him feel.

"So what is the problem? I am looking at a guy that practices the four F's to the max," Crawford stated looking at his long time friend.

"Not with this one, Dan," Tanner stated, taking a deep sigh.

"What? Are you trying to tell me that you are falling for this chick?" Crawford uttered in bewilderment.

"I think so," Tanner slowly admitted to him.

"She should have kicked you in the head, instead of the shin," Crawford complained as he shook his head and stated. "She is a commitment in which you don't need."

"Hell don't you think I know that?" Tanner sighed, as the other two guys who shared the room came in and soon the lights were out, but for one it didn't mean sleep as Tanner tossed and turned in the rack below Crawford.

20

Concentration was not easy when you lacked sleep from tossing and turning most of the night and tried listening to a person with a boisterous voice. Instructor Forster, Reddy took noted, was a big man with a voice to match. Patrolling the isle he told them. "In this class you will find there is no laying back and no free rides. Pausing long enough for effect he then went on. "When your life is on the line, you want to know that the person standing next to you is alert. That he knows what he is doing, as also, this person expects the same from you.

When you are putting your life on the line, your job and your know how are tested to the limits. . Safety is your main concern. You get to make only one mistake…Sometimes that may mean you are history" Again Instructor foster paused for effect and looking around the room, his eyes settled on one of the two girls in the classroom. With long strides he was soon standing at her desk. "I take it you belong in here?" he spoke in a tone with authority. His attention fully focused on the sleepy eyed girl.

"Yes sir," Reddy replied giving him a definite look of reprisal.

Well this should be interesting, Instructor Foster thought as he told her. "Mr. Foster will do now that I am retired."

"Yes Mr. Foster," Reddy spoke with a definite sharpness.

Giving her a stern look with warning of, "don't push it," Instructor Foster went on to tell the class. "Before you leave this class, you will know all there is to know about engines and then some. I take great pride in turning out the best and trust me, you will be the best or you will not be in this class very long. Do I make myself clear?" Turning again his attention was directed to the girls. That includes you Miss Reddy and Miss Cooper," he concluded with.

Having the feeling that she was making his day, she couldn't avoid his look of contempt. "This should really be fun," she groaned inwardly as Instructor Foster went on to tell them. "Your first assignment will be covering PMS, (Planned Maintenance System). There are nine reasons why the PMS was established. I want to know what they are and the benefits and limitations of PMS. Many sailors are sent to a basic 3-M school for instructions on the entire system. But all the necessary manuals and instructions are on every ship and an expert work supervisor can show you what is to be done, and how to do it. The best source of information is the 3-M manual; read it and ask questions of the work center supervisor or the 3-M coordinator and you'll become a reliable part of the Navy's 3-M system. There are also several self-training courses available on the system. You will find them lying on the table in the back of the room. Don't forget to sign them out, if you need to use them."

Instructor Foster added, as he told them. "Break."

As everyone left the room, Reddy walked back to the table where the self-training books were lying. "I'll be the judge to whether I need to bother with this or not," she thought, picking up one of the 3-M manuals, and signing the log book, turning she walked back to her seat.

Instructor Foster glanced up as Reddy took her seat. Getting up from his chair, he walked over to her desk. "Not taking a break?" he asked, as he remembered Roy Hamilton telling him, "keep your eye on the blond. I think she knows what she is dong…?" Time will tell, his thoughts as she looked up and again her eyes showed signs of defiance as she answered. "No, I would rather stay in here and read," answering him, she opened the book to start reading. "Maybe you should take a break, eight hours of lectures can turn out to be a rather long day," Instructor Forster added before turning and walking back to his desk.

Their next instructor covered advancement and how to earn it. "A most useful rule you can learn about a subject is how to find out more about it?" Instructor Roberts begin his lecture with. "Those wanting to achieve the most in advancement are willing to go that extra mile in training. People the training is out there for you to get," his eyes roaming the classroom. "You're learning objective; identify the engineman rating. List some of the duties and responsibilities of the personnel who hold this rating. I want to know who listens," he stated looking around the classroom as he put questions before them.

Taking notes to what ship's engineman were assigned to Reddy soon learned if you were a male it was anything that floated. Girls, on the other hand were limited to tenders, some tugs, repair ships and some tankers, mainly those in port. Their assignments wee to A or M division where they operated and maintained ship propulsion machinery and associations with what she hoped to be doing.

Before they were released for break, Instructor Roberts added to his comments. "If you demonstrate integrity and do the best of your ability to perform your job things will run smooth for you and the department you work in. You will find that every job is important in the Navy, no matter how large or small the task may be. That 'teamwork' depends on being able to get along with your coworkers," as again he reminded them of how important safety came first above all else and without teamwork hazards rose quickly.

By the time lunch rolled around Reddy was getting the feeling that she was going to have a hard time proving she was where she wanted to be. That being an engineman in the Navy was the right career for her. Especially after meeting her third instructor of the day. Instructor Harry Garfield, like Instructor Foster, wasn't to please about having a girl in his class and not missing words he told her. "Don't think for one minute that I will show you favoritism. Not when I feel that women don't belong in here."

Oh! How she wanted to tell him her opinion also, but a 'Captain Mast' she wasn't quite ready for as Instructor Garfield walked away and Matthews leaned towards her and whispered. "Beginning to feel like maybe you chose the wrong field?"

"Not for one minute," Reddy whispered back with her attitude in tact as she let her eyes follow Instructor Garfield to the front of the room. Her determination even more set to prove him wrong in his thinking of her. How does he do it? Reddy was thinking as Instructor Garfield told them about the POD. Her pencil quickly moved to keep up with him as she wrote in shorthand. How does he expect us to keep notes if he doesn't breathe now and then? She complained inwardly to his rapid way of speaking. "I am here to teach you the routines of the ships. What is expected of you when your ship is in port or underway? The routine varies from one ship to another, as you will soon find out. POD is the word. The daily schedule of events, I would advise everyone each morning to take a good look at the POD, if you don't you will be wondering what in the hell is going on and wondering where you should be."

At break Reddy had most of the guys in her class standing around her. "How far did you get with Garfield?" Matthews was the first to ask her, since he knew she always took notes in shorthand.

"I'm not sure if I got everything he said," she admitted with a smile as some guys standing around her looked down at their notes and told her what they had been able to write down. "I kept waiting for him to turn blue," Miller spoke up when she had finished reading most of what she had.

"I kept wanting to yell slow down," another guy complained.

"Well why didn't you?" Reddy insisted turning towards the blond-headed guy who was talking. "Because I didn't think I could get the words in," Simpson replied, as laughter broke out among the group.

As classes resumed for the day again a different instructor told them. "You will be engineman only when I feel that you have earned the title." Like Instructor Foster, his job was to teach them about engines. Instructor Martin stood in one place, his backside learning against his desk. His legs crossed over each other. His expression relaxed as he told them. "Some of your work as an engineman requires your ability to read and work from mechanical drawings and blueprints. We will briefly cover this area since I am to assume you had mechanical drawings in high school and basics." Then moving from his rather relaxed pose, he walked to where each girl was sitting and insisted. "I am to assume you had both?"

"Yes," both girls replied, as Reddy wondered if they all thought she was taking this class for amusement. No wonders there were few girls in the engineman program. Her attention drifted from Instructor Martins words of telling her. "Good. I wouldn't want you to be totally lost in here," as he turned back to the rest of the class. "With each chapter ahead you will be having hands-on experiences." For the next several hours they discussed the correct use of technical language to describe the principles of operating gasoline and diesel engines. "I don't want to hear anyone saying. "This gadget goes here and etc." Instructor Martin spoke sternly, his look threatening as he scanned the room. "To recognize routing of ship piping, whether it be water lines, fuel, steam, salt, or oil, you will find yourselves painting each line by the ship's color code. Incidentally you will be doing this often if you are assigned to different ships while you stay in the Navy." Then he gave them the color code for the piping route they would be using in training. "Any questions," he finished with as he handed out paper with piping routes. "You need to figure out which colors go with which route. Which routes are connected to the water supply, and which ones are fuel, steam, salt or oil. Until you get them right and know them well," Martin smiled, as he added useful information. "Tomorrow we will discuss what paints are used for certain jobs. This is a basic military subject that must be learned by all hands. You will be responsible for the painting and preservation of your ships working space and compartments."

From the back of the classroom someone made the complaint. "I knew I should have asked more questions when I was told to sign on the dotted line."

Throwing her books on her desk Reddy announced to anyone who cared to listen, "I think I found out who is in command of A-school. Trust me, they aren't pleased about me being in their classes?"

"Having problems?" White asked.

"Problems? Oh I wouldn't go as far as to say that because they don't have any idea yet as to whom they are messing with," Reddy declared, as she went on to say. "I just have some instructors who are wondering why I am wasting their time. Not only did I cross their paths, I seem to have blocked their view. Well if they think for one minute I plan on dropping out…they had better think again!"

"You must have had Foster and Garfield for instructors," White commented, as she told her. "Our last two roommates couldn't handle the pressure Foster and Garfield kept them under, so they dropped out of the classes."

"Well I am not giving in," she spoke with determination as she took her seat and opened her books to start studying. Lost in the world of engines, and military must know, she didn't hear the knock at the door until Reynolds dropped a long narrow box tied in red ribbon down on her books. "Whose ass are you kissing?" Reynolds stated, as Reddy looked up at her.

"Not yours," Reddy answered with a blank expression as she picked up the card, opening it, she began to read. "

"There is nothing I would want to change about you.

For changing you, you would no long be,
The person that I find to be a challenge."
Meet me at McDonalds, Steve."

With very nervous hands she opened the box to stare down at two-dozen red roses.

"Man, someone has some bucks," Logan expressed, as Reddy lifted the flowers from the box and walking over to her locker she took out the vase that the last flowers had came in.

"At least he keeps this room beautiful," White giggled, as she walked over to smell the roses.

"Who does?" Reynolds wanted to know.

"Tanner," White let slip.

"You must be kidding," Reynolds stated, as she reached for the card lying on Reddy's desk. "You bitch!" Reynolds quickly added after readying the card. "Well don't think for one minute you are going to keep him. Not when he realizes how naïve you are? Or are you really that naïve now?" Reynolds insinuated.

Reddy really wanted to ignore Reynolds, for the last thing she needed was a consultation with her. She wanted to believe what Tanner had told her about his relationship with Reynolds. But nobody said she was perfect in having the last word. "I don't appreciate being called a bitch!" And another thing for sure, I don't exaggerate about something that I know nothing about, unless your friend whomever it is likes to brag about getting laid."

"What are you saying?" Reynolds took a tyrant pose in front of Reddy and blocked her from leaving the room.

"You figure it out," Reddy flared, not backing down from Reynolds.

"Here we go again," Logan sighed, speaking to White.

"Yeah," White answered watching the two and thinking that this time fist might fly.

"Answer me, damn it." Reynolds made a grab for Reddy. She landed on the floor so quick that it took minutes for her to realize what had happen. Reddy was sitting on her, her arms pinning Reynolds to the floor. "Don't ever assume that I am afraid of you. And the next time you say something about Steve Tanner it better be the truth. Understand?" Reddy's face now was in Reynolds.

Both White and Logan stared in disbelief. "Remind me not to mess with Reddy," White chuckled as she turned to Logan and did her best not to laugh.

Logan also was having a hard time holding her composer as she answered back. "Tell me."

"Get off of me!" Reynolds declared, her expression full of hate as she returned Reddy's stare.

"Sure," Reddy replied, moving and standing up.

"You haven't heard the last of this," Reynolds warned as she picked herself up from the floor.

"Do I look scared? Reddy asserted, as she picked up her purse and books and without another word left the room.

Tanner watched as Reddy entered McDonalds. I think I am in trouble, his thoughts as she came closer to where he was sitting. "Got a problem?" He asked, as she sat down across from him. "No!" she snapped and he wondered if his head was still in tack. Nor nothing could have prepared him for what she said next.

"I know it's rally none of my business, but are you seeing someone else besides me and does she know Kathryn Reynolds?"

"Man! You don't miss words," he stared at her and couldn't believe she was asking such a question.

"I try not too," she answered and hoped he didn't notice that her voice was shaking. "Well!" she added determine to find out the truth.

"Isn't that a little personnel?" Tanner asked, not taking his eyes from hers.

"I guess it would all depend on how you look at it." she said knowing she couldn't back down now regardless of what his answer would be.

270

"Reynolds has been talking again?" Tanner surmised why she was asking questions about seeing someone.

"Yes, she answered, her voice lowered.

"And you believe her?" The questions continued between them.

"Do I have a choice? She can be very convincing." Reddy stated, as she turned her glaze away from his and looked around McDonalds, which didn't have its usual crowd.

Tanner had never been put on the spot like this before and it was a little unnerving to say the least. "Who are you ready to believe, her version or mine?" he questioned her next.

"Hers I have heard," Reddy stated continued as she now looked at him.

"And now you are waiting to hear mine?" The cold stare of his eyes met hers.

Something like that," she confessed, not blinking to his obvious anger.

"No I am not seeing anyone else," Tanner answered, wanting to end the questions.

"Who is Wagner?" Reddy threw at him next.

"A friend," Tanner admitted.

"That's it?" Reddy showed doubt on her face.

He had it with the interrogation as he snapped, "look you either trust me, or get the hell out of my life!"

"I can do that," staring to rise, but he stopped her by reaching out and touching her arm. "Sit!" his voice commanding. For several minutes they said nothing, their eyes questioning as to where they would go from here.

She didn't even nowhere the thought came from or even why she would speak something so off the wall for her. "Should I ask for a medical clearance?"

At first he didn't know what to say, then slowly the little boy grin crossed his face as he said. "Not unless you are planning on sleeping with me?"

With her eyes avoiding him, her head bent, she shyly told him as the color rose to her face. "I don't think I am quite ready for that!"

"I didn't think so," he replied but the humor was gone from his face, as he thought to himself. If I had any doubts about how innocent she was, she just confirmed it for me. Crawford was right, I don't need this type of commitment. But even him thinking this, he was even more intrigued with her honesty.

Seeing the factious expression on his face, she felt that there was something she had to explain to him. "You need to know that I was raised by a domineering mother, a protecting father, and a grandmother who I promised that I would be thirty until I made a commitment to anyone."

"I am not out to make a commitment," he insisted although he couldn't avoid the irresistible magnetized field she was pulling him towards. "How old did you say you were?" he found himself asking as the little boy grin played at the corners of his mouth.

"I am eighteen," she replied.

"I think we've got a while," he added, trying to make light of the conversation. Then looking at his watch he told her. "We've got to be going." since they both had watch duty on Wednesday nights.

21

Instructor Foster was trying to cram all he could in to them before 'stand-down' was called for Thanksgiving. They were going over the constructions of a mock engine. Instructor Foster wanted to know how much they knew about engine parts and how they were related to one another. Calling on Reddy he told her. "Since Miss Cooper and you are the only girls in the class, I guess you get to go first. Miss Cooper. You first," Instructor Foster stated handing her the pointing stick I need you to tell me every thing you know about this engine?"

Looking at the mock engine, Cooper begins to point out diesel generators, chilled water plant, motor generator sets. It was when Instructor Foster started asking questions as to how they were all connected that Fireman Cooper ran into problems. "What is the purpose of a diesel generator?" Instructor Foster, ask the questions.

"To make the ship run I guess," the girl looked at her instructor and shrugged her shoulders.

"Do you agree with her Fireman Reddy?" Foster turned to Reddy and asked the same question.

"Diesel generators are used during emergency." Reddy replied as she gave several description of how diesel generators were used.

"Does everyone agree with her?" Instructor Foster turned to the gentleman of the class. All but two of the guys agreed with her, and as Foster turned to them, he told them. "You better be reading further into the chapters of your manuals, she is correct." As the class continued several male sailors were called upon to point out parts of the engines also. Out of the class of thirty-two people one girl and ten guys made mistakes.

To Reddy's surprised, Instructor Foster called her out before she left for Lunch. "You have heard of teamwork?" Foster questioned her.

"Yes sir,' wondering what he was getting at.

"Then why don't you give Fireman Cooper some help?" Instructor Foster insisted.

"Yes sir," Reddy relied, which Instructor Foster stated. "Good then I can expect improvement from her?"

Once Reddy was in the galley, she walked over to where Fireman Cooper was sitting with a group of girls. Reddy waited until there was a break in the conversation that she asked. "How would you like to study with me for awhile? I am on the third floor of building 332?"

"Why would I want to do that?" Cooper turned looking at Reddy with a surprised expression.

Reddy was speechless for a few moments, then she answered. "I was asked to give you some help to improve your scores."

"Honey, I know how to improve my scores," Cooper insisted, as the other four girls sitting around her stated laughing.

"Excuse me!" Reddy declared, sensing that Cooper was not referring to engineman classes.

"I don't believe I have to draw you a picture, or do I.!" The girl looked at Reddy with a steady eye.

"No, you are coming across loud and clear," Reddy, stated, as she said to Copper and the others sitting around her. "Excuse me." Walking away from Cooper and her friends, Reddy shook her head and mumbled. "Don't say I didn't try."

Instructor Garfield was their next instructor for the day. He started the lecture by telling them. "There are nineteen rules you must know for the hazards of electricity and observing all safety precautions when working with or near electrical systems and equipment. I doubt if I need to remind you, that you must know all nineteen by the end of the week." There were plenty of groans from the classroom as he passed out the weekly test papers. To some it meant they probably wouldn't get leave, and to others it meant they probably were out of the school.

They seem to be falling into a pattern of having everything thrown at them during the first part of the week, and then broken down to discuss through out the remainder of the week as on Friday they were given test to see where they placed. 85% was passing, below 75% you failed. You were given three tries to improve your scores as you were sent back a week in class.

As far as engine went, Reddy figured there wasn't much more to learn. She would be glad when Thursday arrived, even if she was standing watch for the day. The instructors had warned them that things would become harder after the holidays.

Standing duty on Thanksgiving Day was not a pleasant thought, not when; you had memories of it being more festive with families getting together. Standing watch on the quarterdeck, Reddy had plenty of time to think of home. I wonder if Jeff and Linda came home? Probably not, not with Linda so close to having the twins? Her brother, a father? The idea struck her, as if wasn't hard for her to imagine Jeff being one. There was something about her brother that attracted kids to him. As a teenager, he seem to get all the calls to baby sit. The more she thought about her brother, the more she made a mental note to give him a call when she was relieved of her watch.

Walking past the lounge later she looked to see how long the telephone lines were. Groaning, after seeing that there was still going to be some time before she could even think about calling home. A letter would make it faster, she surmised, going on down to her room.

"I hope we are not going to be looking at your moody face for the rest of the day?" Logan remarked, when Reddy entered the room.

"No, you could go and sit in the lounge and call me when the phones are available," Reddy offered, walking over to her locker and taking out her radio and headset. Turning she was greeted by White handing her a note. "It's from Tanner," she whispered.

"What does he want?" Reddy grumbled, since he seemed to be avoiding her the past week.

"I don't know, why don't you open the note and find out?" White suggested

Doing as White suggested, Reddy read, "Meet me tomorrow by my car, Tanner." Listening to the words of *"You're the Inspiration"* by *'Chicago',* she wondered if she could make a commitment to him that would last forever? What about the way I have been raised? Can I deal with that?" the questions seem to run through her head as she glanced at her watch. Reddy still had two hours left before she had to report for rounds again. Leaving the room, she walked back down to the lounge. At least the lines are shorter, she thought stepping up behind one of the girls waiting in line. It was almost an hour before she finally got to use the phone. Her father was the first one to answer, "We were wondering if we would hear from you today?" Her father stated after telling her hello, and letting everyone know she was on the phone.

"You wouldn't believe how long I have been waiting to get the phone. I think everyone on the third floor is calling home. Was Jeff able to come home?" Her voice wishful as she wished she too had been able to go home.

"He did," her father laughed, as he told her. "Linda went into labor on the plane. Everyone is fine, that is Linda and the boys, but the Marine is not doing so well. First of all, he left Linda's parents at the airport, he called us but forgot to mention which hospital he was at, and that Linda's parents were not with them. Mr. and Mrs. Miller called us and we picked them up at the airport after your mother called every hospital in Indianapolis to find out where they were."

277

"Oh my gosh! I am glad everyone got where they were suppose to be." then becoming excited about the twins being born, she threw questions at her father. "What did she name them? How much did they weigh? Who do they look like?"

"Here I will let you talk to your mother. She can give you all the details," her father replied and the next person she heard was her mother. "Hi dear, how is things going for you?"

"Okay, I just whish I was home. Dad tells me that Linda had the boys?"

"Oh yes, they are so darling. She named them after their grandfathers. Thomas Andrew who weighs six pounds, and Jason Roy who weighs five pounds and three ounces. They look a lot like Jeff and you can't tell them apart. Linda will be staying here until she is up to traveling again. Jeff is bringing them home from the hospital tomorrow. Then he is leaving to go back to the base."

"I guess then that Thanksgiving isn't the usual feast?"

"Oh but it is," her mother laughed. "Surly you don't think this family wouldn't get together? Why your grandmother wouldn't hear of it. She even packed a special picnic basket so Jeff could eat dinner with Linda. We are all going over to the Inn later to eat. That is after the parade and the football game. Heaven forbid if we miss a football game. Peggy's friend Mark Greene is here. He is such a nice young man. Did you know that he is becoming an officer?"

"Yes. Peggy wrote me about him." Joan answers with restrain.

"Well dear, I guess I had better let you go, I hope you have a nice day." And the next thing Joan knew she was listening to a silent phone. "Love you too," Joan murmured as she sat the phone back down on the base.

Standing duty with Tanner for the day was something his three roommates were not looking forward to. Lately Tanner was like a sleeping bear that had been woke during hibernation. Not only was he making life hell for the three of them, he seem to be making Chief Molson days. Tanner was letting his scores drop and was risking his chances of staying in school.

"I think you had better get your proprieties straight?" Crawford warned as they waited to make rounds again. His reply was Tanner turning and giving him a troublesome look. Running his hands through his short hair, his eyes brooding, he answered. "You're telling me?"

Man this girl was tearing him apart, Crawford realized. He had never seen Tanner this confused before. "Aren't you forgetting something?" Crawford reminded him again. "I thought you wanted to be an officer?"

"Did! Still do? Hell, I don't know what I want anymore?" Tanner stumbled with the words. Damn her, who does she think she is? He moaned inwardly. Lately he had been living the life of a saint. For what, so she could keep telling him no?

"I was wondering if you had scored with her? I think the expression on your face has answered my questions." Crawford stated.

"Hell I have been living the life of a saint lately?" Tanner told him, expressing his feeling aloud. "She has been raised so strict that I am surprised she is able to breathe on her own." Tanner groaned.

"Why do I have this feeling that is not your only problem?" Crawford looked steady at his friend.

"It's not," Tanner sighed, as he thought about how he really felt about Reddy, to the person who had been his best friend since childhood he admitted. "I love her Dan."

Surprised by his answer, Crawford stared at him in disbelief and shaking his head answered. "You what!"

Shocked that he had admitted his feelings aloud, Tanner murmured "I love her," and saying it again didn't really make him feel that much better.

"That's what I thought you said!" Crawford looked at him. "I hope the hell you know what you are letting yourself in for. As I said before Reddy came with a commitment, one I don't think you need." Crawford expressed with concern.

Things were not much better in building 332, room 347. Logan was yelling at Reddy. "Will you stop your damn bawling? I am trying to sleep," throwing her pillow over her head.

"I'm sorry," Reddy sniffed. Sitting up in her rack and reaching for a tissue to blow her nose with.

"What is it with you! Did someone in your family die?" White complained as she jumped down from her rack and walked over to Reddy's. Standing on the corner of Reynolds rack White insisted as she looked up at Reddy. "For the past week we have listen to you bawl every night. You know you could make your life a little easier if you just sleep with him. Trust me, it isn't all that bad."

"What isn't?" Reddy continued to blow her nose.

"Sex," Reynolds yelled as she added. "I wish you all would shut up and go to sleep."

"Well I just can't sleep with him," Reddy retorted as she added. "Go to hell!"

"Go to hell? Well we are," Logan insisted getting up from her rack. "Why don't you go call Tanner and tell him you have changed your mind? Tell him you are ready to get laid?" Her temper rising.

"Yeah Reddy, do that," White added. "Then maybe Reed and the others in Tanner's room wouldn't feel that they have to walk around on tiptoes when Tanner is in the room."

"Leave me alone," Reddy cried throwing the covers over her head.

"Why don't you grow up?" Logan remarked, as she climbed back into her rack At least with Reddy's head covered they couldn't hear her bawling as much.

Waking the next day the girls in room 347, kept pretty much to themselves as they did field day and waited for inspection. All having plans of their own, they didn't know if Reddy was going to keep her meeting with Tanner or not, and further more for once Logan didn't care as she left the room with Reddy sitting in it.

Reddy made up her mind to catch a train to the mall. Doing some window shopping and buying a few items for Christmas gifts, she was making her way through to a restaurant around lunchtime.

Finding a seat she begins to pick at the food she had bought and rechecked the shopping list she had made out. "Why didn't you meet me by my car?" Tanner asked her as he took a seat across from her.

"Because you didn't say what time," she stated, looking up.

"You sure didn't bother to look either when you came out of your building?" Tanner spoke with chagrin impatience, as he remained sitting straight in the seat across from her.

"How did you find me?" she wanted to know.

"Easy. I saw you getting on the train. I knew the train stopped at the mall," he explained, the boyish grin crossing his face as she stated. "I guess you are lucky that I didn't go to Chicago." her comment made with a straight face.

"Probably," the smile continued as he looked at her. For some reason unknown, silence fell between them. Tanner finally broke the silence as the impetuous magnetism pulled at them. "Spend the weekend with me?"

"What?" Reddy answered raising her head to look at him, their eyes making contact.

"You heard me," His eyes holding hers as he waited for an answer.

"Shouldn't we know more about each other?" Her voice shaky to what he suggested.

"I think we know plenty about each other," his words direct as he searched her face and saw the confusion that was there.

If she said yes, she knew there would be no turning back. Then what, could she make the commitment without regrets later? All the emotions that he had been causing to stir lately seem to intensify as she questioned herself. Nervous being an understatement, as to how she was beginning to feel to the butterflies attacking her stomach, "I need to do some shopping," she gave him as an answer.

21

Hidden Pines was what you would expect a place to be named that sat back among pine trees and a remote distance from the main road. The exterior design resembling a Swiss Alps Inn, with the wood and white tile front, with flower boxes sitting below each dormer windows filled with poinsettias and Christmas greenery. "Been here often?" She questioned him, rather contemptuous, since he didn't seem to have trouble finding the place.

"Would you rather I turned around? Tanner asked not looking at her.

"No," she snapped. Wondering why she was shaking so.

Not wanting to fight with her, Tanner explained. "My parents stayed here when they came to my graduation. I haven't been back here since, he added, pulling into the parking lot. "Would you like to stay in the car while I register us?" His manner quite calm compared to what he was feeling. Crawford warning seems to be ringing loud and clear in his head about her being a commitment.

Joan did manage to shake her head yes even though she didn't turn and look at him.

As he walked toward the office to register them, Crawford warning returned. "Just remember, Reddy comes with a different commitment. One in which you will find walking away from not so easy my friend." Tell me, Tanner thought walking through the Inn's doors and up to the counter.

Sitting in the car waiting for Steve to return, her grandmother's words seem to taunt her. "Let there only be one man in your life Joan." That was what she wanted also one man, Steve Tanner. "Try and understand Gram's," she whispered, as she saw Steve coming back to the car.

It took several trips around the complex before he finally spotted their cottage. Talk about being nervous, his thoughts as he parked the car. Getting out of the car she reached for her tote bag in the back seat and as she straighten Steve took it. "What have you got in here?" He commented since the tote bag seem extremely heavy.

"My books," Joan stammered, as she recalled him laughing, when she had ask that she take her back to the base.

"Different," Steve mumbled to himself taking her hand and leading her towards the motel room. Once inside the room he leaned against the door to close it and welcomed the support it gave when she turned and looked at him.

It was there in her damn intriguing blue eyes, the wanting but yet scared expression. Their glaze holding, as he moved away from the door and towards her, again he felt calmness as he said. "Afraid of me?" the alluring grin appeared on his face as he moved closer and reached out to her. She was trembling and he asked. "Are you cold?"

She couldn't find the words to answer him as she shook her head yes, and as he moved away from her he turned to the fireplace in the room. "If I remember correctly they have a coffee pot and coffee somewhere in here over on the other side of that bar," he pointed towards a small kitchen nook, which she hadn't even noticed when she had walked into the room. "Coffee?" she looked at him, then towards the kitchen. She didn't have the first idea of how to make coffee. As she walked towards the area where Steve had pointed, she begin to have second thoughts. "I am so stupid, what am I doing here? Why couldn't Logan have been a little more frank about what to do? She started to turn and tell Steve she didn't know how to make coffee. As she turned around, she came face to face with him. "I…I do---not, her words cut short as he bent his head and begin to brush her lips with his. Dropping her eyelids, she let the warm feelings rush to soar against her senses.

In the stillness of time she became undressed and as he stood to remove his own clothing, her eyes masked by long lashes glazed at the power he possessed. His skin a light bronze with the fading of a summer tan, her eyes ventured slowly over the masculine physique, as it was unveiled. The image of him being a Greek God seems to come to mind as he moved to lie beside her.

His look tender his touch gentle, he soon brought new sensations to the girl who found the demands of a young woman seeking to come forth. With the denials of how she had been raised pushed to the back of her mind, she cried out. "Steve…!"

Becoming exultant with her soft cries, the response of her body brought a low moan from him as he fought the building passion he had been holding back. from wanting her, his body aching deep in his very soul.

Although it was no longer cold in the room, Joan found herself not being able to stop trembling as he shifted his weight and moved above her. Apprehension was soon placed with fear as she tensed up to the intrusion. Pains seem to come from nowhere to engulf her as she felt the intrusion. Tears ran down her face as she tried moving away.

Lost in his own needs, his own passion, there was no stopping as he sat the rhythm making her, his. Then he was still except for the labored breathing. She felt guilt, humiliation, anything but the excitement of earlier. Why did I agree to… to this? I want to die! Continuing to cry she told him through clenched teeth. "Will you get off of me?" When he didn't move to her demands, she added. "Move…Damn it! Her fist striking blows at him.

"Will you stop?" Trying to ward off her pounding blows by grabbing her arms and pinning them over her head as he came to his knees and towered over her. "Get off of me!" she grated resentful to the fact that she had let things go this far. Twisting and turning she tired freeing herself. The eyes that had been filled with passion only moments ago, where now ice cold.

Trying to reason with her, Steve insisted. "Joan look at me. Don't do this to us?" As she turned her face and looked at him, he saw the guilt written on her face, the tears flowing freely. With concern he tired holding her. "I'm sorry. I didn't mean to hurt you," hoping to console her. From the look he received, he knew she wasn't listening to any reasoning. Not when she spoke with rage. "I don't need a lecture on sex. Now will you turn off that damn light so I can get up?"

"Whatever," he mumbled, moving and turned off the light as she rose and left the room.

Placing pillows behind his head, he lights a cigarette, a contented look on his face. She's yours Tanner, definitely yours. A feeling of possession took hold as he stood and turning caught a glimpse of his back in the mirror. "Tiger sir, one small tiger," the boyish grin appearing to his next thought. "Are all virgins this difficult?

Standing in the shower she cried harder as the tears streamed with the flow of water. "Oh God, how can I face him again? What will he think of me now? I guess I have lived up to my mother's expectations of me . . .Gram's? As the guilt and remorse took over her thinking, her subconscious mind was giving her hell. Her brain was telling her, no regrets, this was your decision; you were not forced into anything. You made it all on your own? Now face it, she felt anything but calm as she leaned against the coolness of the bathroom door before opening it.

In the other room Steve Tanner stood looking out into the brisk cold afternoon. Pulling back the curtains to the sliding glass doors, doing some thinking, his thoughts rambled. Do I tell her I love her? Would she believe me? Damn, why did I think I needed this commitment? I don't need this . . .? Letting the curtains fall he turned when the bathroom door slowly opened. "I thought maybe you had drown in there?" He stated, as she walked further into the room.

"Thought about it," she replied, her eyes downcast, afraid of looking at him. Afraid of what she might see in his eyes, the repulsion that might be there.

"Are you okay?" He asked, taking steps closer to her.

"Yes," she answered hesitantly backing away from him.

Tanner knew that if she backed away now, things would never be the same between them. Not with the guilt she was feeling. Stepping closer in her directions, he reached for her. Taking his free hand, he tilted her head so that she was looking up at him. She had thought of him being cocky and arrogant. He could only imagine what she felt towards him now. Even with his concern for her, he still couldn't bring himself to tell her how he felt. "I don't think any less of you," he did comment, as he dropped his hands and moving past her, he took her place in the bathroom.

Madeline J. Wilcox

Leaning against the coolness of the sliding
doors she took his place to look out into the early
evening of the day. It had started to snow; huge
snowflakes begin to gather on the small patio outside
the room. She shuddered to the coldness, her thoughts
mixed and confused. "Well Reddy! If you are dumb
enough to make love with out marriage? Then you
better be smart enough to accept the consequences.
Regardless of the outcome you now can't change
things. The taunting words her mother spoke haunting
her. "Well we all know why you were so eager to
leave, you can do as you well please!"

The tears started again with an endless flow as
again she thought of her grandmother. "Gram's, I ask
you to understand but how can you when even I
don't?" Whispering, making an effort to brush teas
away, crying she confessed, "I love you, Steve."

She hadn't heard Steve enter the room until he
spoke. "Are you okay?" he asks again, when she
turned to face him. I wonder if he heard my
confession? She thought as she answered him, "Yes,'
then added. "I guess I acted like an idiot earlier?"

With the boyish grin appearing, he made a
move closer to her. "I wouldn't know. I suppose under
the circumstances you acted in a normal response. You
are mine, you know?"

"How do you figure that?" Her voice trailing as
she couldn't take her eyes of him clad only in his
jeans.

"You left your branding marks on me," his
stupid grin broadens as he turned his back to her. "I---I
did that?" her voice filled with surprise.

Looking over his shoulder, chuckling as he answered. "I am government property you know?"

"I know," her voice soft, reaching out she touched his back. The touch of her cool hands causing shudders and the muscles in his back to ripple, taking a deep breath he exhaled slowly, turning he faces her. "I want you," wondering if she would refuse.

Waking he reached out to find her no longer beside him. Sitting up he searched the room for her, he saw her sitting not far away at the breakfast bar, a cup in her hand, which she was slowly sipping. Her posture positioned so that her head was resting on her knees, her look serious. "Why do I have this feeling that I am in deep trouble?" he commented, as he reached for a cigarette, lighting it he continued to sit on the bed.

"Conscience bothering you," she answered, not looking across at him, but knew he was looking at her.

"Probably not, what about you?" Steve threw back at her, assuming that she was on a guilt trip again. Not getting an answer from her, he then said. "Is there more coffee?"

"No, but I can make some more," she answered, moving to a standing position and walking around to the kitchen side of the breakfast bar.

Ah, she speaks," Steve said rising and slipping into his jean, walks over to the breakfast bar, and took the other bar stool. "If you are worried about your reputation, don't be," he said with assurance.

"I wasn't," she answered glancing away from him. Her thoughts returning to why he would be wasting his time with her as again she compared his features to hers. He is handsome and I am so plain…"You didn't ask but I am taking birth control pills." she found herself admitting. Thinking that it was important for him to know.

"To tell you the truth, the thought never cross my mind," he admitted to her as he continued to watch her as she turned and was facing him.

"Weren't you afraid I would become pregnant?"

"Not really. I figured you to be smarter than that," he implied, since she had brought the subject up.

"Should I take that as a compliment or what?" She stubbornly asked.

"Probably," he grinned, getting up and walking around to where she was standing and reaching into the cupboard beside her, he took out a coffee cup, and remembering her saying something about a medical clearance he chuckled as he told her. "You don't have to worry about anything, I just had a physical."

She laughed, a deep throaty laugh. Which coming from her was quite sexy? "What's so funny?" He couldn't resist asking pouring himself a cup of coffee.

"Us. Here we are after spending the night together, saying things that should have been said, I guess earlier?"

"I don't think that discussion ever crossed our minds," he said as a matter of fact, as he added. "How shall we spend the day?"

"Could we go shopping?"

"How about us going into Chicago?"

"More sightseeing?" she questioned.

"I could think of something else," his eyes teasing, his look wanting.

"Sightseeing," she said quickly as she moved away from him and made her way to the bathroom to dress in the new clothes she had bought yesterday. When she reentered the room Steve suggested breakfast, and complimented her on her choice of a red jumper and a white blouse.

"I don't do breakfast," she stated looking at him.

"No wonder you are so slim? Hasn't anyone every told you that breakfast is the most important meal of the day?"

"Not when you had to run the grinder afterwards," she stated, as she took a seat in the area designated to be the sitting room, with a large over stuff chair, and a loveseat, with two end tables, and a coffee table. The area was made comfortable by a fireplace sitting directly across from the loveseat.

"I take it you didn't like the grinder?" Steve commented, taking a seat in the overstuff chair.

"I never was good at running a marathon," she replied, smartly.

"I thought that was in all tomboy hand books," Steve insisted with a chuckle.

"Maybe, but not mine," she said, looking at him. "Mine said to get my hands dirty. Learn about engines, climb trees and drive my mother crazy."

"Which you did?" Steve chuckled.

"All of the above," she found herself telling him. "I was always driving my brother to the limits as I hung around him and his friends wanting to learn all I could about fixing cars. Which really wasn't Jeff expertise, he is more a leader, than a doer."

"He is the Marine?" Steve questioned.

"Yes, I believe he is a drill instructor at Camp Lejune at the moment, before that he was in recon at Twenty-Nine Palms in California. I think dad said something about him being transferred to Camp Pendleton after the first of the year."

"Is that where you would like to be, California next to your brother?" Steve ask next .as he rose from where he was sitting and stirred the logs in the fireplace.

"It would be nice. Jeff and I are rather close, or at least we use to be. He has a family now. His sons were born the day before Thanksgiving," giving him the details of Linda going into labor while on the plane, and her brother freaking out.

"He actually left his in-laws at the airport?" Steve laughed.

"According to dad, he did." Joan responded.

"I bet he was taken off the Christmas list," Steve chuckled.

"Probably," Joan responded, as she looked at Steve who had turned from the fireplace. "Make love to me?" she surprised him with next.

"What?"

"I didn't stutter," her voice a whisper.

. It would have taken Michelangelo to capture the look on his face. The fierce eyes tender, his voice filled with emotions as he spoke. "Do you think then you could drop the guilt trip?"

"It may take some doing," she admitted slowly as he moved towards her. "I think you got dressed for nothing," he whispered, huskily.

The windy city of Chicago was dressed for the seasonal holidays with the windows done in Christmas finery. Once again Steve Tanner was in awe to the girl walking beside him. "I thought you were familiar with all of this," he mentioned to all the Christmas decorations.

"I am, but I still get excited to how things are so different from Wellsburg. You must visit it someday?" She insisted, as she stood back to watch the crowd of people hurrying from store to store to get the best sales for Christmas shopping.

"Maybe I will," Steve answered, as he added. "Let's find a place to sit and have lunch," since they had missed breakfast, and food at the moment sounded very tempting.

As the days passed they went to a movie, took in more shopping and enjoyed being together. He told her about his way of life and in the manner which he had been raised.

"Why did you, choose the military," she questioned as doubts were raised once more to how different they were.

"I am not sure," he remarked, sensing her mood becoming serious.

"I think you told me it was because you found yourself drunk," she reminded him.

"I think there was more to it than that," smiling to think she had remembered him saying it.

"Probably," she returned his smile.

"Whatever the reason . . .Trust me baby, I am here to make the best of it," he assured her with a fierce look.

"With no commitments?" she murmured more to herself than to him.

"If that is the way it has to be, yes," He answered her rather seriously.

"I had to ask, she thought fighting tears. "How much longer do you have left?" she then asked. Not sure if she wanted to know the answer.

"Two months, then it's off to Florida. What about you?"

"I am not sure where I will be stationed, but I think my school is either the end of March or April. I do know it's eight months or so before I will be finished."

It was late evening; she lay with her head resting against his chest. His heart slowly ebbed to a more normal beat as his breathing returned to a more normal pace. His arms were snugly wrapped around her. "You are dangerous," he spoke when he could talk from their fierce lovemaking.

"I thought I was a challenge?" She spoke sleepily.

"That too," he admitted kissing the top of her head. He knew that no other girl would ever be able to replace her. That no other girl would fill his needs again like this one. He felt a sense of loneliness as he realized that they really didn't have much time left together. "I love you," he whispered rising to look at her, and saw that she was asleep.

22

Logan frantically paced the room looking at her watch, Reddy's rack and the door. "Where is she?" she frantically thought. Walking over to White's rack she vigorously shook her. "Where is she? She demanded from White.

Rubbing her eyes, and trying to focus them, White stared at Logan. "Where's who?" Grumbling she made an effort to cover her head and shove Logan away at the same time.

"You know who? Reddy! Where is she?" Logan shouted.

"How would I know?" White continued to grumble.

"Your boyfriend is a friend of Tanner's?" Logan insinuated shaking her again.

"So! And your point is?" White grumbled under her covers.

Poking her again, Logan provoked. "Are you sure you don't know where Reddy is?

"No, and if you want to keep those fingers, get away from my rack." White threaten.

Logan being persistent all but screamed at White. "Get up?"

"What? What for?" White complained, as Logan was determined to get her up.

"You are going to call your boyfriend and find out if Tanner is in the room?"

"I am doing what?" White stated, uncovering her head to make sure she heard Logan right.

"You are going to---" Logan started and was cut off by White saying. "I am not calling Jay for any reason, besides he wouldn't tell me if Tanner was or wasn't in the room," then glaring still as Logan she insisted. "You're not her mother?"

"I know. Her mother would kill her if she is with whom I think she is." Logan declared.

"Good now that is settled, do You mind if I go back to sleep?" White repeated, as Logan gave her a downhearted expression. "You do know where she is, don't you?"

"All I know is that Jay and I saw Reddy and Tanner leaving the mall together on Friday, He hasn't see Tanner since, and I haven't wasted my time looking for Reddy. If she is with Tanner, then she is okay."

"Probably is in heaven," Logan laughed, as she climbed up on Whites rack and made herself comfortable.

"Good. Then you wouldn't mind joining her and finding out all of the details," White stated, kicking Logan off of her rack.

Hitting the floor Logan let out a yell. "Ouch" Reynolds sat quickly up in her rack from the noise and insisted to know. "What in the hell are you two doing now?"

"Nothing," they both answered as slowly the door to their room opened and Reddy tiptoed in. With the room bask in darkness it was easy for Logan to quietly get up and walk over to Reddy once the door was closed.

Assuming that everyone was asleep, Reddy reacted to Logan's voice with a scream. "Now what in the hell is wrong?" Reynolds complained as she rose from her rack and getting up walked over to switch on the light by the door. Looking at Reddy who was dressed, she commanded. "You coming in?"

"What do you think?" Reddy answered, as she walked over to her locker.

"Good. Logan go to bed, the baby finally made it home," Reynolds remarked as she turned off the lights, and switched them back on again. "Where have you been?" She asserted as it dawned on her that Reddy had been gone the entire weekend.

"Out," Reddy expressed as Logan whispered. "How was Tanner?"

"Who said I was with Tanner?" Reddy whispered back to Logan who was still standing beside her. As she threw her backpack into her locker.

"Who else have you been seeing?" Logan questioned with a smile.

"My shadow," Reddy smiled, as she moved to pull her dungarees out of her locker and to dress for the day.

"Sure, and I am suppose to believe you?" Logan stated, as she commented. "At least he put a smile on your face.

Navy Girl

"Come on Tanner, get your butt in here," Crawford declared, as he watched the clock then the door. "Five minutes to muster," Crawford complained, continuously watching the time tick away.

"He's not going to make it," Reed stated, becoming concerned for their roommate.

"He better," Crawford sighed as the door flew open and Tanner hit the room like a whirlwind. Clothes coming off in all directions as Crawford threw his dungarees at him and Reed threw him his shirt. "Did you forget to put in a wake up call?" Crawford yelled at him.

"No. We got pulled over for speeding, Tanner mumbled, pulling his tee shirt off over his head.

"Better have a ticket to prove it, we have inspection this morning," Reed informed him.

"Thought I saw the chief as I crossed the quarter deck," Tanner groaned, beginning to change his clothes, his back to Crawford

"Holy cow! What did you tangle with?" Crawford commented after seeing Tanner's back.

"Tiger, one small tiger," Tanner managed a grin as he turned and looked at Crawford.

"Hope the tiger had its shots?" Crawford snapped shaking his head.

"Better hope she is taking the pill," Reed groaned, as he thought of his own predicament and White's condition.

"She is," Tanner admitted, turning and looked at Reed. "You got a problem?" he asked.

301

"Big one. I got a feeling my time is limited here," Reed stated taking a deep sigh as a hard knock came to their door. "Inspection," Chief Molson shouted as the door to room 356 opened and the four persons who occupied the room stepped outside. With his face only inches from Tanner's, Chief Molson voice raised several octaves as he yelled. "Almost missed it, didn't you Mr. Tanner?" His facial expression grim as he looked at the guy who seem bent on throwing away a good career.

"Sir!" Tanner answered realizing the mistake the second after saying it.

His nose almost touching Tanner's, Molson yelled. "How many times do I have to tell you? I work for a living?" Then he stepped back, a satisfied smirk on his face. "I believe boy you are unsat," Molson declared taking note of Tanner's appearance and no shoes. "I hope you kissed the broad long and hard. It may be a while before you see her again. Get my meaning?"

With a regretted sigh, Tanner only knew to well what the chief meant. If he had doubts, Chief Molson was ready to refresh his memory. "I think you are beginning to enjoy EMI's. I guess you know where you will be for the, shall we say, next two weeks? Maybe it will help you to remember where you are suppose to be at 0500. That is if you are still here?"

One thing about having a chief chew on you early in the morning it did nothing to start your day off and it gave you something to think about as you did EMI's. Why in the hell did I think I needed a commitment to her? But it doesn't have to be this way. I will just dump her. That is if I get out of this and still remain in school," Tanner thought as he cleaned the heads.

"Tried to warn you," Crawford stated, as he stood just inside the door of the heads.

"Yeah you did," Tanner groaned as Crawford added. "Going to breakfast?"

"Be there," Tanner acknowledged, his expression troubled.

Things were not going well for Reddy either. Logan and White seem bent on teasing her and trying to find out what it was like to sleep with Tanner. "Shall I write Rourke and tell him he won?" Logan laughed.

"You do and Thomas will have to find someone else to sleep with," Reddy warned her.

"Do I look worried," Logan continued to laugh.

"Better be," Reddy threaten, hiding her smile.

"Na, you wouldn't hurt a hair on my head."

"Don't count on it," Reddy insisted.

"I'm not. You wouldn't do anything to threaten your not seeing Tanner," Logan continued to laugh.

"You may have a point there," Reddy answered, as a small laugh escaped her lips..

Having heard enough, Reynolds butted in. "Well I guess you are no longer a challenge?" A cynical laugh following her remark as she walked over to the door, opening it wide, she stepped out into the hall and announced. "Reddy got laid over the weekend, Tanner finally scored."

"I am going to kill her," Reddy ranted making a lunge for the door to step out in the hall and deck Reynolds.

"Oh no you won't," Logan grabbing her, stopping her.

Madeline J. Wilcox

"Give me one good reason why I shouldn't drive her through a wall," Reddy stated, glaring at Reynolds who was laughing as she came back into the room.

"Because she isn't worth the trouble you would be in," Logan warned her. "You got away with it once, don't think for a minute that Reynolds would let that happen a second time."

"Do you think I could get away with staying in the room today?" Reddy sighed, making the comment in a low voice.

"Oh hell, just look at it this way. You got Tanner as a boyfriend and the rest of them are drooling," White chuckled.

Well Reynolds announcement sure brought her back to reality as they stood muster and she had to listen to insults and crude comments, which she figured she could do without. Guilt and what they were suggesting did nothing to help matters as she marched to the mess hall. Facing Steve, she realized would merit problems.

"Here comes grumpy," Crawford mentioned, seeing Reddy enter the mess hall. "Damn old buddy, I thought for sure you could put a smile on her face," Crawford chuckled, as Reddy walked up to the food line.

"Tried," Tanner replied, in a somber mood, as he pushed his seat back, "excuse me," then he walked to where Reddy was getting a tray.. "How are you doing?" He leaned and whispered as he stood beside her.

Turning on him, she almost leveled his head with her growl. "I have a bone to pick with you," Her eyes furious as she stared at him.

"Now what?"

"You know darn well what?" Her voice was low and grating. "Even my collar won't hide it," she told him, making motion towards her neck and the mark called a hickey which was plainly clear for all to see.

"That's it? You should have been in my room. They swear I tangled with a tiger," he grinned as he continued on down the food line with her as she picked out fruit, and a bowl of oatmeal to eat. At one point she did say she was "Sorry," as she tucked her head down as she poured coffee.

"It's okay we both will survive," he lightly laughed, as he added. "I have EMI's to do for getting back late."

"Didn't you mention the ticket?" Joan questioned him as they walked to where Tanner usually sat with his roommates. Sitting down, she couldn't avoid the fact that Reed and Crawford were staring at her. "What! She glared at them.

"We have a problem and we need your help?" Crawford spoke up.

"About what?" she asked, missing the humor in Reed and Crawford eyes, as he turned to the person sitting next to him. "Well actually we have several problems," Reed added. "One you need to get our buddy back on time for muster. Two, he says you were pulled over for speeding?" Reed said managing a straight face.

"We were pulled over for speeding," she admitted as again the guys with the steel gray eyes spoke. "Wouldn't mind telling our Chief that? He seems to think different, like maybe you forgot to put in for a wake up call." Crawford chuckled, as he added. "You do need to do something about your nails, after all, our friend is government property and they would mind literally if you destroyed it."

Her attitude was far from being under control as she turned on Tanner. "My reputation? Ha. Big joke? What did you do, go back and tell them all that you finally scored with the dumb hick? Well you should get with your friend, Kathryn Reynolds since you both seem to think a like." Her voice low, but there had been no mistaking her anger as she slammed her chair into the table and stormed away.

"You going after her to explain we were only joking," Crawford asks Tanner. Shaking his head in distress, he answered Crawford. "You go I have enough problems to deal with."

23

It had been days since Reddy and Tanner had a falling out. Getting ready for bed the girls in room 347 were laying down the rules to Reddy. "You start bawling tonight and I assure you I won't be responsible for any actions that I may take," Logan made a threat to Reddy as she climbed into the rack below Whites.

"Yes," White and Reynolds both agreed. "We don't need to loose any more sleep due to your bawling every night."

"Why don't you just walk up to Tanner and tell him you are sorry." White suggested.

"She may have a problem there," Reynolds snickered, "I think my friend Ann Wagner is taking care of his needs so to speak."

Both Logan and White looked over at Reynolds with contempt. "You just had to open your big mouth?" Logan glared at Reynolds and then she turned on Reddy. "Don't listen to her. You know how she loves to get you riled?"

"She is probably right for a change," Reddy expressed a forlorn expression on her face as tears started falling again. To her crying Logan rose and walked over to Reddy's rack. Taking her arms she marched her over to stand in front of the mirror. "Would you look at this person?" Logan demanded.

Reddy found the person staring at her unbelievable. She appeared thinner, her eyes looked dull. She truly looked horrible. "I---I can't face him. I feel so guilty about what we did?" Reddy sobbed.

"Oh hell, unless you are pregnant there is nothing to feel guilty about," White insisted, hopping down from her rack and thinking that again sleep was going to be impossible.

"Boy! Wouldn't that throw a kink into Tanner's plans," Reynolds laughed picking up on White's remark. Only Logan caught White's unsaid words as she asked her. "You got a problem?"

"A big one and Reed doesn't want anything to do with me," White begins to cry.

"Oh great! Now White is bawling," Reynolds groaned looking at her and adding. "So what is your problem?"

"I'm pregnant," White confessed. You could have heard a pin drop in the room and three girls stared at her. They knew the consequences of finding yourself pregnant. They would kick you out of school, and be sent to shore duty, or worst be kicked out of the military. (One other option was open you could sign a waver to let someone else raise your child.)

"I take it you told Reed he is going to be a father?" Logan responded reviving from the shock.

"I did and he told me there was no way his career was going to be ruined because I was stupid," White sniffed with a fresh flow of tears.

"Do your parents know?" Reddy asked, feeling sorry for White.

"Not yet, I plan on telling them when I go home for the holidays."

"What do you want to do?" Logan then asked White.

"Marry Reed of course," White answered, as she walked back to her rack and climbed up into it.

"That would be the best solution," Reddy agreed, her problem now seen small compared to White's.

Sitting in the classroom waiting for Instructor Foster to start the lecture for the day, Reddy's thoughts were more on Tanner than what was being said. Having seen him in the mess hall with another one of his conquests. How could I have been so stupid? Why did I think he would be any different towards me? Ha, I am just another notch in his belt. At least he's not consistent; she continued to think as Instructor Foster continued the morning lecture. "I can not begin to express the importance of safety. As you are aware we have been going over and over PMS checks. We have been doing PMS tag out logs. Well today isn't going to be any different. You will be reminded that safety comes before anything else. Safety is a job for all hands, twenty-four hours a day. Some danger exists in every single operation aboard a naval vessel. Going to sea involves working with powerful machinery. You will be working with high-speed equipment, intensely high temperature and pressure steam, volatile and exotic fuels and propellants. The list goes on and on. It is the responsibility of everyone aboard ship to observe all safety precautions," He looked around the room as he added his usual comment. "Or all of you will be history."

Reddy, whose attention had been listening to only half of what Instructor Foster was saying, commented. "History! Great Tanner, just what I want to be," Instructor Foster stepping up to her desk and in his boisterous voice loud enough to drown out the snickers and guffaw laughter, startled her as he said. "Would you care to repeat that remark? There are a few who didn't quite understand it. Including me."

Seeing Instructor Foster and his look of contempt towering over her, she realized the mistake she had made. Shrinking down in her seat, she did her best to avoid looking at Instructor Foster. "Well we are waiting," he spoke with a stern chaffing.

"Sorry sir," stammering she finally looked up at him.

"Sorry! Is that all you have to say? Well being sorry won't help your fellow shipmates when you are the reason they have been blown to smithereens. You had better pay more attention to what is going on in this room or Tanner won't be the only thing you will be history with. Get my meaning?" His look full of disgust Instructor Foster turned his back to her and called lights. As the lights dimmed a safety film aboard ships flashed across the screen.

Sitting across from Matthews in the galley during lunch she had to listen to him. "What is going on with you and this character, Tanner?"

"Nothing," she objected to his question.

"Nothing! Hell I'm not stupid," Matthews glared at her. "I see how you have been letting yourself go lately. How you seem not to be paying attention in class. You had better get your head out of you ass," Matthews continued to preach, "or you will find yourself doing shore duty and odd jobs for the Navy. Get my meaning?"

With tears forming in her eyes and looking in the direction of where Tanner was sitting, she mumbled, "I love him Brian!"

"What? I thought you said things weren't serious between the two of you?"

"They weren't' until Thanksgiving," she tired explaining to him without saying too much.

"You slept with him?" His look total disgusted with her. Then thinking about what he had just said, he spoke in a more subdued tone. "I'm sorry. It's none of my business what you do?"

"Your right it isn't!" She spoke rather sharply some of her old spirit showing.

Realizing that their friendship was at risk, Matthews told her. "Look, I didn't mean to pry or make judgment on you. Shaking his head at her and thinking she was falling for a lost cause, he felt like getting up and going over and punching Tanner's lights out. Damn him, of all people why did he have to hurt her? "You going to be okay?" Matthews asked with concern reaching over and laying his hand on top of hers to let her know he cared.

"Yes," she spoke softly.

Great! Reddy thought having to sit in class and deal with Instructor Foster glaring at her for the remainder of the day. "Okay people, this morning we went through PMS checks and tag out logs. Now we will be dealing with 3-M maintenance, material and management."

Instructor Foster kept the pressure on them, as each day they were given pop quizzes on safety. Come Wednesday and the test that said you stayed in the same class or went back one week was given. Reddy had, had no problems staying with the others until her ordeal with Tanner, now concentration seem difficult as she tried answering the questions. It was the first time since being in school that she went below the 75% level.

On Friday as Instructor Garfield was calling out names of who passed and who failed he stared at the name in which he was about to call. Ms. Reddy failed. Mr. Johnson failed.

Tanner was having a difficult time paying attention to what Instructor Adams was saying about electrical components as intense blue eyes, a pert nose, and sensuous mouth kept invading his thoughts. Damn her, he cursed, his thoughts continuing to trouble him "Going to break?" Crawford asked, tapping him on the shoulder.

"Be there," Tanner replied looking up and seeing Instructor Adams headed in his direction. Now what? Moving he sat straighter in his chair. "I received word this morning that you are to report before the disciplinary review board on Monday." Instructor Adams began towering over him.

"So," Tanner arrogantly replied, closing his books and started to stand. Far from excusing him, Instructor Adams blocked his way. "You amaze me Mr. Tanner. I seem to have a problem understanding why you waste your time and mine by showing up for this class?"

"I guess because it's either here or the brig. I would much rather see your smiling face any day," Tanner remarked with his usual insolence.

"I wouldn't push it son!" Instructor Adams warned. Especially when it comes to where you will be on Monday." His stare didn't move from the guy whom he figured could have anything he wanted from the military but made it rather difficulty by his attitude. With no further words said, Instructor Adams stepped aside and excused Tanner.

Having been waiting just outside of the classroom, Crawford remarked when Tanner joined him. "You know one of these days he is going to write you up for insubordination."

"I doubt if he will get that privilege since I am going before the disciplinary review board on Monday," Tanner informed Crawford.

"Thought you were spending too much time out of the room," Crawford sighed as they walked into the crowed lounge. Moving towards a window again Tanner's thoughts were focused on Reddy. The dark brooding eyes staring out the window were troubled to how easily Reddy could invade his thinking. Reddy had managed to get at him in every available sense. If he continued to let her do so, Chief Molson and Instructor Adams would be getting their wish, he would be sent to the fleet, his career shot to hell!

It was unusually quiet in room 347 with just Logan, Reynolds and Reddy. White had been moved to TPU thanks to someone going to the Petty Officer in Charge. Both Reddy and Logan has surmised who had opened their big mouth since she seems to be staying out of their way. Slipping her headset on and listening to the words of "*You're the Inspiration*" she tired concentrating on cold iron watches, and the need to know for tomorrows class.

"We have rounds," Logan reminded Reddy as she tapped her on the shoulder.

"Okay," Reddy responded closing her books and looking at Reynolds asleep on her rack. "Who is going to wake up sleeping beauty this time?"

"Oh! Let me," Logan laughed as she gave Reynolds rack a good hard shake. "What!" Reynolds yelled turning to see who was disturbing her sleep. "We've got rounds," Logan informed her.

"So make them," Reynolds snapped turning her back to Logan. which was a mistake as Logan threaten, "get your lard ass out of that rack before I dump it." Beings that Logan was the 'officer of the watch' no one was going to sleep while she was on duty, not when they had a watch to stand.

Still complaining Reynolds came off her rack. "All right, you don't have to make a big deal about it?" For some reason that no one understood, Reynolds never made an attempt to argue with Logan, but did whatever Logan suggested or told her to do. "Did you put the fear of God into her," Reddy had asked one day. "No, but I have been tempted," Logan had remarked back to her. Well whatever had happened between the two girls, Reynolds seemed mellower lately and was easier to get along with.

After making rounds, Reddy decided to call her grandmother. "Grams I need some of your wisdom," she spoke as soon as her grandmother accepted the call.

Laughing, Maude answered. "I don't know if I can give a sailor any wisdom. Maybe you should be calling your father on that subject."

"I wish it was that simple," Reddy sighed, and her grandmother heard the seriousness in her tone of voice. Having received a letter only today from her granddaughter and telling her about a certain young man, she was almost expecting to hear from her. Jumping to conclusions Maude answered with alarm. "Oh no! Joan your not?" finding the words to express the rest of her concern difficult.

"What?" Joan answered with despair as she absorbed her grandmother's question, the words that were not spoken. "Oh Gram's I never expected you to judge me," she sobbed, before hanging up the phone.

She wasn't sure how long she had been sitting in the lounge, her eyes glued to the darkness of the night, her face tear stained. I can't keep going on like this?" I've got to get a grip on reality, she warned herself. "Reddy!" Logan screamed at her. "I have been looking all over for you. Did you forget that we had watch?"

"Oh god, I'm sorry. Are we late?" Reddy stared at her in disbelief that she had forgotten something so important as 'watch'!"

"Not yet we aren't," Logan assured her as both girls hastily left the lounge and headed for the quarterdeck where they were standing watch.

The next evening Reddy was sitting in McDonalds studying identification symbols for shipboard machinery, piping and valves used in the engine room. "Do you mind if I have a seat?" Looking up to see who was asking, Reddy came face to face with Ann Wagner who was making herself comfortable across from her. Knowing who she was, Reddy replied. "Looks like I don't have much of a choice. So what do you want?" Reddy asked with a blank expression.

"To talk about a mutual friend of ours," Wagner let her know.

"I guess then you are wasting your time. I am not interested in anything that has to do with Tanner,' Reddy retorted.

Wagner wasn't going to give up as she told her. "Do you know he went before the review board this morning?"

"And your point is?" Reddy answered.

"I think you are the reason that he is having problems," Wagner added.

"'Oh really!" Reddy offered with no remorse at least any that she was willing to show, as she added. "And what makes you think that?"

"Because he was fine until he became involved with you," Wagner accused.

"I don't believe that we are involved with each other," Reddy asserted, looking at Wagner who was busy rolling her eyes.

"Oh no? Just what kind of games are you playing?" Wagner glared at her.

"I am not playing any games," Reddy then insisted.

"Aren't you? First you gave him this come on, then you backed off when things got where you couldn't handle them. You couldn't leave well enough alone, you kept teasing him with your innocent act. You are so stupid, you can't even see that he is in love with you!" Wagner snapped at her, and tired of the conversation she rose leaving Reddy alone.

It was later that Logan and Reddy were sitting in the room, Reynolds was out, and they were talking about going home for the holidays. "Are you eager to go home," Logan questioned Reddy.

"Not any more I'm not," Reddy answered thinking about her phone call home and hanging up on her grandmother.

"Why, because you slept with Tanner?" Logan surmised with a chuckle.

"Probably. I talked with my grandmother yesterday. She assumed that the reason I was calling was that I was in trouble?" Reddy stated looking at Logan with a forlorn expression.

"Damn! Maybe you had better stay here," Logan suggested.

"Oh sure, you already complain that I spend too much time in this room."

"Yes I know I do, but are you trying to change? Hell no. You keep mooning over someone who doesn't give a damn about you," Logan insisted even if she doubted her own words. But yet, she wanted Reddy to except the fact that Tanner wasn't coming back.

It was then that Reddy confessed. "I had a visit with Ann Wagner. It seems that Tanner is going before the board?"

`"I heard rumors to that effect. Did she say anything else?"

"Yes. But I am not sure if I should believe her. She said Tanner was in love with me?"

"What?" Logan looked at her in surprise.

"Steve loves me," Reddy repeated in a lower, softer tone, as if she finally believed it herself.

"And you have doubts about it?" Logan said, ready to change her words about her earlier comment.

"I'm not sure what I have, or what I am feeling. I do know that I don't want Steve to get kicked of the military because of me," Reddy stated with assurance.

"Then you had better let him know of your feelings," Logan warned her as she added. "Speaking of getting kicked out of here, how are you doing?"

"I passed my last test," Joan responded, thinking that she was back on the right track. "It seems funny not having Matthews around, but at least there are more girls in this class and the pressure doesn't seem to be as heavy on me although I still have the same instructors."

"They are probably waiting for you to fail again." Logan responded, as she yawned. "So are you going to tell Tanner how you feel?"

"Probably, I guess I should be honest with him...But I don't want to be hurt any more either." Reddy uttered with a sigh.

"I don't think you will be hurt," Logan stated as she recalled how Tanner would look at Reddy. The guy had it bad then laughing she said, "Since you aren't sure if you are going to see Tanner again, tell me, his he as good as he looks?"

"I thought Reynolds cleared that up for us?" Reddy responded, with a smile on her face.

"Reynolds is gay, so she wouldn't know what Tanner is like," Logan stated as Reddy's expression turned to total shock. "She's what! How do you know?" Reddy stammered.

"Caught her and one of her girlfriends here in the room going at it." Logan answered, with a serious expression on her face.

"Oh my gosh!" Reddy added, shaking her head in disbelief. "Now I have an ideal why she is always jumping to your least little whim. She is afraid you will turn her in?"

"It's none of my business what her preference are as long as she is not putting the make on me," Logan remarked, as she changed the subject and asked again. "Are you going home?"

"Do I have much choice?" Reddy stated.

"You really didn't tell your grandmother that you slept with Tanner/" Logan asked with skepticism.

"Do I really look that stupid?" Reddy declared.

"Sometimes," Logan responded, as Reddy picked up her pillow and flung it at her.

"Well you mother can relax now," Logan, continued to laugh, "You finally got laid. Just show her Tanner's picture, she just might have a change of heart about killing you."

"She might," Reddy added, as she stood and walked over to her rack. Before closing her eyes Reddy informed Logan. "We have only one more week left before we go home for the holidays."

"I know," Logan answered sleepily.

24

Going before the disciplinary review board made one think about where they were headed. Especially when you had a Captain breathing into your face and declaring. "Give me one good reason Mr. Tanner why I shouldn't be kicking your ass out of here?"

With an obstinate stare and looking straight ahead, Tanner had his own thoughts as to why he was here and to why he should be able to stay in school. Expressing those views he knew would not do him justice, since he was not give permission to speak. Tanner tried not to appear alarmed about the fact that one wrong word could send him to the fleet instead of the nuclear program. There were his test scores; surly they would take them into consideration. They had been good up until now? He had been hours ahead of the others when it came to hours spent in the classroom. But he wasn't stupid either; he knew if he stayed in school this time…There couldn't be a next time of going before the board and for what, a piece of ass?

No, that wasn't true? Reddy meant more to him, his thoughts continued while he was raked over the coals and warned. "One more time Mr. Tanner and you will be out of here so fast that you won't have time to pack. Get my meaning boy? Now get out of my face!"

Minutes later standing in the hall, Tanner leaned against the wall for support, "Whew I don't think I want to do that again?" Tanner groaned as a guy waiting to go before the board asked. "What's it like in there?"

"No worse than a drill instructor chewing on your butt in boot camp," Tanner remarked casually as he moved to leave the building.

Crawford was eager to find out how things went the minute Tanner entered the room that evening. "I still have my ass," Tanner remarked, reaching behind him and placing his hands on his backside. "Smaller but still there," he commented

"Man! You are one cool dude for someone almost getting kicked out of here," Crawford stated shaking his head.

"Really? Well let me tell you looks are deceiving," Tanner admitted to his friend thankful that no one else was in the room, continuing to confess Tanner added. "What am I going to do Dan? I can't get her out of my mind, she is everywhere I turn." Then in a lower voice he told him again. "I love her, Dan."

"I tried to warn you she was a commitment in which you didn't need," Crawford reminded him.

"So you did, only I didn't pay much attention," Tanner sighed with a troubling expression.

"Better start unless you want to go to sea earlier than you expect."

Tanner raised his head and for a second he was the old Tanner. "I think someone else just reminded me of that fact also. I believe his rank was a captain." Tanner grinned.

"Well if you won't listen to me, I am sure you had better listen to him." Crawford commented as his friend lay down on his rack with a grim expression on his face. "Maybe things will look better after being away from Reddy for a couple of weeks?" Crawford stated as his friend slipped a headset on.

"Yeah, sure," Tanner grumbled tossing and turning to find a comfortable spot to sleep in. With his efforts becoming uneventful he rose and telling Dan, "I need to make a phone call," Tanner redressed and left the room.

"Won't be seeing him until morning," Dan muttered to the closing of the door.

With only a couple of days left before going home, Reddy was in the Laundromat doing her laundry. It was quiet and at 2200 there were few people to contend with as she threw clothes into a washer.

"We need to talk?" Tanner spoke to her as she didn't bother turning to look at him, put kept putting clothes in to washers and she responded. "I don't think we have anything to talk about. You made it very clear how you felt about me. Now if you will excuse me," she straighten and turning walked pass him to where her books were laying on a table, "I have some studying to do."

After what he had been through today he was finding it hard to control his temper as he moved again to stand beside her. "I am sorry for what happen in the galley, but Dan and Jay were only teasing you," He begins to explain.

"Yeah right," Reddy stated not excepting anything he had to say and then she turned and finally looked at him. "What happen did you lose your civilian chit again? Noticing that he was dressed in his dress blues.

"I had a meeting today," he replied in a sober tone.

"So I heard. I take it you are still here?" She flatly stated.

"Something like that," Tanner remarked continuing to play her game for the time being. "Would you like for me to be somewhere else?" He then asked.

"Probably," she quickly replied, continuing to turn pages in her engineman book, without giving him any encouragement at all.

"Spend the night with me?" Tanner found himself saying next.

"What happen did you run out of dates?" she asked with a cynical stare.

"Nope have one," He answered, closing her book and demanding her attention.

"I am not one of your tricks," She bated trying to free her book from his clasp.

His temper finally reaching the limit, he sternly replied. "I don't do tricks."

For the next hour as her clothes went from the washers to the dryers it was a standoff between Steve and her, as her clothes started drying Steve began to pull them of the dryers. Walking over to the table where she had started folding her clothes he grabbed her ditty bag and along with her books and threw every thing in it. "Meet me outside your building in ten minutes?" He sternly spoke to her.

In your dreams she was thinking as he handed her ditty bag to her. Walking across the street with Tanner close by her side words weren't spoken until they reached her building. "You better be back down here in ten minutes." He warned her.

Logan was still in the room when Reddy returned and dropped her ditty bag into her locker and turned speaking told her. "I have a problem," looking at Logan and wondered why she had never put motels on her list of attractions? It seems the place to go if you wanted to settle an argument.

"What kind of problem?" Logan asked, continuing to look at her books lying on the desk in front of her.

"Tanner is downstairs and wants me to spend the night with him?" Reddy stammered.

"That's a problem?" Logan smiled to herself.

"Yes," Reddy quickly asserted. "I don't want to become just a casual thing with him,"

"Well I guess you are on your own here?" Logan stated closing the book she was reading and turning looked at Reddy. Once more she found herself smiling inward to Reddy throwing items into a backpack. "You going somewhere?" she couldn't avoid asking.

"Out," Reddy answered throwing the backpack over one shoulder and headed for the door. Waiting to cross the quarterdeck, Reddy could see Tanner outside the building pacing back and forth and checking his watch. Once outside and walking up to him she watched at the irresistible grin crossed his face. "I'm glad you decided to come?" He said taking her arm and directing her across the street to his car.

After asking her if she was hungry, and her answer had been yes, he pulled into McDonalds and order food for the two of them. They sat outside the Crow's Nest Motel eating as he told her. "I feel that I need to explain my actions as to why I didn't see you?"

"You don't need to explain anything. I think your actions were loud and clear," she commented looking over at him.

Knowing of her attitude and how quick it could change, Tanner didn't want to start a fight with her, but he did want to apologize for his actions s he declared. "I had no intentions of hurting you.'

"A challenge, I believe you said I was?" she reminded him, her stubborn glare turned on him as he made the move to get out of the car to order a room for them. "Don't I wish that is all you were?" He murmured, walking into the building.

Lying beside him in the warmth of the covers and his arms, tears stinging her eyes as she thought, once again I let you make love to me. I'm not sure Steve Tanner if you are the best things that happen to me, or the worst. I have changed so much over the past few months. My life has taken a different turn and it's not easy accepting all the changes that have been made. Tomorrow---Tomorrow we will talk, letting out a deep sigh she let sleep take over and her dreams became a nightmare of what her life had become in the past weeks.

25

Home for the holidays were the main topic as they girls in room 347 packed for going home. "I can't believe that this time tomorrow I will be home?" Logan expressed, putting the last of her things into her sea bag and looking over at Reddy who seemed not as thrilled about the idea of going home. "I thought you would be jumping up and down with joy?" Logan laughed, "or did someone steal your lollipop again?"

"Don't I wish," Reddy grumbled, as she seemed to move in slow motion to packing. The CPO had told Logan and her to take all of their things out of their lockers and desk after inspection this morning. Also, she told them to turn in their bedrolls, as there was a good chance that they probably would be assigned to different rooms when they returned from stand-down. They were also in for a surprise when Reynolds announced that she would not be returning.

"Well not for two weeks anyway," Logan commented.

"Longer than that," Reynolds snickered, "You two won't have to put up with me when you return. I will be in TPU." (Transit Personal Unit).

"What?" The other two girls simultaneously spoke at the same time.

"You know, adieus, farewell, goodbye, I am out of here," Reynolds repeated as she turned on Logan and Reddy. "I think one of you did some talking?"

"Not us," Logan insisted, as the two girls shared a knowing look. "Probably you put the make on the wrong person," Logan commented also.

Reynolds didn't have a come back and grunted a reply as she walked over to Reddy and stated. "Don't think for one minute that you have won Tanner back. My friend still has a few tricks up her sleeve."

"Do I look worried?" Reddy retorted as she checked her locker to see if she had missed anything.

Reynolds continued in a sarcastic tone, "You should be since Wagner and Tanner come from the same hometown."

"As I said before what is your point?" Reddy repeated, trying hard not to doubt Steve and his feelings for her.

"Time will tell won't it," Reynolds added as she ducked out the door of the room.

Logan who had remained quiet turned and looked at Reddy. I guess things between you and Tanner have been settled?"

"Working on it," Reddy replied.

"Well then you should be in a better mood?" Logan laughed, as Reddy tossed a pillow at her. Catching it, Logan Added. "You better stay clear of your mother for the next two weeks, mother's have a way of knowing when certain changes are made? Speaking of which, I got a card from Warner. I guess now I can tell her you got laid." Logan continued to tease Reddy.

"You heard from Warner? When? Where is she stationed at?" Reddy asked full of questions.

"Here you read it," Logan said, handing her the Christmas card, "it is meant for both of us." Receiving the Christmas card, Reddy began to read.

"Hi. I am sending this card to wish you and Reddy a Merry Christmas

and wondering how things are going for the both of you. As for me, I am having

the time of my life. I am learning to be a medical technician. Rubbing elbows shall

we say with all the right people. Mother is keeping her fingers crossed for a doctor. Not me being a doctor, but marrying one. Well not for now that is, I am having too much fun.

How is Reddy doing. Probably still innocent?" (don't I wish), Reddy thought as she

continued to read: "Wouldn't believe whom I ran into the other day? Darrin McCall. He really is a nice guy.

Do you two get leave? I do, I am going home. It's going to seem strange you know. I'm in the military and my friends are all in college. Wow! What a comparison. Take care and write. That goes for Reddy also. P.S. Take note of my address. I am going to be here for a while. Please write, Ann."

"Nice letter," Reddy mentioned as she handed it back to Logan, but not before writing down Warner's address. "I will drop her a line about Steve when I get home," Reddy expressed as she put the finishing touches on her packing.

330

"Send her a picture. It will say more than words can tell," Logan   laughed as the two girls were interrupted as Reynolds came back into the room. "You want to know something Reddy?" she began. "Tanner thinks of you as a country bumpkin. Wagner is more of his class. Think about it, you will be in hick town, Indiana and Wager will be in Tanner's arms. Merry Christmas and a lousy New Year." Reynolds snickered as she grabbed her luggage and hurried towards the door.

"Coward," Reddy yelled after her.

"Don't let her get to you?" Logan stated seeing the depressing look on Reddy face.

"But maybe she is right? Maybe Steve does think of me as a country bumpkin," Reddy stated as doubts rose in her mind,. "I mean I didn't know him very long when I slept with him,' guilt pushing at her doubts.

"Will you stop it? The guy loves you," Logan expressed as she picked up her luggage and started towards the door. "How are you getting to the airport?" She remembered to ask Reddy, as she stopped and turned to look at her.

"Steve is taking me. We both are leaving around noon," Reddy replied.

"Good he can help you with your luggage," Logan smiled as she watched Reddy struggle with two sea bags, her hat box, her dress uniform carrier, a carry on bag, and two suitcases, Plus a duffle bag full of gifts.

"I think I am going to have to make several trips?" Reddy sighed as she left some of the luggage in the room and made towards the door to follow Logan down to the quarterdeck. Standing on the quarterdeck Reddy could see Tanner pacing back and forth outside.

"Well it looks like your chauffer is waiting?" Logan stated, as she too waited patiently to cross the quarterdeck.

Tanner looked again at Reddy's building about the time that she walked out. "Got everything?" he asked, walking up to her and reached for one of the sea bags she was carrying and commented. "I take it you packed everything in here?" he questioned to the weight of her sea bags.

"Almost I have to go back and get a few more things." she stated as she let him carry the sea bags for her.

"Could you hurry a little bit? I would like to be on my plane when it leaves," He mentioned as she turned to go back into her building. "I'll try," Reddy called back over her shoulder.

Finding her seat on the plane a feeling of nostalgia crept over her as she thought of the entire festivity-taking place for the holidays. Home, it would be good to see her family and friends again. I wonder if Maureen will be home?"

Maureen? She probably will refuse to call me a friend. I really haven't kept in touch with her since arriving at Great Lakes. But then, her letters haven't been that many either, she continued thinking about her high school friend who now was a model with some agency in New York. She defiantly has made a name for herself, Reddy smiled looking down at the magazine laying in her lap. Maureen's picture was on the front cover, and there was an article about her on the inside.

"I didn't know you were into fashions?" Steve had teased, when she had bought the magazine at the airport. Her response had been. "There are a lot of things you don't know about me?"

"Yea, but I am learning. So how do you know the person in the magazine?" He then had asked.

"She is my friend," Joan had responded slowly looking at him.

"Really?" Tanner had remarked, as his personal thought were. "WOW! Now there is someone I could really enjoy?"

Sensing that she had lost him for a few moments, she moved closer to him. "Going to miss me?" she asked, her look almost defensive.

Regaining his senses, Tanner replied. "Maybe," avoiding the tempting blue eyes and pouting lips, as he made the pretense of looking around the airport.

"Steve?" she spoke again not sure of his feelings for her as the moment. Shaking her head to clear her thoughts and reminding herself of where she was, she forced herself to think of home.

Approximately one hour later, Joan Reddy's plane landed at Indianapolis International Airport. Searching the terminal in the crowd of eager travelers hurrying to get home, it took some time before she spotted her father. Seeing him, the longing and excitement that had been missing invaded her as she picked up her steps and headed in his directions. "Dad! Dad!" she cried out, waving her hand high in the air and jumping up and down to attract his attention.

Tom Reddy was looking in all directions from where he was standing. Thinking he had heard a familiar voice, he turned just in time to see his daughter jumping up and waving her hand like crazy. Moving past several people he was soon standing at the gate as Joan stepped through it and into his arms. "Boy have I missed you!" Tom Reddy stated, giving her a big hug.

"Same here dad," she expressed as he took a step back to take a good look at her. There was something about her, something different, he sensed it right away, but couldn't put his finger on it. "You look great!" he finally spoke again, and added. "Do you have more luggage?" since she was carrying a backpack, and a carry on bag.

"Do I have luggage," she laughed, as she slipped her arm through his and they began to walk towards the area where you collected luggage. Once they were away from the main crowd of people, Joan asked. "Didn't anyone else come with you?"

"Sorry, it's just your old dad," Tom answered; smiling down at her and seeing the disappointment look on her face. "I thought Peggy would be here?" she somberly expressed.

"Peggy's friend Mark his here with his parents and his sister. Peggy is busy entertaining them." Tom casually spoke.

"Oh," Joan responded as she saw some of her luggage coming around, turning to her father she was about to warn him, "Dad their heavy," as he stepped forward to lift the sea bags that Joan had pointed to. As they waited for the rest of her luggage Joan answered her father's questions about school and how things were going for her. "I am doing quite well for being one of two girls in my class of thirty-five guys. Did you know that if I pass this part of school, I would be going to more schools?"

"I think your Uncle Matt, said something to that effect just the other day," Tom smiled.

"Remind me to thank him," she soberly expressed as she added. "Instructor Garfield seems to be treating me a little better. I think he finally has realized that I know what I am doing."

"Well that must be a big relief for you," Tom answered, still trying to figure out the change in her.

"It sure is. We have been learning about the basic in boarding ships, and what to expect once we are on them. Which won't be for a while," she said, taking a deep sigh.

"Oh time will fly, you just wait and see," Tom spoke with pride as he again stepped forward to retrieve a garment bag, hat box, and a suitcase in which Joan pointed out "Are you sure you brought everything," her father chuckled, as they pushed a luggage cart towards the parking lot.

"Everything," she laughed as she added. "I hope you brought the van."

335

"I thought about it, but since there would be just you and I, I brought the old egg beater. Thank goodness it still has a top over the bed of it." He commented, as they continued to walk towards the parking lot.

Once they were in the old pickup and moving away from the airport Joan asked. "How is mother and Grams?"

"Your mother is busy entertaining all the guest at our house," Tom answered, as Joan interrupted. "Just who all is there?"

"Well let me see there is Mark, his sister Jill, and his parents. Then there are Linda's parents, your mother and your sister, plus you and I." Tom smiled, omitting the fact that Jeff, Linda, and the twins were there also since it was to be a surprise for her. "Your grandmother is anxious to see you and she also said to tell you that she was sorry for jumping to conclusions the other night? About what she didn't say," he added, with raised eyebrows as he looked over at his daughter. "Care to fill me in off what was said?" He then questioned her.

"It was nothing of importance," Joan, responded, as she turned her head to avoid further conversation about her grandmother, her father turned his attention back to driving and she began to take in the winter scenery passing by. I have missed this, she realized thinking all the base had to offer was; a lot of tall buildings, few trees, and plenty of cold spaces which whipped chilling air through as you stood at attention in front of your buildings waiting for the CPO to release you. Here was scenery, with snow-laden trees, and decorated houses here and there. This was home, she found herself smiling as her father reached the village limits. Once more the village had been transformed to days gone by. The antique lampposts had been wrapped in sprigs of evergreens with bright red bows tied just below each lamp.

Each store window displayed a scene of the Christmas spirit in animation. At the curb stood horses donned in collars covered with silver bells, red reins for leading to pull the six-passenger sleigh hooked behind them. In the horse drawn sleighs were brightly printed quilts to snuggle under as you rode through the hills and valleys of the countryside.

Madeline J. Wilcox

Tom feeling that there was more to this conversation letting it slide for the time being as he suddenly realized, his daughter was no longer unsure of herself, she had finally grown in to a young lady. Why do I have a feeling that the young man Peggy and Kathryn have been talking about has something to do with it?" His thoughts as he again took a glance over at his oldest daughter who glaze was glued to watching the scenery go by. Why do I have a feeling, that she no longer is my little girl? The questions plague him as he turned off the main street of town and drove down the street in which they lived on.

As her father pulled into the driveway, Joan's feelings of apprehension increased as she saw her mother standing at the front window. Her look was very anxious. Great! Were Joan's thoughts, as she opened the door to the truck and stepped down? Walking to the back of the truck to retrieve her luggage, she didn't see the person as he stepped out of the garage.

Busy pulling her sea bag out of the back of her father's truck, she heard "Would you like some help?" A shout of joy that would have jarred the earth broke out as Joan screamed. "You're here? You're here?" she continued to yell, as she wrapped her arms around her brother after she let go of the sea bag she had been tugging on.

"Hell yes I am here. Did you think I would miss seeing a half-pint sailor?" Jeff laughed, as he inspected her appearance. "You're looking good. I take it what's-his-name as been taking good care of you?" His eyebrows raised, he spoke in a teasing manner.

"He has," she managed as her face turned a deep crimson color.

"Good," her brother laughed again, as he reach for the two sea bags. Lifting them he remarked. "You did pack everything?"

"Everything," she assured him with a smile.

"Damn, my sons don't even weight this much put together," with a grimace expression he continued to complain.

"They are here!!" Turning with excitement, she almost caused her brother to fall over her.

"Yes. Did you think I would leave them at home?"

"I'm not sure," she laughed as she begins to tell him. "Peggy wrote me all about you leaving Linda's parents at the airport, and how you called mom and dad and told them the twins were born, only you forgot to say which hospital."

"So I got excited," Jeff snapped,

"Careful big brother, your attitude is showing," Joan responded as she reached for the lighter items to carry and asked. "What kind of mood is mother in?"

"I think you are in for a surprise. Our mother has made a complete turn around. She is actually human. She's decorated the house; baked enough food to feed an army, and even is worried about where you are going to sleep. Now if there are any more questions, can we answer them in the house? My feet are freezing," Jeff claimed as he stomped his feet in the fresh snow.

Looking down at her brother's bare feet, she started to laugh, "At least I have enough sense to wear shoes."

339

"So do I. Now move it before I kick your small behind." Jeff said giving her a push towards the house.

There had been two women watching as Joan got out of the truck. "She looks smaller?" Kathryn expressed to her daughter-in-law.

"I was thinking the same," Linda agreed, "But it has been a while since we have seen her," she added to Kathryn's concern.

"Oh how I do want us to get along," Kathryn sighed.

"You will, just keep smiling," Linda commented, hoping to assure Kathryn doubts as they both heard Jeff and Joan enter the kitchen, and Jeff calling out, "Hey where is everyone?"

"Right here," Kathryn spoke, as she stepped from the hall into the kitchen. Walking over to Joan, she slipped her arms around her. Hugging her, Kathryn realized it had been a long time since she had done so. "Welcome home, dear," Kathryn said, searching for words.

"It's good to be home," Joan answered, accepting her mother's hug with uncertainty. Releasing her, Kathryn then told her. "Come you must see the new family room."

"But my luggage?" Joan replied, feeling a bit apprehensive to her mother's warm welcome. "Let your father and Jeff take care of it for you," Kathryn added, as she took Joan's hand.

They went down the side steps that usually led out to the garage, but Joan hadn't notice the three steps across from them, as now they walked up them and her mother led her down a small hall. "We have put in another bathroom here," Kathryn stated, as she pointed to a close door. "And this is the family room," she stated, as she opened two swinging doors. A huge crowd greeted Joan. "Welcome home," they all shouted. There were her aunts, uncles, cousins, family friends, and most important, her grandmother. "We thought maybe you would enjoy a surprise?" Maude smiled, hugging her.

"Thank you," Joan responded returning her hug.

"Oh don't thank me. This was all your mother's idea," Maude stated, as Joan's expression turned to bewilderment. "Mother thought of this?" Surprised to think she had done something special for her.

"Yes," Maude acknowledged as Kathryn stepped up to them. "Mother Reddy, I hope you don't mind if I steal Joan?

"Oh heavens no, I don't mind, besides I have to be getting back to the Inn. We will see you later Joan?"

"You can count on it," Joan assured her,

Leading her towards a striking couple about her mother and father's age, her mother said. "I don't believe you have met Captain Miller and his wife. This is my daughter Joan, and these are Linda's parents." She remarked, as Joan spoke when Captain Miller held out his hand, speaking, and his eyes sparkled with mischievousness. "I understand that you like being in the Navy?"

"Yes sir," She replied,

"Why didn't you come into the Marines? We could use a few good engineman," He winked at her.

"I don't think the Marines could handle two Reddy's' in the same branch," Joan answered as her brother and father stepped up along side of her. "Not when the two of them have the same type of temperament." Tom insisted, as Jeff added. "Yeah, but I can keep mine under control, the little sailor can't."

"I try," Joan laughed, as Mrs. Miller held out her hand. "You have to excuse my husband, he enjoys keeping pretty young ladies to himself. Have you seen the twins yet?" she added, wanting to show off her new grandsons.

"No, I don't believe I have," Joan responded as Linda seem to come from out of know where holding a small baby. "This is Tyler," she said, moving back the blanket so Joan could see him.

"Do you think they favor their old man?" Jeff bugged her as she again looked down at the wrinkled face and the baby's eyes opened. "Oh, his eyes are blue too," Joan excitedly responded as the baby open his eyes and stared at her. "Where is Josh?" She then asked, remembering the other baby's name.

"Mon has him," Jeff let her know, as Joan turned and saw her mother gently talking to the baby in her arms. I think I am in for more than just a surprise, Joan surmised as she excused herself when Peggy and Mark entered the family room with a girl whom she assumed to be was Mark's sister, and the couple following them had to be Mark's parents as he favored the man.

"You didn't wear your uniform?" Peggy complained as she gave her sister a hug.

342

"We were told it wouldn't be a wise idea with all the high-jacking going on." Joan expressed, as Mark said, "a mutual friend of ours said to tell you hello if I saw you."

"How is Darien?" Joan responded, as Mark answered, "great!" then introduced his parents and the girl who sort of stood off to the side from the rest of them.

Joan had a feeling that she wished she were somewhere else than being in Wellsburg. Happy this person wasn't as Joan held out her hand in welcome. "Hello," Joan spoke to her. "Has Peggy showed you all of the sights yet?"

"I've seen enough of this quaint hick town," the girl grumbled with boredom.

"Jill you apologize to Joan, right now!" Mrs. Greene reprimanded.

"Oh mother, get a grip!" Jill glared at her.

Ah, this person has an attitude worst than mine? Joan thought, as her Uncle Matt and Aunt Maggie walked over to the small crowd. "You doing me proud?" Her Uncle Matt laughed, hugging her.

"Working on it!" Joan smiled returning his hug, as her Aunt Maggie spoke. "You two can swap war stories some other time." Hugging her, her Aunt Maggie whispered. "How do you like the change in your mother?"

"So far, so good," Joan responded, as her aunt added. "Give her a chance okay? She wants to be your friend as well as your mother."

Madeline J. Wilcox

"Really? I would like that also," Joan spoke with skeptics in her voice as she looked over to where her mother was talking with Mrs. Miller. She seemed more relaxed and opened with people, as her attention was drawn back to her aunt who was saying. "I understand there is a young man in your life now? When I heard that you were seeing someone, I thought to myself, no this couldn't be our Joan?"

"I know, and would you believe I didn't kill him." Joan blushed slightly.

"Well I am impressed." Her aunt smiled, as Joan's mother announced, "there is sandwich, salads and drinks set up in the dinning-room. As friends and family started filing for the dinning-room. Linda walked over and asked. . "How do you like what your mother has done to the this room?"

"It's pretty. I think mother has done a terrific job in decorating it.," she answered also, giving praise to the room, which looked like a picture out of a Good-housekeeping magazine. At one end of the room there was a large fireplace with bookcases on either side. Above the mantel was the painting of large flowers in soft pastel color of yellows, blues, and a light touch of pink. "Peggy?" Joan stated, knowing that it was her sister's artwork. Her mother had chosen the colors in the painting to decorate the overstuffed rattan furniture with. Also in the large room, was a matching rattan table, with four overstuffed chairs? Large plants were placed here and there adding to the atmosphere of comfort.

Linda's next question was as she followed Joan out through the doors that led to the deck outside. "Did Steve and you make up?"

344

"Yes, He is supposed to call sometime this afternoon." Joan answered, adding. "So what made the change in mother?"

"She has been seeking help. It got to the place where she couldn't stand herself, let alone anyone else. Your father gave her the alternative, either a divorce or seeks help. She also has enrolled in a class at the University, and is studying interior decorating." Linda informed her.

"She is?" Joan expressed with surprise mother was going to college. "How does dad feel about mother going back to school?"

"He is very proud of her. I think you are going to see a big change in your parents." Linda added, as Kathryn spoke from the doors leading to the kitchen. "Would you two like some hot chocolate and sandwiches?"

"I know I would" Linda responded, "It's getting pretty chilly out her. What about you Joan, care to join the other guests?"

Turning Joan looked at her sister-in-law then her mother. "I'm not really hungry."

"Well I am," Linda suggested lightly, as she stepped towards Kathryn, and walked past her. Once Linda had left, Kathryn reached for a throw lying across one of the chairs, carrying the throw outside she walked up to her daughter and asked.. "Are you okay?" taking the throw and placing it around the two of them. "It's a little chilly out here," Kathryn said, explaining her move.

This is not my mother, Joan kept thinking as she felt the comforting warmth of the throw put around her, her mother's arm resting lightly on her shoulder as she held the corners together with her left hand. "I love to come out here and just look at the scenery. It is rather beautiful with the snow clinging to the trees." Kathryn expressed softly.

"Yes it is. I miss the trees and the quiet serenity of the hills and surrounding scenery. We don't have very many trees on the base, just a lot of space and buildings for the cold wind to whip around; and having the wind come off of Lake Michigan it can be very cold."

"In some of the letters that Peggy shared with us, she mentioned that you went to Chicago several times?"

"I did. Have you ever been to Chicago?" Joan answered, wondering if this was confession time as her mother answered. "A long time ago. I did go up to the top of Sears Tower. Did you ever go up there?"

"Yes, I love the view from up there. On a clear day you can see forever. And at night, the scenery is unbelievable."

"I take it being in school is a lot better than being in boot camp?"

"Boy, you got that right. When I am not standing duty on weekends, or on Wednesdays, I am either with Steve studying or at the library looking up vital information, or doing laundry."

"You do laundry?" Kathryn laughed. "Wouldn't I love to see that."

"Would you believe I have even managed to keep my white's white?" Joan expressed enjoying this moment with her.

"Your father says you are doing quite well in school. I think we are all a little proud and a little surprised of you," Kathryn said, looking at Joan and seeing the sad look on her face. "You okay?" Kathryn again expressed with concern.

Joan's eyes fixed on the trees that surrounded the back forty didn't see the look on her mothers face as she answered her with. "Probably no one as been more surprised than me. I have some instructors who at first were not sure that I belonged in their classes. I think I have proven to them otherwise."

"How does Steve feel about you wanting to be an engineman?" Kathryn asked, remembering her lover's name, and wanting to bring back the subject of the two of them.

"Steve is not sure about dating someone that wants to get her hands dirty." Joan answered, looking up at her mother with a forlorn look coming to her eyes.

"Why don't you tell me about Steve?" Kathryn then stated.

"Steve! I don't know if I can explain him? Logan says he wears clothes like an advertisement, and he does. His chief says he's arrogant, and he can be. He has brains; is studying E double E, He wants to be on a submarine." As Kathryn listen to Joan speak with fondness for the young man in question, she knew that the old Kathryn would have been throwing a fit by now.

"How old is Steve?" Kathryn then asked next.

347

"Twenty-three. At least he will be next month."
Joan replied.

"Isn't he a little old for you?" Kathryn
questioned her lightly."

"Not really. We seem to get along pretty well,"
Joan responded, thinking to herself that age shouldn't
matter. "Isn't dad older than you by several years?"
Joan questioned.

"Yes, but I was older than you when we met."
Kathryn stated.

"By what, one-year?" Joan reminded her.

"Back when I was your age, girls seemed to be
more mature," Kathryn reminded her also.

"Are you saying I am immature?" Joan
questioned her mother's logic.

Kathryn had to stop before saying the wrong
thing, and then she said. "The last thing I think you
are, is immature? You have always been one step
ahead of the girls your age. Do you know that I never
figured you to follow through with going into the
military? I always figured that you would back out.
But you didn't, you followed it through, even when
things were rough, you continued to stick it out. And
whatever has happen between Steve and you, I am sure
you have had a great deal of guilt haunting you?"

"Oh that I have," Joan deeply sighed, as she felt
her mother's arms tighten around her. "I was afraid of
coming home, of having to face everyone. I know
saying I love Steve doesn't make if acceptable, not
from how I was raised anyway. Gram's once told me
to only let there be one man in my life. That is what I
want also." Joan ended her confession with.

Kathryn not sure of what to say suggested that they join the others in the kitchen and dinning room. Enter the rooms her Aunt Maggie walked over to her. "Is everything okay?" She asked Joan who had moved away from her mother to get a cup of coffee.

"Yes," Joan replied as her cousin Zack walked into the kitchen with several of his friends. Zack looked quite different from the person she remember him to be. As if reading her mind her Aunt spoke again. "Zack is going to IU."

"Zack is going to IU?" Joan repeated with surprise.

"Oh yes," her Aunt Maggie spoke with pride. "And doing very well, I might add."

"Well miracles cease to amaze me," Joan laughed, as she looked at her cousin, who had been nothing but trouble for her Aunt and Uncle for the past few years. "So Zack, what are you studying?" Joan asked him.

"Research medicine."

"Wow! When did you inquire brains?" She looked at him in surprise.

"About the time that you lost yours," Zack replied, looking at his cousin and thinking that she had changed quite a bit. She looked almost feminine, as he recalled Dave Wright telling him that she wasn't so innocent any more. Which he could care less about, he never did like her as his father was always putting him down and telling him that he should have more gumptions like her. "So Joan," he began in a scrutinize tone. "I understand you are not so, shall we say, innocent anymore?" You could have heard a pin drop as everyone seem to quit talking at the same time, and caught the tension that seems to develop between the two cousins.

Joan didn't want to continue the conversation from across the room, so with dignity she walked over to Zack. With a tone matching his she replied in a lower voice. "To whatever you have heard, trust me, I will not stoop low enough to condemn myself. Do I make myself clear?"

"Perfectly." Zack replied with a devious grin. "At least you are not denying It." as he turned and walked out of the kitchen and headed for the family room with his friends.

Taking a deep sigh of disgust and preparing to answer Zack, she stood with her mouth gaping as he left the room. I will get even with him, she thought to herself, as her father walked over to her and stated. "You have a phone call." Was it her imagination, are did her father appear just a little angry with her? Looking again at him as she answered the phone, she saw the querying look on his face. 'I think I am in trouble?' she thought as she said, "hello."

350

With in minutes of calling the Reddy's home, Steve was hearing the girls voice who could make his blood run hot and cold at the same time. "Hi babe,"

"Hello," she answered back recognizing the person who could make her smile just thinking about him. "I see you made it home okay. How are your parents?"

"They are fine. How about yours?" Steve answered, knowing how worried she was about going home and having to face her family.

"Okay. My mother and I are actually speaking." Joan replied, as she turned her back to Peggy whom seem to have appeared out of know where and her expression seem to be taking in every word she was saying.

"Is this something different?" Steve inquired, as he realized that Joan hardly ever mentioned her mother.

"Considering that we generally fight, yes, I would say it was quite different," Joan smiled, imagining him with the little boy grin on his face.

"Then you received a better welcome that I," Steve answered grimly. From the time his father had picked him up at the airport, they had been in a heated discussion as to where Joan would fit into his career with the military. The fact remaining was his father had seen fit to have Joan checked out. "What's the matter dad didn't you trust my judgment?" Steve had argued with his father.

"Your mother and I have dealt with your judgment before," Stephen Tanner had expressed with annoyance towards his son.

"Well you had better get use to the fact that I love her. That I will keep on seeing her," Steve had blasted at his father with defiance as to whatever else his father was thinking.

"I understand that you went before the Review Board," his father had continued to reprimand. "Did the girl have something to do with it?" Then with out giving Steve a chance to answer, his father warned him. "Screw up and you will be disinherited from this family. Get my meaning?"

"Steve! Steve? Are you still there?" Joan broke in to the silence that prevailed.

"Yeah babe, I am still here. Miss me?" he answered with a regretted sigh.

"Very much so," she answered, blushing lightly.

"Same here. Wish now that we had stayed at the base?" he then asked.

"Maybe, but it has been good seeing my family. Everyone was here when I got home, including my brother and his family. The twins are identical. They have the same color of eyes as Jeff and I." She told him.

"So what are your plans for tomorrow?"

"I am not sure. Peggy wants me to go ice-skating with Mar and his sister Jill."

"Who's Mark?" Steve then questioned her.

"Remember me telling you that he was in my brother company?" Joan answered.

"You sure that Darien McCall isn't hanging around? If I remember right, he also was in your brother company with this Mark person. Or did you forget that you told me about him?" Steve stated, as Joan heard doubt in his tone of voice.

"Do I hear a note of jealousy?" She slightly laughed.

"Hell no," Steve quickly answered, as he added. "Crawford, Ann and I are going skiing tomorrow. Does that sound like fun?"

Her mood quickly changed at the mention of Wagner. "Probably," she retorted.

It was his turn to ask. "Do I hear a note of jealousy?" Steve questioned because after the round with his father, the last thing he wanted to deal with was Joan's attitude.

"Tell Wagner hello," then Steve was listening to an empty dial tone. "Damn it," Steve uttered, slamming the receiver back on to the phone jack.

Joan had retrieve to Peggy's room to get away from all the holiday chatter, and to sulk, as Logan would put it. She hadn't realized she had dozed off until her mother was shaking her. "Joan are you going with us to your grandmother's?"

"Yes," Joan replied, drowsy from sleep as she moved to sit up. "Do I need to wear my uniform?" She also questioned her mother, still feeling the need for more sleep.

"I think dressing casual will do," Kathryn answered, as she turned and left the bedroom.

Maude Reddy glanced up from where she was working at one of the tables as another group had arrived to help fill baskets for the homeless and families who were unable to have Christmas without help. She smiled when she noticed it was Tom and his family. "Well I see you brought extra people along?" She mentioned to the new faces among the group.

"They didn't want to miss the fun," Tom smiled, as Mrs. Miller remarked, "Tom has told us about this event of filling baskets for those who wouldn't be having Christmas with out the help of the town. And I couldn't think of a better way to spend the holidays by helping others. Just tell us what we need to do?"

"Well we need gift wrappers, stocking stuffers, list checkers. Oh heck, just pitch in where the help is needed." Then seeing her son, Matt, she called out to him. "We have more willing volunteers." It was in no time that the guests and family members were up to their elbows in wrapping paper, fruit, candy and each, working diligently so that every name on the list would receive something for Christmas.

"You look like you have lost your best friend?" Maude Reddy questioned her granddaughter's expression as she had walked over to where Joan was working.

"I probably have," Joan stated in a sober tone.

"Would you like some hot chocolate and a shoulder?" Maude chuckled, as the two made a move to leave the dinning area, where everyone was working.

"The hot chocolate sounds great," Joan agreed, following her grandmother to the back part of the Inn, where her residences were. There was a transition made as the girl who was always considered a tomboy began to speak about the person that had made changes in her life. "I did the dumbest thing Gram's. Steve called me today, and instead of being happy just to hear from him, I hung up on him when he told me he was going skiing with an old girl-friend."

"And now you are thinking that he will not call back?" Maude questioned her.

"Yes," Joan sighed. "I have his phone number Gram's, should I call him and apologize?" Joan then asked her grandmother.

""Why not wait and give him the benefit of the doubt?" Maude answered.

"If I do that Gram's I might never hear from him," Joan regretted with a sigh.

"Oh I think you will hear from him again," Maude eyes twinkled, and her voice carried a merry sound to it. It was only about twenty minutes ago that a young man had called and wanted to know how to get to Wellsburg and he didn't want a certain young lady to know he was coming. He had also added something about a bear, and not letting her push any buttons on it in front of a crowd.

With the next day being Sunday, it was Church in the morning and the rest of the day everyone seem to be busy doing last minutes shopping, cooking or whatever took up their time. Joan sat in the family room curled up in a chair with a book stuck under her nose. "Are you sure you don't want to come with us?" Peggy pleaded for the umpteenth time, as all their old friends were going ice-skating, and then over to Sam's Pallor, where all the young people gathered to talk, play pool, dance and eat.

"No," Joan snapped at her sister. "I am not in the mood. Now if you will leave me alone, I just might get this chapter read?" She added, without looking up at Peggy and missed seeing her hurt expression.

"Don't say later that you weren't invited," Peggy growled at Joan as she turned away and headed for the kitchen.

"Wouldn't dream of it," Joan murmured to herself as she returned to reading about engines, or at least making the pretense of reading. Her thoughts were more on Steve and wondering if he would call her again. How come she felt so insecure about their relationship? Was it because she was here and he was in Oklahoma? Or maybe, she questioned her feelings; I have always felt this way but just didn't want to admit it? I knew that soon we would be separating and I just getting a taste of the torture that I am going to be feeling when he heads to where ever he will be stationed, and I will be, God only knows where? Lost in her thoughts, Joan did not hear her mother enter the family room until she spoke. "I thought maybe you might enjoy this?" Kathryn spoke to her oldest daughter as she handed her a cup of coffee. "I looked in here after Peggy left, and you looked so engrossed in what you were reading that I did not want to disturb you. You really do like what you are doing?" Kathryn spoke more with pride than a question.

"Yes, I guess so," Joan admitted as she sat the book aside and accepted the warm steaming cup of coffee.

"Got time to talk?" Kathryn then asked, glad to have some free time with her daughter.

"Sure," Joan smiled, as her mother took the rattan chair that matched the one she was sitting in.

"How much longer will you be at Great Lakes?" Kathryn started out with

"I should be done with school about the first part of April. From there I do not know where I will be going. I will fill out what they call a dream sheet, which gives me different choices of bases that I could be transferred to"

"Do you have a preference as to where you would like to go? Her mother then asked.

"I am thinking California. I think I am ready for a warm climate," Joan answered with a laugh as she added. "I have already seen Florida, and they can keep it."

" I believe Jeff is being transferred to California in February. I think he said the base was Camp Pendleton. Is that close to any Naval base?"

"I think the one in San Diego is close to Camp Pendleton." Joan expressed, as her mother's next question was. "Will Steve be any where near you?"

"I don't think so. Steve will be going to a nuclear base, or to a submarine base." Joan expressed with a sigh of regret.

Madeline J. Wilcox

"It must be difficult knowing that you will soon be separated from him?" Kathryn added, as she reached over and laid her hand on her daughter's arm in a comforting manner.

"I try not to think about it. Gram's always told me, let there be only one man in my life. Well that is what I want also," Joan again sighed.

"And you feel that it may not be that way?" Kathryn then questioned, as she saw the unsure look on her daughter's face.

"I'm not sure. I don't know," Joan, answered with confusion, as tears fell down her cheeks. "How can it be when we will never see each other again after we leave school," she answered with regret as tears dampen her face.

"How much longer does Steve have?" Kathryn asked softly.

"He should be done with school by the end of February." Joan answered, taking another sigh.

"Oh Joan, I am so sorry. I wish I could say something to help you through this. I know it must be very hard to have to say goodbye to your first love?"

"Did you have a first love? I mean other than dad?" Joan questioned her mother as she turned and looked up at her and watched as her face took on a gleeful look.

Laughing Kathryn remarked. "I don't remember. I think I have always been married to your father."

"There is a change in you," Joan then stated.

Smiling, Kathryn told her. "I have been seeking help. I got to the place where I couldn't even stand myself. I was always snapping at everyone around me. It seems that my hormones were out of whack. I was going through the change of life early. Your father gave me an alternative. Either a divorce or I seek help. I sought help," then laughing, she added. "I think we both have changed?"

"I wish Steve and Logan could hear you say that," Joan joined her mother in laughter. "Logan keeps telling me to grow up, and Steve keeps saying I need to do something with my attitude."

"Your attitude, is what makes you unique, what makes you your own person." Kathryn assured her, as she added. "Maureen is home for the holidays. What not give her a call? I am sure she would like to hear from you."

"I did earlier, but Mrs. Colby said that Maureen had to fly back to New York this morning for some retakes. But she was sure she would be back in town on Christmas Day."

"Maybe then you two can get together," Kathryn stated, as looking at her watch and seeing that it was almost time to fix supper for her guest. "Guess I better get back to the kitchen, there is going to be a lot of hungry people coming home pretty soon."

"Would you like some help?" Joan asked, following her.

"Would love the company," Kathryn responded, realizing how wonderful it was to be able to talk to her daughter without fighting with her. Kathryn listens steadily as Joan talked about school and how much she had been teased at first, and now was being accepted by her peers. "At first when I started classes I didn't think I would ever fit in, but now, I am actually enjoying what I am learning. I just hope that I will be able to do it aboard a ship?"

Still finding it hard to believe that her daughter wanted to be an engineman for the Navy, Kathryn shook her head in disbelief as she commented. "So you really do want to continue with this career?"

"Yes, Its fun learning about what makes a ship move. Mom, not only does a ship in the military carry weapons, but it's also a floating factory, for fixing those that become dead in the water. We carry supplies to all the ships, and I can't wait to be a part of it all." Joan concluded.

"Well I guess then you have found your adventure," Kathryn smiled, as the back door open and her other family members and guest started arriving home for the evening.

Christmas Eve had been a hectic day for everyone as they made the rounds to different homes delivering boxes of gifts, food and etc, so that everyone in the area of Wellsburg county could wake up to a Merry Christmas, and small eyes would stare in belief as their parents shook their heads in amazement. In the Reddy household everyone was sitting around at the dinning-room table taking in the luxury of just relaxing after eating one of Kathryn delicious meals.

Navy Girl

"I believe this has been the best Christmas yet?" Tom Reddy mentioned, as everyone seem to agree with him.

"I am not sure they will allow us on the plane," Mrs. Greene remarked, "I think I have gained several pounds, after eating Kathryn's good cooking." Which in agreement the rest of the guest agreed. "I want to take some of those recipes home with me," Ruth Miller added, as she looked over at Kathryn, and holding up her glass of wine, she said. "Here is a toast to our perfect host."

"Here ye, here ye," added Kathryn's family as well as her guest, as Kathryn's face turned a rosy color, and Tom reached over and kissed his wife on the cheek. Then as if on clue, each one arose and left to repair for the candle light service at the church.

Getting ready in Peggy's room the three girls were in consistence chatter about the past four days. "I must admit I am having a good time," Jill stated, as she slipped into her dress.

"Well I can't understand why?" Peggy laughed, "I think you have all the boys falling at your feet."

"Yes, I think I have," Jill laughed, as she turned to Joan. "Have you heard from your boy-friend?"

"No, I think I really made him mad when I hung up on him." Joan responded.

Then to change the subject, Jill asked. "Do you take birth control pills?"

"Isn't that kind of personal?" Peggy chimed in looking at Jill then at Joan.

"It's okay Peg," Joan responded, as she added. "Yes, I take the pill."

"So do I," Jill informed them.

361

Madeline J. Wilcox

"You do?" Peggy said with shock as she looked ay Mark's sister who was a year younger than her.

"Well yeah! I don't care to become pregnant," Jill, responded as a knock came on the door. Turning to the door that was slightly ajar, Joan watched as her mother stepped in to the room. "I just wanted to remind you to wear your uniform," Kathryn spoke to her oldest daughter, and to the other two, she said. "Better get a move on it, we will be leaving soon." Then Kathryn closed the door, and stood for a few minutes to catch her breath from the conversation she had just heard. The old Kathryn would condemn Joan, Kathryn realized. She had talked to her doctor about her feelings and the fact that she had read one of Joan's letters to Peggy. Doctor Martin had told her to take a deep breath and deal with it calmly. That it wasn't an uncommon thing with young people these days. Well she is taking precaution; Kathryn pondered still not wanting to accept the fact that Joan was having an affair with this Steve Tanner.

With everyone standing in the kitchen to leave for church it was quite impressive, when Captain Miller walked into the kitchen in full dress uniform. Jeff, Joan and Mark snapped to attention and saluted him and as he returned the salute Peggy snapped a picture of them.

Tom Reddy stood back watching with pride and thought he had a lot to be thankful. He had one child that was a Master Gunnery Sergeant in the Marines. A daughter who showed promise of going places in the Navy, and a daughter who was making plans to go to college. Yes, Kathryn and I have a lot to be thankful for he thought again as they all left the house.

Every one sat in the Reddy family room waiting anxiously to see what was under the tree for them. Kathryn Reddy had seen to it that her guests as well as her family had something under the tree.

"Hey I drove a van up here, not a semi," Jeff complained, "How am I supposed to haul all of this stuff back home/" Jeff asked as he made inventory of two highchairs, two playpens, and everything that would make his sons comfortable. "Honey, we won't have to buy the kids clothes until their teenagers?" He mentioned to Linda laughing.

"I know, isn't it great?" Linda replied as she thanked everyone for the gifts.

"We could send some of the things to you?" Tom mentioned as he turned and pulled a huge box from behind the tree. "I guess it's time for Joan to open this big box and end all our curiosity?"

"We have shook, rattled, lifted and even turned that box upside down," Kathryn laughed, as Joan looking it over couldn't find out who it was from, only that it came from Chicago. Eagerly tearing the outer wrapper off she was confronted with a plain large box, which she rapidly tore open, only to find wrapping paper again. Ripping it off, she stared again at another box. "This better be the end," she mumbled, while her family laughed and made statements among them. Excitement filled the air to what might be hiding behind the next box or wrapping paper. Tearing the box apart, she had to contend with dark packing paper. As she tore it away from the object it covered, she found herself staring at a huge bear dressed in a black smoking jacket, a red ascot, a pipe in one hand, and a silk red rose in the other. What made the bear so unique was her thinking, 'Damn Tanner did you pose for his face?' for the bear was wearing a stupid lopsided grin. Pinned to the lapel of the jacket was a note. "I am a radio and a tape player. Please lift my jacket in the back to turn me on." Turning the bear around she found the buttons. Pushing the buttons she wasn't quite ready to what it started saying. "Holding you in my arms and making love to you I have come to realize that your are unique. That there is nothing I would want to change about you. For in doing so, you would no longer be the person I have fallen in love with. Steve."

"You could have heard a pin drop everyone was so quiet. If was Jeff that finally broke the silence, as Joan tried to recover from the color of her face without choking." Well sis, I don't think there are any more doubts as to how Steve feels about you?" He said, looking to his parents whom didn't seem a bit amused by the bear.

Her reply to her bother was as she managed to turn and look at him. "Do you think I could fit into one of those boxes? "Where do you want to be shipped to?" Jeff laughed.

"Oklahoma, I am going to kill someone," Joan responded as she looked over at her parents and sensed that they were not impressed by what the bear had to say. Rising as quickly as she could, she grabbed the bear and made an exit to Peggy's bedroom.

"Tom is there any more present under that tree?" Kathryn asked trying to remain calm and still be civil at the same time.

"I don't think so, that was the last present." Tom answered avoid looking at anyone in the room.

Rising from where she had been sitting, Kathryn told her family and guest. "Breakfast should be ready by now. We are eating over at the Inn. Peggy you want to get your sister?"

"I'll get her," Linda said, getting up from where she was sitting and handed the baby she had been holding to Jeff.

"Nice bear," Linda laughed, walking into Peggy's bedroom where Joan was standing and looking out the window. "Someone is going to think nice," Joan responded as she turned from the window and looked at her sister-in-law. "How am I going to face everyone?"

"By not making a big deal out of it. I was three months pregnant when I married Jeff. Everyone either knew it or guessed it. I walked down the isle with my head high, for all the gossip in the world can't change the fact that Jeff and I love each other."

"Keep reminding me of that," Joan half smiled as she followed Linda from Peggy's room. "I think I will ride with Jeff and you," she commented as they neared the kitchen.

"Coward," Linda laughed as Joan and her went outside to join the others.

Maude had set up tables for Tom's family and guest off to one corner of the room next to Matt's family. As always red and green plaid tablecloths decorated each table, with a white or red poinsettia's decorating the center of the tables. A candle had been placed above each place sitting. For those who were guest at the Inn, had the pleasure of listening to the choir from the high school fill the dinning room with Christmas Carols? It was a Christmas Morning in which they would remember, as the host of the Inn made sure each guest had a small gift which would signify their visit.

Everyone was enjoying the excellent meals of the breakfast bar, which consisted of; coddle eggs, scrambled eggs, bacon, curd ham, Pastries of all sorts, hush puppies, hash brown potatoes or American fries, sausage gravy, and biscuits and ff you went away hungry, is was your fault.

As Tom, his family, and guest were waiting for their turn Mark, Joan, and Jeff shared some of the anticlimactic stories of being in the military Mark even brought up the subject of Joan and McGuire on their trip to Disney World. "We were all wondering how long it would be before she would kill him. "Didn't he go to Great Lakes?" Mark questioned Joan who sat across from him, her look half amusing, half irritated, with exasperation Joan answered. "He did."

"I take if you don't see him?" Mark continued to question her.

"Not if I can help it," She assured him.

"And I was thinking you had your attitude under control," Jeff butted in teasing her.

"Only with certain people," Joan glared at her brother.

"Yeah I know. I was wondering why he didn't come home with you?" Jeff's eyes filled with laughter as his sister's face turned several shades of red. She had a feeling that her brother was about to build a fire under their parents. "Come on sis tell us about the guy that has put a sparkle in your eye, and has sent a bear to confess all." Jeff went on.

Looking at her parents, Joan caught the petulant look on her father's face. She had a feeling that there was another set of words he would have considered using.

As she did her best to talk without embarrassment, the guest of the Reddys saw a transition made as the girl who was always considered a tomboy began to speak about the person that had made changes in her life. "I don't know if I can explain him. He is lanky and aristocratic. My friend Logan says he wears clothes like an advertisement? And he does, his chief says he's arrogant and he can be. He has brains," she continued, as her sister-in-law asked. "Do you have a picture of this incredible character?"

"Yes," Joan answered reaching behind her and taking her purse off the back of her chair where it had been hanging. Taking out the picture of Steve she handed it to Linda.

Looking at Steve Tanner's picture Linda got the strange feeling, that he would hurt Joan, maybe not intentionally but he would hurt her she surmised before handing the picture to her mother. "Oh my, I don't think I can breathe," Mrs. Miller commented looking at the handsome young man in the picture. "Where did you say he was from?" she laughed as she passed the picture to Mrs. Greene.

"Oklahoma," Joan responded, as Steve's picture was passed around the table.

"Well I don't know about the rest of you?" Mrs. Greene smiled, "but I am making a trip too Oklahoma," handing the picture to her husband, who declared. "Yes dear I know, but you never go," Winking at her. "So I guess he is safe."

"Wow! He's even better looking here than the one you sent me. Of course the one you sent me, he is standing about a mile from the camera. How did you meet him again?" Peggy added.

"By tripping over his feet and landing in his lap," Joan replied, becoming a little annoyed with her sister. "You don't have to memorize it," Joan declared as she reached for Steve's picture.

"Well let me take a look at this person," Jeff stated, taking the picture away from Peggy. "I am sure mother and dad would like to take a look at their future son-in-law," which he received a swift kick from Linda under the table for making the remark.

"What!" Jeff whispered at her.

"You know what?" Linda grimace

Joan was still trying to recover from Jeff's earlier remark about the bear as she looked at her parents, and sensed that they didn't find the comment too amusing. She was about to say something in her defense, but was saved by everyone rising to go to the breakfast bar.

"Here is your picture back, " Jeff stated as he fell in line behind his sister and commented. "I was just kidding with you."

"Sure you were?" Joan spoke in a low gritting tone as she threw food on her plate instead of her brother.

26

With Christmas behind her and not wanting to spend the day at home, Joan decided to take a stroll through town without Peggy and Mark along, although in all honesty in the last few days she hadn't seen much of them. Not after Peggy had received her engagement ring for Christmas. They had been to busy making plans of a summer wedding. Maybe it's me and wanting to get away form all the big ado about a wedding, she thought, feeling a little envious towards her sister again.

Shopping she bought two outfits for her two nephews. Leaving the store she first thought about making a visit to her grandmother's Inn and having coffee, then laughing she changed her mind and headed for the large house sitting on Cherry Street. Knocking on the door, Maureen's mother answered. "Hello Mrs. Colby, is Maureen home?" Joan asked as she was invited in and Mrs. Colby informed her. "Yes. Maureen arrived late Christmas Eve. We were gone all day yesterday," explaining to Joan why Maureen hadn't called her.

"That's okay, I understand. I didn't try and call because we had a house full also, Jeff and Linda are home with the twins." She informed Mrs. Colby.

"Are they still here?" Mrs. Colby asked.

"Yes. I believe they are leaving after New Year's Day." Joan informed her, as Mrs. Colby added. "I was planning on taking Maureen up her breakfast. How would you like to do it?"

"Sure I won't wear it," Joan laughed, excepting the tray and headed up the stairs. The Colby home was a two story with long pillars and a winding porch that went clear to the back of the house. There were four bedrooms upstairs, and each bedroom consisted of patio doors and plenty of windows to look out over the surrounding view. Two of the bedrooms, had been turned into bed and breakfast rooms, as each bedroom had it's own bathroom. The bedrooms were done in colonial style; with overstuff feather beds, ruffles and warm colors to make the couples feel welcome.

Knocking on Maureen's door Joan yelled out to her. "Hey get up, we got things to do? Places to see?"

A sleepy voice answered back, "Who is it?"

"Who do you think?" Joan answered.

Still feeling jet lag, Maureen wasn't in the mood to play games. Yet there was something familiar about the person on the other side of her door. As it donned on her who it was, she let out a scream and bounced out of bed. Throwing the door open wide, she stared at the person on the other side who was holding a tray with fruit, grain coral, coffee, juice and toast. Maureen started to throw her arms around her, but stopped short as Joan stated. "I don't care to wear your breakfast," Laughing, Maureen took the tray and turning around walked over to the table sitting by the window. Sitting it down she turned back to Joan who had followed her into the room. "Am I aloud to touch you?" Maureen asked.

"Yes," Joan responded and the two long time friends hugged each other. As Maureen ate her breakfast the girls chatted aimlessly about Maureen's career, Joan's life being a sailor. They talked about Joan's mother getting therapy, about how she had changed. "At least you have a man in your life,' Maureen complained. "I don't even have that?" she stated, as Joan begin to talk about Steve and meeting him.

"Do I have to beg to see his picture?" Maureen interrupted as Joan was telling her about the trips to Chicago and the things she saw, the places he took her to.

"Yes," Joan laughed, reaching into her purse and pulling out her billfold. Handing the picture to Maureen, Joan told her. "I love him."

"WOW! This is Steve!" Maureen's eyes glued to the picture of the guy with a stupid grin on his face. He was very alluring in the picture, there was no shirt covering his chest. His physique neatly built. He was dressed in white pants, his shirt thrown over one shoulder, and his hat was cocked to one side. Maureen found herself taking a deep breath as she handed the picture back to Joan.

Feeling insecure Joan stated. "I know what you are thinking, what does he see in me?"

"Are you crazy? I was just wondering if he has a brother?" Maureen laughed then added. "I know what he saw in you, other than you being cute." Maureen insisted.

"What?"

"Your lousy attitude and dry sense of humor," Maureen stated as she said in a more serious tone. "Don't go cutting yourself down," as again she looked at the picture and saw the phenomenon look on Steve's face. This guy was in love; there was no doubt about that. "Was this taken before or after your little escapade?" She question Joan.

"Before. Why?"

"Oh nothing," Maureen sighed thinking that she would give anything to have a guy look at her like that. "You wrote that he went to college. Why didn't he become an officer? Isn't that the route they usually take?"

"I think so. He tells me that Crawford and him went out drinking one night and enlisted. Which I truly doubt they did. I do believe that someday he probably will be an officer though."

"You say that with some skepticism?" Maureen mentioned, as she watched Joan's expression change to sadness.

"Only about us. Officers are not aloud to date enlisted personnel, " Joan explained sighing deeply. She slowly added. "It really doesn't matter what he will be. I doubt if I will ever see Steve Tanner again."

"Why not?" Maureen asked.

"Because he called and I hung up on him?"

"Do I dare ask why?"

"Because I was jealous over some girl he knew," Joan explained, and then she went on to tell her about the bear. "I thought for sure someone was going to have to revive mom and dad. I still think dad is waiting to say something, for he has been rather cool towards me."

"You are probably exaggerating, your father wouldn't say a word to you, but on the other hand aren't you glad your mother has changed?" Maureen chuckled as she dressed and added. "We are going shopping."

They drove to Indianapolis to do their shopping. Maureen was out to buy out the stores Joan has the feeling as they went from one large department store to another. "Are you broke yet?" Joan asked, as they took a break and were eating a light lunch.

"Not yet, but almost," Maureen laughed as she added. "What are your plans for New Year's Eve?"

"I plan on doing some studying, and probably will baby sit for Jeff," Joan replied, casually.

"What! Jeff can find a babysitter, and you will not stick your nose in to books. Not while I am at home you won't," Maureen insisted, giving her friend a trying look. "I know for a fact that your parents always go to the club. I think it's time you show Wellsburg the new Joan Reddy?"

"New Joan Reddy? What do you mean?" Joan looked at Maureen cautiously and wondered what she had on her mind.

"As I recall you like to dance and from all presumptions of talking to you today, I know you have changed," Maureen stated with a mischief look to her expression. "So how would you like to knock this opinionated town off it's feet?"

"I am not sure if I know what you are getting at?" Joan expressed concerned as to what her friend might have in mind?

"Trust me," Maureen tipped her head back and laughed.

They walked from store to store. Joan believed she had never tried on so many clothes. "Would you mind telling me what we looking for?" Joan finally became discouraged with Maureen.

"A dress," Maureen stated, with a serious look on her face as she pondered over another rack of dresses as yet another sales person asked. "May I help you?"

27

Joan had decided to get dressed over at Maureen's. Her parents were upset that she wouldn't be going with them. Peggy was irritated that Joan wasn't wearing her uniform. As she started out the door, Jeff stopped her. "Why do I have this feeling that you are about to blow the roof off the Country Club?"

"I wouldn't dream of doing such a thing?" Joan answered trying to keep a straight face. "This is me we are talking about," She added, closing the door and walked out to her mother's car which she had borrowed. As she drove to Maureen's she recalled the other day and the endless stores that Maureen had dragged her through in Bloomington. "This is the final store," Joan had complained. "If we don't find something in here, I will wear my uniform to please Peggy."

"We will find it," Maureen insisted, as they walked up to the sales lady and Maureen told her. "I am looking for something slinky and sexy for my friend."

Joan was sure the woman had walked away laughing after muttering, "a size three I believe you said?"

Maureen's parents left for the club early leaving the two girls alone. Maureen had applied Joan's makeup and had fixed her hair as Joan sat in a chair speechless. "Okay you can put on your dress," Maureen told her, "and don't look in the mirror yet."

"Okay," Joan replied walking over to where the dress was hanging on the back of the closet door. Once the dress was on, Joan begged Maureen. "Can I look now?"

Maureen applying makeup to her own face turned, her mouth dropped open, and her eyes stared in astonishment. "You can look now," Maureen stammered to the effect that the dress with the no back and a low cut front with two very thin straps were holding it up around Joan's slim neck. The bodice and skirt were of a deep blue with metallic sliver blending in with the royal blue chiffon over light blue satin skirt. A split up the front extending just above the knees gave a glimpse of leg as Joan posed this way and that. "What do you think? Do I look military?" Joan laughed.

"I don't think so," Maureen answered not believing that this was her friend whom she had transformed into a girl. "I think you are going to knock a few country boys off their feet," Maureen commented as Joan turned and looked in the mirror hanging on the front of the closet door.

Joan stared at the person looking back at her. It was one time in her life that she thought she looked stunning, and looked older than her nineteen years.

Crawford had been driving while Tanner caught some sleep. This is the strangest thing we have done yet," Dan complained to himself. Dan had done a lot of arguing, trying to talk Steve out of this crazy notion of his. "What will I do while you spend time with Reddy?" Steve's answer had been. "From what I hear about this quaint little village, there will be plenty of things for you to do. Who knows you just might get lucky?" Steve expressed to his buddy.

"I doubt it. I don't think there are two of Reddy?" Dan mentioned as Steve turned and looked at him with a questionable stare. Which Dan gave a quick reply to? "Don't worry I am not about to step in to your territory."

"See that you don't," Steve spoke only he wasn't smiling.

"Boy! Are you sensitive this morning? Let me guess your old man pissed in your cereal bowl before we left?"

"Do you know he had her checked out?" Steve sighed.

"I heard a rumor to that fact," Dan stated glad to know that he hadn't been given away, since he was the one that had given Steve's brother the information on   Reddy.   "
So what does your father think of her?" Dan had to ask after a few minutes of silence.

"I think his words were," Steve expressed. "Well I guess I should be glad that she isn't your usual fly-by-night date."

"Sounds like she may have passed his approval," Dan made the effort to smile.

"Who are we kidding? Dad didn't make the quest to find out who she was to give his approval, he made the effort to find out because he didn't want his son to screw up again."

Waking Steve, Dan asked if he could drive. "Sure," Steve responded. It was after they made a stop that Tanner took over driving. Having traded seats getting back in the car Dan tilted his seat back and went to sleep. His words later when waking up were, "Where are we now?"

"Almost there," Steve answered, as he pointed to a magazine laying on the console between them as he turned on the overhead light so Dan could see the book.

"When did you start buying modeling magazine's?" Dan commented, picking up the book and looking at the front of it after Steve told him too.

"I haven't. But the name on the front cover caught my attention. Maureen Colby is a friend of Joan's. I remember Joan's grandmother saying that Joan had been spending a lot of time with her this past week." Steve explained.

Turing to the article and picture of Maureen Colby, Dan Crawford let out a wolf whistle. "Wow this is Reddy's friend, Maureen Colby?" Staring at the picture he couldn't believe his luck. "You say she is a friend of Joan's?" he repeated.

"Yes, quite a looker wouldn't you agree," Tanner grinned.

"That she is but aren't you forgetting something, the reasons why we are making this foolish trip to Wellsburg?"

" I haven't forgotten, trust me. But I thought maybe you could use a little excitement in your life," Tanner chuckled as a vision of Joan crossed his mind. No way was he ready to jeopardize their future on a pretty face. I wonder if she is expecting me?" Tanner chuckled again as he could imagine his reception.

On the way to the Country Club, Joan and Maureen had dropped Joan's mother car off at Joan's house. Getting back into Maureen's car her thoughts were miles away as a sadness filled her eyes. Maureen seeing her friend's expression said. "It's going to be okay, trust me?"

"What's going to be okay?" Joan stated, looking back at Maureen.

"Tonight," Maureen smiled.

"What are you going to do, go around and beg someone to dance with me?" Joan expressed, still not sure as to how she looked.

"I don't think I will have to. So did Steve call today?" Maureen questioned her,.

"No. I guess it's really over between us. I have watched the mail, set by the phone and still there hasn't been one word from him.

"Sorry, Now put a smile on that forlorn face," Maureen insisted as the ten minute drive to the Country Club seemed to have gone by rather fast. Stepping out of the car Joan's heart begin to race from the anticipation of walking into the Country Club, and the reception that she probably would receive.

The Wellsburg Club was packed with tourist, as well as home folks as the girls entered the club. Wellsburg took great pride in their club. The décor more than said it all with the crystal chandeliers, the highly polished wood floors, and mirrored walls, with frosted floral designs. The grand entrance that led down to the main part of the club was decorated with potted poinsettia's sitting here and there. The palm trees and shrubbery that added their splendor to the scene. Strobe light of different color reflected off the dance floor and spotlighted the ladies and gentleman in their finery.

Jeff who had been watching for his sister, wanted to see the reaction of the people when Maureen and her made their grand entrance. He didn't have to wait long as he turned and saw the two girls entered the main entrance to the ballroom. "I think you better had watched this," Jeff spoke to his dad who was sitting next to him.

'What?" Tom answered, to the loud noise and music.

'Turn around and looked towards the entrance," Jeff smiled, for his sister definitely looked stunning as she moved down the steps and towards their table. Not only was Tom Reddy looking at his daughter but also several young men were taking note of the two girls who were making a grand entrance. Dave Wright being one of them wished that Betsy would take a hike and he could spend some time getting to know the person he knew was no longer an iceberg!

"I think they approve," Maureen chuckled as she walked along side of Joan.

"Who?' Joan questioned.

"The country boys," Maureen laughed as they neared Joan's parent's table.

"Keep cool," Maureen whispered as she left Joan to join her parents who were sitting at the next table. "I believe you two just pulled a show stopper." Maureen's dad smiled.

"Yes, I think so. Do you think they remembered who we were?" Maureen smiled.

"No, but they are thinking," John Colby laughed.

At the Reddy table, Tom Reddy rose and said to his daughter. "As I recall you like to dance?"

Laying down her purse she accepted her father's hand. As they moved towards the dance floor, Joan asked. "Dad where is Gram's?"

"She didn't feel like coming tonight," Tom explained, not looking at his daughter so she wouldn't see the expression on his face, and know that he was lying.

"Is she okay?" Joan asked with concern.

"She is fine, she just wanted to relax. Surly you remember that tomorrow is going to be another big day for her?"

"I remember," Joan answered and added. "You're a pretty smooth dancer for an old guy."

"Old guy! I have you to know I still have movement in this old body as you put it. Just wait until a fast song comes along. I'll show you who is old?" Tom laughed.

As her father kept her on the dance floor for several songs, she realized it was him who gave Jeff, Peggy and her the rhythm to dance. Cause as he had stated he could still move to a fast song, even though he had to beg for a rest after the third fast song.

Maureen and Joan's seats never got a chance to warm as they were kept on their feet dancing to one song after another. Joan was returning back to her table, when Dave Wright walked up to her. "Would you like to dance?"

"Sure," Joan replied not wanting to appear rude as she followed Dave Wright to the dance floor as she was thinking. I would like to eat before midnight.

"I have been reading quite a lot about you," Dave started, once they were on the dance floor and dancing to a slow song.

"Should I ask whether it was good or bad," Joan replied.

"Different, I would say," Wright laughed. "So is the guy here?"

"What guy?"

"The one who branded you?" His look cynical as he laughed.

She wanted to slap the smug look off his face, but a scene she didn't need. "And I thought your manner's would improve?" Joan stared at him.

"Not hardly," Wright grinned.

"So does Betsy like the new you?" She changed the questions to him.

"Probably, although she's not very happy with me at the moment. She was expecting a ring and didn't get it. So how long are you home?"

"Until the fifth." she stated, as she asked. "How about, how long do you have home?"

"I leave tomorrow," Dave expressed with a sad puppy look, as he added. "I guess that means you and I won't be able to have that date?"

"Gee it must be my lucky day," she said and couldn't resist smiling at him.

"But we have tonight? Why don't you meet me later at a motel?" Dave suggested.

"Excuse me! I may have made one mistake, but trust me I am not about to make another one." then stopping from dancing with him, she turned and left Dave Wright standing alone on the dance floor.

28

Maude Reddy had checked everything twice to make sure her home looked just so. Then she glanced at her watch about the same time that the doorbell rang. Assuming who it was, she remarked as she answered the security call box. "Right on time," she said to herself as she asked. "May I help you?" She inquired of the two young men standing on her porch.

"Mrs. Reddy, it's Steve Tanner."

As Maude Reddy opened her door, she was greeted by two very nice looking young men and as she welcomed them into her home, she had the pleasure of seeing the irresistible grin that Joan had told her about as the young man with the deep piercing eyes asked. "Is Joan here?"

"No she has already left for the dance," Maude answered, as Steve Tanner realized this is not quite what he was expecting Joan's grandmother to look like. He was expecting someone with a little more full figure with an apron tied around her waist...Instead he met a lady who was very prim and perfect like the living room they were standing in. Everything in its place. The furniture a perfect example of a lady who respected antiques.

The room more a show place than seating for comfort. It wasn't until walking into the kitchen that Tanner began to relax. Off to one corner the room had become an office, at the other end of the kitchen was the usual stove, refrigerator, dishwasher, and etc. and as you looked further to the side of this area was a spacious sun room,

As the two young men took seats at the round oak table, Mrs. Reddy served them hot coffee, and cinnamon rolls. It was at this time that Dan Crawford rebuked the idea of going to a dance. "Dance?" You didn't tell me anything about a dance? I thought we were just coming here to visit Reddy?"

"Do I look stupid?" Steve replied, as Maude again saw the irresistible grin, but even with the lighthearted mood of this young man, Maude sensed the authority that he reeked of. It was his mannerism and the way he carried himself.

Maude was brought back to the conversation, as the young man called Dan, continued to argue about going to the dance. "Since you didn't tell me about a dance? You wouldn't be too disappointed if I didn't go," Dan insisted as Maude took a seat at the table and enjoyed the thought of having to fine looking young gentlemen sitting at her table.

"Look at it this way old buddy, you don't have a choice," Steve lightly warned him.

"So that is why you insisted I bring my tux?"" Crawford groaned again.

"Yelp," Tanner laughed. As Dan added. "I should have known there was a catch to coming here?"

Begging for a break Joan was about to take her seat when Maureen tapped her on the shoulder. "Did you see what just walked in? They are definitely not local?" She spoke of the two young men getting ready to step down the steps that led to the ballroom. They both were in tuxedos, but it wasn't the clothes it was the way they carried themselves, and lo and behold Maude had her arms looped through their bent elbows.

Turning towards the entrance to where Maureen was directing her attention, Joan's mouth dropped and her heart stop beating for a few seconds from holding her breath. Then when it did return it was pounding in her ears. "Steve?" her voice a whisper as she glanced at her father.

"Well don't just stand here girl. Go get him," her dad said giving her a light shove.

"We will never find her," Crawford complained to the place that was packed with people.

"Just look for a short sailor," Steve laughed.

"She is not in uniform," Maude chuckled, watching the two young men search the crowd for Joan.

"Great, we won't find her," Crawford complained again.

"Want to make a bet," Steve smiled, as he saw Joan making her way through the crowd, as least he thought it was her, as his eyes became hypnotized to her appearance. The low wolf whistle slowly left his lips as she stepped closer.

"Reddy?" Crawford said, stunned by Reddy's appearance. His eyes glued too her also. For this was not the spitfire, tomboy that usually was ready to take on a good fight with his friend.

"I. . .I think so," Tanner answered, his voice a little husky.

Maude had taken a step back from the two young men as her granddaughter laughing and crying at the same time called out. "Steve. . .!" Then she was in his arms, her face tilted up to look at him. The dark fathom eyes held hers as questions were answered without words spoken, the little boy grin planted firmly on his face. His look of approvable bestowed upon her. "You defiantly look different?" he mentioned not being able to take his eyes off of her. Tanner didn't care if there were plenty of eyes on them, as he lowered his face, and kissed her.

"How? When?" Joan stammered as he released her, and the little boy grin remained on his face, as he spoke to her. "Can we discuss this later?"

As Joan was about to answer, Dan Crawford spoke. "You talk to her Tanner. I am going to find the bar."

Maude still standing near them made the suggestion with a chuckle, "Would you like to meet Joan's parents?'

Releasing her with difficulty Tanner shook his head in agreement to Maude's suggestion. "You do remember how to dance?" Steve asked, taking her hand and letting her lead him to where her folks were sitting. "I can keep rhythm," she replied as they walked along with Maude following them.

"Kathryn, you need to turn around and look towards the entrance," Tom stated to his wife, as he watched Joan and the young man with her walk towards them. One thing about it, Tom thought, they do make a striking couple. He couldn't recall when his oldest daughter looked more beautiful.

Walking up to her parents, Joan was saved by introductions, as Maude introduced Steve to Joan's family.. "This is my son Tom Reddy, his wife Kathryn, their daughter Peggy and her finance Mark Greene, His parents, Gladys and Ken Greene, her brother Jeff, and his wife Linda, her parents Captain Miller, and his wife Ruth, Their daughter Jill is sitting at home babysitting with the twins."

After meeting her family and guest, Joan took Steve's hand and told him. "There is someone else I would like for you to meet. Then she led him to where Maureen and her family were sitting. Maureen gave her look of approvable the minute Joan arrived at her table. "I think you got their attention," she whispered, as Joan said. "This is my best friend, Maureen Colby."

"Hello," Steve replied, thinking the girl with the creamy complexion and dark eyes was striking, but knew she couldn't hold a candle to the spitfire standing beside him.

Joan became the girl that Wellsburg didn't know. She became alive as she moved to the music and to the one that could set her heart afire. The girls who use to snub her were now breaking their necks to speak to her, and to get a closer look at the guy whom Joan was with.

"Well it looks like both our daughters have found their mates," Kathryn remarked as Tom and her went to dance.

"It would seem that way," Tom responded, as he again looked at Steve and Joan.

"They defiantly stole the show," Tom commented also, although he wasn't too sure about Steve Tanner and the affair he was having with his daughter?

"I would agree," Kathryn smiled as she added. "I believe he does love her."

"Yes, I guess you could say that, after hearing a bear declare it," Tom replied, rather strict, as Kathryn looked up at him and saw the disprovable look on his face. "I thought you would be happy for her?" Kathryn stated.

"Why?" Tom replied, shaking his head at her and thinking that Joan was out for one huge fall.

Dan Crawford had found the bar with out too much trouble and getting a drink, he had turned to look the crowd over. His eyes stopped their roaming as they fell upon the dark haired girl moving in his direction.

She was more than just striking with her cream colored skin and dressed in what he assumed was the latest fashion. She moved with the grace of a cat seeking prey. Pulling himself to a straighter position, he was hoping to become that prey.

Maureen had one objective in mind as she walked across the room toward the bar area, to know what's-his-name a little better. "You lost sailor?" she spoke in a soft demure tone as she stepped up beside the guy who had come in with Steve Tanner.

"Not any more," Dan declared with a smile, showing white even teeth. His steel gray eyes lighted with laughter as he looked at the stunning girl in the red evening dress.

"I think we have mutual friends here?" Maureen continued to tantalize him with her soft voice.

"All depends on who you are referring to?" Dan replied as she mesmerized him.

"Joan Reddy and Steve Tanner," Maureen let him know as she continued to make eye contact with him.

"I am sure you don't care to continue this conversation about who we know, or who we don't know for that matter," Dan stated as he added. "Care to dance?"

"Would love to," Maureen answered as he took her hand and began to lead her toward the dance floor. "The model?" Dan spoke as it hit him who she was. He almost had second thoughts, for he didn't care to be involved with anyone who would be vain about their looks, and since he wasn't vain about his own looks he suddenly felt that anyone looking this good probably admired herself immensely."

"I would prefer to be called Maureen," she replied, hoping that he wasn't going to disappear as he made it quite obvious that he was about to change his mind.

"Dan Crawford," his voice sounded different as he decided, "What the hell was a few days and not knowing anyone other than Steve and Joan? Why not take Tanner's advice and enjoy!"

In the days that followed Joan and Maureen showed Steve and Dan the quaint village of Wellsburg Taking them on a sleigh ride through the countryside, the wind rustling through the ice laden trees, the ground covered in a crust of white snow.

It became a night of winter wonderland as they snuggled under heavy quilts. Their laughter rang through the trees as the two young men serenaded them with songs.

The two sailors from the big city were taken back in time as they ice-skated on a frozen pond to the music from a carnival arcade. They drank hot chocolate and ate fried donuts with the blaze of a bonfire for warmth. They bobsledded down hills that took them screaming and yelling around trees. They built snowmen, made angels and had snowball fights.

Sitting before the fireplace in the early morning hours at her grandmothers house, Joan and Steve were finally alone. "I am glad Dan thought to bring along a camera. I don't think we could make any one believe where we have been just by telling them," Steve commented as Joan sat at his feet.

"Have you really enjoyed being here?" She questioned, since they really hadn't spent much time alone together.

"Immensely.. Your grandmother has made Dan and I feel very welcome. She is a great lady," he added, complimenting his hostess for the days he had been in Wellsburg. "As a matter of fact your whole family has been rather pleasant to be around. I take it your mother and you have settled your differences?"

"We have. There has been a major change in her," Joan remarked.

"I had a long talk with your brother," Steve mentioned next. "I take it you two are very close?"

"We are," she admitted turning to look up at him as she placed her hands on his knees, and rested her chin on top of them.. "So what did my dear brother have to say about me?" Steve had to take a deep breath as she looked at him, her eyes competing with the fire in the fireplace, "That I should make love to you until the dawn comes," he managed with a husky voice.

Laughing softly she replied, "I doubt if Jeff said that?"

"But it does sound interesting," Steve added.

"Maybe," She spoke softly, then laughing, she added. "I should be angry with you. I enjoyed the bear, and so did everyone else."

"I take it you weren't alone when the bear began to talk?" His eyes danced with laughter as he could almost imagine everyone trying to avoid looking at one another.

"What do you think? It was Christmas and everyone was opening gifts."

"Sorry," he apologized with a laugh.

"Sorry you say. I thought I was going to have to revive everyone in the family room after the first sentence, and that included me," she told him, as she listens to his laughter.

You wouldn't be up to parking?" he asked when he could stop laughing, he lay back against the pillows behind him and pulled her up closer to him. "Tomorrow," she yawned, curling up next to him. Soon the two young people were asleep.

29

Rising early from force of habit, Steve walked into Mrs. Reddy's kitchen in search of the coffee he had smelled brewing as he had showered and dressed. To his surprise, he found Joan's father sitting at the kitchen table. "This is the only place I can find peace and quiet," Tom remarked. "Plus I figured if I wanted to see my daughter before she leaves today now was as good a chance as any." He looked at the person who had taken up her time in the last four days.

Tom Reddy had this habit of taking first impressions of a person. Usually his perceptions of a person were correct. Shaking Steve Tanner's hand, he had found his grip firm and there was a sense of authority on him, even if he did appear to be arrogant, he recalled looking at Steve as he took a cup from the tree mug.

Feeling Joan's father on him, Steve wondered if this was what Mike had meant when he told him once. "Little brother, you are going to meet the father of one of your conquests? Don't be too surprised if he's not impressed with your relationship with his daughter." I think I have met him Mike! He continued to think as Joan's father continued to speak. "I believe you are more involved with my daughter than I would care for you to be?" His tone rather sharp, his look of disapproval staring at him.

Steve Tanner's fierce eyes were defying Tom's as he told him. "Whatever is between Joan and I, I believe is of our own choosing, sir."

Meeting him with his own deep blue eyes and not looking down, Tom Reddy answered, "what you think and what I feel are two different views. I know my daughter and how she was raised. I am just wondering how much pressure was put on her?"

"None that I am aware of. The decision was totally hers to make," Steve assured him.

"You expect me to believe that, when the two of you have known each other only for a short time?" Skepticism was in her father's voice as he looked at Steve.

"Guess sir, you will have to?" The fierce eyes did not waver, as he lifted the cup of coffee to take a drink.

To his arrogance, his voice stern but not harsh, Tom Reddy fought to get a hold on his temper. "I don't have to believe anything. Nor do I have to accept it?" Then with warning he added, "I don't want to see her hurt. . .For believe me, this world would not be big enough for the both of us!"

"Sir I love your daughter and I do plan on marrying her. Maybe not next week or even next year, but mark my word, she will be my wife," Steve declared, not wanting to make Joan's father his enemy

"Wouldn't want me to hold you to that?" Tom remarked as he rose to pour himself more coffee and didn't wait for an answer, as he asked. "You ready for more?" as he held up the coffee pot to pour more coffee. .

Steve hoped he meant coffee as he let out a deep sigh now that Tom Reddy's stare was no longer on him, and as he was about to answer yes, when Joan walking into the kitchen saved him.

"Good morning dad," Joan spoke walking up to her father and started to kiss him on the cheek. Turning away from her, Tom Reddy asked his daughter, "Did you forget where home was?"

"No," she looked at her father with a questionable stare. Moving over to the table she took a cup from the coffee tree. "I hope there is enough for me," she said, walking back over to where her father was standing with the coffee pot still poised in his hand.

"There is," Tom replied, as she held out her cup to be filled.

"I need a cigarette," Steve mentioned as he rose from where he was sitting and moved past Joan and her father but not before whispering to her. "He's all yours." as she took a seat at the table.

With Steve gone, Joan asked her father. "How do you like him, dad?"

"Time will tell, wouldn't you say?" Tom said taking his seat again at the table.

"I love him, dad," Joan said to her father's doubts.

"You don't have a clue as to what love is all about," Tom spoke harshly, " Love, for all you two know about love is to find a motel and spend a few nights together. You seem to forget that I was in the Navy. Let me tell you about his love. The minute you are no longer around to please him, someone else will."

She had never stood up to her father before, but she wasn't ready to deal with any shallow remarks about Steve. Especially when the person speaking didn't know him. ""Excuse me, I think you are wrong and whatever is between Steve and I, is of our own choosing. I am on my own. I figure whatever mistakes I make I will have to live with them."

"Hold it young lady! This is your father you are talking to, I may be old but I know a thing or two about what that young man is thinking! Don't think for one minute he will remember you after a year and you are no longer around.

Again she said. "I think you are wrong, Steve loves me. Plus we both know what is a head of us." . She had always been open with her father, and she wasn't thinking of the consequences when she added. "I am taking birth-control pills."

"You are what?" Tom Reddy grated, his face turning beet red.

She was almost afraid to repeat her self, as she had never seen her father so angry before. "I am taking birth-control pills," she repeated slowly.

"Who's wild idea was that, your boyfriends? Surly not yours, for you were to damn green to even know what they were for before you join the military." Tom retorted.

"My friends from boot camp recommended them," Joan flatly replied.

"Am I supposed to be relieved to know this?" Tom stated. "Well you certainly have proven your mother right?" Tom said still angry with her.

Biting back tears, she couldn't believe this was her father she was talking to. He uses to be fair in his opinions, and didn't judge a person so cruel. Looking directly at him, she accused. "I never thought you would stoop to call me names, that you always listen to the other persons side. I love Steve, and nothing you say will change my feelings for him." With that said she started to rise from the table, but her father stopped her with his hand being placed on her arm.

"When you leave today don't bother coming back home until you come to your senses." Tom flared, looking at her.

"Then I guess its goodbye dad," she said, holding her head up and looking directly at him, as she added. "I am sorry you feel this way."

Having said their goodbyes, the three sailors were ready to leave. Saying goodbye wasn't so hard after all, Joan surmised. Again she had promised Peggy she would write. Her grandmother had made her promise to call when she got back to the base. Her father did not bother to see her off, and her mother had promised that she would talk to him after she had said goodbye, and wished them a safe trip.

Once they were on their way, Steve asked, "How did things go with your father after I left the room?"

"They went," Joan replied, turning her face to look out the window, and hope Steve didn't see the tears that seem to continue every time she thought about her dad and his behavior. It was so unlike him to accuse her of being the names that her mother had once called her. It was as if her parents had traded places. Her mother now was charming and accepting, where her father was unreasonable, and rejecting.

"Have I lost you," Steve questioned her silence and the forlorn look on her face.

"Not really," she turned and looked at him. It was now or never, she decided as she asks. "What would you do if I was to become pregnant?"

"Is there something I need to know?" Steve asked keeping his eyes glued to the road, his knuckles turning white from gripping the steering wheel so hard as he waited for Joan's reply.

"No," she finally answered after a long pause, her eyes stationed straight ahead.

"Good, so why the question?" Steve asked, slowly letting out his breath.

"Oh just curious," she slowly answered as she heard Dan in the back seat starting to go into a coughing fit as they waited for Steve to come up with an answer.

"I thought we settled this conversation about a month ago?" Steve finally spoke after drawing a quick breath.

"We probably did, but I had the question put to me today?" she stated still not looking at him.

"By your father?" Steve asked, glancing over at her.

"Sort of," she replied.

. " I thought we understood where we were headed? That our careers were first and foremost important to us?" Steve stated, hoping she would see his viewpoint.

Looking at him and trying to figure out where she stood with him, she asked without thinking. "Tell me again why I am sleeping with you?" pausing for a few minutes before she added. "Damn, I keep for getting that I am a challenge, but obviously I am not that anymore, am I?"

Crawford was about ready to choke to death in the backseat of the car and Steve almost lost control of the car. "Do you think we could discuss this when I am not driving?" Steve stated once he was over the shock of her last comment. and to change the subject, Steve asked Dan. "Where are we suppose to meet Maureen in Chicago?"

"At the Hotel Continental on Michigan Avenue," Dan informed them.

"Is she making reservations for all of us?" Steve then asked.

"I think so," Dan commented, as Joan turned around and looked at him. "I thought we were going to the base?"

"Nope been a change of plans, Maureen staying over in Chicago for the night, and I thought Steve, you and I could join her." Dan informed her.

"Well obviously Steve and you made the plans without consulting me?" Joan declared crossing her arms across her chest once she turned back around to face the front of the car.. How dare him to think I would just drop everything and go to a motel? She thought, again taking a glance in Steve's direction.

Glancing at Joan and seeing her pouting face, he inquired. "Am I getting some of your attitude here?"

"No," she flatly stated, and for the next several hours it was quiet amongst the three people on their way to Chicago.

Once in the room at the hotel, Steve was ready to settle the score of their careers, and their lives together. "Look I don't know what your father said to you, but you have been sulking every since we left that damn quaint village.

"Why should you care at all about what I think? You will be leaving soon and God only knows when we will see each other again." She stammered dropping the tote bag she brought with her in the nearest chair. Then taking off her coat, her eyes caught the ring on her left hand, third finger. The blue sapphire ring had been Steve's grandmother, and as he had slipped it on her hand New Years Eve, he had told her. "For the blue of your eyes," Her eyes and his irresistible grin what a combination for love. Was her father right? Did they really know what love was, what lie ahead of them? "You sure you wouldn't want to take this ring back?" She asked him, making the move to remove it.

"Why? Why would I want it back?" he questioned her motive.

"Because you don't give a person something this expensive if you don't plan on seeing them again?"

"Guess that should tell you something," Steve stated, walking towards her. Reaching her he tipped her face upward to look at him as soul-searching kiss followed. As he released her, looking down at her he saw her mood hadn't changed as tears slipped down her face and crying she told him, "You can not see me anytime that you want. We are in the military, our chances of being together are very slim."

"Baby I may be in the Navy, but they don't own me. Especially where my personal life is concerned," Steve declared.

"I don't believe I am worth a court martial," she came back with as the fierce eyes held her attention. Then his eyes changed and a playful look filled them. "You may have a point there?" he said cheerfully hoping to change the gloomy mood that was beginning to come over them.

"See didn't I tell you so," she said, not seeing any humor in the topic.

With laughter in the corner of his eyes, the fierce look gone, he began to chuckle. "You wouldn't be willing to make a trip to Florida and remind me of why I would take a risk for a court martial?"

"Why wait until Florida?" she replied slowly, her eyes now looking up at him.

The magnetism that always seems to pull them together was in full force to attack their senses as they tried not to think about the time they had left together.

31

Dropping her one sea bag, suitcase, garment bag, and her books down in her new assigned room, she looked around. Not much changed. She thought as she looked around the room. Well some she decided, the room was larger and the desk was no longer sitting in the middle of the room, but along the walls at the end of the racks. The lockers still lined one wall, and the color still remained the same, gray?

I wonder who my other roommates are? Since no one was in the room when she had arrived. She took locker four, and beds four, which put her on top of three. After unpacking and making up her bed, she left the room and walked down the hall to call her grandmother. It was several rings before she heard her grandmother accept the call. "Hi Gram's she started with. "I am settled into my new room. Logan and I are no longer together. She is still on the third floor and I am on the second. Haven't met my new room mates yet."

"Is Steve still next door to you?" Maude then asked.

"Yes," Joan replied.

"I had a long talk with your father a short while ago, he is ready to say he is sorry for not saying good bye to you."

"Is he?" Joan spoke with a hurt tone to her voice.

"Honey, you just have to remember that he is still trying to get over the fact that he is not number one anymore," Maude lightly chuckled.

"Dad will always be number one to me," Joan stated, biting her lip to hold back the tears, as she added. "But Gram's he told me to never come back home?"

"Oh poo, he was just angry that you have taken matters into your own hands and somewhere he lost the little girl that you once were."

"Should I give him a call?" Joan asked next.

"Why don't you give him a week or so before you call," Maude lightly stated.

"I can do that," Joan replied, thinking that her father was still was angry with her. "Gram's I love you, and I hope you are not to disappointed in me?"

"Heavens no, why would I be disappointed in you?" Maude questioned, although she had some idea as to where the question was leading.

"Steve?" was all Joan said back to her.

"Do you love him?" Maude questioned her.

"Yes," Joan said with out conviction as she reminded her grandmother, "Dad said that mother was right about my leaving Wellsburg?"

"That I know, and he is sorry for saying it." Maude told her, as she added. "I know he hurt you, but please try and forgive him. He loves you and he still cares about what happens to you."

"Gram's I have to go. Someone is waiting to use the phone." Joan lied, as she didn't want to continue to talk about her father.

"Okay, but just you remember, I am still here for you if you need to talk to someone?"

"Okay," Joan replied, before letting her go.

It was much later Sunday evening that she met the other three girls in the room. All three were in the engineman classes. Maxwell and Cramer were fresh out of boot camp. Maxwell was a tall, thin, black girl with delicate features. She had light brown skin and was very pretty. Cramer, on the other hand, was white and snooty. The third person was Jackson, who also was black. She was about five feet, and stocky built. Jackson had strike for school, was a petty officer coming from San Diego, and was complaining as she slipped off her coat. "What was I thinking to have left California in the middle of winter?

"You haven't seen nothing yet," Maxwell declared. "It gets much worse."

"Where you from, sister?" Jackson asked Maxwell,"

"Chicago. But I have been in Florida for the past nine weeks." Then Maxwell turned to Reddy and Cramer. "Where you two from?" Cramer answered, New York." Reddy told them. "Indiana," as she asked, looking at Jackson. "Where you from?"

"L.A." Jackson laughed, as she took note of the smallest girl in the room, and asked. "What are you taking in school?"

"Engineman." Reddy answered, as Jackson declared. "But you are so tiny. Do you think you can do the work?"

"Trust me, I don't think my size will be my problem but I am not sure about my mouth," Reddy laughed.

"Why do you talk a lot?" Cramer stated, looking at her with disgust.

"No, I have problems with my attitude." She continued to laugh, looking at Maxwell and Jackson and asked. "Have you started school yet?"

"Not yet, but we have been told we will start on Tuesday."

"Let me clue you in on a few instructors. Hamilton doesn't believe girls should be in engineman classes, and neither does Miller, who is the worse. Foster, although he has a voice that barks, he is okay. The best thing to do is to take notes and listen. They are tough, but if you are determine to be an engineman, they will back you up."

"So how are you doing?" Cramer asked her in a doubtful tone.

"I am staying at the top of the class," Joan informed her.

"Would you give us help if we need it?" Maxwell then asked.

"Sure." Joan replied.

Cramer, who had been looking Maxwell and Jackson over rather sternly, finally had her say to them. " Well don't expect help from me and you two better stay away from my things?"

"Don't worry girl, you have nothing we want," Jackson informed her.

As if ignoring her, Cramer went on. "Don't drown yourselves in perfume. I am allergic to it.

"Wouldn't think of it," Maxwell remarked, looking at Jackson and Reddy.

"Take it you two weren't in the same company at boot camp?" Jackson remarked, looking at Maxwell.

"Thank God," Maxwell murmured as Jackson walked over to Cramer. "You see these stripes?" pointing to her sleeves. "They say I out rank you. I won't give you any trouble, as long as you don't dish out any. Get my meaning?"

Trying to change the tension in the room, Reddy asked Jackson. "Were you on a ship in San Diego?"

"Honey, I was on shore duty which I don't recommend. I was on a tug." Then she proceeded to tell them about her experiences. "We were pulling up to one of the ships to unload their bilges. I being new was getting initiated. I was told to stand in the bow and keep an eye on the barge we were pulling up to. Little did I know that the tug master had a trick up his sleeve? Here I am hooking up the bilge hose, when wham! I was hit with everything. Garbage slime and you name it. It was bad enough that I smelled to high heaven, but I was told to clean up the mess." She exaggerated with expressions.

"I would have died," Reddy laughed.

"Don't think I didn't," Jackson went on to tell them about walking in to the men's restroom. "We had been on a paint detail painting every thing blue on the pier. It was extremely hot, and I think the fumes were getting to all of us. Well anyway, I had to go to the bathroom. Without thinking to look at the sign on the door I went through I walked into the men's restroom. You should have seen the surprised look on the guys faces in there," laughing she gave a few details. "When I came back out, the petty officer in charge asked me if I enjoyed the view? I told him that I had seen better."

"How did you make petty officer/" Maxwell wanted to know.

"Oh girl, that was easy, I passed the test." Jackson answered, still laughing, and then added. "By doing my job and keeping my nose clean," pausing she added. "Well most of the time."

"I think my brother is a little more colorful than you about making rank." Joan smiled, as the three girls had taken seats on the floor and continued to talk.

"Is your brother in the Navy also?" Jackson inquired.

"No, he is a master gunnery sergeant with the LAV, (Light Armory Division} in the Marines He is stationed in North Carolina right now, He's married and got a set of twins that are just a month old.

Cramer, who had climbed in to her rack when the other three had started talking, was beginning to complain. "Why don't you three shut up? I am trying to get some sleep up here."

"We will when taps are piped, until then just ignore we are down here." Jackson answered. "Here I will turn out the lights," Jackson added, as she got up and went over by the door and turned off the lights.

"You know, I think she does have a point about sleeping." Joan spoke softly. "We do have to rise early in the morning," As if agreeing with her, Maxwell stood up also, yawning, she said. "I have to agree, I am sleepy.

"Well not me, I am still on California time." Jackson informed them, as she picked up her coat and purse. "Do you know if they have a petty officer's club around here?"

"It should say on your map where it is," Reddy stated, as she climbed above Maxwell to get into her rack.

"I hope you don't twist and turn in your sleep?" Maxwell stated, as Reddy flipped first one way and then another, and answered her. "I don't know I am usually asleep."

"Will you two shut-up?" Cramer complained again.

"Oh throw a pillow over your head," Maxwell told her, as a pillow came flying her way. "Thank you, I was wandering where I was going to get another pillow from," Maxwell declared, as she flung the pillow down to the foot of her rack and told Cramer, "If you want it, you've got to come and get it!"

Instructor Foster taking his usual pose in front of his desk had a rare smile on his face. "Okay people," he started the lecture. "You will need to know the piping system of your ship. Since you will be on different ships, I assume that you will take the time to learn the piping designated for that ship. For now we will assume this piping route and you will do the diagrams according to it. Fresh water-blue, salt water-red, steam-white, fuel-yellow, and oil-green. I want to know where the hook ups meet. Whether it is for fuel, air or water. I want to know where the strainers are located. This should keep you busy for a while. Oh! Don't forget the steam traps, and drains." Then still smiling, he said, "Welcome back."

"Damn, I hate these pop quizzes," several mumbled as they picked up pencils to answer the questions on the papers in front of them. Patrolling the aisle, Instructor Foster could almost pick out the ones who would still be in class after their big test on Friday. They were halfway through the course and some of the sailors were still dragging their feet. This week would be one of the roughest weeks they had to deal with. It consisted of recalling everything they had learned so far.

Staying in her room for the week, Reddy kept her nose stuck to her books. She saw Tanner only in the mess hall. He too was sticking to his books, since he was being tested all week. There were no plans made for the weekend, as they both had watches to stand.

It was Thursday, and evening meal, as usual she was sitting with Tanner and Crawford. "Where is Reed?" She questioned Tanner, since he usually was sitting with them.

"In TPU, he dropped out of the Nuclear Program." Tanner informed her with disgust.

"You sound disappointed?" Reddy questioned him.

"I probably am. I hate seeing him throw away a good career." Tanner added, as he looked at her. "Not only did he drop out of the nuclear program, he married White over the holidays."

"Really!" Reddy said with surprise. "Well I am glad he took on the responsibility to be a father to his kid."

Looking from Reddy to Tanner, Crawford commented, "I wouldn't touch that my friend," he told Tanner.

But ignoring Crawford, Tanner was ready to argue with Reddy. "White should have taken precautions?"

"So should have Reed," Reddy disagreed with him. "Why should it always be the female to make sure nothing happens?" she went on.

"Look out, she is setting you up," Crawford insisted, continuing to warn his friend.

Reddy had raised Tanner's attitude and still ignoring Crawford, he declared. "Because you are the ones that take the pill. Not us."

"What!" Reddy glared at him, and uttering in a low tone she told him. "Go to hell!" Then rising she left the table.

"Looks like you need to pull your shoe out of your mouth," Crawford lightly chuckled.

"Glad you are finding this amusing" Tanner groaned, looking at Crawford.

"Well you can just be lucky she's not pregnant," Crawford stated, but not laughing any longer.

"Trust me, I am." Tanner stated, as he remember his father's warning. "You screw this career up and you will no longer be a part of this family."

They had been back in school one week when Matthews showed up in class. "Where have you been?" Reddy asked, standing beside him in the break room.

"On leave, I took fifteen days, Jenny and I were married over the holidays," he told her. Seeing the expression on her face, he laughed as he added, "Guess who else is married? Your friend Logan, she married Matt Thomas. They are living down the hall from Jenny and I."

"I was wondering why I hadn't seen her around," she mentioned to Matthews as she thought to herself. Did I miss something? Damn there must have been a blue light special on weddings this holidays? "Joan---Joan did you hear me?" Matthews questioned her.

"Yes I heard you," she snapped turning to look out the window.

"Gee I can't wait to tell Jenny how happy you are for us?" Matthews complained.

"I am happy for you," she declared, turning and looking at him again. "I am just sorry I missed the weddings," she lied.

"Sorry you missed them, or wished one of them had been yours?" Matthews insinuated sort of smiling.

"Stupid I'm not," she asserted, realizing that she had probably made him angry, as she saw the expression change on his face. So what, she was here for a career, not a husband! Turning she left him rather than have to explain her answer.

Instructor Foster stood before them and insisted they had better be alert for the next few months. "This is your critical stage," he warned, as he begin calling out names for those reporting to the trouble-shooting class and telling them where to go. Troubleshooting was just as the class indicated. They had eight engines to break down, find the problem, and put them back together again. Instructor Tucker put the two girls in the class with Mr. Cole. "You have engine number three. What I want from you is the problem, and how to fix it? Oh and to help you move quickly, you will be timed?"

"Okay girls. So we won't get this wrong, let me do the work," Cole stated, telling them to stand back and watch.

"Wrong," Reddy objected. "I am not standing back and watching nothing. I know quite a bit about engines, and I am not going to let you mess me up. I think all three of us should work together. You know, teamwork?"

As they started in on the engine, Reddy heard him mutter, "great! Two stupid broads to work with," and if that wasn't bad enough, they were on the third try, when the instructor called time, even though Reddy had told Cole, "there is nothing wrong with the engine," that resembled a ship engine, only in smaller size. "Is there a problem here?" Instructor Tucker questioned, walking up to mock engine three.

"I say we have a valve problem." Mr. Cole stated, and Ms. Reddy says there is nothing wrong with the engine."

"You should listen to Ms. Reddy. She is correct," Instructor Tucker stated is a voice that only the three heard before he continued on to the next three people. "Thanks smart ass, you just lost us a point," Cole spoke to Reddy in a low gritting voice.

"Your welcome," Reddy replied, as they were all told to move down one engine. Again it was tearing the engine down and making repairs. Instead of letting her ego prove Cole that he was wrong about most of the engines, she made suggestion so that all three could agree on the problem.

What really through them off was when Instructor Tucker threw pop questions at them? "This tells me who knew what, when you were troubleshooting the engines." Then looking around the class, he chose Ms. Brooks to start with. "During the compression stroke in a 4-stroke Otto cycle engine, assume that a piston moves seven-eights of the total distance from BDC to TDC, what is the compression ratio?

"6 to1." Ms. Brooks spoke with out hesitation.

"Very good, Ms. Brooks. Now for you Ms. Reddy, let me see how good you study. "We are still on Otto cycles. I want to know, which characteristic of the Otto cycle occurs in the actual diesel cycle but not in the theoretical diesel cycle?"

"When rapid pressure increases during combustion," Reddy spoke with assurance,

Madeline J. Wilcox

"Does every one agree with Ms. Brooks and Ms. Reddy? If not, you had better go back and study pages twenty-four through sixty." Then to continue the lecture, he called again on the ladies in his class as they continue to answer questions on Reciprocating Internal-Combustion Engines.

It was easy reading your books and staying in the room when you wanted to avoid someone. It was also easy to avoid the person when your friends invited you over for the weekends. Reddy had been invited over to Jenny and Brian's apartment several times. Even Logan and Thomas had, had her over for a few meals. Logan, I have got to stop calling her that, Reddy corrected herself. It's Thomas now. She even surprised herself, as she was civil with Matt Thomas, even if she still didn't care for him.

"I hope we get spouse duty," Logan had told her the last time they saw each other.

"I hope you do too. By the way, I think you are good for Matt, he is more civil."

"Think so, for he said the same about you. He said your attitude is calmer. Speaking of which, how are Steve and you doing?" Thomas finally asked, since she didn't see him with her.

"We're not." Reddy somberly answered.

"His he still here?" Logan asked next.

"I don't know," Reddy replied.

"What! What happen between the two of you?"

"We had a huge disagreement and I haven't seen or heard from him since," Reddy said, fighting back tears.

Thomas wanted to ask more questions, but she felt that it was best to leave things as they were. Wanting to bring Reddy back to a good mood, she did say. "You are looking a little ragged, but I just assumed you were spending less time in the building," Logan laughed, hoping to bring a smile back to Reddy's face.

"Oh aren't we funny. No I haven't changed that much. I still stick to the grind stone," Reddy admitted, looking around Thomas apartment. It diffidently was different than Jenny and Brian's. They hardly had any furniture in the living room. They did manage a table and chairs for two. One bedroom was cluttered with clothes, and the other held a bed, and a lamp. Other than that, the apartment always looked clean. Turning to Thomas she asked her. "What can I get you two for a wedding present?"

"Nothing," Lori expressed, "we have tons of stuff back home in storage. We just decide to leave it there until we find out where we will be. I know your intentions are good, but you wouldn't believe what our family and friends threw on a short notice."

Lori added.

"You truly love Matt, don't you?" Reddy said with surprise.

"Yes. We are good for each other," Thomas stated, the glow on her face agreeing to the testimony.

Moving into February they had covered transmissions, pumps and were starting into the last phase of school. The auxiliary equipment, "you should have thorough knowledge of air compressors, their construction, and care," Instructor Foster stated, looking over his class of fewer people. "You will find

417

that compressed air serves many purposes aboard ship and that several outlets are installed in various suitable locations through out the ship. The uses of compressed air include, but are not limited to, the operation of pneumatic tools and equipment." he went on listing things they would need to know.

"Math again," Reddy grumbled, reading from her textbook on distilling plants. "Where is Tanner when I need him," she also grumbled, as Jackson asked. "Having problems?"

Reddy's reply was. "I have reached my limit on numbers, verse letters. We are studying mechanical kinetic energy. I think it refers back to Newton's law's?"

Taking a look over Reddy's shoulder and reading her textbook on the principles of steam engineering, Jackson begin to work out a formula for her. "Great! You know how to do, now show me," Reddy laughed, when she was finished.

"It's easy, just remember that PE=potential energy, W=total weight of the object, D=distance between the earth and the object. Potential energy, in foot-pounds, weight-pounds, distance-feet. Got that?"

"If not, I know whom to call on," Reddy commented, going back to reading her text.

32

Instructor Garfield sat behind his desk looking out over the few people who had chosen to remain in their seats during break, their eyes glued to their books. As usual his eyes stopped on the girl who stood out at the top of his class. Moving from his chair, he walked over to the desk across from her and made himself comfortable by leaning against it. "Instructor Foster says you are good. You seem to be proving him right," Instructor Garfield, stated. "Have you decided where you want to be?"

"Yes, on a ship in a warm climate," Reddy replied, not looking up from where she was reading about compressed air systems and distilling plants.

"He also thinks that you would make a good instructor someday," Instructor Garfield added.

"So he told me," Reddy replied as she marked her place and looked at him, her expression seemingly bored with the conversation. "I believe he also said that I would need rank and rate?" Recalling the conversation in which she had with Instructor Foster only days ago. "You know Reddy," he had begun, "I usually don't make recommendations to any of my students, but I have this feeling about you. When you

419

get some rank and experience under your belt, you should think about becoming an instructor. I think you would make one hell of a teacher?"

"Sure I wouldn't put you out of a job?" Reddy declared.

"By then I would be too old to care," Instructor Foster had laughed.

"You sure about that? I might make rank faster than you expect," she said, not letting him down for her attitude remain stubborn.

"Na, I'm not too worried about that. You are still young, and wet behind the ears, and a female."

"I don't think my being a female should effect my career," she rejected his remark.

"Then you have a lot to learn," he had commented, before moving back to the front of the room. "You know the pressure is on you to stay ahead of the game. There are a lot of young men in this class that are equal to you when it comes to engines and know how."

"Naturally, I wouldn't think otherwise," she replied, as the rest of the class returned from the break room. As she thought about what he had said, he told them that the last two hours of the class would be learning about barring devises and interlocks.

It was the same procedure as always; taking notes, drafting and comparing functions. "This I am sure of," she concluded as she finished doing her work.

Maxwell was gone for the weekend. Jackson and Cramer she hoped would be making an exit soon since she was trying to study, and the two were making the effort impossible with their usual bickering. Gathering up her books, she made up her mind to go to the library. At least there it would be quiet.

On the way out the door, she was greeted by the BDO, who was passing out mail. "You seem to have hit the jackpot," BDO Garrison mentioned as she handed Reddy her mail.

"Thank you, ma'am," Reddy answered, making a u-turn and went back into her room, and walking over to her desk, took a seat and started reading her letter. The first being from Peggy. Peggy started with the up and coming marriage of Maureen. "You wouldn't believe who is getting married. Maybe you already know. Maureen is marrying that guy who came home with Steve Tanner. I understand from Mrs. Colby that he comes from a wealthy family. Did you know that?"

I had an idea he was, Reddy thought to herself, as she read on. It was several times going over the same lines, that it finally sunk in. "Mother is gone. She has asked Dad for a divorce. She is living in Florida with Grandpa and Grandma Cole. I don't know what happen to make her so angry. I came home from school and dad was staring out the front window as she packed her car. I asked what was going on, Dad just shrugged his shoulders. Would you have any idea as to why mom would leave?" continuing to read, Peggy complained about all her plans being ruined. "I guess I will not be having a graduation party, and I surly don't plan on having my wedding here. I don't plan on it being ruined by mother and dad fighting. Our parents are so selfish. How dare them to do this to me?" Peggy.

Not wanting to read anything more about her parents, she laid aside the letter from her grandmother, and opened the one from Florida, as her heart took up a different beat after reading the postmark. The letter was from Steve. "Joan, You don't know how many times I have tried writing you. I'm sorry for leaving the way I did. But as you once said, we knew that sooner or later we would part. I just wish now it had been on friendlier terms. Think about you, I do nothing but that. I still care about you, and what we meant to each other. I will get over you, it may not be the easiest thing to do, but sooner or later the aches will go away.

Are you ready for this? Dan is marrying your friend Maureen. I don't think a date has been set as of yet. He has asked me to be his best man. So we probably will be seeing each other again. (Not if I can help it, she thought to herself.)

"Nuclear School is anything but easy. You probably won't believe this, but I am keeping my nose to the books. Also you are right about Florida, it is hot here. Take care, and have a great adventure. Steve."

Reddy was mad, Jackson and Cramer watched as she stormed around the room. In an eight by ten area with furniture and four girls' belongings taking up space, there wasn't much room left. At least we are getting the room cleaned, they agreed silently. Reddy told them to move, and they weren't about to argue with her. "Damn the Navy!!" Reddy cried throwing mop water around like it was her destiny with fate.

422

"You knew the score when you came in," Cramer reminded her. "Nothing lasts forever. Not even a bad love affair, besides, what's your beef? There are plenty of others to take his place?"

"Cramer do me a big favor. Shut-the-f---up!" Reddy asserted, glaring at her.

Come Monday morning, her mood was not the best to say the least. Reporting for Instructor Weaver's class, she realized that she forgot her manual on firefighting, flood control and damage control. "Today we will report to damage control training class. For those of you moaning, I certainly hope you read your books. We wouldn't want any casualties. Now, would we?"

"I think this is going to be another hands on experience," the guy standing behind Reddy commented, as she turned around and told him. "For some reason I think you are right," in a low voice as they followed Instructor Weaver to a different training area of the school. "Okay people, pay close attention to the people in the tank area. You will be getting a chance to do the same thing in a few minutes."

The object of damage control is to repair a ship while having water pour in on you at a rapid pace. "I don't think I am going to enjoy this?" Reddy mumbled, watching the group in the tank area, which was made up like a mock ship, with a gaping hole in one side of it.

"Sure you are," Instructor Weaver assured her. "Plus we have spotters to help you out of trouble," he informed her as he said. "Okay people, take your places."

Their objective was to shinny a steel plate over the gaping hole in the hull side then get out of the area. "You have fifteen minutes in which to do this," they were informed by an instructor standing a top of the hatch on the mock ship.

"Heck this easy," Mike Decker mentioned, as water trickled over his head. They didn't feel rushed, nor did they feel the need to panic. Finding boards to brace the steel plate, they were doing it with ease. They didn't even seem to notice the water rising around their legs, as time was yelled at them. "Ten minutes left," then wham!! All hell broke loose as water came at them in all-different directions.

Cursing burst out from more than one person as they dropped what they were doing and swimming for the escape hatch, all chaos broke loose. Reddy found herself being trampled, shoved, pushed and whatever as it became all for one, one for all as they headed for the hatch. Reddy felt someone grab her and shove her upward with a strong thrust. Whoever had done the pushing, pushed so hard that the catcher almost missed her as she came through the hatch, and almost sent her to the other side of the plank in which the guy was standing on.

"I am not going back in there," She flatly refused to move from the spot she was standing on, and talking to Instructor Weaver when she joined the others in her class.

"Oh but you are," Weaver assured her. "You will do it over and over until you do it right!"

"Excuse me! I don't think so," Reddy was ready to argue.

"You really wouldn't want to be put on report?" Weaver warned her.

"No, but I don't want to drown either," she continued to argue.

"I can assure you Ms. Reddy, that we won't let that happen," Instructor Weaver stated, knowing something of the girls attitude.

It took several tries through damage control for the eight people to get it right. On the last try, Reddy made sure she was the first one to reach the hatch, as she clawed, kicked and climbed her way to the hatch. By stepping on arms, legs, shoulders and even heads. When she came out of the hatch, she found four instructors trying to regain their composure from laughing so hard. Brushing her hands together, she stated, "now that was easy!"

It was the end of March and four weeks to go before school was done. Reddy had just returned from doing her laundry. It was the weekend and the room was empty when she returned. What to do? She pondered, grabbing her purse and thought about making a trip to Lakehurst Mall. Starting to open her door, she was greeted by a knock. "Who is it?" she called out.

"Messenger of the watch," the person answered.

As Reddy opened the door, the girl asked. "You Reddy?"

"Yes."

"You have a visitor on the deck," the girl informed her.

Probably Lori or Matt," Reddy mumbled, locking the door and following the messenger. Crossing the quarter desk, she stepped outside. The weather for March was still under the spell of a late winter. Turning around she saw Lori. "What?" she was ready to question her.

"I got this crazy call early this morning. I was told to bring you to the Crow's Nest." Lori informed her.

"What? Who called you?" Reddy again questioned her.

"How would I know? They woke me up," Logan declared, pointing across the street where Thomas was waiting in an old beat up car.

Arriving at the Crow's Nest, which hadn't even open their doors. She looked around. "It's about time," she heard the person say, as she turned to face them and a dozen red roses were shoved in her face. "They are a little wilted, but they will work," Tanner said, lowering the flowers and giving her one of his little boy grins.

"How? When? You're here?" Questions flew out of her mouth. Her eyes not believing what she was seeing. "I'll answer questions later," Tanner said, taking her arm and leading her towards the car he had rented.

"I hope you are buying breakfast," she told him as they pulled away from the Crow's Nest.

"Later," he smiled, turning and looking at the person who had been invading his dreams, and making his life, pure hell.

She didn't want to argue with him. He was here, for now that was enough. "Where are we going?" she did ask though.

"To Hidden Pines," he answered, glancing again at her.

"Could we stop at the mall first?" she asked next.

"All depends," he grinned, "on how much shopping you have to do?"

"Please," was her response?

Looking in the mirror her eyes were only slightly red, her mouth slightly swollen. "This is not how I planned on looking," she mumbled, turning to where the box lay open. Carefully, she opened the tissue papers that protected the white silk negligee. The soft folds of silk shimmered her lithe frame as she slipped it on. "I need a tan," she thought, as she picked up the perfume bottle and lightly sprayed herself with the perfume that Steve said reminded him of roses.

"Steve," she spoke softly as she stepped into the outer room and as he turned from where he had started a fire in the fireplace. She had to catch her breath to the sight beholding her eyes, the fire casting a soft glow on the Greek God that was her love, her heart's desire. He was more than alluring, sexy, as he stood clad only in jeans. He had turned his fading tan, into a dark one.

Madeline J. Wilcox

As Joan moved toward him, he found himself hypnotized. To him, she never looked so soft, so feminine. Then long white negligee hugging her small breast. His eyes ventured lower, the smallness of her still amazed him as the gown embraced her like a whispering caress. Taking a deep breath and letting it out slowly, he reach out and lifted her to him. "You are mine. Don't ever forget it."

"Never," she managed to reply before he claimed her mouth insistently to find that she was more than willing to accept his passion.

She was in his arms. They were sitting in front of the fireplace, their bodies spent from making love. "Did you go UA?" she was finally asking questions.

Steve didn't say yes, or no. He only told her, "I am here." as he lay a kiss to the top of her head.

"Steve, you could get into some serious trouble," She stated, even if she was happy to see him. She didn't want him to be caught by the shore patrol. She didn't want him to receive a court martial, just to be with her.

"I have it covered," he assured her. "It's Easter weekend, and everyone is on 'stand down' until Monday" he added, turning her face to look at him, leaning he covered her mouth with his. With a gentle tenderness he lowered her to the pillows behind them.

With the expertise of a lover, he began to turn sparks into flames as he tasted the slender throat, caressed the contour of her body, the heat of her building under the silk folds of the gown she was wearing.

She was everything he needed. This crazy tomboy that had come into his life. Undressing her, he devoured her with his eyes; again they made love, matching the heat from the fireplace as they lay in front of it. Lying in the crook of his arm, his body close to her, she asked. "Where do we go from here, Steve?"

"To hell," he sighed, his voice containing a note of sadness, which she knew only too well.

"A year-an-a-half really isn't all that long," she tired assuring them both.

"Do you know where I will be? What I will be?" the clarity of the unspoken words so obvious that she hid her face in his chest. She knew it wouldn't work, not with the continent of the United States between them. Him probably an officer?

"Joan look at me," he whispered. They forgot about the cold winds of March. They tried not to think about what lay ahead of them. It was their night to fill their dreams and fantasies, and to make promises that neither expected to keep.

It was late Sunday morning, Steve had a plane to catch back to Florida, and they were eating a light breakfast in their room. "Are you still on the pill?" he asked, between bites of his food.

She did her best to avoid looking at him. She had not taken the pill since arriving back to the base in January. She had hunted for them when she first had returned, but with her not dating, she just let it slip her mind until now when he asked about them.

Steve looked at her, his expression no longer caring, he was angry, as he stated. "You trying to trap me?"

"What!" surprised that he would even dare say such a thing. Then letting her attitude take over, she declared. "So what you are saying? If I was to become pregnant? You are telling me it's my problem? Not yours!' becoming angry with him, she rose quickly, only to be followed by him. Throwing money on the bed, Steve told her, "You know how to call a cab? Then grabbing his coat, his tote bag that he had brought with him, he walked towards the door.

Staring at the closing of the door, she would have thrown something, but there was nothing close by. When the reality hit her, she cried, until she didn't think any more tears could fall. "I wasn't trying to trap you," she yelled to the silence of the room. "I didn't even know you were coming here?"

33

Their last week in school was doing tests and learning how to report for sea or shore duty. Taking notes, Reddy soon learned that if you were a male, it was anything that floated. Girls, on the other hand, were limited to tenders, some tugs, repair ships and some tankers, mainly those in port. Their assignments were to A or M divisions, where they operated and maintained ship propulsion machinery and associated was what she hoped to be doing.

Before Instructor Foster released them for break, he added to his comments. "If you demonstrate integrity and do the best of your ability performing your job, things will run smooth for you and the department you work in. You will find that every job is important in the Navy, regardless of how large or small the task may be, that 'teamwork' depends on being able to get along with you coworkers. Also, remember that safety comes first above anything else. Without teamwork, hazards rise quickly. Good luck ladies and gentleman on your new jobs." then he excused them.

The ceremony wasn't until 1400, so Reddy spent the time packing and getting ready to move to TPU, to wait for her orders. "It might be a short stay at sea," she thought, unless something happens real soon?"

"Got a problem?" Maxwell asked, as she saw the expression on Reddy's face.

"Hope not," Reddy answered with a defeated sound in her voice.

"Oh girl friend, you are just nervous about getting new orders," Maxwell declared, as she added. "I hope you get San Diego."

She had the certificate that declared she was a qualified engineman, and a certificate stating that she was a diesel mechanic. There was something missing in the girl's eyes as she had received the two certificates. It was as if she no longer cared to be the best that the adventure was no longer hers to seek.

Calling home, she was surprised when her grandmother answered the phone. "Hi Gram's she spoke glad to hear her voice.

"Hi yourself, what a pleasant surprise. How are you doing?"

"I am great, did Peggy tell you I was graduating today?" She answered, hoping to hide the unhappiness in her voice.

"No, come to think of it, I don't believe she did." Maude replied as she added. "Was it anything like the ceremony in Florida?"

"It wasn't anything special," Joan lied as she added, they just handed us our certificate and wished us good-luck. Has any one heard from Mother?"

"No, just her lawyers. I guess you know she doesn't live here anymore?" Maude replied.

"Yes, Peggy wrote me. How is dad holding up?"

"Oh you know your father, he is not saying to much." Maude stated. "Its Peggy who is having a hard time excepting it."

"Is she there?" Joan then asked, thinking maybe she could talk to her.

"No, but I will tell her you called. So when do you get leave to come home?"

"As soon as I get my orders," Joan informed her. "They told me it will take about two weeks. I am hoping to get San Diego. You know warm weather all the year around." She smiled.

Maude with some hesitant asked. "Have you heard from Steve?"

"Yes. He came up one weekend in April," she said, not adding that he left angry with her.

"Where is he stationed at?" Maude continued the conversation.

"In Florida." Joan soberly added.

Maude sensing that maybe this wasn't a good subject to keep on, asked her about school and where did she place in her class.

"Let's say I was in the top ten," Joan responded, as she added. "Boy do I have a lot to tell you when I come home." excitement heard for the first time in her voice as she talked about school. Well Gram's I need to let you go. I am moving into TPU today. Tell everyone I am sorry I missed them. Love ya,"

Moving her things to TPU by taxi cost her ten dollars. Complaining, she told the cab driver. "I could have saved myself ten bucks and drugged it over here. We didn't even go two blocks!"

433

Checking in and getting her assigned room, again she found herself dragging the entire luggage up a flight of stairs. Unlocking the door to her room she noticed she had a roommate. "I wonder who it is," she mumbled as the bathroom door opened and Ann Wagner came into the room.

Both girls stopped and stared at the other. "Oh great! Just the person I want to spend the next ten days with," Reddy grumbled to herself.

Ann Wagner couldn't believe her eyes, as she declared, "You stay out of my way, and I will stay out of yours!"

"No problem," Reddy assured her. Tension began to build in the room between the two girls who loved the same person.

Standing muster at 0545 and listening to her barracks duty officer telling her what she would be doing the next ten days did nothing to enhance her mood, not when she was sharing a room with Ann Wagner. Nor did meeting CPO Dixon help the matter. His voice and mannerism reminded her of an old salty sea sailor. He was near retirement and one thing for sure. . He wasn't going to let anyone forget it. "You!" Pointing at Reddy, as he took several large steps and stood in front of her, he asked. "Who let you in the Navy?"

"Probably my recruiter, sir," Reddy boldly spoke back.

"Well Ms. Reddy, I see you have some back bone. Let's see how good you are with it. See that door over there? In it you will find brooms, mops, buckets and etc., for cleaning restrooms and offices." I think you can keep yourself busy for the rest of the day. I want everything to shine when you are done. Oh! And if you have any questions as to what you will be doing for the rest of the week. Let me inform you now, the same. That way, you can get busy the minute you arrive."

For the next ten days, she became a go-for as she stood duty, cleaned offices and whatever else they could come up with to keep them busy as they waited for their orders.

She actually welcomed the duties of scrubbing floors, emptying ashtrays, answering phones, and making coffee. Anything beat going back to her building at night and having to face Ann Wagner.

On the second week, third day, she received her orders to report to San Diego on May twenty-third. That meant she had two weeks leave starting Friday. "Yes!" she let out a yell that would have rocked the nation's capital. "I'm out of here!"

Finding a phone, she put in a call home during lunch. Peggy answered, and Reddy quickly told her, "Tell Uncle Matt to pick me up Friday at Midway. Sorry I can't talk longer. Have to go. See you soon."

"Two days," she thought. "Two days and I am out of here." She was so excited that she almost forgot about work detail. She slid into the room just as the clock was striking 1300. "Almost didn't make roll call," the guy standing next to her remarked, as CPO Dixon walked into the room. "Tell me," she whispered back, as they were told. "Get to work, don't just stand here."

On the morning that Reddy was leaving, Ann Wagner broke the silence that had become a wedge between the two girls. "How is Steve?" Wagner asked, as Reddy was packing.

"I am sure you are aware of the fact I have not heard from Mr. Tanner," Reddy turned on her, and for once truly looked at her. She was so much different than me, she was tall, lanky, and had dark hair and fair skin. Wagner was pretty in a sense, Reddy surmised, as she continued to speak. "I am sorry. I guess he led you on also?"

"You could say that. Now if you will excuse me. I need to call a cab." Reddy continued to be cool towards Wagner.

"I have the day off. I wouldn't mind driving you to the airport," Wagner offered

"I would be willing to pay you for the gas," Reddy accepted the offer, and informed her, "I am flying out of Midway."

"I really cared for him," Wagner said with a sad voice as she helped Reddy with her luggage. Reddy felt uncomfortable to Wagner's confession and wasn't quite sure how to answer her. She wasn't ready to admit anything, nor was she ready to give up on Steve quite yet. Reaching for the last of her luggage, Reddy did tell her. "I didn't mean for you to get hurt."

"I know. I doubt if Steve ever mentioned the fact he was dating me?"

Not wanting to hurt her further, Reddy ignored the question as she picked up the last of her things and left the room with Wagner following her. The truth was, Steve had not mentioned her, or the fact that he was dating her. Only Reynolds had made that obvious.

Wagner and her waited around the airport for several hours, then Reddy decided maybe she should check with information to see when her Uncle's plane was coming in. "I'm sorry," the lady behind the counter stated. "But there is no flight plan for a Matt Reddy today."

"What? Peggy you're dead," she remarked, marching over to a phone. It was several minutes before she heard her father speak. "Hello, Tom Reddy here."

"Dad, it's Joan. Didn't Peggy tell you I was coming home today?"

"Home! No I don't think so. Where are you calling from?" Tom answered with surprise.

"Midway Airport. I thought Uncle Matt could pick me up here?"

"Your Uncle Matt isn't even here. He is in Washington D.C. on business. Peggy knew that." Tom was confused as to why Peggy hadn't mentioned that Joan was coming home today.

"Great!" Joan stated with disgust. "Now I will have to wait for a plane to go home, and it's going to cost me a fortune. Tell Peggy I said thanks." Then she told him. "I will call when I get to Indianapolis." Getting off the phone, she walked over to Wagner. "Would you mind taking me to O'Hara?

"Sure," Wagner laughed with agreement. "Did someone forget you were coming home?"

"She's going to think forget." Joan stated, as the two girls walked out to Wagner's car. Her first call arriving at the airport was to the Credit Union to see how much money she had in the bank? The next move was walking over to American Airlines.

"I have a red-eye flight leaving at midnight," the lady told her checking her schedule.

"I'll take it," Joan answered, as the lady told her, "that will be three hundred and twenty nine dollars round trip." After paying for her ticket she found a place for her and Wagner to eat dinner. "You don't have to stick around," Reddy told her.

Having no idea as to where Joan was headed, Wagner said, "Are you sure you will be okay here by yourself?"

Looking around the airport, she smiled when she answered her. "I think I have a lot of sailors to keep me company."

"Yeah I guess you are right," Wagner agreed, as she got up to leave, and thanked Reddy for the gas money and dinner.

"Who said planes left on time?" Joan thought as one delay after another kept her waiting at O'Hare. Finally, at last they were told they could board. It was like a zoo as one hundred and eighty angry people boarded the plane for Florida, she being one of them. Finding her seat, she realized she probably would have to make motel reservations.

It would be better to go there first. Then I could call Steve's barracks to see if he was in. If not, I could always see Disney World again. Thoughts rambled through her mind as she made plans. As the plane landed, she had one goal in mind, walking over to a pay phone; she took a small address book out of her purse. It was several rings before she heard someone answer the phone. "Hello, Cole residence."

"Hi mom, it's Joan?" she said hesitantly.

"Joan? Oh my goodness! Are you calling from Chicago? Kathryn said excited to hear from her.

"No, I am here in Florida. I needed someone to talk to, and I thought maybe you and I could talk?" Joan spoke still with some doubt in her voice as to whether her mother would talk seriously to her. "I have graduated from school. I have two weeks leave, and then I have to report to San Diego. Can you believe it; I got a warm climate, with beautiful weather all the time. There was a girl in my room, who was stationed in California, and she said it was nothing like Florida."

"Where are you at?" Kathryn was able to get a word in, when Joan took a breath.

"At the airport, here in Orlando," Joan answered, with a laugh.

"Stay there, I am about an hours drive from the airport," Kathryn commented.

Even though it was early morning, Kathryn and her parents had already started the day. Kathryn had just finished getting ready for work, and her mother and father had risen early from habit. "Who was on the phone dear?" Her mother asked, when she had lay the phone back on its cradle.

"Joan. She is here. I mean she is at the airport in Orlando." Kathryn spoke with excitement.

"Oh my goodness!" Elaine Cole expressed "Do you think she would mind if dad and I showed up with you?"

"She would probably love it?" Kathryn stated again with surprise for at Christmas, they refused to even discuss Joan. It wasn't until after she had showed up in Florida that they began to speak of Joan. As they pulled out of the driveway her parents began to speak incessantly about Joan. They talked proudly as they mentioned how much spunk she had shown the other girls in Wellsburg by leaving. "I never saw her look more lovely than at the New Year's Dance. Is she still seeing that nice young man?" Mrs. Cold asked.

"I am not sure. I do know that at Christmas time, she mentioned that he would be going to Nuclear School at the Naval Base down here." As the conversation continued about Joan, they arrived at the airport in no time at all. "Did Joan say where to meet her at?" Stan Cole asked.

"No," Kathryn laughed, "I simply forgot to ask, since I was so excited just to hear from her."

" Why don't we try the cafeteria," She probably is hungry, as well as being tired." Stan Cole suggested, as he looked around the airport. This early in the morning, there were few people in the airport. It was Elaine Cole who spotted Joan first. "There she is sitting up at the counter." About the same time that Mr. Cole noticed her, Joan turned around and groaned inwardly when she saw her grandparents with her mother.

440

Nervous, Joan wasn't sure how she would be accepted by her grandparents, she was ready to walk past them and get a cab out of there. It was her mother who made the first move as they came closer to her. "You look so young?" Kathryn remarked, as she slipped her arms around her daughter. For the moment the two cling together, each comforting the other although no words were spoken. "You must be awful tired?" Kathryn stated, as she released her.

"Not really," Joan expressed, as her grandmother stepped up to her, and to her surprise, she slipped her arms around her. "I hope you are going to spend a few days with us down here?" Elaine Cole asked.

"Plan too," Joan smiled, returning her grandmother's hug.

"Well don't I get a hug too," her grandfather said, stepping up to her.

"Sure," Joan responded, turning to him and giving him a hug also, as he said. "I know a cheaper place to eat."

"Well lead the way," Joan added, basking in all the attention. With her grandparents in the lead, Kathryn and Joan followed. "Do you have other luggage?" Kathryn expressed, to the backpack that Joan was carrying.

"No. I sent the rest of my luggage home. Trust me, I won't do it again. Wow! Did it cost?" Joan informed her mother, who was looking at her. "Are you okay?" Kathryn asked, as she had taken a good look at her, she didn't have that perky step about her but was pale and drawn.

441

Joan confused her mother by saying. "Sure, I have had one miserable day at a time, but I will survive."

"I guess you are wondering why your father and I have separated?"

"It has crossed my mind?" Joan expressed.

"Is that why you are here?" Kathryn inquired.

"Some, but not my main concern. I figured if you and dad are having problems that we are old enough to accept the fact that things happen, whether we like them or not." She answered, as they came closer to her grandparents car, "Well we thought you two had gotten lost?" her Grandfather spoke as Joan and her mother took the back seat.

"Sorry dad, we were just catching up?' Kathryn answered her father, as she reach over and took one of Joan's hands. "I am so glad that you came to see me?"

"So am I," Joan said, laying her head back against the seat. She hadn't realized that she had fallen asleep until her mother woke her. "Joan, we are here?"

Her grandparents lived in a large condo in Melbourne Florida, as they walked into the living room, Joan knew just from looking around that her mother had decorated it. It was done in rich amber, dusty rose, and deep garnet. The sofa and love seat were covered in a floral pattern and to make the area in to a conversational area, her mother had chosen deeper reds for solid pieces such as the side chairs with ottomans. "We even have a large balcony to over look the ocean." Her grandmother Cole stated, as she began to show Joan the condo. In the center of the room a huge coffee table with drawers sat so the guest could place their drinks on, Her mother had placed scented candles a decorated cigar box, and an arrangement of roses and faux greenery. "Now if you will follow me I will show you where you can sleep?" her grandmother Cole spoke with kindness. Walking down a hallway, Joan stopped behind her grandmother as she opened a door. "I hope you like it, we only use it as a guest room," her grandmother said, stepping aside and letting Joan into the room. The room was refreshing as a bright, sunny day! Vibrant yellow walls with sky-blue carpeting and accents made waking up a joy! Under the only window in the room set a vanity table, flanked by a pair of candlestick lamps, and a collect of different sizes bottles that once held perfume. "Your grandfather, is fixing us breakfast, and if you can remember, he does one swell of a job," her grandmother chuckled, as her mother entered the room. "We can go shopping later today if you wish? I took the day off just to be with you?" Kathryn informed Joan.

"That sounds like a plan to me," Joan smiled, sitting the tote bag down that she was still holding and followed her mother and grandmother out to the kitchen. Everything in the condo spoke of her mother's interior art designs. Even the kitchen was a cooks dream, with counter space and pot's and pan's hanging down from a metal turn-style above the counters.

"Mom this place is utterly beautiful," Joan expressed, turning her head in every direction.

"I try," Kathryn smiled, pleased that Joan liked her work. "I have been extremely busy since I moved down here. I have been using mom and dads place as a symbol of my work, plus the pictures I took of the house back in Wellsburg."

"We are so proud of your mother and the accomplishments that she has made down here," her grandmother spoke up."

"I will have to take you by my office," Kathryn added.

"Oh don't do that," her grandfather said, turning to Joan. "You never will see anything else." he laughed, looking at his only daughter with pride, as he began to sit the table with coddle eggs and ham, hash-browns, and whole wheat toast. Dear ladies, breakfast is served as once more he turned to Joan. "I bet the Navy never feeds you this good?"

"You got that right," Joan stated, as she started to eat. "Gramps, this is very good," she complimented him. As they ate breakfast, her grandparents wanted to know all about her life in the military. She had them laughing, when she mentioned the episode which happen in damage control. "Let me tell you, it didn't take me long to figure out I was going to be the first one out the hatch." She finished by telling them, you wouldn't believe all that I have learned? I am just hoping I will get a ship so I can practice it?'

"My daughter the sailor?" Kathryn laughed as her parents stood and left the kitchen area. "It's good to see you smiling again," Kathryn mentioned to Joan, as they lingered at the kitchen table finishing another cup of coffee. "Have you talked to anyone back home?"

"I talked to dad yesterday when no one showed up at Midway. I guess Peggy forgot to tell anyone that I was coming home? So I had to make different arrangements. I was going home, but then I decided to come down here to see you and Steve."

444

"I was wondering if your mood had something to do with your father and I?" Kathryn looked at her, and saw that the forlorn look had returned.

"Probably, What happen mom? Why did you decide to leave Dad?"

"At first I hadn't planned on leaving, I just needed to get away for a while to think things over, after all the house was so crowded over the Christmas holidays, and when ever one left, it was quiet, so quiet?" Kathryn stated remembering back to the holidays and how congested the days had been seeing people had clean beds, towels and plenty of food to eat. I wish there had been room at the Inn," Kathryn added with a smile. "I wanted to spend time with you and get to know you again. We had so many disputed years, that I just wanted to say I was sorry."

Reaching for her mother's hand that lay on the table, Joan lay hers over it and spoke softly. "I am here now." And for a moment their eyes met and words were not needed, as the mother and daughter both expressed their feelings by the tenderness in their eyes. "Do you plan on seeing Steve while you are down here?"

"I---I am not sure?" Joan said with hesitancy.

"But you did come down here to see him?" Kathryn stated.

"Yes," then Joan explained why she didn't think Steve would see her. "The last time we were together, he accused me of trying to trap him. When I was home my birth control pills came up missing. Upon returning to the base, I became so involved with school. Steve and I were not speaking, let alone dating, so I just didn't think about getting them again."

"Your pills came up missing? Who would have taken them?" Kathryn asked.

"I am not sure, I really haven't given it much thought." Joan answered, as she stood to clear the table and to do the dishes, she wasn't sure if her mother would accept the true reason as to why she was in Florida,

"Is there anyway you can contact him?" Kathryn asked next.

"Yes, I have his address, and I can call his barracks." Joan answered.

"Why not give him a call. It's ten o'clock I am sure he is up." Kathryn added.

"Yeah, up and gone," Joan responded with a mumble

"Well you won't know, until you call." Kathryn smiled, as she handed her daughter the phone, and took over her duties of cleaning the dishes.

The phone rang several times before someone finally answered it. "Mason Hall, Hurst speaking."

Her voice sounded nervous as she asked. "Is there a Steve Tanner on your floor?"

"Probably," the guy said and asked. "Who wants to know?"

"Joan Reddy," she stated, as Hurst told her. "Hang on, I will see if he is in?" Several minutes later the voice that could make her blood run hot and cold was saying.

"Hello Joan," although he didn't seem to pleased to be talking with her. Maybe I should just hang up, she thought as again she heard him say. "Where are you calling from?"

446

"Would you believe Florida," she answered, her voice calmer.

"I would believe anything that you would pull," a ghost of a smile tugging at his lips. "Do you know how to get here?" Tanner asked next.

"I am sure a cab does? What are your plans for tonight?" she added.

"Seeing you," he answered, "Hell it's Saturday, I am not standing duty. Why not come and make my day for me now?"

"Can't. I have plans to go shopping with my mother?" Joan informed him.

"Then it's going to be a long day," Tanner uttered with a deep sigh.

"Probably," she laughed, "but it will give you something to think about," again he heard her deep throaty laughter. "Thanks," he grumbled, as he told her. "See you later, then."

"You can count on it," She answered. After talking to Steve she turned to her mother, "He sounded tired, but okay. He wants to see me."

"I am sure he does!" Kathryn smiled, as she put the last plate into the cupboard. "Okay, shall we be going? I doubt if you would like to meet Steve in the same clothes you probably have wore for days?"

They went shopping and looking. "What are we looking for?" Joan wanted to know as her mother drug her from one store to another. "A special dress," Kathryn smiled.

"You are as bad as Maureen?" Joan complained, following her mother yet into another store. Why can't I just buy a new pair of jeans, and a shirt?"

Madeline J. Wilcox

"Because," her mother stated, searching through a rack of dresses in the Sears store. They walked from one rack to another, until her mother stopped dead in her tracks. "This one!" Her mother stated, pulling a dress off the rack with a pink strapless bodice and full skirt. "Mom, I think Jeans and a sweatshirt will do just fine." Joan complained looking at the dress.

"Don't you want to look nice for him?" Kathryn stated, not quite understanding what was wrong with the dress.

"I came here not to impress him, but to talk." Joan somberly stated.

"Oops I think it's time for coffee," Kathryn implied, as she put the dress back on the rack.

They were seated in the restaurant drinking coffee and splitting a club sandwich between them. "Is there another reason as to why you are here?" Kathryn asked with concern.

"Not that I am aware of," Joan stated looking down at the plate in front of her.

"Your not pregnant?" Kathryn asked in a low tone as she reached across and laid her hand gently on her daughters.

"Not that I am aware of," Joan added, looking down at her plate.

Laughing, Kathryn then brought up the bear that Steve had given her at Christmas. "The look on your face was worth a thousand pictures. Our guest were embarrassed along with your father and I. Did you ever thank Steve for the nice gift?"

"Yes, only I believe I wasn't so pleasant about it." Joan stated, as she finally smiled at her mother. "Is the bear still in Peggy's room?"

"No, it's put away in your closet with the rest of your things. I was a little surprised that you didn't take it with you?"

"I wanted to, maybe I will take it with me to California." Joan said, looking at her watch and couldn't imagine where the day had gone. "If I am going to buy something to wear tonight, we had better be going mom?" she remarked, regretting the fact that she had made plans to be with Steve.

Dressing was easy, she picked out the extra pair of jeans and a sweatshirt that she had brought with her walking out of the bedroom she was staying in, her mother handed her the keys to her car. "Just take interstate 436 back into Orlando. I think you can get to the base by staying on it."

34

Arriving at the main gates Joan had to search her purse for her military ID to show the Shore patrol attending the gate. After telling her to "carry on," he gave her the directions to Mason Hall. Standing on the quarterdeck of Steve's building it was her doing the pacing this time. "Come on Tanner. I am waiting," she mumbled to herself.

The Rover knocked on room 436. Tanner's roommate Lowe Martin answered the door. "Tanner in? He has a visitor on deck," the rover told him.

"Hey Tanner it's for you," Martin said, turning and looking at Tanner, who as usual had his nose buried in a book.

"What's up?" Tanner asked, walking over to the door.

"You have a visitor on deck. She told me to tell you that your challenge was here," the rover explained, repeating what the girl had told him to say.

Tanner stared at the guy in disbelief. He had talked to Joan earlier today, but he didn't actually believe she was in Florida. "What does this person look like?" Tanner then asked.

"She has blond hair and is wearing a navy blue sweatshirt and jeans. Has deep blue eyes and stands about as high as a Western grasshopper," the guy laughed.

"Reddy!" Tanner yelled, "Tell her I will be right down. Never mind," he added quickly as he tore around the guy and headed for the quarterdeck. He was half way down the stairs when he saw her pacing back and forth. Without a word said, he made a u-turn and walked rapidly back to his room. Throwing clothes in a bag, not taking time to see what they were, he uttered with a chuckle. "Probably won't need them anyway?" The boyish grin spreading across his face.

Martin stared in amazement Tanner was actually going out? Must be someone special to get him moving this fast and packing a bag? "I better check this out?" Martin thought, as he left the room. Walking down to the quarterdeck, he found himself smiling as he looked at the girl standing on the quarterdeck, whom matched the picture on his roommate's desk. "So you decided to come to him. About time!" Martin uttered, as he turned and went back up the stairs to his and Tanner's room. "She's cute," Martin stated, as Tanner whip past him.

It was not a dream. She called out his name, as he took her further and further into a raging inferno as the heat traveled through them. It was hunger and greed that made them one. "Thank you mother for making me a girl," she laughed against his chest.

"Ssss, don't move," he whispered.

"But I want to," she spoke softly.

"I know," he answered, looking down at her, the little boy grin slowly crossing his face.

She wanted to scream, to cry out, as he kept her pinned in one position, holding her in limbo as wave upon wave of intimate desire flooded her. Drunk with desire, she became a tigress. Her nails etching scores along his back.

Grabbing her hands and holding them out away from him, he controlled her and once again she felt the power of him. She clung to him gasping for much needed air. as he laid above her, the scent of her perfume filling his nostrils, "I don't think I will ever get enough of you?" he spoke softly, as he moved to lay beside her. Then laughing he added. "It's a good thing I had my physical last week. They would swear I ran into a tiger if they saw me now. Give me your hands. One thing I did remember," then he reached over the edge of the bed and finding his tote bag, took out a pair of nail clippers he moved back onto the bed, taking her hand he began to trim her nails as she laid laughing.

She woke stretching only to find Steve gone. "He was here," she thought as a contented feeling came over her. Then she heard a knock on the door. "Steve?"

"Yes. Want to get the door? My hands are full."

"Just a second," she replied, reaching for the sheet to wrap around her. "Why didn't you take a key?" she questioned when she opened the door.

"I did, but as you can see I still need your help. Would you take one of these bags before I end up wearing coffee?"

"You always need my help," she stated, giving him a coy look. Taking the sack from him, she walked over to the table and sat it down just as the sheet slipped off of her from him stepping on it. "Cute," she remarked, turning to face him.

"Got that right," he answered, letting his eyes move slowly over the slim frame and then coming back to her face. Sitting the coffee's down on the table, we walked with purpose to cradle her face into his hands. It took a different move to cradle her into his arms as he carried her over to the bed. "Do you want to eat cold food?" she managed to say, as he began to lead her through the maze that would leave them breathless.

Sitting at the table across from her, he laughed, as he answered her early question. "I always eat cold food, or wear it.

"Complaining," she teased looking at him.

"Do you know that Chief Molson was concerned about me running out of uniforms?"

"He was? Well he should have had my cleaning bill. My dad was wanting to know what I did with my paychecks. He couldn't believe I was having to clean my uniforms every week," she laughed, looking into the bag of food as they sat eating. "Is nuclear power hard to learn?"

"It all depends on who is teaching it. Instructor Adams was good. Even if we didn't always see eye to eye on everything. I think he saved my ass from getting kicked out of school." Steve also mentioned.

"Aren't you afraid of accidents?"

"Hell, yes I am, but I try not to think about it. It has its hazards just like any other job," he stated, sitting back in his chair and looking at her as she continue. "Yes, I know that. But other jobs won't wipe out millions," she stated firmly.

"Great, I fall in love with a girl who is going to question my job. I can see it all now. Tanner, your wife is out there picketing again."

She didn't know why she became angry, as she sat up straight in her chair and looked directly towards him.

"Wife! Isn't that thinking a bit premature? In case you forgot. We are in the military. Going in two different directions."

As if this was the first time he thought about it, he said in surprise. "You want this career of being an engineman?"

"Yes. Did you have doubts about it?" She asked, wondering if he really did have doubts about her career as she added. "I want my career as much as you want yours."

Pushing back his chair, Steve stood and pacing he asked. "Don't you want to be married and have kids?"

"Probably some day, but not now. I was promised adventure and traveling, As you said, I want this career, and I don't believe being in the military would give me the chance to handle both, that is being a wife and a career person?"

"Am I getting some more of your damn logic?" he questioned looking at her again, and wondering why he had let the affair go this far? Why hadn't he seen this side of her earlier in their relationship?

Joan turned and looked at him as she answered. "Probably. I want our relationship to be more than just hello, and goodbye. I love you Steve, I never had doubts about that. But I will not stand in the way of your future. I saw your face that day you took me on the submarine. Even if you do love me, you need to follow that dream."

"So this is why you came to Florida. To tell me goodbye?"

"No," she replied, trying hard to hold her bottom lip still, to hold back the tears; knowing that she would no longer see him after this weekend.

Looking at her seeing her tears, the guy who had made a promise that no one would ever get close to him again, walked over to the girl whom he had let into his private world. "I love you, I want you to know that more than anything" His own voice was filled with sadness as he realized that also he would soon be saying goodbye to her

She spent the next few days with her mother during the day and the evenings with Steve. Sitting in the airport waiting for Joan's plane, Kathryn had walked away so Steve and her could have a few moment alone. "I don't want to leave," she whispered as tears stung her eyes.

"Don't go getting soft on me," he replied, having trouble seeing out of his eyes also..

"You will write? You will call?" she questioned as she heard her plane being called and saw her mother walking back towards them.

"Yes," he replied, as he turned and too saw Joan's mother coming towards them. After saying goodbye Steve and her mother stood watching as Joan walked to board her plane. Staring at her, and as she turned to wave goodbye to them, Steve cursed under his breath. "Damn you, why did you come here?" as the pain of watching her leave was tearing at him. "No problem Tanner. You forget the girl and make the career top priority," he finally decided as he followed Joan's mother back to her car.

As she looked out the plane window, she let the tears flow. The image of him printed on her mind. "I love you Steve, but I can't let you keep tearing me a part. I've got to let you go. I have to, if I want to keep my sanity."

The cramps has started on the airplane, but she really didn't think much of them until the pain begin to increase. Once in the lobby, she made it to a phone and called her Aunt Maggie who happen to be a nurse. "I think I've got a problem?" Joan stated, when she heard her aunts voice on the phone.

Joan awoke not sure of where she was, but she saw her Aunt Maggie sitting beside her. "Am I...?"

"No," Maggie answered patting her hand. "Did you say anything to Steve?" Maggie then asked.

"I tried, but I couldn't tell him. I couldn't even tell mom." Joan confessed.

"Well then I guess it's yours and mine secret." Maggie stated looking at her niece.

35

Kathryn had called Tom the morning that Joan had left to go home concerned about her. "Tom, I believe there is something wrong with Joan. I believe there was a major reason as to why she came here other than to give Steve back his ring. You two are very close, please talk to her and find out what is wrong?"

For three days Maude and Tom wondered and worried about where she was. They had even called Jeff to see if there was anyone to contact incase she didn't show up.

."Joan is not stupid, she knows what is ahead of her," Jeff told them as he knew where Joan was after having talked with Linda and her only a couple of hours ago.

It was the evening of the third day when Tom Reddy had come home to find his oldest daughter sitting at the kitchen table. She was very pale and drawn. "Where in the hell have you been?" Tom started yelling at her.

Her look forlorn, her voice sad, she answered him. "Dad, please don't ask questions, so I won't have to lie to you," she pleaded, her eyes now down cast from him.'

"Can I at least ask how you are?" he questioned her, as he sensed something was wrong as she answered. "Yes," then looking at him, she added. "I am okay."

"Why in the hell don't I believe you," Tom sighed, looking at her and trying to control his anger and wanting to kill Steve Tanner. "He hurt you?" Tom uttered with disbelief.

"No more than I hurt him," she remarked, only there was no smile only a forlorn look as tears stung her eyes.

Walking over to her, Tom pulled her up from the chair she was sitting in and hugged her. "I feel that you have learned a hard lesson but with time it will heal. You will go on with your life," Tom commented as he thought that he too was going on with his life.

"I love you dad. I know I have let you down, but I hope you don't hold that against me." Joan sighed, accepting the welcome hug from her father.

"How have you let me down? You have made me very proud, and knowing you, you will keep doing so. As far as your personal life, that's just it Joan. It's your business."

After her dad returned to work she went to her room. Removing the bear from the closet, she turned it on and sat listening to the voice that she longed for and didn't hear the knock, or notice the person who entered. "Thought I would find you in here," Her grandmother spoke entering the bedroom.

"Hello Gram's." Joan spoke looking up with out rising from the chair she was sitting in.

"I had a call the other day from Steve." Maude informed her, "He wanted to know if you had arrived safely? At that time your father nor I had any idea as to where you were," she spoke hoping that she could find out where Joan had been?"

"How nice of him to be concerned," Joan spoke with bitterness, as she turned from the bear to look at her grandmother.

Maude tried not to look alarmed to Joan's drawn appearances. "What happen when you saw him?" Maude question with concern

"Nothing. We told each other lies, and that was all there was to it. Now I can get on with my life," Joan stated, adding. "One thing about Steve and me. If we were not fighting, we were making love!" Her statement not surprising her grandmother as she continued, "I just wonder how long I can keep on handling the feelings he awoke in me?" Turning away from her grandmother, she looked out the window, the sun feeling good as it came through the window to warm her.

"I think you will handle those feelings Joan," Maude answered, as she joined her at the window. "I am here if you need me," Maude also expressed, as she laid a comforting arm around her granddaughter.

"I know Grams," Joan stated, continuing to look out the window.

"I feel that you have been hurt deeply, please don't dwell on what ever it was? You are far too intelligent to mess up your life, or the career you want so badly. If you keep busy you will be able to handle anything." Maude added, kissing her granddaughter on the cheek.

Madeline J. Wilcox

"I hope you are right Grams," she replied as she continued to look out beyond her bedroom window, her thoughts lost to where she had been the past three days.

It was time to say goodbye again, as she packed up her duffle bag. Hearing a knock on her door, she turned as her father walked into the room. "Can I take some of this luggage out to the car?" Tom asked, as he felt he was intruding in on her.

"Sure dad," Joan responded, telling him. "I am almost done. I packed away my winter clothes and put them in the closet with the rest of the things that mom has already packed.

"Are you taking the bear?" Tom questioned to the stuffed bear sitting on the chair. "I haven't made up my mind yet," smiling she turned and looked at the bear with the stupid grin on his face. Walking over to it, she lifted the bear and giving it a hug, told her father. "I told gram's that I would send for it someday. Did mother and you have a good talk last night?" she then asked changing the subject.

"I think so. At least we are willing to work things out now," Tom assured her.

"That's good. By the way where is my sister?" Joan added, sitting down the bear, and walked with her father as they left the bedroom and walked towards the kitchen.

"I think you will find her in the family room. While you say goodbye to Peggy, I will take these final things to the car.

460

During her few days that she had been home, Joan had saw little of Peggy. She was usually in school, or at work, or staying at a friend's house. What time they were together they seem to have little to say. The tension was thick, usually from their arguing over their parents. She was still going through with her marriage to Mark, only it had been put on hold for a year. "I just came in to say goodbye," Joan expressed, as she stepped into the family room.

"I wish you could be here for my graduation," Peggy said, without looking up from the magazine she was reading.

"I wish I could be here too. It's too bad I cannot extend my leave for another week"

"Yeah, that would be nice, but I know you can't," Peggy answered, the strain still evident between the two sisters.

"Maybe I will be able to come to your wedding," Joan responded as she turn and started to leave the family room, only to have Peggy call out to her. "Wait," then Peggy was standing at her side. Turning to face her, the sister's hugged. "You have changed," Peggy declared," releasing her.

"I hope for the better," Joan smiled, as she heard her dad calling her. "Come on Joan we've got to be going."

With the long drive to the airport, little was said between father and daughter. To Joan quiet mood, Tom sensed that she had finally grown up.. "Jeff called last night," Tom remembered as he told her, "he will try and meet your plane."

"Do I hear a sound of relief in your voice now that I have a big brother watching out for me," She slowly smiled.

"Could be," Tom returned her smiled.

"Don't worry dad, I am going to be fine," were her final words to him before she walked down the ramp that led to the plane headed for California.

As the plane accented upward, she thought about her last night at home, of talking with her grandmother. "Why Grams?" she asked as she laid her head on her grandmother's lap and staring out across the room. "Why did Steve and I make commitments that we both knew we couldn't keep?"

With a gentle hand touching her hair, Maude tried to give her a reason. "You were young, impressible. Steve Tanner is experienced, older. He was the first person you took a chance with. Men! They can declare their dying love, yet some need, something more than what they have. With the distance that will developed between Steve and you, maybe the pain will go away."

Oh well her grandmother had been right about one thing, she would have plenty of time to erase him from her mind. The ring that he had given her, she had handed to her mother who promised to return it to Steve..

It was as the announcement was made over the intercom, that the excitement of being in California became visible. It was looking at the folder laying in lap that made her realize she was about to report to the home of the Seventh Fleet.

Walking out of the airport terminal after collecting her luggage, she turned her face upward and let the California sun soak in, a smile lighting her face, a sparkle in the deep blue eyes as she took note of her surroundings. Sitting her luggage down and rising again, she threw her arms wide. Doing a little twirling dance, she shouted. "I am going to love it here!"

Drew Adams stood watching the girl doing a little dance. There was something familiar about her. It wasn't until she had stopped dancing, that he recognized her. He had met her a couple of times over at his sister's back in Chicago. His ebony eyes taking in the view of the sailor, the view well worth the look for she was smiling. Something he rarely saw on her face. Generally, he recalled, she was ready to take on a good verbal fight. "Well this is different attitude I am seeing. I think they should have sent you here sooner," he remarked watching her face turn a deep crimson color.

"Hello sir," Joan answered, coming to attention and saluting the warrant officer.

"At ease, sailor," Drew called it, still laughing at her.

Falling to 'at ease', she added. "You saw me! Just now?" recovering as her eyes did their own assessment of the guy with the rugged, dangerous looks.

"I saw it. Cute," he replied, laughing he asked, "Do I pass inspection?"

"Probably," she commented, realizing who he was. Remembering the comment he had made during a casual meeting at Jenny's about her being an engineman on a ship. He wasn't sure who side she would be on if they were at war. The enemy's or them!

"I take it you are stationed here?" Drew asked.

"No. I was sent here for a vacation," her light mood intriguing. "Yeah I bet. So did you get a ship or shore duty?" Warrant Officer Adams, asks next.

"A ship. I am not sure which one though. They said I would find out when I reported in," she answered as a cab pulled up to the curb. "I would give you a lift, but I am being picked up," Drew explained helping her load her luggage into the cab.

"That's okay. Thank you for helping me," her voice pleasant as she took a seat in the cab.

Drew leaned against the window and told her. "Maybe I will see you again. Jenny and Brian live here. He's on the Kitty Hawk for the time being."

"That would be nice," she stated, as the cab driver asked. "Where to Miss?"

"To the Naval base," Joan replied not knowing that there were several Naval Bases in the area. It took fifty-one dollars on the meter reading and a tour of Miramar, Coronado, and Point Loma, before she finally got it across to the driver who couldn't speak a word of English, which base she was reporting to.

The Yeoman in the 'pass and decal' cage unknown to him was about to have his day made?. He was having a hard time keeping a straight face as he watched the girl in the sailor uniform struggle with a garment bag, sea bag, suitcase and a hat box making her way towards the building. Her mood from the

464

expression on her face was going to be anything put pleasant. He was correct as she snapped. "I hope I am suppose to be here?" Then dropping everything down to the floor, she handed him her folder.

"Why don't you take a seat while I check this out," the Yeoman stated, as he lifted the folder up and sort of waved it in her direction. As she took a seat, he checked out the name on the folder, and going down his rooster of new personal arriving today, he read. Fireman Reddy, Joan Marie, 555-22-9082. Leafing through his log, he came across her name for new sailors reporting aboard ships. Her name was listed under the USS Spirit. "Yo, Reddy, you want to step forward?" he called out. As she neared the counter, he told her. "You are in luck your ship pulled in this morning. Sign here," he told her, pushing a clipboard towards her, then he told her. "You need to go out the first door down there on the end. Go to pier 6, the USS Spirit is tied up there."

As she neared pier six, she stopped to stare at the huge ships tied there, her eyes wide with anticipation. "Are you ready to take me on my adventure?" she spoke in a whisper. Then she stepped up to the pier sentry standing at the gates of pier six. "Your orders?" the guy said as she came to attention, saluted and handed him her orders.

Checking the daily log, the guy called personnel. Reading her name and number off the folder, he waited for a few minutes while she was checked off. Then getting the okay for the main deck, he told her. "Carry on."

Lifting her head, and squaring her shoulders she walked with a strut of pride up the gangway. As she neared the center, she sat down her luggage, and turning toward the bow, she saluted the Ensign. When she had returned to walking, she heard from behind her. "Need some help?" as two sailors took some of her luggage, and saying "thank you," she welcomed any help that she could get. Reaching the quarterdeck, once again she came to attention. saluting the Officer of the Deck, she handed her orders to him. "State your name and business;" the Officer of the Deck commanded. "Fireman Reddy, Joan Marie, 555-22-9082 reporting for duty."

Checking through with personnel, the OOD told her. "Permission granted to cross my quarter deck."

About The Author

Madeline Wilcox, with the desire to write began writing short stories while a young girl in the Children's Home at Knightstown Indiana. She continued this love of writing through her marriage of 39 years, the raising of two daughters and a son. Being a wife and mother, she also worked outside of the home.

Her short stories covered many aspects of her children, family and friends lives that she met through working in factories, restaurants, and public relations with people.

Navy Girl, based on her oldest daughter being in the Navy, is her first attempt of being published.

Printed in the United States
17700LVS00001B/34-168